I0594792

The Talismans Rising

Zodiac Universe - Book 1

Kyrie Dunphy

ZODIAC

SEA OF NEPTUNE

OCEAN OF THE
FIVE ELEMENTS

OCEAN OF THE
FIVE ELEMENTS

STRAIT OF VEDIC

STAR OCEAN

SHENG XIAO

ZODIAC

Astrologia
Dendera
Vedic
sea of neptune
Ged
YANG TEMPLE
Souris
Dingo
PILLAR OF
BALANCE TEMPLE
Felidae
Statera
X's FORTRESS
Coinin
IMPERIAL
BAY
Unknown
Wilderness
Cochan
IMPERIAL CITY
Kusini
Doragon
Saanp
Fahal
Alkahyl
Explosivo
Ocean of the
five elements
strait of vedic
Listra
Mico
YIN TEMPLE
Star Ocean

To my family and friends

for believing in me

♥*Kyrie*

Table of Contents

Prologue: The Cat's Honor

The Qing River roared like a beast unleashed, its sapphire rapids slashing through Sheng Xiao's rolling hills under a blazing midday sun. Foam sprayed from jagged banks, its wild surge hinting at nature's unyielding challenge.

In the distance, the Imperial City gleamed: golden-roofed temples and spires carved with qilin guardians, their horned forms twisting in an eternal dance.

Cherry blossoms spun in the breeze, their sweet scent tangling with the smoky warmth of festival feasts wafting from far-off clans. The crowds pulsed with Souris lumber workers with calloused hands, Kusini farmers sturdy as their plains, and Listra dancers in flowing silks from jungle valleys.

The Great Race, decreed by Emperor Tanzanite, would lock in the Zodiac's order: twelve spots for those who conquered shale cliffs, tangled thickets, and the river's relentless surge. A celestial wheel, bound to the Emperor's pact with Heaven, whispered of the Prophecy that could shift the world's fragile balance.

Banners snapped in the wind, clan emblems blazing: ox for endurance, tiger for ferocity, rabbit for grace, dragon for might, snake for cunning, horse for speed, and more. Mark of the Ox Clan stood like a mountain; dark eyes locked on the horizon.

Jasmine of the Tiger Clan prowled restlessly, amber gaze sharp as blades, braid whipping like a tail. Mariah of the Rabbit Clan fidgeted, auburn curls bouncing with nervous energy. Shiro of the Dragon Clan adjusted his scale-etched cloak, regal and unflinching. Saanp healers of the Snake Clan murmured blessings over serums, Ged traders of the Goat Clan gripped spears tight. A Horse Clan runner bolted past, mane-like hair streaming as a Rooster Clan racer dodged thorns with a cocky smirk.

Mark let out a low grunt, steadying his stance as the crowd pressed closer, his ox strength a quiet anchor amid the chaos.

Tai, the Cat Clan's swiftest scout, scanned the cliffs. Black hair tied back, his heterochromic eyes-- one vivid green, one piercing blue--shimmered with quiet fire, a mark of his bond to Li Shou, Sheng Xiao's shadow guardian.

My shadow feels heavy today, Tai thought, its edges sharp as if eager to move, a secret pulse only he sensed.

Beside him stood Vladimir of the Rat Clan, his friend since boyhood days under cherry trees. Vladimir's sly grin flashed, lean frame taut in a tunic stitched with a rat's curling tail.

"Bet I outrun you, cat!" Vladimir said with a laugh, clapping Tai's shoulder.

"Keep dreaming, rodent," Tai shot back, but a sharp edge in Vladimir's voice made his gut twist.

Just race nerves, he thought.

Memories flickered: late nights by crackling fires, swapping stories, hands clasped in oaths of loyalty.

We'll cross that line together, Tai thought, trusting in their bond as solid as stone. That spark drove him to carve the Cat Clan's name among the stars.

The Emperor's gong crashed like a storm breaking, and the racers surged forward, dust exploding in their wake. Tai's legs burned as he sprinted, blossoms snagging his hair. Mark barreled through, parting the crowd like a plow through earth.

Jasmine snarled, "Move it, boulder!"

Shiro chuckled, "Try keeping up, stripes!" as he hauled a Tortoise Clan racer from a vine snare, his dragon emblem catching light like an ember.

Thorns tore at Tai's tunic, drawing thin streaks of blood, but the cliffs loomed closer, jagged and unyielding. A Crane Clan racer slipped on loose shale, her lithe form twisting in panic, but the race spared no one. Vladimir darted alongside, breaths quick and sharp.

He's pushing too hard... Tai thought, unease coiling tighter, but their friendship held firm in his mind.

The Qing River surged ahead, a churning wall of fury, froth snapping like angry spirits. Jasmine sliced through waves with a roar while Shiro weaved like smoke and Mariah leaped stone to stone, curls plastered flat. Tai skidded onto the muddy bank, knees sinking into slick earth, Vladimir panting beside him.

"No way we swim that beast," Vladimir said, eyes wide.

Tai spotted Mark plunging into the current. "Mark! Haul us across?" Tai shouted. Vladimir nodded fast, his gaze darting sharply, almost calculating.

Mark grunted, "Climb on," his massive frame cleaving the river like a blade through silk. Tai gripped tight, icy water slamming his skin, numbing his hands.

Halfway across, the current roared wild, waves crashing like jaws. Vladimir's grip tightened, a heartbeat of hesitation flickering in his eyes. Tai's fingers slipped--then twisted into a deliberate shove.

"Sorry, Tai," he sneered, voice laced with false regret, eyes cold as steel.

Betrayal stabbed like thorns in Tai's chest as the river yanked him downstream, rocks battering his sides, lungs searing with mud-choked water. The ache of broken trust burned deeper than the bruises, a raw wound where friendship once thrived.

Vladimir's mocking laugh faded as he scrambled to the bank and bolted on. Tai's vision blurred, the world dimming.

Tai snarled, kicking fiercely, limbs heavy with sludge. Vladimir's smirks, those broken oaths, twisted like vines in his gut. He clawed upward, bursting to a distant bank with a ragged gasp, the palace a hazy smear far upstream.

Drums thrummed. Vladimir stood first, flanked by Mark, Jasmine, Mariah, and Shiro. Tai dragged himself from the bank, tunic shredded, body trembling.

"For my clan," he growled, feet pounding toward the palace under a sky streaked in pink and gold.

Hills darkened under gathering dusk, stars sharp and cold. Vines lashed like whips, blood mixing with sweat, muscles screaming. Amber eyes gleamed from the underbrush—a wolf, its snarl vibrating low.

Tai bared his teeth, Li Shou's sly ferocity in his blood, blade gleaming in moonlight. The beast slunk into the gloom. Palace lanterns flickered ahead, gates yawning, a crimson banner torn and flapping uneasily. Steel rang out, and a cry sliced the night.

Tai sprinted to the throne room, blade drawn, his shadow pooling like ink across cobblestones, floral tang undercut by iron's bite.

Emperor Tanzanite battled three hooded assassins, violet eyes blazing, blood staining his robe like spilled wine. Guards lay lifeless, marble slick with crimson, sandalwood censers toppled.

The assassins' cloaks bore venomous knots—twisted threads pulsing with faint, greenish glows, their edges frayed as if torn from some ancient, forbidden craft.

Tai leaped, dodging a whistling sword, rolling to slash his blade across the first assassin's throat—scarlet sprayed hot. The second lunged before Tai tripped him into Tanzanite's waiting sword. The third whirled, knife arcing. Tai sliced his steel across the man's back, opening a path for the Emperor's final thrust.

Tanzanite's magic surged, fenghuang carvings flaring with a radiant pulse as the assassins crumpled. Tai slumped against a pillar, breath ragged, his mismatched gaze locking with Tanzanite's, a silent vow forged in blood.

The Emperor knelt, voice steady despite the chaos.

"You saved me, Tai of the Cat Clan," he said, words ringing like a gong's echo. "Vladimir claimed the race, but your honor guarded Sheng Xiao's heart. Li Shou's shadow-weaving is yours."

A warm pulse surged through Tai's mind, like a golden thread weaving into his thoughts, linking him to Tanzanite's steady resolve. Their bond ignited with a faint, golden chime.

"Serve as hidden advisors, for threats like these will rise again. The Prophecy stirs—one with eyes like yours will wield the talismans to restore our world's balance. Listen close, for its whisper echoes through the stars: light and dark must dance in eternal rhythm, shadows embracing flames to weave balance where opposites clash. Without this union, chaos devours all— clans shattered, rivers run dry, heavens unraveling like thread from a loom. And through you, Tai, a legacy will emerge, its shadows destined to rise."

Tai straightened, blade heavy in his hand. "Where, my lord?" he asked.

Tanzanite's whisper carried starlight as he said, "Felidae, part of Dendera."

Air folded like silk around them, weightless and chill. Tai's shadow rippled like midnight silk, cool and alive, cat-like forms flickering within as blood's tang faded. It swelled, enveloping his clan: elders with lined faces full of wisdom, children clutching woven cat charms that glimmered faintly. In a breath, they vanished into the dark, reappearing in Felidae's glowing square.

The Cat Clan staggered, eyes wide with confusion, until Tanzanite's voice followed, resonant and clear: "For your courage, Tai, I gift you Felidae, a city of gold and bloom in the land of Dendera, blessed by Li Shou's grace, its riches a testament to your honor. Thrive here as Sheng Xiao's secret guardians, shielding its balance from the shadows."

The clan gasped, elders bowing as golden stone warmed under moonlight, a towering cat statue with jewel eyes pulsing like heartbeats, its sapphire and emerald depths reflecting the oasis's tranquility.

Temples shimmered with onyx veins, orchards heavy with ripe figs and pomegranates, their sweet aroma mingling with the lapping of tranquil pools mirroring the stars. Children chattered against the water's soft hum, their awe weaving a fragile hope.

Tai stood at the cliff's edge, the oasis sparkling below. His mother's voice drifted in the breeze: "Our clan endures—we outsmart the fiercest storms."

Leaving Sheng Xiao ached, a raw wound in his chest, but Felidae bloomed with promise—a sanctuary where his shadow could shield the future. His mismatched gaze lingered on the statue, sensing a tremor in Sheng Xiao's heart, a faint echo of the Prophecy's dance.

Tanzanite's voice lingered, telepathic and starlit: "Your eyes awaken the dance of light and dark, binding fates anew."

Vladimir had seized victory, but Tai's resolve lit the path for the dance to come. Far in Mico's Yin Temple, a scroll pulsed, stirred by that same dance, awaiting a struggle where light and dark would clash.

Chapter 1: The Lowest Point

The Mico outpost clung to the jungle's edge like a forgotten scar, its bamboo walls slick with damp under a moonless sky. Flickering holo-torchlight danced across the rough-hewn table where maps lay sprawled, their edges curling in the humid air like dying leaves.

X leaned over them, his grey eyes burning with a cold, unyielding fire that seemed to suck the warmth from the room. His dark brown hair was cropped short, practical for the field, and a faint scar traced his jawline, a remnant of battles long past, now a constant reminder of losses he couldn't afford to forget.

As X leaned over the maps, a memory surged of his love's laughter under starlight, a fleeting melody that warmed the night. Her joy vanished with her loss, a sting sharpened by Vincent's whispers— "Jade's light betrays her"—twisting his grief into vengeance.

The starlit glow pulsed in his mind, his sword vowing to shatter Sheng Xiao's balance, his heart a storm against her radiant crown.

Across from him stood Vincent, his serpent-shaped scepter gripped loosely in one hand, the ancient knots etched into its surface pulsing with a venomous shimmer, like veins of forbidden power whispering secrets from long-banished crafters.

"The Yin Scroll will break their harmony," X growled, his voice low and rough, carrying the weight of a predator's snarl held just in check.

His broad shoulders tensed under his tactical vest, muscles coiled from years of relentless training, the silver ring on a chain around his neck catching the holo-torchlight—a delicate band engraved with swirling zodiac motifs, a token from a life stolen away.

A memory clawed at him: her silhouette sprawled on cold stone, her glow dimming to nothing, the air thick with the scent of blood and ruin. He lunged forward, pulling her limp form into his arms, hugging her tight as his tears fell, mixing with her blood on her dress in a cruel, crimson blur.

His hands trembled as he pried the ring from her lifeless finger. Vengeance ignited, a wildfire consuming his grief, a pain that haunted every step he took.

Vincent's dark blue eyes glinted in the dim light, unreadable as ever, his light brown hair falling slightly over his forehead in a way that made him look deceptively casual. He traced a finger along the scepter's knotted length, its venomous shimmer flaring like a serpent's gaze.

As Vincent traced the scepter's knots, a memory surged of an Ogham grove, its mossy shadows cloaking ancient stones.

His scarred hands traced cryptic runes, their glow whispering dominion—Sheng Xiao kneeling, Jade's light dimmed under his will. A crest-like rune sparked resentment, her crown a taunt to his isolation.

The moss-scented air pulsed in his recollection, fueling his ambition to unravel her reign with Ogham's long forgotten forbidden power, a dark fire kindling in his heart.

"And reshape Sheng Xiao in our image," he murmured, his tone smooth and measured, laced with an undercurrent of a deeper drive he kept buried, his fingers tightening with a flicker of tension.

"No mistakes, Vincent," X warned, straightening to his full height, his presence filling the cramped outpost like a storm cloud. The ring shifted against his chest as he clenched it in his fist, the metal warm against his skin, a ghost of her touch. "We go to the cenote at dawn, eclipse by evening. The clans' peace ends tonight."

The air thrummed with their pact, the canopy outside pressing in with its chorus of nocturnal hums and insects droning, leaves rustling like whispers of warning. The outpost's bamboo creaked under the weight of the night, sealing their scheme in the heavy silence, the scepter's eerie glow casting serpentine patterns on the walls, as if the banished crafters themselves approved from their lost realm.

Outside, the pre-dawn haze clung to the Sapphirine River's banks, the water's deep blue surface rippling under the first hints of light. Lucas stood at the edge of a makeshift dock, his broad shoulders casting a long silhouette against the water's gleam.

His blonde hair was matted from the humidity, and his light blue eyes scanned the cluster of Monkey Clan scouts gathered nearby—wiry figures with quick hands and quicker grins, their tech-nets slung over shoulders like shimmering spiderwebs.

The nets pulsed faintly with embedded energy circuits, a blend of Mico's ingenuity: vines woven with micro-generators harvested from the hydroelectric falls upstream.

Lucas shifted his weight, his tunic already sticking to his rippling muscles from the muggy air.

He owed X... owed him big, from that night years ago when X had pulled him from a collapsing mine, saving his hide when no one else would.

The gratitude swelling within him fueled his resolve, a second chance he'd seized despite his past treason. X knew and still spared him.

"You know the cenote paths?" he asked, voice gruff but steady, crossing his arms, jaw set against the unease.

One scout, a lanky young man with sun-bronzed skin and a mop of curly black hair, stepped forward, his net humming as he adjusted it. "Better than anyone, outsider. But that place is holy, pixiu statues don't take kindly to thieves seeking its riches."

His companions nodded, eyes darting to the thicket's edge, where vines swayed like watchful sentinels.

Lucas pulled a pouch of coins from his belt --gold from Kusini's plains mingled with Coinin's tech-chips-- and tossed it to the leader. "Double if you get us there quiet. Half if you talk."

The scouts exchanged glances, the clink of coins sealing the deal. The leader pocketed it with a nod, his grin sharp. "Dawn's breaking. Follow close, thicket eats the slow."

Lucas turned back to the outpost, signaling the team with a low whistle.

Hiring locals wasn't his idea, but X had insisted since the Monkey Clan's knowledge of traps and tech would cut hours off the trek.

As the scouts melted into the undergrowth ahead, Lucas felt the weight of his purpose settle heavier, like the machete at his hip.

X knew his betrayal yet gave him a chance—this job had to succeed.

The thicket of Mico wrapped around X's band like a living snare, its dense canopy a tangled green veil slashed by shafts of midday sun that turned the air into a steaming haze.

The Sapphirine River twisted alongside their path, its deep blue waters surging with a wild roar that drowned out footsteps, the spray misting their faces with cool droplets laced with the scent of wet earth and blooming orchids.

Here in Sheng Xiao's southernmost clan lands, the Monkey Clan buzzed with ingenuity—the distant hum of hydroelectric falls echoed faintly beyond the groves, where villagers wove tech-nets that blended seamlessly with the vines, pulsing with subtle energy harvested from the river's fury.

The scouts led the way, their steps quick and silent, nets slung low to avoid snags. X pushed ahead, his dark tactical vest melding into the dappled gloom, sweat-soaked fabric clinging to his taut frame, boots sinking into the damp earth with deliberate precision.

Orchid perfume hung heavy in the air, cloying and sweet, mixed with the sharp drone of insects and a distant bird's screech that sounded almost like a warning.

Vines brushed his shoulders like unwelcome fingers, the canopy fighting back every step, roots twisting underfoot as if to trip the unwary.

Lucas swung his machete ahead, broad shoulders bulldozing through the undergrowth, his tunic streaked with green sap and clinging to his rippling muscles like a second skin. His blonde hair matted under the relentless heat, light blue eyes scanning the path for threats.

A flicker of hesitation slowed his swing—gratitude from that old debt gnawing deeper, the memory of X saving him in the mine flashing unbidden: the cave-in's roar, dust choking his lungs, X's hand yanking him free.

"Why me, a traitor?" Lucas had gasped then.

X's reply: "Because everyone deserves a second chance, don't waste it."

"Path's opening up," Lucas grunted, wiping sweat from his brow with the back of his hand, the words a thin mask for the resolve bubbling underneath.

"Keep sharp," he added, voice dropping low as his eyes flicked to a snapped twig, too clean, too deliberate, a trap's mark. The canopy pulsed with hidden dangers, every rustle a potential ambush.

Bella trailed close behind him, sparks dancing idly at her fingertips like restless fireflies, her crimson scarf a bold streak against the endless green.

"This humidity's wrecking my hair," she griped, smoothing frizzy red strands that framed her sharp features, amber eyes flashing with restless energy.

Her lithe build moved with a cat-like grace, but the heat made her steps heavier, her usual swagger tempered by the thicket's oppressive weight.

"Watch it, Bella," Lucas said, glancing back with a sharp grin that didn't quite reach his eyes. "You'll set the whole canopy ablaze before we even reach the temple."

She shot him a glare, lips twitching into a half-smile despite herself.

"Your machete's lagging like your jokes, Lucas. Pick up the pace!" Her bravado masked the fear gnawing at her edges, but her loyalty to X burned bright, his rescue from the wildfire's curse had given her purpose, a gratitude that steadied her steps. Their bond, forged in the crucible of X's desert missions, flickered like her flames.

Dolore kept pace a few steps back, lightning crackling faintly along her hands like nervous sparks, her light brown eyes sharp behind fogging glasses.

Her dark brown hair was pulled back tight into a practical braid like the locals, but stray strands escaped in the humidity, framing her determined face.

Her pulse raced whenever X's gaze swept past, his grey eyes cutting through her without seeing the longing she buried deep—her heart ached with a love she dared not voice, sparked by his rescue from a shrine collapse, his words "You're worth more" echoing in her soul.

Her sparks flared protectively, a silent vow clashing with the doubt Vincent's calm stirred.

Vincent glided at X's side, his rune-stitched scarf shading his light brown hair from the sun's glare, dark blue eyes unreadable as a still pond.

"Temple's near," he murmured, the scepter's knotted length humming with a sickly green pulse that made the scouts' nets flicker uneasily. Vincent's fingers tightened, a flicker of tension in his jaw hinting at buried drives, his calm a mask honed by years of silence.

The canopy's vines swayed like serpents in the midday haze, their arcs sparking a memory X couldn't shake, pulling him into the past with vivid force.

Years ago, in Kusini's sunbaked plains, he'd overseen a training session under a vast sky streaked with harvest dust. A young fighter sparred in the ring, his knives flashing in a fluid crescent sweep, disarming his opponent with precision that drew gasps from the onlookers.

"He's got the captain's form," one soldier muttered, awe in his voice, as the boy landed a flawless parry. The boy beamed as he won, knives sheathed with a flourish, the crowd cheering.

"Gonna ask the captain to teach me more," the boy said to his opponent, wiping sweat from his brow. The memory lingered like a ghost; the vines' sway a cruel echo of a life lost to war's chaos.

The vines snapped him back, their curves twisting mockingly as Lucas hacked through another thicket. They'd pushed off at dawn, the Sapphirine River's roar their constant companion, guiding them deeper into Sheng Xiao's wild heart.

Midday haze had thickened, hours blurring in the relentless humidity, the sun dipping toward early evening's promise as gloom lengthened across the path.

Mud tugged at boots, roots snagged ankles like grasping hands, the river's surge peeking through gaps in the foliage, foam flecking its blue fury with white caps that crashed against rocks.

X's piercing eyes, once lit with a lover's warmth, stayed fixed ahead, his dark brown hair matted with sweat, features hollowed by endless nights of planning. *They took her from me,* he thought, his fist clenching around the chain at his neck until his knuckles whitened, the ring's engraving biting into his skin.

The memory clawed deeper, dragging him to her side, her body limp, glow dimmed to nothing.

The thicket snapped him back from that chaos, its gloom tightening like her vanished pulse as Lucas shouted, "Clear ahead!"—grief fueling the fire that burned hotter than Bella's sparks.

A guide whispered, voice low and trembling, "Legends speak of ancient knot-crafters, foes of zodiac harmony, banished long ago to their shadowed groves."

X ignored it, his rage drowning out the myths. He drove forward, the canopy's crush no match for the storm coiling inside him.

One scout called out, "Vine trap ahead—glyphs flaring!"

A vine snapped taut across the path, glyphs flaring faintly—Monkey Clan traps, woven with tech-net precision that hummed like angry bees. Lucas hacked it down with a grunt, but thorns erupted from the earth, barbed and gleaming with poisonous sap that dripped like tears.

Bella's sparks flared brighter, incinerating them in a burst of heat that singed the air, her crimson scarf fluttering as embers danced around her.

"This place hates us," she muttered, her voice edged with a mix of bravado and fear, the scarf clutched tight in one hand as if it were a lifeline.

Lucas reached back, steadying her with a firm hand on her arm, his light blue eyes meeting hers with a steady gaze. "Easy there, firebrand. I've got you."

She rolled her eyes, smirking through the tension. "Keep up, muscle, or I'll roast you too." Their bond, forged in the crucible of X's desert missions, flickered like her flames.

The path had narrowed to a rickety bridge creaking over a tributary, frayed planks swaying precariously, its ropes groaning under their weight.

The scouts balked, eyes wide with fear, one whispering legends of cursed crossings, their nets trembling as glyphs flared along the ropes. X led them across next, his boots thudding with authority, the scouts following with hesitant steps, their breaths shallow.

Lucas gripped the ropes, guiding Bella, her sparks flaring to light the way, their breaths syncing with the creak of wood. Dolore's lightning cast jittery blue glimmers on the planks, her glasses fogging as she whispered prayers, her dark brown braid swaying with each cautious step.

Vincent glided across last, his scepter's knotted length steady, its green pulse a stark contrast to the scouts' trembling. Solid ground welcomed them, but the rustle ahead shattered the relief.

A panther emerged, eyes like molten gold, its growl rumbling low through the vines, Mico's primal guardian baring fangs that gleamed white. Its claw swiped, grazing a vine near Bella, the reverberating snarl echoing through the thicket.

The scouts froze, nets trembling in their grips as the beast prowled closer, muscles rippling under sleek black fur. A female scout gasped, her net shaking, murmuring a prayer to Monkey's cunning.

Vincent lifted his scepter, its glow flaring with twisted etchings, chilling the air with an unnatural frost that made the leaves brittle. The beast stilled, golden eyes narrowing, then slunk back into the undergrowth, claws snagging Bella's scarf on the way, tearing a small rip.

"Next one gets roasted," she spat, flames dancing hotter along her fingers, but her hands shook slightly, the tear in her scarf a small wound that mirrored the cracks in her resolve.

Lucas chuckled, clapping her shoulder with a rough hand. "Save the fire for the real fight, hothead." Their banter cut the tension, a flicker of normalcy amid the wild, but beneath it, Bella's unease grew—she'd borne too much from fire's judgment, scars of exile she couldn't erase.

Another trap triggered—vines lashing like whips from the trees, glyphs flaring red with zodiac patterns that twisted like living tattoos.

X dove forward, his dagger slicing through the air in a precise arc, sap spraying and burning his skin like acid.

The scouts shrieked, one net sparking wild as a ritual-fueled serpent struck from a crevice, fangs grazing a wiry arm, venom foaming at the bite.

Vincent's scepter pulsed, a green wave calming the beast mid-lunge, but his gaze lingered on X, unreadable, a scheme coiled tight like the vines themselves.

X nodded at Vincent, trusting the man's power without question, the pact between them forged in shared loss. Dolore's sparks flared protectively, her loyalty fraying at the edges as Vincent's scepter gleamed, his eyes hiding depths far beyond the trembling earth.

The river tightened, foliage peeling back to reveal the cenote's yawning depths, jagged black stone walls gleaming under Bella's sparks and Dolore's crackling blue light.

Pixiu statues loomed at the edges, their lion-like forms carved with fierce precision, protective gleams in their eyes warding the sacred drop as if Sheng Xiao's harmony depended on its vigilance.

The walls shimmered with zodiac etchings—Horse's flowing mane, Dragon's shimmering scales, Snake's coiled grace, Monkey's nimble tail—all twelve clans coiled in starlit harmony, weaving the cycle's balance like threads in a grand tapestry.

The cenote, Sheng Xiao's deepest wound, thrummed with veiled power, its teal-veined waters rippling with ancient runes that pulsed like a living heartbeat, a sacred pulse resisting the scroll's corruption.

Glyphs vibrated along roots, dripping stone mingling with fertile earth, ritual-fueled serpents hissing from crevices like Mico's untamed fury, their scales glinting with the scepter's influence.

The scouts balked, nets flickering unsteady, one whispering, "The pixiu... they'll awaken if we disturb the temple's heart."

Vincent's grip on the scepter tightened, eyes narrowing—a wordless command that silenced them.

As the team paused, a chill swept through the air, heavy with unseen eyes watching from the gloom. A vine trap snapped, glyphs flaring as thorns lashed out, forcing Lucas to duck and slash with a grunt.

Dolore's glasses fogged, her lightning dimming as a vision gripped her—an Oracle's whisper, unbidden: "The balance fractures, chaos swallowing harmony, clans crumbling unless restored."

She gasped, clutching her chest, her heart torn further by X's silhouette below, the warning fading as X's growl pulled her back.

"It's down there," X growled, his unyielding eyes flashing with that tragic fire, the ring a cold weight against his chest.

Lucas saluted, his light blue gaze steady despite the weight pressing on him. "We're right behind you, boss."

Vincent raised a hand, his voice cutting through the tension. "X must descend alone—the runes demand it."

Dolore's sparks faltered, concern etching her face as she glanced downward, her heart aching with unvoiced love.

Bella huffed, "We can't help?"

Lucas shifted uneasily, machete gripped tighter.

Vincent passed X a leather spellbook, runes etched green and thrumming like a heartbeat.

"You'll need this," he said, the scepter's knotted length projecting runic paths into the depths, guiding X alone down the spiraling stairs, damp air chilling his skin to the bone, Dolore's lightning flaring one last protective surge.

The staircase twisted tighter, moss slick under his boots, each step echoing like a heartbeat in Mico's chest. Glyphs pulsed on the walls, zodiac patterns—Dragon's scales glinting like fire, Rabbit's leap frozen in stone—whispering of ancient balances that had held for centuries.

A ritual-fueled serpent lunged from a crack, fangs dripping venom that sizzled on the stone. X slashed his dagger in a swift arc, its body thudding wetly to the steps, but another coiled from the shadows, tail rattling like bones.

He ducked, dagger flashing again, a thorn grazing his palm earlier, blood mixing with sweat as he gripped the spellbook, venom splattering his vest and burning like fire on his skin. Her memory urged him deeper, her loss burning in his mind like an eternal flame.

The sanctum yawned open at the bottom, walls aglow in silver light that danced across the water's surface, zodiac carvings shimmering like a cathedral of clans united under the stars.

A stone plinth jutted over the cenote's inky waters, the Yin Scroll perched atop it, its parchment surging with veiled chaos—a heartbeat that could unravel Sheng Xiao's core.

A silver vortex whirled around it, spectral tendrils lashing out like angry spirits, harmony's edge teetering on the brink of collapse.

X's lips curled into a snarl, grief igniting into pure fury— *This will shatter their precious world, just as they shattered mine.*

He flipped open the spellbook, runes crackling green and casting stark patterns on the walls, the air thickening with the scent of ozone and ancient dust. His voice rasped the ancient chant, each word laced with fury, the green tendrils clashing against the vortex like clashing swords, spectral wails echoing through the chamber as silver barriers fractured with sharp cracks.

Vincent's scepter pulsed brighter from above, fueling the ritual through some unseen link, the air thick with the bite of burning runes.

He chanted louder as he advanced, the sanctum trembling, glyphs flaring wild on the walls, ritual-fueled serpents slithering faster from crevices, their hisses a chorus of chaos rising to a fever pitch through the chamber.

X forged ahead, boots slipping on moss-slick stone, a dart grazing his arm with venom burning through his veins like liquid fire, but her memory burned hotter, pushing him forward.

He chanted louder, the spellbook's pages fluttering like trapped birds in a gale, green light searing the air and illuminating the zodiac carvings in eerie relief.

A grim smile cracked his face, the scroll's power surging like victory through his veins—he clutched it tight, a fleeting triumph flashing in his eyes, vengeance within reach at last.

A root burst from the plinth, zodiac glyphs glowing fiercely, wrapping the scroll in a protective coil like a mother's embrace. X's runic chant, amplified by Vincent's distant scepter, shattered it with a thunderous crack, blood from his palm mixing with sweat as he gripped the spellbook, his rage a storm swallowing every doubt.

The barrier exploded in a crystalline shatter, shards dissolving into the depths with a final hiss, the waters swallowing the light like a starving beast.

The spellbook parted the cenote like a veil, a misty path glowing green and rippling unsteady across the dark surface. X stepped forward, boots firm on the ethereal bridge, air sparking around him with residual energy, the scroll's warmth jolting through him like a promise.

As the sky bled red, Vincent's scepter flared green in eerie contrast, the cenote's depths glowing with the same venomous hue, chaos painting the wilds in clashing colors.

"They'll all pay," he snarled, seizing it in a firm grip, its power thrumming through his veins like a second heartbeat.

The ground bucked violently, limestone chunks plunging into the water with resounding splashes, the temple's hum twisting into a wail as Sheng Xiao's harmony cracked wide open.

The sky above was crimson through the canopy, the world deepening cold across Mico's vast expanse, disharmony chilling the air like a winter frost in summer.

Above, the pixiu statues groaned to life, their eyes dimming as cracks webbed their stone forms like veins of lightning. The scouts screamed, nets sparking uselessly in panic, one collapsing as a ritual-fueled serpent struck true, venom foaming at his mouth in agonized bubbles.

Lucas hauled him up, machete slashing vines that surged like living traps, his gratitude fueling his resolve: an old debt weighing heavy, the mine's dust still in his lungs.

Bella's flames roared, burning a path through the chaos, but her bravado cracked wide, amber eyes wide with genuine fear.

"We broke it," she whispered, scarf clutched tight in trembling hands, the tear from the panther a harbinger of the fractures to come.

Dolore's lightning surged, fending off serpents with bursts of blue energy, but her gaze locked downward, heart aching for X below. *Is he safe?* she thought.

The guides bolted into the undergrowth, nets sparking wild as they cried, "The harmony fractures!"

Lucas grabbed Bella's arm, his light blue eyes wide with the quake's fury. "We did it," he said, her smirk crumbling entirely, flames dimming as fear gnawed at her edges.

"This... this is bigger than us," she whispered, fingers clutching her torn scarf, the fabric a fragile reminder of home.

Lucas forced a grin through the panic. "Stick together, firebug—we always do."

The henchmen regrouped, breaths ragged, while Vincent stood apart, a faint smirk betraying his satisfaction at the scroll's power, his scepter humming softly.

Dolore's lightning sputtered, her unvoiced love for X clashing with the mission's toll, loyalty fraying like the bridge's ropes as her heart tore further.

The eclipse deepened, stars vanishing, Sheng Xiao's balance splintering like a carved serpent hissing chaos, light and dark teetering on eternal fracture, the cenote's echo lingering like a whisper of unraveling fate.

Chapter 2: Beacon of Balance

The Imperial City gleamed a thousand miles from Mico's tangled jungles, its golden-roofed temples pulsing under fenghuang holo-lanterns that cast a radiant glyph shimmer, like starlight trapped in glass, across the throne room's vast marble expanse.

Empress Jade stood before her family's grand portrait, her amethyst gaze—sharp as cut gems, framed by flowing red hair that spilled in fiery waves over her sapphire-threaded silk robe, its intricate embroidery glinting like a night sky--lingering on her father, Emperor Alexandrite. His steady presence loomed like a mountain she feared she'd never climb, silver hair etched with a wisdom that felt like an unreachable star, his violet eyes a mirror of her own yet brimming with unshakable resolve.

Her mother, Empress Liora, smiled gently beside him, kind eyes a distant memory lost to illness a decade ago, a void that carved a hollow in Jade's chest, her delicate features a reminder of a warmth the palace no longer held.

Her twin siblings, Onyx and Opal, stared back—Opal's warm smile a fading light lost to tragedy, Onyx's stern eyes a mystery since his disappearance, leaving Jade adrift in a silent ache, her heart twisting at the empty spaces where their laughter once echoed—Opal's playful jibes, Onyx's quiet intensity.

Her sharp cheekbones caught the glyph shimmer, her regal poise masking the doubt gnawing within, her slender fingers trembling slightly as they brushed the portrait's gilded frame, the cool metal grounding her against the tide of grief.

Jade's fingers lingered on the frame, a memory flashing of a childhood lesson with her father under the Great Race mural, its zodiac glyphs pulsing with Sheng Xiao's promise. At ten, his violet eyes shone, tracing a dragon motif on a tapestry.

"Your heart leads, my pearl," he said, incense curling in the air.

Now, his absence and X's chaos loomed, Jade fearing her crown would chain her love for Cade, her identity torn between empress and girl. The mural's hum urged her to weave duty with heart, a vow kindling her resolve against the gathering storm.

Can I ever fill his throne without crumbling? she wondered, frustration simmering like a slow-burning ember as her fingers traced the frame's intricate zodiac carvings—Horse's mane flowing like wind, Snake's coils twisting with cunning grace—a silent judgment from the twelve clans she ruled.

The Fenghuang Throne loomed behind her, its seat shimmering with embedded holo-crystals that pulsed in rhythm with the city's heartbeat, qilin horns curling from the arms like guardians poised to judge, their mythical forms a symbol of the balance she struggled to maintain, the throne's weight a constant pressure against her resolve.

Above, a mural of the Great Race sprawled across the vaulted ceiling, Vladimir the Rat sprinting in victory—a taunt from five centuries ago that mirrored her doubts, his triumphant stride gleaming under the glyph shimmer, a challenge that seemed to trap her in its coils.

Jade's lithe frame, honed from diplomatic travels across starlit courts, her sapphire robe whispering with each step, tensed as she brushed the throne's armrest, energy weave flickering unsteady at her touch, magnetic pulses shimmering the air like waves in a still pool, their faint hum mirroring the waver in her resolve, her breath catching as she fought the urge to shrink beneath the throne's looming presence.

Her amethyst stare hardened, a silent oath to weave balance from her father's ashes, the throne's weight a forge for her strength.

The palace hummed with blended elegance, servants gliding across the marble, polishing with jasmine-scented cloths under holo-torchlight, the sweet bloom mingling with the hum of zodiac-aligned holo-screens displaying celestial alignments and prosperous trade flows: bustling markets brimming with silks, thriving harvests of grains and herbs from the clans.

Guards' steel glinted in the sleek glow, their armor etched with fenghuang wings for imperial balance, their disciplined steps echoing softly as they patrolled the hall, their presence a quiet reassurance of order.

A young female guard, her dark eyes sharp under a helm, murmured to her partner, "She's holding steady—more than I'd manage under that glare," her voice low with respect, adjusting her stance as the hall grew still.

A male guard adjusted his helm, his deep voice replying, "The Empress is tough."

Courtiers murmured in tight clusters, silk tunics rustling like unwelcome whispers, their eyes weighing Jade's every move as holo-displays flickered with reports of steady commerce—spices flowing freely, tech-chips traded briskly, and starlit omens heralding peace, the city's pulse a constant reminder of the harmony she was sworn to protect, a burden that felt heavier with each sidelong glance from the court.

Lord Huan approached, his hawkish nose sharp under thinning gray hair, his angular face carved with lines of calculated ambition. His voice carried a gruff edge, a promise to Alexandrite to forge her strength, though his stern gaze felt like a lash, rooted in reverence for the throne's zodiac traditions.

"Your Majesty, the trade guilds await your tariff ruling on medicinal exports. The clans grow restless under this...uncertainty," he pressed, his tone mean but protective, hands clasped behind his back as if guarding the throne's legacy, his reverence for its rites evident in his rigid posture.

Jade's throat tightened, her fingers fumbling the frame's edge.

Why's it always me they doubt? she thought.

Her cheeks burned with the memory of three years ago, her first decree stumbling out in this very room at sixteen, barely a year after her father's sudden death.

Courtiers' sneers had rippled through the hall like poison from a hidden viper, their whispers— "Too young, too weak"— cutting deeper than any blade, leaving scars she still felt under their gazes.

Now, at nineteen, she bore that legacy, her voice clipped but steady as she replied, "Tomorrow."

Huan bowed deeper, a hint of approval in his narrow eyes despite the harshness, fueling her resolve to prove her worth.

Jade paced to the alcove, seeking refuge from the throne room's oppressive weight, the marble cool under her embroidered slippers, her silk robe whispering against the floor like a faint sigh.

Her thoughts drifted to a sunlit afternoon seven years ago, when she was twelve, the throne room bathed in incense from distant vineyards, the air thick with the scent of cedar and jasmine, holo-lanterns casting a golden sheen across the marble like liquid sunlight.

Alexandrite knelt before her, his silver hair gleaming as he summoned energy weave with a graceful wave, light and dark energies swirling in perfect harmony like forging balance from chaos.

"Feel the scrolls' pulse, Jade," he said, his voice steady as a river, guiding her small hands to mimic the weave, the air humming with his magic's warm pulse, like a heartbeat binding the clans. "Yin and Yang, Light and Dark, hold Sheng Xiao's heart: one lost tips disharmony, talismans anchoring the clans to steady the storm."

Young Jade nodded, her weave flickering unsteady, the rough texture of his robe brushing her fingers as he pulled her close, a rare embrace that lingered like a promise, the cedar scent clinging to his sleeve, his violet eyes a beacon of hope, the holo-crystals pulsing in sync with his words.

She pressed her cheek against his robe, the fabric coarse yet warm, his hand steady on her shoulder as he added, "The clans rely on you, but you'll never stand alone." He smiled, a rare softness breaking through his regal demeanor, his voice a low murmur: "You'll be the balance, Jade, stronger than you know."

The throne room's marble gleamed around them, the holo-screens flickering with zodiac motifs—Rabbit's leap, Rooster's cannon—as Jade's small hands tried to hold the weave steady, her father's patient nod igniting a spark of courage she clung to even now.

The memory faded, her resolve trembling but kindled. She'd prove him right, even if the throne felt like a cage forged of expectations, her fingers tightening on the alcove's edge as his words echoed like a distant drum.

Another memory surfaced: Percy, Alexandrite's Cat Clan advisor, under cherry blossoms five years ago, when Jade was fourteen, petals drifting like snow in a gentle breeze, the air sweet with bloom and the faint tang of palace gardens.

His gentle voice wove tales of Li Shou's shadow guardians shielding the throne, his laughter a warm shield against court sneers, a dagger in his hand a symbol of quiet loyalty.

"You have a strength all your own, Jade," he said, warm eyes steadying her as petals caught in his dark hair, his tales sparking her courage amid the palace's cold marble.

"Li Shou's guardians stand unseen, always ready for the crown," he teased, tossing a blossom her way with a twirl of his dagger, its blade catching the light like a star, his smile warming the spring air.

"You'll outshine their sneers, Jade, just wait," he added, his voice a soft promise as the petal landed in her palm, her fingers closing around it like a vow, the breeze carrying his laughter like a melody.

The garden's grass crunched softly under their feet, the cherry trees swaying as Percy spun another tale of Li Shou's stealth, his dagger flashing in a playful arc, Jade giggling as she ducked a falling petal, her heart light despite the court's weight.

His presence bridged her father's wisdom and her uncertainties, but now, silenced by murder in the chaos that claimed Alexandrite, his loss lingered like a wound, yet his warmth lived on in another, a blue-green gaze that echoed his brother's legacy.

That warmth bloomed in Cade, Percy's younger brother, his loyalty a steady anchor, their bond a secret grounding her amid the storm.

A childhood memory flickered: under those cherry trees a decade ago, when Jade was ten and Cade eleven, his boyish grin promised, "I'll always stand by you, Jade," his green-blue gaze sparking with roguish charm, evoking Tai's in old tales, his dark brown hair tousled by the breeze as he clutched knives like treasures from their shared adventures.

They played at weaving shadows, his small hands mimicking her energy weave, laughter echoing as he teased, "You're the empress, but I'm your guardian," his lean frame hinting at the fighter he'd become, the air sweet with petals and promise.

He tossed her a cherry blossom, his fingers brushing hers, the spark of his touch lingering as he laughed, "Gotta keep up with you, Empress," his voice bright with a loyalty that rooted deep, his small frame darting through the grass as she chased him, their giggles mingling with the rustle of leaves.

The sun filtered through the trees, casting dappled light across their faces, Jade's red hair catching the glow as she tackled him, both tumbling into the grass, their laughter a vow that bound them through the years.

His eyes lit up at the tales of Li Shou, a heritage he barely grasped, raised in the palace yet drawn to a clan he longed to claim, their vow binding them to an unspoken passion she buried deep, his touch lingering like a spark in the petal-strewn grass, her heart racing even then at the boy who'd become her anchor.

Cade stood by the throne room's edge, his knives glinting under holo-torchlight, a memory flashing of a Doragon spar with Percy. "Protect Jade," Percy had grinned, blades clashing, but Cade doubted—a Cat Clan outsider worthy of an empress?

Now, her summons stirred fear, her amethyst eyes a spark, urging his loyalty. The holo-torchlight flickered, his heart vowing to be her shadow in Sheng Xiao's storm, knives ready for the Prophecy's trials.

Another memory surged, vivid and raw—four years ago, at fifteen, when Cade returned to the palace after training across Sheng Xiao's courts with Commander Calix.

Jade stood in the throne room, her silk robe brushing the marble, heart racing as he strode in, no longer the scrawny boy of their childhood. His lean muscles rippled under a fitted tunic, dark brown hair tousled from travel, emerald and storm-blue gaze blazing with quiet intensity.

His knives gleamed at his belt, and whispers of his skill— "Calix's best, knives like lightning," guards had said—echoed in her mind.

Seeing him now, she believed them, struck by his rugged charm, his sharp jawline and steady strength, a mind honed by Calix's lessons as brilliant as her own diplomatic wit, his presence commanding the hall like a quiet storm.

"Still the palace's shadow, Cade?" she teased, her amethyst stare locking with his, heart skipping at his roguish grin.

"Only for you, Empress," he shot back, voice low and rough, his gaze lingering, awestruck by her flowing red hair, sharp cheekbones, and commanding poise that made her every bit the ruler she doubted she was.

Their eyes locked, a spark flaring in the glyph shimmer, a vow unvoiced, his loyalty a flame she felt in her bones, their childhood promise now a fire neither could name, the air thick with the scent of jasmine and unspoken longing as he stepped closer, his breath catching at her presence, her own pulse quickening as she met his intensity, the throne room fading around them, the light casting their silhouettes in a dance of tension.

The chill sliced through like frost from Ged's peaks, yanking Jade from her daydreams to the trembling present, a low hum vibrating through the marble, a pre-tremor warning that set her nerves on edge.

The air turned biting cold, the holo-lanterns flickering erratic as if gasping for breath. The ground bucked without warning, chandeliers clattering like frantic chimes, dust sifting as gloom veiled Vladimir's victorious stride, making it seem ready to falter, an ominous warning tracing the mural's lines.

Fenghuang lanterns surged wild, an eerie gloom flickered over the portrait, visible through the alcove's arch, tracing the twins' faces in an omen of chaos, the qilin horns on the throne vibrating with the quake's growl.

The sky outside darkened, the moon's halo bleeding crimson, disharmony chilling the air like a wound reopening.

Citizens spilled into streets below, clutching prayer beads, shouts rising from temples now dim under a crimson veil, the sky shifting to early evening as disharmony spread, merchants shuttering stalls in panic, children clinging to parents' robes, priests chanting desperately against the quake's roar, the city's pulse stuttering uneven like a heart in distress, the cobblestone streets trembling as if the earth itself mourned the loss of balance.

Jade's energy weave shimmered involuntary, a vision gripping her—an oracle-like whisper of imbalance: "Scrolls shift, light and gloom splintering harmony, a pulse from Mico's depths."

She sensed Cade's distant fear, their telepathic bond flaring to life, his surge of surprise mirroring her own, his presence a steady hum amid the chaos, a lifeline she clung to as the vision's weight pressed against her chest.

The tremor subsided, but the warning lingered, suspense coiling tight like a spring ready to snap, the portrait's eerie gloom a silent promise of chaos yet to unfold.

Cade burst through the throne room doors, drawn by their bond to the alcove where Jade stood, his mismatched gaze blazing as he rushed to her side, his dark brown hair disheveled from racing frantically, his broad shoulders tense under a fitted tunic, lean muscles coiled with energy, his rugged charm a quiet fire in the flickering light.

"You okay, Empress?" he asked, voice low and urgent, a surge of fear thrumming through their telepathic bond, his dual-hued stare locking on hers with roguish intensity that steadied her heart.

His gaze scanned her, protectiveness flooding like a wave, knives flashing ready at his belt, long sleeves hiding a cat-silhouette tattoo that pulsed faint with his clan's hidden power, a royal tie binding him to her in ways words couldn't touch.

His cat-like grace, honed by years of training with Calix, a reminder of secrets they shared, the air humming with unspoken tension as he stepped closer, his sharp jawline and tousled hair catching the flickering glyph shimmer, her heart racing at his nearness, his breath steady but quick, a silent vow in his stance.

"I felt it too," he said, the bond humming between them, his voice a low rumble that sent a shiver through her not entirely from the cold.

Jade's red hair caught the flickering light, her frustration easing at his nearness, her amethyst stare softening as she met his gaze, the palace's weight lifting slightly in his steady presence, her energy weave calming as his presence anchored her like a star in a storm.

"The Yin Scroll's gone," he added, words cutting sharp, the Prophecy's darkness closing in, his knives shifting as he paced, his lean frame taut with urgency, muscles flexing beneath his tunic, his roguish charm a quiet fire that warmed the chill of his fear—*Can't fail her now, not when she needs me,* his doubt whispered.

"We can't let X tip the scales," she replied, voice trembling but steeling, her energy weave steadying as she placed a hand on his arm, the contact sending a spark through their bond. "I'm not the ruler Father was yet, but I have to try."

Her father's lessons echoed—scrolls as Sheng Xiao's fulcrum, one lost tipping all toward disharmony.

"Head to Ged, the Yang Temple. It's our only counter." Jade sent the courtiers and servants to ensure the palace and city's safety, clearing the alcove for her and Cade alone, her tone softening, trust warming the bond like sunlight breaking clouds. "Be careful, Cade."

He nodded, shadows coiling at his edges in secret, a gold-blue glow thrumming faint from his tattoo, his green-blue gaze lingering on her with that intensity that made her heart race.

"You worry too much, Empress," he teased, winking with that grin that sparked something deeper, his voice laced with affection he tried to mask. He lingered a moment, their eyes locked, the alcove's quiet amplifying their bond.

"You've grown too pretty for this palace, Jade," he blurted, then froze, vulnerability flashing as he realized his slip, her breath catching as she whispered, "And you're too reckless for my peace."

Their shared smile held a promise, the air thick with unspoken longing before he vanished into a swirl of midnight silk, shadows rippling like Li Shou's grace, cat-like forms flickering as he melded with the dark, the alcove's glyph shimmer fading behind him.

In Ged, atop Sheng Xiao's highest peak where starlit winds howled like restless spirits under a star-flecked night, the Yang Temple stood radiant, white marble walls bathed in holo-beacons' golden light, a stark contrast to Mico's dark cenote, defying the thin, frost-laced air that bit like invisible fangs.

Jagged cliffs ringed the plateau, biting cold stinging Cade's skin as he materialized, breath clouding in the chill, his dark brown hair ruffled by the gusts, emerald and storm-blue gaze narrowing against the wind's assault.

The entrance loomed, a towering archway flanked by pillars etched with zodiac clans: Rabbit's leap frozen in grace, Rooster's cannon vigilant and bold—a haunting melody in the carvings' glow, the air humming with ancient power that made his tattoo pulse in response. The temple's silence stretched, its emptiness a mirror to the Yin Temple's isolation, warding him with spectral stillness.

Cade exhaled sharp, the freeze piercing like needles—*I'm no hero, but for Jade, I'll push through*, he thought.

His unworthiness gnawed, the Cat Clan's vow burning in his dual-hued gaze, Jade's amethyst eyes a fire in his mind, her trust steadying the doubt that threatened to freeze him in place.

Inside, white tiles bore zodiac motifs—Snake's coils twisting with wisdom, Horse's mane flowing independent—a symphony of light that pulsed with Yang's energy, the air heavy with polished stone and incense, frost mingling with the hum of chants that echoed like a distant storm.

A marble pedestal held the Yang Scroll, its parchment radiating sunlight warmth, a beacon against encroaching gloom— its golden script a heartbeat anchoring the clans.

Pressure plates gleamed along the floor, edges etched with Rooster's vigilance, guarding with traps that could crush the unwary, the pixiu illusions shimmering faint, weaving through the air like spectral guardians.

Cade's heart pounded, shadows surging toward the scroll, but a pixiu ward blazed gold, shoving him back with a jolt that

burned his fingertips. He gritted his teeth, eyeing the first tile—
step by step it is.

A low hum built, the temple's pulse quickening as he leaped, landing with a thud on the first tile, the ward's glow steadying as zodiac carvings brightened, the chill seeping into his bones as doubt whispered, *I'm not enough for her,* his knives twitching at his belt as he braced for the next move.

Halfway across, a tile clicked like bone snapping under pressure. A spectral groan rose from the temple's core, and Cade teleported, shadows straining, his tattoo searing with Li Shou's fire, just as obsidian spears—etched with Pig's hammer for prosperous force—erupted from walls, grazing his cloak with a rip that tore the fabric like a scream, one shattering tiles in a deafening crash, dust choking the air in a vow of destruction.

Glyph beams flared, Rooster's motifs surging hot. Searing paths he dodged with a shadow blur—self-doubt clawing. *She's counting on me—time to earn it.* The wind outside howled in mockery, his breath ragged as he steadied himself.

The next tile cracked, ceiling buckling as marble chunks rained down, splintering floors with thunderous booms that echoed like coastal storms, the temple's hum rising to a roar that vibrated through his knives.

He teleported again, debris whistling past his ear, knives slashing a falling shard mid-air with a metallic ring, the fragment exploding in sparks.

A spectral zodiac spirit materialized, coils like Snake's wisdom lashing wild, forcing another desperate leap, its cry fading as Cade landed, sweat beading cold on his brow despite the inner fire of Jade's trust, his muscles burning from the strain, his tattoo pulsing like a second heartbeat.

Crystalline spikes thrust up, Goat's motifs glinting lethal with mild persistence turned deadly, and he dodged once more, the air electric with near misses that singed his tunic, the frost biting deeper as he pushed forward.

A glyph trap flared, Dragon's scales igniting a fiery burst, and he rolled, knives clashing against the heat, the temple's pulse a frantic heartbeat matching his own, shadows straining at his command. Three tiles left, each teleport a prayer to Jade's trust, the quaking floor a test of his soul.

He reached the pedestal, the Yang Scroll's warmth flooding him like summer's embrace, golden sparks cascading like zodiac embers, illuminating the tiles in a dance of light and gloom. The temple quaked, walls splintering, zodiac carvings trembling as spears flared in warning.

The moon's halo bled crimson outside, winds howling disharmony's cry, the scroll's glow dimming as Cade clutched it tight, its heat a vow sealing in his palm, its surge a promise as he teleported to the entrance.

He staggered from the teleport, the scroll's warmth his only anchor as shadows receded, dust settling, the hum falling silent, his breath ragged but triumph surging through the bond to Jade.

On the jungle outskirts, almost free of Mico's grip, en route to X's fortress in the Unknown Wilderness, X's band camped, fire crackling as they savored a victory meal, roasted meat sizzling under the canopy, vines framing their makeshift haven. Bella smirked, sparks dancing playful at her fingertips, her crimson scarf fluttering in the humid breeze.

"That cenote was a pit of snakes and traps—guides ran like scared kids!" she laughed, tossing a twig into the flames, her amber eyes glinting with fire's defiance.

Lucas chuckled, machete resting across his knees, his blonde hair matted but spirits high. "Their nets sparked out—useless! But X went in alone like a beast, pulling us through," his light blue gaze flicking to X, admiration mixing with guilt, the mine's dust a heavy weight, his treason a secret X forgave, his machete gleaming as guilt fueled his grip.

Dolore's lightning crackled faint approval, her gaze on X warm.

"Fearless, descending that cursed heart," she murmured, her braid swaying, devotion softening her edges.

Vincent glided silent, scepter in hand, his dark blue eyes hiding calculations, a cryptic glance stirring the fire, runes pulsing unsteady, his voice low, "Our move strengthens—watch the clans squirm."

X allowed a rare grim smile, the Yin Scroll secure, savoring a fleeting triumph, his grey gaze ablaze with a conqueror's glory, the scroll's pulse a war drum in his hands.

But the scroll pulsed erratic in his hold, its shadowed chaos reacting to some shift, and then the ground bucked again, harder than before, the eclipse deepening darker, crimson halo bleeding thicker, the air turning heavy with disharmony's chill, the canopy's vines trembling as if alive.

X's eyes widened in surprise— "She got the Yang already? I'd planned for both."

Vincent frowned, confusion flashing before his cryptic mask returned. "How? She's no match for true power—weak, unworthy of that throne."

The scepter's green runes thrummed unsteady, plans shifting in the quake's echo, his fingers tightening as firelight danced across his unreadable face.

Bella's sparks flared, "What now? Another quake?" her voice sharp as she stood, flames licking her fingers.

Lucas gripped his machete, "Not again—this jungle's cursed!" his voice rough as he scanned the trees.

Dolore's lightning sputtered, her eyes on X, "What's causing this?! Will it harm you?" her voice trembling with concern.

"We accelerate," X growled, resolve hardening as he clutched the silver ring, the chain cool against his skin. "Target the talismans now."

Vincent's lips twitched, saying, "As you wish," runes whispering chaos like a gathering storm, the group's mood shifting from celebration to grim determination, the fire's crackle fading under the jungle's sudden silence, the air thick with the weight of their next move, the roasted meat forgotten as they braced for what lay ahead.

As the eclipse deepened, the moon's halo crimson and ground rumbling, Jade stood firm—Cade had the Yang Scroll, disharmony surging like a tide, holo-screens still dim from the quake's chaos, their feeds stuttering as the city reeled, priests' chants echoing faintly through the palace walls.

Stars faded, Sheng Xiao's balance teetering, her resolve hardening like steel. Lina trembled nearby, clutching a broom that clattered to the floor, fear widening her dark eyes as aftershocks growled, her simple tunic dirtied from the dust, hands shaking like leaves in a gale.

Jade knelt swift, helping Lina to her feet, energy weave shimmering soft around them both, her voice warm amid the chill, amethyst gaze meeting Lina's with genuine care.

"We'll protect Sheng Xiao together," she said, her hand steadying Lina's shoulder in a gesture of solidarity, the throne room's mural above seeming less judgmental in the moment's humanity, her heart steadying as she rose, a leader emerging from doubt.

Lina clung to her hand a moment longer, whispering, "You're our hope, Empress," her gratitude a quiet strength that bolstered Jade's resolve.

Cade's green-blue gaze flashed in her mind, his roguish charm a spark against the dark, their bond humming with his triumph.

The scrolls were faltering, balance fracturing, Sheng Xiao's fate resting on her shoulders, but in that instant, with Lina's hand in hers, Jade felt the weight shift—she was ready to lead, the Prophecy's dawn breaking through the gloom, her amethyst stare lifting to the mural, Vladimir's stride no longer a taunt but a call to rise.

Chapter 3: The Call to Arms

In the Imperial City's library, Empress Jade and Cade pored over a holo-table, its surface aglow with maps of Souris's riot-torn markets, the air thick with aged ink and polished oak, the faint scent of jasmine from Jade's cloak mingling with the musty tomes.

Jade's scarlet tresses spilled over her sapphire-threaded cloak, her amethyst stare glinting with resolve strained by doubt as she traced a flickering holo-file, its interface unveiling secrets of talismans forged post-Great Race to unify Sheng Xiao, glyphs pulsing like a heartbeat.

Cade leaned close, his green-blue gaze sharp with strategy, dark hair swept back, rugged leather jacket framing broad shoulders, knives glinting at his belt under the holo-lanterns' golden pulse.

"Rat Clan's too sneaky—I don't trust them leading Souris," he said, voice low, his telepathic bond sparking with Jade, his finger tapping a holo-screen, reports of looted trade routes flickering, his mistrust rooted in the Great Race's betrayal five centuries ago.

Jade frowned, her fingers brushing his, a spark flaring at the touch, "That's why they'll lead—their cunning will outsmart X where brute force fails."

His grin flashed, a spark of defiance, "You're too trusting, Empress—Vladimir's legacy is a curse."

She shot back, "And you're too stubborn, Cade—their cunning is our edge."

Her heart skipped, their eyes locking, a near-confession hovering—Cade's gaze softening, words catching in his throat, "Jade, I—" her breath hitching as she pulled back, the moment heavy with unspoken longing, the holo-screen's glow casting their silhouettes in a fleeting dance.

A guard burst in, voice urgent, "Pardon the interruption, Empress, Cade, the envoys need briefing—now."

Cade hesitated, his gaze lingering on Jade.

"It's okay, go ahead," Jade said. Cade nodded, slipping out, leaving her alone, the holo-files casting zodiac motifs— Rabbit's leap graceful, Rooster's cannon bold—across the shelves, the air humming as Jade's courage grew, their bond a quiet anchor in the storm.

Jade lingered alone, the library's silence wrapping around her like a heavy cloak, the guard's footsteps fading, leaving only the hum of holo-lanterns.

She traced a picture of a talisman in an ancient book, its worn leather cool under her fingers, glyphs pulsing soft with energy that whispered of kin—her sister's laugh a fading shield against loneliness, her brother's scowl a lingering thorn of abandonment, a captain's grin a lost spark of joy.

Afternoon light slanted through arched windows, bathing the oak shelves in a warm gleam that danced across volumes etched with zodiac motifs—Rabbit's leap graceful, Rooster's cannon bold—but doubt weighed heavier than her scepter's burden, its fenghuang emblem glinting like a phoenix ready to rise.

A memory crashed in: the palace gardens under dappled sun, 12-year-old Jade sparring with Cade while Percy watched, her wooden staff wobbling in sweaty palms, the grass soft under her feet, cherry blossoms drifting like confetti in the breeze.

Percy's laugh rang warm, his dark hair catching the light as he leaned against a tree, dagger twirling in his hand.

"Guard up, little phoenix—Li Shou didn't weave shadows by hesitating," he teased, his voice a steady anchor, easing the knot in her gut as he demonstrated a quick parry, the blade whistling through the air, its gleam catching Opal's green eyes as she clapped from the sidelines.

Her healing glow warmed the garden, a soft aura that chased Jade's fears, while Calix cheered beside her, his grin broad and infectious, his voice booming, "Swing harder, Jade!"

Onyx kicked a stone nearby, his scowl sharp as a blade, arms crossed in silent judgment, but Cade's shout—"You've got this, Jade!"—bolstered her swing, his mismatched eyes alight with belief, his small frame darting forward to adjust her stance, his touch a spark that made her laugh despite the staff's weight, the breeze carrying their giggles like a promise.

Percy leaped to a shadow, vanishing and reappearing with a flourish, "Think where you want to go—shadows obey," his voice guiding Cade's first shadow step, the air crackling as he stumbled, then steadied, Percy's laugh warm, "She'll need you, Cade, more than she knows."

The scene blurred, Jade's fingers clenching the book until knuckles whitened, glyphs mocking her wavering resolve, her aura pulsing faintly like a hesitant shield, the Yang Scroll's glow a faint taunt on the table.

Why do they see strength when I feel like I'm crumbling? she thought, eyes stinging with unshed tears, the Prophecy's weight pressing like a storm on her heart, her bond with Cade flaring briefly, a distant pulse of his unease tugging at her heart, her resolve hardening.

The library's oak doors creaked open, advisors sweeping in with sharp murmurs of unrest, their footsteps echoing off the high ceilings like distant thunder.

"Cochan's grain hoarding fuels unrest," Lord Huan reported, hawkish eyes probing her expression, a sneer curling beneath his bow as he adjusted his cloak, zodiac embroidery glinting. "Souris markets burn with riots; stalls toppled in quake-fueled curses. Saanp's healers report venom shortages amid unrest. Your command, Majesty?" His voice pressed, a gruff edge of traditional reverence, hands clasped as if guarding the throne's legacy.

Jade's hands trembled faintly, aura pulsing as doubt clawed—*What if I choose wrong again?* she thought.

She drew on Percy's lessons, straightening her posture, her scarlet tresses catching the holo-light as she steeled her voice despite the storm raging inside, the book's glyphs pulsing in sync with her courage.

"We're assessing options," she said, her tone measured, masking the uncertainty twisting her gut, her resolve flaring as she met Huan's gaze, a silent vow to rise above the court's doubt.

Cade returned, slipping from the shelves' gloom, mismatched eyes locking on hers, his knives catching the holo-light in a gleam of readiness, his cat tattoo pulsing faint beneath his sleeves, a royal secret binding him to her in ways the court could never know.

"Your father said the Guardians would rise when scrolls faltered," he said, voice low and urgent, his mismatched stare carrying fierce loyalty thrumming through their telepathic bond, a silent assurance that steadied her like an invisible hand.

"It's time. Rat Clan's cunning can lead—Omar's stubborn but loyal, known him from Kusini's arenas," he added, a flash of memory—his knives clashing with Omar's mace under a blazing sun, sweat and steel forging respect, a nod sealing their bond.

Jade nodded, Cade's words steadying her resolve, her aura flaring brighter.

"Send envoys," she ordered, scepter pulsing in her grip, fenghuang emblem radiant as it cast a warm glow across the room.

"We call the Guardians," she declared, her voice firm, the advisors' murmurs fading as she drew strength from Cade's presence, Huan's sneer faltering under her resolve, the Yang Scroll's glow flaring brighter on the table.

A low hum built, footsteps echoing as the twelve Zodiac Guardians filed into the throne room a week later, their boots clattering on the marble, waiting for the empress, their clan symbols embroidered on varied attire—leather jackets, vests, cloaks—a vibrant tapestry of Souris's cunning Rat, Listra's fierce Tiger, Kusini's loyal Ox, Ged's creative Goat.

The throne room buzzed with anticipation, afternoon light streaming through high arched windows, qilin carvings pulsing on marble pillars, their horns shimmering like starlight as if sensing the gathering's weight, the Great Race mural looming above, Zodiac signs—rabbit's leap graceful and swift, dragon's soar mighty and bold, pig's warmth steady and true—casting restless gloom across the polished floor, glyphs flickering with talisman lore, a constellation of Sheng Xiao's teetering balance that made the air hum with tension.

The Guardians' voices murmured low but tense, anticipation building as priests' chants echoed from distant temples, their rhythmic pleas against the quake's shadow mingling with palace staff whispering of unrest in hushed tones, the cobblestone paths outside alive with nervous footsteps, temple bells tolling softly, their mournful clang carrying the city's fear.

Veronica of the Rat Clan leaned against a pillar, her pistol holstered at her hip, short brown hair framing sharp green eyes that gleamed with wit honed by Vladimir's legacy, her slender frame radiating cunning confidence in a black leather jacket, the shame of her clan's dishonorable legacy burning like a hidden flame, driving her to wield cunning with honor.

"Ox, your frown's carving trenches—lighten up, or we'll mistake you for a statue," she teased Omar, her voice sharp with wit, her Rat emblem curling like a maze on her jacket as she crossed her arms, her eyes scanning the room, sharp with cunning, her fingers twirling her pistol in a deft spin, ready for any chaos.

Omar of the Ox Clan adjusted his mace at his belt, his dark brown eyes narrowing under bushy brows, his sturdy frame like a wall of endurance, broad shoulders tense in a heavy linen vest, the weight of family duty forging his gruff voice and unyielding loyalty.

"Rat, focus—this isn't a festival," he rumbled, his Ox emblem standing firm like a plow through earth, a spark of trust flickering beneath his stubborn crust as he met Veronica's gaze, his dark skin catching the light as he shifted, recalling Kusini's dusty arenas where Cade's knives met his mace, sweat and steel forging a bond, his hand flexing with readiness.

Tate of the Tiger Clan smirked, flexing his claw gloves with a flourish, his black hair flashing with vibrant energy, his athletic build coiled like a predator in a fitted leather vest, amber eyes sparkling with competitive ego that veiled deep insecurities, his fear of failure a shadow he buried.

"I'll snag the Rat Talisman first—watch me," he boasted, his Tiger emblem roaring on his vest, cockiness a mask as he leaned forward, claws glinting in the holo-light, the pressure to prove his bravery a weight he hid, his smirk faltering as he thought to himself, *What if I'm not enough?*

David of the Dragon Clan gripped his katana's hilt, his sturdy frame taut in a scale-etched cloak, brown eyes fierce with temper honed by high family expectations, his muscles straining against the fabric.

"Keep dreaming, Tiger—your stripes won't save you," he growled, his Dragon emblem surging with power, his voice a rumble of controlled anger.

The jab was a release for his frustration as he stepped closer, the air crackling between him and Tate, his katana half-drawn in a flash of steel, his stance rigid with pride.

Hana of the Horse Clan cracked her whip sharp, her white headscarf framing sarcastic blue eyes, her lithe form radiating free-spirited defiance in a flowing desert cloak, flirting with David's glance.

"Back off, Dragon—save the roar for later!" she snapped, her voice slicing through the din, her Horse emblem snapping with grace as she flicked her whip again, the crack echoing like thunder, her blue eyes flashing defiance, a playful smirk teasing David as she twirled the whip's handle, her stance bold as she tossed her hair, confidence masking her rebellion.

Alice of the Rabbit Clan's tablet sparked in her hands, her auburn ponytail bouncing as she muttered fixes, her cautious intellect a shield against a bullying past, her slender fingers dancing over the screen in a soft linen tunic.

"If we don't focus, we'll all fail—these tests aren't games," she said, her Rabbit emblem glowing with quiet resolve, her voice soft but firm, her eyes darting nervously as the room's tension pressed against her, her fingers tracing her tablet, mind racing to prove her worth, whispering to Melissa and Sam, "Heard Jade lost her family—hope she's kind," her voice low, her Rabbit emblem glowing as she shared her concern, her cautious eyes glinting with empathy.

Doug of the Dog Clan wavered, his sword at his side, fear of abandonment shadowing his loyal heart, his brown eyes darting as he tried to rally in a sturdy canvas jacket.

"We've got to stick together," he muttered, his Dog emblem dimming slightly, his sturdy build shifting uncomfortably, his voice cracking under the pressure of the group's discord, whispering to Gerry, "Tate and David are too aggressive—let's keep it steady," his hand twitching toward his sword, his loyalty a quiet fire.

Gerry of the Goat Clan ducked behind a pillar, his spear clutched tight, skittishness from family caregiving duties making his courage falter, his light hair falling over wide eyes in a loose woven cloak, his creativity a spark waiting to ignite.

"This is too much—what if we mess up?" he whispered, his Goat emblem standing mild on his cloak, his voice hesitant as he gripped the spear tighter, replying to Doug, "We need to calm Tate and David—too much bravado," his creativity buried under doubt, his fingers twitching as he steadied his spear.

Patricia of the Pig Clan stood by a side table, her hammer at her belt, her generous naivety a light in the tension, her warm smile trying to soothe in a homespun tunic, her clan's sharing ritual a quiet strength.

"Let's not fight—we're in this together," she said, her Pig emblem blooming with sincerity, her round face softening as she offered pastries, untouched by the group, her warmth faltering slightly, her gentle eyes shining with hope to bind the room.

Ryder of the Rooster Clan's quip stumbled, his cannon slung over his shoulder, boastfulness hiding parental disappointment, his cocky grin faltering in a bold red vest.

"Yeah, let's blast through—easy win!" he boasted, his Rooster emblem crowing faintly, his energetic frame leaning in, doubt clouding his perception as he tried to rally the group, his cannon shifting as if ready to fire.

Melissa of the Monkey Clan admired the chaos with a grin, her axe at her side, cleverness masking burnout from overprotective parents, her braid swinging in a sleek jungle cloak.

"This discord's a puzzle—let's solve it before it bites," she said, her Monkey emblem dancing with charisma, her voice light but strained, burnout hidden behind her wit, whispering to Alice and Sam, "The empress's got fire—bet she's tougher than this lot," her grin teasing.

Sam of the Snake Clan observed silently, her bow slung across her back, wisdom steadying her guarded heart, her dark hair framing enigmatic eyes in a flowing silk cloak, her gaze a quiet strength.

"Unity wins battles—squabble, and we lose," she said, her Snake emblem slithering with cunning, her voice calm but sharp, a steady thread cutting through the noise, whispering back to Melissa, "Jade's young, but her resolve's like steel—watch her lead," her bowstring tightening as she scanned the room.

The shouts peaked, Veronica's tease igniting Omar's rumble, Tate's boast clashing with David's growl, Hana's whip cracking the air like a storm, Alice's tablet sparking in frustration, Doug's doubt rippling through Gerry's shyness, Patricia's warmth lost in Ryder's falter, Melissa's grin strained, Sam's wisdom ignored—a pillar's qilin horn cracking faintly under the tension, the room's chaos a storm ready to break.

Jade and Cade entered, her scepter pulsing, fenghuang emblem illuminating the mural, glyphs flaring to calm the discord, the room's chaos stilling slightly as Jade's scarlet tresses caught the light like a phoenix's flame, her amethyst gaze sweeping them with a command she willed into existence, her regal stance in a flowing velvet cloak steadying despite the tremor in her heart.

Cade's rugged poise in his leather jacket stood firm beside her, his green-and-blue eyes a silent anchor.

"Your discord fuels this chaos!" she declared, aura surging, gold light stilling the mural's restless gloom, her voice echoing with a strength drawn from Cade's nod, their bond sparking with shared courage.

Jade raised her scepter, gold light intensifying, elegance commanding despite her heart's tremor, the fenghuang emblem casting a warm veil across the room. "The Yin Scroll's been stolen," she announced, aura a golden veil that steadied the air. "We must retrieve the twelve talismans, forged after the Great Race, to fulfill the Prophecy. Start with Souris's Rat Talisman—X seeks to unravel Sheng Xiao's harmony," her voice carrying the Prophecy's weight, glyphs flaring with destiny's call.

Jade raised her scepter higher, channeling its energy to etch glowing tattoos on the Guardians' arms—Rat for Veronica, Ox for Omar, Tiger for Tate, Dragon for David, Horse for Hana, Rabbit for Alice, Dog for Doug, Goat for Gerry, Pig for Patricia, Rooster for Ryder, Monkey for Melissa, Snake for Sam—each pulsing with their clan's essence, binding them to her cause with a unity's light that flared briefly, a ceremonial bond deepening their resolve.

Glyphs glowed on the mural, depicting talismans' essence—rat's cunning, rabbit's grace, dragon's might, pig's heart—binding Sheng Xiao's balance in a shimmering display, the room's hum rising as if the zodiac itself approved, the qilin horns pulsing brighter, harmonizing as the Guardians stood united.

After her speech, Jade assigned teams, her voice firm: "Veronica, Omar, Doug—lead for Souris to secure the Rat Talisman, prepping with pistol drills and mace swings. Tate, Sam, Melissa, Alice, Ryder, prepare for Kusini's Ox Talisman next, studying maps and tech. Hana, David, Gerry, Patricia, train in the palace for future quests by sparring in the courtyard." Veronica's pistol twitched, a cunning grin spreading as she spun it deftly, her eyes scanning the room, sharp with cunning, Omar's mace thumped the floor, his nod steady as he flexed his hand, ready for any fight, and Doug's sword gleamed, loyalty shining through doubt as he tested its edge, ready to guard his team.

Tate flexed his claws, smirking, "We'll outshine Souris."

Sam's bowstring tightened, her eyes sharp as she studied a holo-map.

Melissa's axe swung playfully, "Let's not botch this."

Alice's tablet flickered, her mind racing as she traced its screen. Ryder's cannon shifted, his grin cocky but focused. Hana's whip cracked playfully, David's katana lowered with a huff, Gerry's spear steadied with a nervous nod, and Patricia's hammer glowed with warmth, her smile steadying the group.

The Guardians received holo-link tablets, screens flickering to life with zodiac interfaces, ready to coordinate across Sheng Xiao, the devices humming with tech-magic that linked their emblems: Hana's whip coiling around hers, Alice's tablet syncing seamlessly, Doug's sword hilt vibrating in sync, the air alive with their unified pulse, their tattoos pulsing faintly in rhythm.

Jade noticed Patricia's pastries on the side table, her voice softening, "Almond cakes—my favorite," sparking smiles as Patricia beamed, offering them to the group, the sweet scent easing the tension, her Pig Clan's sharing ritual warming the room, pastries shared, her warmth binding the group.

"Omar, didn't think you could get stronger—look at you," Cade said, clapping his shoulder, their Kusini sparring days flashing in a shared grin, "Good to see you, Cade," Omar replied, his chuckle warm, memories of dusty arenas and clashing steel lightening the mood.

The Guardians relaxed, Jade's words sparking laughter, emblems glowing as Veronica grinned, tossing a quip, "These cakes might outshine Souris."

Omar chuckled, his mace resting easy as Tate relaxed, claws still. David's huff turned to a smirk, sharing a pastry with Hana while Alice's cautious eyes brightened, nibbling a cake as she nodded to Sam. Doug rallied Gerry with a pat, his loyalty infectious and Melissa's grin widened, axe gleaming as she teased Ryder.

Sam's bow steadied, her wisdom softening as she nodded to Alice.

Ryder's cocky grin softened, his cannon at ease, the group's laughter a harmony against the city's unrest, temple bells clanging, staff murmurs of unrest echoing from the palace halls.

"Let's not turn Souris into a bonfire, yeah?" Ryder asked, his Rooster emblem crowing faintly, his quip easing the tension, his cannon shifting with newfound focus.

Doug nodded, Dog emblem steady, "We've got this," his grin sparking, loyalty shining through his doubt as he clapped Gerry's shoulder, rallying the skittish Goat with a nod to their earlier talk.

The Guardians smiled, tension easing, ready for Souris, their emblems and tattoos a constellation of resolve, the throne room's light warming as Jade's command took root, the city outside trembling with the weight of their mission, temple bells clanging, staff murmurs of unrest echoing through the halls.

In X's gothic fortress deep in the Unknown Wilderness, jagged spires pierced a storm-heavy sky, shadow-draped turrets looming over gnarled vines that clung to cracked stone walls, the air heavy with the scent of damp earth and ancient magic. The fortress groaned, runic maps flaring faintly within a war room carved from obsidian, jagged artifacts trembling with the Yin Scroll's chaotic pulse, forbidden knots etched into the walls pulsing green in the dim holo-light.

Vincent's eyes glinted beneath his rune-stitched cloak, fingers tightening on his serpent-shaped scepter, green runes thrumming cryptic plans as he traced a map's edge, his resentment simmering like a hidden flame, his schemes coiling like a viper ready to strike, his cloak billowing as he paced, eyes glinting with menace.

"We hired locals to spark Sheng Xiao's unrest—price gouging and hoarding now ripple across the realm," Vincent said with a smirk, spellbook flaring, Sheng Xiao's unrest a cover for his deeper schemes, the air humming with the scepter's venomous energy, his fingers twitching as if eager to unleash chaos, his voice low and threatening, "Kusini's caravans, Saanp's healers, Cochan's granaries—all teetering on collapse, their collapse fueling our rise."

Bella tossed a report of hired riots, her amber eyes glinting in a rugged leather jacket, "My thugs lit the markets—Souris burns tonight."

Lucas's machete gleamed at his side in a worn canvas cloak, his blonde hair matted as he growled, "Got my plan set—merchants hoard, prices soar," his blade steady, a promise of violence.

Dolore's lightning crackled, dark hair loose in a dark woven tunic, her glasses reflecting the holo-map's glow as she murmured, "Cochan's grain vanishes next—our hirelings move fast," her loyalty to X fueling her menace.

X's fingers traced a battle map, his strategic mind plotting Souris's fall, his sapphire ring a bloodied memory fueling vengeance, the metal cool against his skin as grief flashed in his grey eyes, the fortress's gloom amplifying his resolve.

The spellbook's pull darkened his gaze, Vincent's voice a blade slicing through his thoughts.

"Sheng Xiao's unrest beckons, doesn't it?" Vincent murmured, his dark blue eyes hiding a hunger for chaos, his cloak shifting as he leaned closer to the map, his smirk a promise of ruin.

"Lucas, deploy to the markets," X growled.

Lucas nodded, his machete gleaming, Bella's report clutched tight, Dolore's lightning crackling with quiet approval, their readiness a storm brewing in the war room's gloom, the holo-map flickering with images of Souris's burning stalls, Kusini's looted caravans, and Cochan's hoarded grain, the air thick with the promise of realm-wide imbalance.

In the palace gardens, Cade stood under starlight, jasmine scenting the air, incense clouds a distant veil from the temples below, their chants a faint hum against the night's quiet, temple bells tolling, staff murmurs of unrest echoing from the palace halls.

Jade's resolve glowed—she was the Empress, he was her shadow, his heart aching with unworthiness despite the bond's pulse, his knives gleaming in the moonlight as he scanned the horizon, his rugged poise in his leather jacket a quiet strength.

Hana's stare unnerved him from afar, her blue eyes sharp with curiosity, as if probing his secrets, making his stomach twist.

Veronica's wit sparked, her glance cutting like her pistol, testing his resolve, her smirk a challenge he felt unfit to meet. Omar's gruff nod carried respect, but his gaze weighed heavy, measuring Cade's worth, a weight he couldn't bear.

Doug's glance offered trust, yet Cade felt it undeserved, his loyalty a burden he feared he'd fail.

Melissa admired Jade's fire with a grin, her braid swinging, but her eyes lingered on him, questioning his place.

Tate smirked at Jade's scepter, his amber glance flicking to Cade with hidden awe, making him shrink.

Alice's tablet hummed, her analytical stare making him shift uncomfortably, his heart racing—unworthy of Jade's trust, a mere protector beside an empress, his bond with her a flame he feared he'd dim.

Jade sensed his unease through their bond, a faint pulse of his doubt tugging at her heart.

She whispered through their link, *Your eyes hold strength, Cade. Don't doubt them,* her words a private balm, steadying his trembling resolve, their bond flaring with quiet intimacy.

A flashback stirred: Percy teaching shadow-travel in a hidden courtyard, knives flashing under moonlight. "Think where you want to go—shadows obey," Percy grinned, teleporting to a distant tree, his voice a steady guide as Cade tried, shadows flickering unsteady at first, the air humming with Li Shou's power.

"You've got the gift, brother—use it for her," Percy said, clapping Cade's shoulder, his dagger glinting as he demonstrated a quick leap, guiding Cade to shadow-step, the air crackling as he stumbled, then steadied, Percy's laugh warm, "She'll need you, Cade, more than she knows."

The memory faded, duty anchoring him, Percy's loss a scar, but Jade's trust a balm, his knives twitching as her voice cut through the bond: "We're bound together, Cade—trust us," her words steadying his resolve.

He nodded, duty before all, Cat Clan's oath burning like a flame in his chest, his mismatched stare fixed on the stars.

Jade returned to the library, talisman maps spread across the oak table, ink smudging her fingers as she traced Souris's layout, unrest reports piling high—burned stalls, Cochan's grain hoarding, Saanp's venom shortages, a city teetering on the edge of chaos, Onyx's absence a thorn in her hope that twisted deeper in the quiet.

Cade's eyes—like Li Shou in Tanzanite's Prophecy—flashed in her mind, his roguish charm a spark against the dark, their bond sparking as she steeled her courage, the holo-files glowing with secrets that promised victory, the quake's aftermath a faint tremor in her chest, her aura flaring as she sensed Cade's distant unease, her resolve hardening.

The scrolls were shifting, talismans calling, Sheng Xiao's fate on her shoulders, her aura steadying as she prepared to lead, the library's glow a beacon in the gathering storm, her amethyst gaze lifting to the shelves as if the zodiac itself urged her forward.

Chapter 4: Into the Forest

The Imperial City's gardens bloomed with jasmine under fenghuang-carved arches, their petals unfurling under the midday sun, their golden glow catching the breeze, casting a sweet, heady scent that mingled with the faint metallic tang of zodiac-etched lotus ponds.

Water rippled softly, reflecting the sunlight in fractured patterns, but Souris's unrest coiled around Empress Jade like invisible thorns, ink-stained reports fueling a fear that gnawed at her insides.

Maps lay strewn across a stone table, their edges curling from the humidity, sigils flickering in erratic distress—lumber stalls looted in Souris's bustling square, riots erupting over hoarded goods, craftsmen clashing with guards amid the chaos.

The Rat Talisman loomed as the first true test, with Kusini's Ox Talisman waiting like the sun on the horizon, each danger a keen reminder of the responsibilities pressing down on her. *What if I can't protect them?* she thought.

Her amethyst eyes darkened, fingers tracing the intricate fenghuang emblem on her scepter, the cool metal grounding her even as her heart pounded like a trapped bird against its cage.

A memory pulled her back: after a grueling council session, Jade lingered in the gardens, the midday heat pressing against her skin as courtiers dispersed, their murmurs fading into the rustle of leaves.

Emperor Alexandrite approached, his silver hair catching the sunlight, his violet eyes mirroring hers with a scorching intensity that steadied her trembling hands. He guided her to a fenghuang-carved bench, pointing to zodiac motifs etched into the stone—Rat's cunning, Ox's strength.

"Balance demands courage, Jade—not perfection," he said softly, his voice a balm as he wiped a tear she hadn't meant to shed.

She'd faltered in the council, misjudging a clan dispute, her suggestion sparking hushed criticism that left her doubting her worth.

"Lead with your heart, and the clans will follow—even when the weight feels too much. You're not alone—your Guardians, your family, will stand with you," he added, pulling her into a fierce hug, his presence easing her fears as she nodded, the weight lifting slightly.

She swallowed the lump in her throat, the weight of his words sinking deep as he squeezed her shoulder, a fleeting shield against her doubts.

Cade slipped from the garden's edge like a silent guardian, his dark cloak hugging his muscular frame, the fabric brushing against the warm midday breeze.

His heterochromic gaze held a softness that always warmed her core, a quiet strength that made her see not just her advisor, but the man whose resolve had lit her darkest storms since childhood.

Their telepathic bond thrummed faintly, a thread of intimacy that connected them beyond words, steadying her in ways no one else could.

Words bubbled up inside her, her heart racing as she teetered on the edge of confession, the empress's mask slipping for a fleeting moment.

She imagined his hands steadying hers, his green-blue eyes locking with hers, their lips finally meeting in a kiss—a vow unspoken but felt in the fierce heat of that imagined touch.

Duty warred with love in her mind, the throne's weight urging silence, but a tender thrum brushed her mind—his unworthiness flickering, a raw edge she ached to soothe.

She masked it with a steady breath, the empress's resolve hardening. Before she could speak, the moment shattered as Hana burst into the garden, her whip looped at her hip like a symbol of swift grace, her white hijab framing dark blue eyes that sparkled with Horse Clan energy.

Hana paused at the sight of Jade, dipping into a graceful bow, her movements fluid and respectful, the hem of her tunic brushing the dew-kissed grass.

"Empress," she said, her voice light but laced with deference, rising smoothly as she straightened. Then, turning to Cade with a teasing smile, she chirped, "Cade, map help? These eastern routes are twisting my brain into knots."

Her hand brushed his shoulder longer than needed, fingers lingering just a fraction too long, that spark in her eyes sending a twist through Jade's gut—like a dagger she hadn't seen coming.

Cade hesitated, his green-blue stare flicking between them, taken aback by Hana's flirtatious energy. A quick thrum hummed through the bond—"Is it okay if I help her?" he asked.

Jade nodded swiftly, masking the jealous sting that burned hot in her chest. *He can't know,* she thought, forcing her mind to shield the turmoil, burying it under layers of duty.

Cade cleared his throat, glancing at Jade again. "Empress, permission to assist?" he asked, his voice formal, a nod to her authority.

"Granted," Jade replied, her smile tight, the word tasting like ash. As Cade and Hana walked away toward the maps on a distant stone bench, Jade watched—Hana playfully tugging at the edge of his cloak, her laughter light and flirtatious as she leaned in close.

The sight twisted deeper, Jade's thoughts a whirlwind: *What if Cade likes her? She's pretty, fierce—everything I'm not when doubt creeps in?*

The jealousy surged, but she turned away sharply, her amethyst eyes steady, the empress's mask unyielding. To distract herself, she raised her scepter, the fenghuang emblem flaring gold as she projected her voice across the realms.

"Veronica, Omar, Doug—Souris's forests hold danger. Stay sharp," she commanded, her tone firm despite the ache twisting inside her. The Guardians' holo-links buzzed in response.

In Souris's dense forests, pines loomed tall and ancient, their trunks etched with the scars of generations of lumber harvests, chill dusting the needle-strewn paths like a veil of forgotten snow.

Golden rays pierced the branches like hesitant spears, illuminating rural camps where craftsmen huddled around hearths, their tools gleaming with fresh resin. The air carried the keen bite of pine sap, mingling with the earthy scent of sawdust and distant smoke from market riots that had spilled into the woods.

In Souris's lumber camp, pine resin scented the air as clansfolk wove zodiac paper charms under frost-dusted canopies.

Veronica watched, the rustle of handmade paper echoing the forest's hum, each charm etched with rat motifs pulsing with Sheng Xiao's energy.

Elders chanted, "Cunning binds us," their hands deft from years of paper production, the charms glowing faintly to ward off maze illusions.

The ritual steadied her, the pine's tang grounding her resolve to face the Rat King's challenge.

Mara, a weathered Souris camp leader with calloused hands and a voice rough from years of bellowing orders over saw blades, gathered Veronica's team near a sacred grove.

"Glyph traps guard the clearing—step light on these forest trails," she warned, her eyes narrowing as she cited old legends of protective carvings passed down from the Great Race itself.

The group formed a loose circle around a low altar, where Mara began the Pine Oath ritual, integral to Souris life as the turning of seasons.

She lifted a bundle of fresh luck charms—small wooden rats etched with protective glyphs—and chanted softly, her voice weaving with the locals' rhythm: "By Rat's cunning and forest's root, ward the path, bind the truth."

The resin dripped slowly, anointing each charm with a protective sheen that thrummed softly, the air shimmering as holo-emitters activated, projecting faint zodiac motifs—tiny sprinting rats that faded like whispers.

Mara pressed one charm into Veronica's palm, a warm gesture of trust.

Veronica clutched her mother's Rat Clan sigil, its worn edges warm, sparking a memory of a Souris lumber camp.

At eight, her mother taught her to weave cunning traps with vine-threads under lantern glow, resin's tang sharp.

"Cunning with honor," she'd whispered, her eyes fierce. Vladimir's betrayal stung, but her lesson fueled Veronica's vow to redeem the clan.

The pine-scented air hummed, glyphs pulsing, urging her to wield wit over trickery, her heart blazing to prove her honor to Jade and Omar.

Veronica turned to Doug, fastening his around his neck with a teasing smile, the closeness making him blush deeply, his light blue eyes darting away as he stammered, "Thanks, Veronica."

Mara then secured Omar's charm with steady hands, handing him Veronica's to fasten. As Omar's fingers brushed her neck, a shiver coursed through them both—the spark igniting, a warmth that lingered in the chill.

Mara nodded firmly. "These will glow warnings against disharmony—carry Souris's strength."

With the charms secured, the team prepared to leave. Veronica adjusted her charm, turning to Omar with a smirk. "Not bad for an Ox in the woods—think you can keep up?"

Omar grunted, a rare smile cracking his stoic face. "Try me, Rat. Just don't trip over your own speed."

Doug, blushing again, chimed in, "Yeah, Veronica, you're like a blur—coolest thing I've seen!"

She ruffled his hair, sibling-like. "Stick close, Dougie, or you'll miss the fun." Doug's sword gleamed in Souris's frost, a memory of a Dingo beach flashing.

At sixteen, a friend's betrayal—abandoning him during a fishing raid—stung, the sea's salt mocking his trust.

"Loyalty binds," he'd vowed, yet pessimism lingered—could he trust again?

Veronica's resolve sparked his, the pine-scented air pulsing, urging his Dog Clan loyalty to prove his worth in the maze.

Omar's mace felt heavy in the maze, a memory of a Kusini festival flashing. Kofi's grin rallied farmers, his charisma outshining Omar's swings in an ox-pull contest, their father's gaze crushing.

"Kofi should be heir," Omar wished, the weight stinging.

Now, Veronica's smirk sparked his Ox Clan strength, the frost-charged air urging him to lead, his heart vowing to prove his grit over Kofi's charm.

The banter lightened the mood, their steps surer as they exited the camp, the forest path calling.

Veronica felt the weight of it all in her bones, the air biting her cheeks as the team headed deeper into the forest toward the clearing, the path narrowing under the pines' watchful gaze. Her fur-lined coat—a gift from her mother, woven during a brutal winter when blizzards had isolated their camp—hugged her slender frame.

Its silver-stitched rat symbol gleamed faintly, a reminder of her Rat Clan heritage, keen features framing her cunning brown eyes that missed nothing.

Her pistol hung heavy at her hip, cold steel a steadying force against the unknown. Two charms thumped against her chest: one, her mother's Rat Clan sigil, worn smooth by countless prayers. The other, the one Mara had just blessed, was pine-sharp with glyphs that vibrated faintly in the chill.

A shiver ran through Omar as he followed, his broad shoulders—built from years of Ox Clan labor in Kusini's sunbaked plains—hunched against the unfamiliar cold, the dense forest a stark contrast to the open fields he'd known, where scorching winds carried the scent of ripe harvests.

Mist curled from his lips, his dark eyes scanning the trees with a steadfast intensity, his sturdy build a quiet anchor in the uncertainty.

What if I botch this? The thought gnawed at him, his loyalty to Jade a fire that burned brighter than any doubt, but the pressure of his clan's expectations—as heir to Kusini's ruler, stubborn duty passed down like an unbreakable yoke—made his steps heavy.

A memory flickered: his father's voice barking orders in the fields, demanding he stay back from a collapsing barn, the sting of being coddled fueling a silent vow to prove his strength— this mace swing now a testament to that resolve.

Doug trailed close, his light blue eyes wide with youthful wonder, his lanky frame buzzing with Dog Clan eagerness, blonde hair tousled by the wind.

His breath clouded the air as he grinned, his luck charm swinging resin-fresh from his neck, loyalty shining in every glance he stole toward Veronica—a crush that made his cheeks flush whenever she turned her keen gaze his way.

"These pines dwarf the Imperial City towers! Back in Dingo, I've traveled the beaches and cliffs plenty, but this is my first time outside—nothing like these towering giants! It's like walking through a living fortress."

But beneath the excitement, a flicker of pessimism lingered, rooted in a coastal raid where friends abandoned him, their laughter echoing as he fought alone—waves crashing, blood-stained sand surrounding him.

Veronica's teasing ruffle now felt like a lifeline, chipping at that wall, though fear of loss tightened his grip on his sword.

Veronica shot him a smirk, her heart skipping at Omar's protective glance her way, the spark between them undeniable: a pull that made her pulse quicken, his steady presence making her feel seen in ways her clan's legacy never had. But Doug's eager grin tugged at her too, his puppy-like admiration endearing, though she treated it with sibling-like teasing to keep things light.

"Eyes on the path, Dougie. Wouldn't want you tripping over your own feet while staring at the trees." She ruffled his hair again, letting her hand linger a beat longer, a silent vow to shield him from past betrayals, her keen eyes catching his grateful blush.

The path twisted deeper, pines crowding the sky like silent sentinels, the chill's bite sharpening with every gust of wind howling through the gaps. Souris's lumber culture thrummed in Veronica's blood, a legacy of Rat Clan craftsmen shaping luck charms in daily rituals that bound community and tradition.

In the distance, a mill hummed with activity, its massive blades guided by holo-glyph projectors that embedded zodiac lore into paper scrolls—interactive holo-chips woven into the fibers, allowing trade logs and clan reports to flicker to life when activated.

These scrolls doubled as ritual tools, blessed during Pine Oaths to summon pixiu wards or reveal hidden trails, a fusion of ancient cunning and tech that made Souris a silent nerve center for Sheng Xiao's wisdom.

She paused at a fork in the road, her mind flashing back to how she'd earned her place as guardian.

The memory pulled her under: Souris's central square buzzed with anticipation, young hopefuls gathered under the elders' watchful eyes for the cunning challenge—a labyrinth of illusions rising from glyph-stones in the chill-kissed ground. Veronica, heart pounding, stepped into the maze, the air shimmering with deceptive holo-mirages of twisting paths and whispering winds that hid pitfalls.

She navigated with keen eyes, dodging an illusionary bramble that grazed her arm, its sting a fake but the fear real.

Midway, she overheard a hushed whisper—elders altering a holo-glyph to favor a rival, its code rigged to collapse paths for others.

Using her speed, she blurred to the core, hacking the projection with a swift override on her wrist device, the rigged glyph flaring red as evidence burst into view.

The crowd gasped, other contestants cheering as the maze stabilized, their voices a wave of awe. The elders' faces paled, their grudging nods betraying how impressed they were, their rigged plan foiled by her cunning, securing Jade's call to guardianship.

Amid the cheers, her mother pushed through, her hands glistening with happy tears for her daughter's clever win, pulling Veronica into a fierce hug as she vowed to herself, "Vladimir's betrayal ends with me."

The flashback faded, a fire kindling in her chest, burning away the Rat Clan's shadowed past.

A stone glowed ahead, glyphs shimmering silver, chill-veined brambles coiled beneath, carved with intricate cloud-patterned lattices that vibrated with ancient energy.

"Trap," Veronica hissed, her sarcasm keen as she halted the group. "Unless you fancy bramble hugs, step light." Omar's mace swung low, slashing a suspicious bramble, his hand steady as he glanced her way, their eyes locking with a spark of unspoken trust—and something more, a pull that made her pulse quicken.

"Don't go soft on me, big guy," she teased, her voice lighter than she felt, though duty clashed with the attraction—his overprotective gaze, born from Kusini's familial yoke, made her wonder if he'd curb her independence.

Doug, ever eager, missed a faint glyph marking, the earth shuddering as brambles surged upward. Veronica blurred forward

with her super speed, shoving him back just in time, her pistol
drawn in a flash.

"Keep up, Dougie!" she snapped, worry lacing her bite,
her heart racing at the near miss—his crush evident in the grateful
blush that colored his cheeks.

Glyph spikes thrust from the ground, pixiu carvings
flaring on the stones, the earth crumbling beneath their feet as
beams flashed, blocking paths in chaotic pulses.

Thorns whipped like serpents, one grazing Veronica's arm
with a searing sting that drew a thin line of blood, the thorn's burn
a keen reminder of Sheng Xiao's fracturing harmony.

Omar roared, his mace crushing a cluster of spikes in a
thunderous arc, shards flying like chill-shattered glass, while
Doug's sword parried a second lunge, his blade humming with
Dog Clan loyalty as he shouted, "I've got your back, Veronica!"

Each step became a gamble, the forest's defenses testing
their every move, the air thick with the crackle of energy and the
metallic tang of blood.

The clearing opened at last; stones etched with pixiu
carvings humming low, twilight cloaking them in deepening chill.

Veronica stepped forward, glyphs flaring underfoot. Pixiu
illusions roared to life, lion-like forms with dragon heads charging
from the mist, venomous brambles surging from the earth like
living whips. Her super speed blurred her into motion, dodging
thorns that grazed her coat, their sting sharp and immediate.

"Stay back!" she shouted, shielding Omar and Doug with her body, pistol firing precise shots at a bramble's root, the recoil steady in her grip.

The illusions lunged, eyes glowing with ethereal fire, but her charms fueled her resolve, the Pine Oath's blessing warming against her skin. She darted through the chaos, luring the pixiu away with calculated taunts, their forms fading as the glyphs dimmed under her cunning maneuvers.

Omar's mace cleared a brutal path, his swings powerful and precise, while Doug's sword steadied them, his loyalty shining as he covered her flank. A fire kindled in her chest, burning away the Rat Clan's shadowed past, the maze ahead a true test of her redemption.

Back at Mara's camp, sawdust swirled in the air like golden dust, the resin thick and aromatic as axes chopped rhythmically against fresh logs.

Mara's team prepared supplies, her axe sharpening with deliberate strokes, while her daughter Lia clutched a carved luck charm, its resin gleaming fresh from the ritual.

Tate, Melissa, Sam, Alice, and Ryder had just arrived, their gear slung over shoulders. They set it aside, helping unload crates and set up temporary tents—prepping for Kusini but lending hands to fortify against riots spilling from the markets.

Tate swung his claw gloves, splintering a log with a grin, taunting Sam as sparks flew. "My claws would beat your bow any day, Snake."

Sam notched an arrow, eyes narrowing in response, her reply keen. "Prove it, Tiger," the tension crackling like dry pine needles.

Ryder hauled a crate, his cannon clanking, steadying Lia with a reassuring nod and a quick joke— "Don't worry, kid, this cannon's louder than any quake"—his lighthearted tone easing her wide-eyed fear as they stacked supplies together.

Melissa adjusted tent stakes with deft hands, her Monkey Clan cleverness shining as she rigged a quick reinforcement. Alice synced her tablet, fingers dancing over glyphs, her focus a quiet anchor.

Ryder's cannon rested nearby, his nod firm as it steadied Lia's nerves, while he hauled a supply crate with Melissa.

Alice's tablet hummed softly, tracking glyph patterns with Rabbit Clan precision, her focus a quiet anchor as she synced it to a local holo-mill's interface, performing a quick upgrade—her fingers flying over the screen to optimize the holo-chips' data flow, ensuring trade logs and clan reports loaded faster for the craftsmen.

Lia whispered to Melissa, "You'll stop the riots? Bring back the harmony?"

Melissa knelt, her voice gentle as she adjusted a tent stake. "We've got you—and Sheng Xiao."

The assurance calmed the girl, the camp's warmth a bulwark against the encroaching storm, the group's assistance forging early bonds that hinted at the unity they'd need ahead.

In Souris's chaotic markets, Lucas fought through a mob of locals—craftsmen wielding glyph-etched axes that sparked with protective holo-bursts, their chants invoking Rat cunning as they defended looted stalls.

The air rang with the clash of steel, sawdust swirling as a burly lumberjack swung his axe, the impact jarring Lucas's arms, resin charms flaring with warning glyphs that pulsed red.

Another charged with a holo-net, its micro-generators humming to ensnare him, the net crackling with energy as it tangled his legs, but Lucas roared, ripping it apart with brute strength, the effort leaving him gasping, blonde hair matted with sweat, light blue eyes narrowed in exhaustion.

A final skirmish with guards—axes glancing off his armor, one grazing his side with a keen sting—drained him further, the riots' frenzy sapping his edge for the ambush ahead.

Fatigue weighed his limbs, fresh from X's Mico heist where he'd hauled the team through the cenote's venomous traps, muscles aching from dodging serpents, every breath a reminder of the dungeon he'd escaped years ago—X's silhouette breaking through steel and shadow to drag him free.

That lifeline, twisted with guilt over his treason, pushed him through the haze, his resolve hardening despite the burn.

In X's fortress war room, runic projections hovered in the air, flickering with unstable green veins, artifacts quivering as the Yin Scroll's energy surged unevenly, the air thick with the scent of ancient parchment and smoldering runes.

Vincent's dark blue eyes glinted beneath his rune-etched cloak, its heavy folds draping like shadows as his light brown hair fell slightly over his forehead, fingers tightening on the serpent-shaped scepter, green runes thrumming with cryptic plans that whispered of deeper schemes.

X stood at the head, his voice a low growl. "Status report—now."

Bella stepped forward, her amber eyes flashing as flames danced along her fingers, her thrill-seeking edge evident in her grin. "Kusini's plains are primed—my scouts have mapped the harvest barns, ready to ignite if we need a distraction. The farmers are hoarding grain already...they won't know what hit them."

Dolore followed, lightning crackling faintly around her hands, her voice hesitant with unrequited longing for X's approval. "Lightning probes are scouting eastern trails—storms brewing in the forests, but nothing solid on the talisman yet. The quake fears are stirring more unrest—clans turning on each other. Your plan is working perfectly, X—your vision guides us."

A holo-link flared, Lucas's face appearing amid static, his broad frame battered and sweat-slicked.

"Market's secured, boss," he reported, voice rough, wiping blood from a shallow cut. "But the locals fought hard—axes, charms, the works. Took everything to clear a path—riots are getting wilder."

X's fingers traced a battle projection with deliberate strokes, plotting Souris's fall, his grey eyes burning cold as he clutched the silver ring on its chain, a sapphire band now bloodied in memory, fueling a vengeance that boiled like magma.

The spellbook's pull darkened his gaze further, and he noted Lucas's heavy breaths and shadowed eyes, the exhaustion etched into every line. Vincent's voice cutting keen, a veiled prod. "I'm locating the talisman—progress, but slow. The clearing's still a puzzle."

"Push through—the Rat Talisman's ours," X growled, his command unwavering despite Vincent's lack of progress and Lucas's fatigue.

A memory seared Lucas: trapped in a rival clan's dungeon, chains gnawing his wrists as traitors' jeers rang out, X's silhouette breaking through dust and steel, a lifeline forged in chaos. That bond, layered with gratitude, burned despite the exhaustion, a tragic tie that deepened his resolve even as his body screamed for rest.

In the palace gardens, Hana and Patricia stood near the edge, watching Cade practice with Gerry, David, and Patricia— the Guardians not tasked with Souris. Gerry drilled with his spear, thrusting at holo-targets projected by a training glyph, the shimmering forms shifting with each strike.

David flowed through katana forms, his blade slicing the air with dragon-like grace, while Patricia's hammer swung in slow arcs, her gaze keen as she assessed the group.

Hana leaned in, her voice a conspiratorial whisper, eyes sparkling as she gossiped. "Look at David—those strong arms wielding that katana like it's an extension of him, his temper hiding a heart of gold. If he loosened up, he'd be irresistible. And Cade? Those mismatched eyes, that build—he's got the brains to match the brawn, doesn't he? Always so focused, but imagine if he let loose." Her tone carried a hint of rebellion, masking a forced betrothal she'd dodged with every flirt.

Patricia chuckled, her Pig Clan warmth shining through. "You're bold, Horse. David's got potential, sure—fiery like his clan. But Cade's got eyes only for duty—or someone."

Hana waved it off with a flirtatious grin, but her admiration lingered, a playful threat in the night air.

Jade watched from nearby, ink from the maps smudging her fingers as she pored over Souris's unrest reports—burned stalls, quake fears rippling through the clans, a city teetering on the edge of full collapse.

Onyx's absence throbbed like a fresh wound; her twin brother vanished after Opal and Alexandrite's deaths, a thorn in her hope that twisted deeper in the quiet moments.

But Cade drew her stare, his form moving with roguish grace as he demonstrated a knife throw, muscles rippling under his sweat-dampened shirt as he twisted in a fluid strike, his black hair falling into those mismatched eyes, blending raw power with the keen intellect that left her breathless.

His loyalty, his spark—I love it all, she thought, the warmth flooding her. A tender thrum through their bond hinted at his focus, and she masked her longing, the empress's resolve hardening.

The Guardians' unity fueled her resolve, the fight rising as Souris's markets became the first battleground, a storm where talismans would decide the fate of their world.

78

Chapter 5: The Rat King's Challenge

The Souris clearing thrummed with an eerie energy, glyphs glowing ghostly silver, casting a restless gloom across the chill-dusted forest floor. The air carried the keen tang of resin, blending with the earthy nip of frozen ground, as Veronica's fingers brushed her two charms—her mother's worn Rat Clan sigil, its edges smoothed by years of prayer, and the newly blessed Pine Oath gift, its carved rat glistening with fresh resin—thumping against her chest.

Her jaw tightened, as if the weight of Vladimir's heritage pressed down, a constant reminder of the legacy she aimed to redeem.

Omar stood steady beside her, his mace drawn and glinting in the dim light, his breath misting in the icy air like a veil of quiet resolve, his calm, dark gaze a lifeline amid the bone-deep cold. Doug hovered close, his light blue eyes darting with nervous energy, the Dog Clan guardian's tracking instincts faltering in the unnatural stillness of the clearing.

Doug scanned the underbrush, his eyes narrowing as he tested the air, his voice dropping to a shaky mutter, his gaze darting to the shadowed pines as he shifted uneasily: "This place feels off… like the forest is watching us."

The pines loomed tall and ancient around them, their boughs groaning under the weight of twilight, needles crackling with chill that sparkled like shattered crystal in the fading light.

The landscape of Souris unfolded in a tapestry of dense, snow-laced woods, its air heavy with the scent of lumber and the legacy of craft, every tree a testament to the clan's resilience.

The air shimmered abruptly, mist rising thick and swirling like a spectral shroud, and the Rat King materialized—a massive spectral rat, its translucent fur gleaming white as fresh snow, onyx eyes glinting like polished obsidian in the dimness, its tail coiling like a whip poised to strike.

The guardian's form towered over them, its body rippling with ethereal muscle, keen teeth bared in a grin that promised death, claws scraping the chill as it shifted.

She recalled clan tales: the Rat's birth in a Great Flood, from an era before the zodiac's dawn, when rivers swelled to drown the clans in a deluge that shattered villages.

 The Rat, a lone survivor shunned for its wily nature, turned its cunning to salvation—crafting vine snares to trap flood spirits, guiding clans to high ridges where they etched glyphs of gratitude into stone under moonlit skies. Its spirit bound to the talisman after death, it became a guardian of balance, its spectral form a paradox of instinct redeemed by selfless leadership, its onyx eyes a beacon of a clan's resilience—a parallel igniting her resolve as she faced its ghost.

As she pressed through the maze, a glyph vision flashed: the Rat sacrificing its strength to shield a child from the flood, its wit a legacy she now honored with every riddle solved.

The maze's glyphs pulsed with flood echoes, whispering of waters parted by the Rat's cunning, resonating with her drive to redeem her clan's honor. Its presence radiated an oppressive power, the air growing heavier, as if the very ground quaked under its spectral weight.

Its voice rasped, reverberating through the pines like a howling wind, "Solve my riddle to breach my maze, or be ensnared—two more trials await the talisman! You, child of Vladimir, seek my talisman. Prove your worth or perish in my maze."

The words hit her like an icy gust, her breath catching as her jaw clenched, fists balling at her sides, the weight of his heritage a burden she'd vowed to lift.

The elders' praise of his "clever victory" in the Great Race echoed, a hollow accolade for a deed lauded as cunning triumph, its details lost to time, but Veronica saw the trickery beneath, driving her to redefine it with true honor.

"Not here for games, ghost," she snapped, her sarcasm a shield for the nerves twisting in her gut, her breath misting as she met its predatory gaze with a defiant glare. "Name your test."

Omar shifted closer, his mace gripped tighter, a silent pillar of support that sent a warm ember through her chilled frame, while Doug edged nearer, his sword half-drawn, his crush on her fueling his protective stance.

"Let's show this rat who's boss," Doug said, earning a rare grin from Omar.

"Only if you keep up, pup," he said.

The ground rumbled with a low, ominous groan, stones sinking into the earth as if swallowed, and a maze rose from the depths—thorny vines weaving walls in intricate, glyph-etched patterns, their ice-laced thorns shimmering with a venomous gleam in the twilight, each tip dripping with a frozen poison that promised searing pain.

The barriers twisted like sentient guardians, rooted in Souris's protective lore, glyphs pulsing with flood imagery—raging waters, rat silhouettes—echoing the Rat King's tale, their etchings humming with ancient whispers of its cunning.

At its center, a gold-blue glow surged—the Rat Talisman, perched on a pedestal of twisted thorn-roots, its rat-carved motif a beacon piercing the gloom, crafted from polished obsidian with intricate zodiac carvings, roughly the size of a clenched fist.

"Enter my maze and solve my riddle," the Rat King rasped, its tail lashing with a crack that sent shards of chill scattering across the ground. "I am not alive, but I grow, I need air, but have no lungs, water kills me. What am I?"

The spectral figure leaned closer, its onyx eyes narrowing to slits, testing not just her intellect but her spirit, the flood survivor's cunning woven into the riddle's deceptive simplicity.

Veronica's mind raced, her charms warming against her skin like a vow of resilience, the Pine Oath's resin scent rising faintly, as if the forest itself lent her strength.

Doug ventured eagerly, his voice breaking the tense silence, "A plant?" His guess hung in the air, hopeful yet misplaced, his light blue eyes flicking to Veronica for approval, his crush driving his desire to impress her.

Omar shook his head, his deep voice cutting through the cold with steady logic, "Plants need water." His presence was a fortress, grounding her, the ember between them flickering in the chill.

Veronica nodded sharply, the answer snapping into place like a lock turning. Facing the Rat King with a defiant glare, she declared, "Fire, ghost," her Rat Clan pride flaring like a torch in the dark, her voice steady despite the spectral threat, the team's unity fueling her spirit against the guardian's test.

The Rat King's onyx eyes glinted with mischievous malice as it sneered, "Proceed, child—your spirit will falter yet."

The maze responded, vines hissing in retreat, their thorns retracting with a slithering sound, the icy walls parting to reveal the path ahead.

"Nice one, Veronica—burn that rat down!" Doug cheered, his enthusiasm lightening the tension.

Her charms pulsed with a deeper warmth, igniting a memory that pierced her like a thorn. At ten, during the Pine Oath festival, Elder Thane—his sly eyes glinting at sixty—had smirked, pressing a false charm into her small hands.

"A gift," he lied, the resin gleaming deceptively under the festival's lantern glow. She'd delivered it to Mira, her friend, but its tainted etchings seared Mira's hand, the sizzle of burning flesh

and her cry of pain shattering the joyous chants, shaming
Veronica before the gathered crowd.

The festival turned to chaos, Mira clutching her blistered
palm as Veronica, with a child's fury, exposed Thane's trick, her
speed unveiling the rigged glyph hidden within the charm.

Yet the elders praised her as "Vladimir's heir," lauding
his cunning as a badge of honor, their words twisting like vines
around her heart.

Loathing their approval, she vowed to reject such deceit,
Mira's sob a scar etched into her soul, fueling her resolve to
redefine her clan's heritage with honor, not trickery. The memory
faded, but its heat flared in her chest, her steps quickening with a
renewed fire in her eyes as she led Omar and Doug deeper into
the maze.

The path twisted onward, vines whispering threats with a
voice like rustling leaves, their icy thorns glinting with lethal
intent, the forest's nip pressing against them like an unyielding
vice. At a fork in the maze, Veronica's instincts screamed danger,
the scent of decay keen and rancid in the frosty air.

"Omar, Doug—left path," she ordered, her eyes scanning
the shadowed gloom, the cold biting deeper into her exposed skin.

Omar nodded, his mace held ready, his touch grazing her
arm as he moved close, a warmth that made her pulse skip
beneath the chill, the ember between them growing with every
shared glance.

The right path beckoned with a deceptive lure, but she shoved the team toward safety, the burn of caution a familiar sting, her super speed itching to race ahead yet held by the bond of her team.

She spotted a glyph trap—silver glyphs pulsing with a rhythmic hum, pixiu carvings flaring with dragon-like roars that reverberated through the trees, their ethereal forms briefly materializing in the mist.

Marking it with a stone, she continued with Omar and Doug, but a vine wall surged, its thorns slashing at Doug.

Veronica blurred to shield him, her speed a blur of silver, as Omar's mace thundered through, chill shards flying, the Rat King's laugh rasping, "Your speed won't save you!"

A thorn raked her arm, drawing a thin line of blood, its sting a sharp echo of Mira's pain, fueling her resolve.

Glyph thorns pulsed, their barbs hissing as Veronica darted past, leading them through the venomous maze, "Keep up, or these thorns win!"

The tunnel loomed ahead, vines weaving a ceiling tight and oppressive, the air growing heavy with poison's bitter bite that stung their lungs. Veronica hesitated, her super speed rendered useless in the confined space, but Doug's nose caught a draft cutting through the sap's sting.

"It's open," he whispered, guiding them through, thorns snagging coats like greedy fingers, his tracking anchoring the team with newfound confidence.

During the pit save, a memory flickered for Doug: a coastal raid, friends abandoning him as waves crashed, blood staining sand—Veronica's shield chipped at that trauma, his resolve hardening. During his mace swing, a memory flickered for Omar: Kusini fields, his father's orders to stay back from a collapsing barn, the sting of being coddled fueling his strength vow.

The tunnel opened into a wider chamber, but the maze shifted again, its walls rumbling as paths rearranged, forcing a backtrack through the chill-laced chaos.

As they navigated the backtrack, the Rat King's voice cut through the mist, its tone dripping with challenge.

"Another test, child of cunning," it rasped, its tail lashing with a spectral strike that sent chill shards spinning. "I fly without wings, cry without eyes—what am I?"

Veronica's mind raced, the air thick with tension. Doug frowned, then ventured, "Rain's close—maybe clouds?"

Veronica built on his insight, her voice steady, "Clouds, ghost!" Omar nodded, "Good call, Doug—teamwork makes the trick," and the vines shifted slightly, parting to reveal a narrow path forward, the Rat King's eyes glinting with reluctant approval as it sneered, "Proceed."

Veronica, Omar, and Doug pressed toward the maze's center, its glow blazing brighter, the talisman's polished obsidian pulsing with a gold-blue glow beneath the chill.

The Rat King towered above, its onyx eyes glowing with predatory intent, its tail lashing with a crack that stirred the mist into a swirling dance.

"Your ancestor's tricks won't save you—break or bow," it taunted, its voice a chilling wind that cut deeper, challenging their spirit. "One final riddle: I speak without a mouth, hear without ears, have no body, come alive with wind. What am I?" The air thickened, charged with an unnatural energy.

Doug whispered hesitantly, "A spirit?" his voice trembling with defiance against the guardian's threat.

Omar frowned, his brow furrowing, "Wind carries sound," his steady logic a bold stand.

Veronica grinned, the answer clicking with clarity, her team's input fueling her resolve. She stepped forward, facing the Rat King, "Echo, your majesty," her voice firm, her clan's honor burning, her defiance rejecting its heritage.

The Rat King nodded solemnly, its onyx eyes flickering with approval before it dissolved into mist, the maze crumbling as vines retreated into the ground with a final rasp, chill cracking underfoot.

A surge of glyphs erupted, the vision intensifying—twin zodiac figures sharpening into shadowy forms, their voices overlapping with a sinister chant, "The bond weakens, betrayal nears."

A glyph ward flickered, its rat silhouette warping into a zodiac emblem—a subtle hint of Sheng Xiao's fragile harmony, hardening Veronica's resolve as she clutched the talisman, its weight surprisingly light yet a shiver of ancient power coursed through her grip.

With the talisman secured, elation swept over Veronica, Omar, and Doug.

Veronica grinned widely, holding the talisman aloft, "We nailed it—take that, rat ghost!"

Omar clapped Doug's shoulder with a hearty laugh, "Proud of you, kid—your nose saved us!"

Doug beamed, his voice bright with relief, "Team effort! Let's tell Jade—the Empress will be thrilled!"

They shared a chill-crusted chuckle, the talisman's golden-blue glow casting a triumphant light as they gathered their gear, preparing to call Jade with the good news.

In the Imperial Garden, Jade's scepter flared with urgent light, Souris updates flashing dire—pines withering under riot-fueled chaos, Veronica's peril a thorn in her chest.

"They must hurry," she murmured, amethyst eyes clouding as jealousy's echo twisted deeper, Hana's flirt lingering like a riddle unsolved.

She'd never imagined Cade with someone else—no ladies chased him in the palace, his quiet loyalty to her a constant—yet Hana's boldness sparked a possessive fear, as if he belonged to her, though he didn't know her feelings.

Torn between the realm's demands and her heart's pull, the weight of her crown felt heavier, her focus fracturing as she gripped the scepter.

A memory surged—sixteen, at the fenghuang festival, Cade's hand brushing hers as they spun, his grin lighting the night, her heart racing until duty yanked her away.

Through the bond, his presence brushed her mind, a phantom warmth against her cheek, his voice steadying, "I'm with you, always."

Her breath hitched, longing warring with duty, the scepter trembling as she masked the ache, her worry for Veronica fueling her resolve. Cade's green-blue gaze flickered in her mind, his festival grin a tether, strengthening their unspoken vow as she steeled herself for the news.

Cade's green-blue eyes scanned Souris holo-reports in the courtyard, worry gnawing as Veronica's team faced the Rat King.

Huan's sharp voice cut in, lingering with pointed disdain: "Know your place, Cade—advisor, not suitor. Why hover over the Empress? Percy was the emperor's advisor, and now you take his place—yet the emperor treated you and Percy like his own, but that doesn't make you royal. Her station demands a match of noble lineage."

The concern was clear, his push to uphold Jade's station laced with jealousy of their closeness, a bond Huan envied but couldn't sever, his words dripping with the sting of their shared history.

Cade noted the envy, seeing truth in Huan's point—despite the emperor's paternal care, his non-royal roots marked him an outsider, unworthy of her throne.

A memory flared: the festival, her hand brushing his, her laugh a spark against his doubt, now mocking his inadequacy. Through the bond, Jade's worry pulsed, her warmth a phantom touch on his palm, steadying him.

I'm not worthy, he thought, knives twitching, her royal fire igniting a vow to shield her—betrothal or not—his heart aching to match her grace.

He sent a silent thrum back, "Your strength guides me," reinforcing their bond as he monitored the holo-feed, her presence a beacon amid his doubt.

In X's fortress, runic maps glowed with unstable green, the Yin Scroll pulsing chaotically. X's fingers clenched the silver ring, grief clawing—a vision of his love's glow dimming in blood and ruin, her laughter stolen by loss.

"The runes hint at the Rat King's maze," Vincent said, his scepter tracing knot-like zodiac runes, hinting at a scheme to harness the talisman's power to destabilize Jade's reign. X nodded, "Lucas, find the clearing and beat Jade."

A memory seared X: her laughter cut short, his rage driving him to clutch the ring, the Scroll's chaos amplifying his grief as he vowed to shatter Sheng Xiao's harmony.

Vincent smirked, "Their balance frays—our time nears," his ambition fueling the plan as he unraveled a rune suggesting the talisman could fracture the zodiac's unity, its energy a weapon to unravel Jade's rule.

In the chaotic Souris markets, Lucas carved a path through rioting locals, their glyph-etched axes swinging wildly, resin charms flaring with protective bursts.

A lumberjack's blade grazed his shoulder, tearing his cloak, the sting fueling his rage as he parried with his machete, sparks flying.

A glyph trap erupted underfoot, vines snaring a mercenary's leg—he roared, slashing free, but a pixiu illusion lunged, its claws raking his chest, his scream cut short as he fell.

Exhaustion from X's mine rescue—venom scars throbbing, muscles aching—slowed Lucas, yet his loyalty drove him onward, dodging a holo-net's crackling snare, his breath ragged as he spotted his target ahead. In a charred Souris market stall, he pinned a craftsman against the wall, the man's hands bound with rough rope.

"The Rat King's maze—where's the clearing?" Lucas snarled, his machete clashing with the craftsman's glyph-axe, sparks flying as the man carved a gash across Lucas's arm.

Fatigue weighed his limbs—venom scars burned, muscles ached—every swing slower, a near-miss as the axe grazed his cheek, blood trickling.

The craftsman spat, "Pine Oath guards our forest—you'll find nothing."

Lucas snapped the man's luck charm, its glyph shattering with a crack, the man's defiance crumbling as he whispered the clearing's path. Lucas's chest puffed, X's mine rescue fueling his loyalty, though exhaustion blurred his vision.

He roared, "Talk, or I'll gut you!" shoving the craftsman harder, the man's resistance faltering as Lucas's mercenaries dragged him away, mapping the north ridge.

A glyph pit swallowed one with a scream as pixiu illusions slashed another, a mercenary's cry echoing as his arm bled out, their numbers dwindling while Lucas pressed on, the clearing's call a spur.

At Mara's camp, the air was thick with the scent of fresh resin as locals carved luck charms under the rhythmic Pine Oath chants, their voices weaving a protective spell.

The Pine Oath's chant wove a loosening spell, truths spilling unbidden as Mara nodded, "The ritual opens doors, lets the truth flow free."

Tate scratched a tiger into a wood scrap, his claw gloves glinting as he grinned, "This beats your bow, Snake."

Sam notched an arrow, her fingers steady despite a nervous laugh, "Crowds freeze me...this is worse than carving," her stage fright slipping out.

Alice's tablet buzzed with a glyph update, her tech stress melting into a chuckle, "I hate when they mock my tech skills."

Ryder teased Lia, "Don't worry, I'm fearless," his cannon clanking as he demonstrated a mock boom.

Her playful shove sparked laughter, but her wide eyes darted to the shadowed trees, "I'm scared they'll come here."

Ryder knelt, "We've got you, kid—Sheng Xiao's with us," his reassurance calming her.

Melissa rigged tent stakes with deft hands, hope rising with the chant's rhythm.

Veronica clutched the Rat Talisman, its glyphs humming, Omar's gaze meeting hers with trust, Doug's nod eager, his tracking anchoring them.

Veronica's wit met Omar's resolve, Doug's faith forging a bond—her fire, his fortress, his steadiness holding firm. Jade's warning spurred her resolve. The talisman's spark proved her honor, Souris's pines their shield.

Chapter 6: The Ambush

Veronica clutched the Rat Talisman, its gold-blue glow pulsing through her coat pocket like a heartbeat, the obsidian rat carving etched with zodiac motifs surprisingly light for its fist-sized form, yet heavy with her clan's legacy. Her arm throbbed from a thorn graze in the maze, venom-like pain a badge of resilience now, not a burden.

Chill crunched underfoot in the Souris clearing, the air hushed with resin's tang, the Rat King's maze leaving a reverent silence, faint glyphs pulsing softly in the earth like whispered prayers, their hum vibrating under her boots.

The quiet there, a sacred hush near the maze and Mara's safe camp, stood in stark contrast to the distant market riots—torches flaring, voices raging over looted lumber stalls. Omar's dark eyes met hers, a warm spark of trust flickering, his mace glinting as he nodded, his Ox Clan strength a steady anchor.

Doug's eager grin flashed, his luck charm thumping, pulsing faintly as if echoing his unease, his tracking senses from the maze still keen. Their bond held firm, shared nods sealing their trust under the chill's bite, a spark of victory in Sheng Xiao's fracturing balance.

"We actually pulled it off," Veronica said, her voice laced with disbelief and triumph, Vladimir's betrayal—a shadow haunting her Rat Clan for centuries—lifting like mist burned away by the sun.

A memory flickered: at twelve, during a Pine Oath festival, her mother's worn Rat sigil pressed into her palm, its smooth edges warm as she whispered, "Cunning with honor, Veronica, not like him."

She meant Elder Thane, whose false charm had burned Mira's hand at the festival, the girl's cry piercing the crowd as Veronica exposed his deceit, her fury burning as elders praised her as "Vladimir's heir" for her cunning, though she loathed their veneration of trickery over her friend's pain.

Mira's cry echoed in her mind, a keen sting that fueled her vow to wield cunning without cruelty, her determination hardening as chill bit her cheeks, her wound stinging like a distant fire.

I'm proving them wrong, redeeming our name, she thought, the clan's shame fading under her grip, the talisman's hum a beacon of her redemption, her heart swelling with pride as she stood taller.

Omar's gaze lingered, a flicker of awe softening his gruff tone as he studied her under the moonlight's glow.

"You led us through," he rumbled, adjusting her torn coat, his fingers brushing hers, lingering a moment too long, sparking warmth she buried under snark.

His strength grounded her, her heart stuttering at the intensity, like a steady flame in the cold.

He trusts me—why does that scare me? The Rat Clan's reputation for deceit makes trust rare, but I'll change that stigma, she thought, shoving the warmth down as her cheeks warmed, the flicker of something deeper bolstering her will.

"Don't get sappy, big guy. Eleven more talismans, and I'm not carrying you through them," she teased, punching his arm lightly, the contact jolting her, her smirk hiding the spark.

Doug chuckled, light blue eyes scanning the gloom. "If we keep winning, maybe I'll get that holo-puzzle rematch from palace drills, Veronica—no 'cunning' shortcuts." His Dog Clan loyalty shone, his crush softening into a sibling-like bond, forged by his "rain" guess sparking her "clouds" answer and tracking safe paths in the maze.

"Efficiency, pup, not cheating," Veronica grinned, teasing, "That maze would've eaten us without that sniff of yours." Their banter wove a fragile shield, laughter drowning the distant unrest's echoes—vendors guarding holo-chips with zodiac codes, artisans hiding relic shards in panic.

Veronica pulled out her holo-link, its chime cutting the night like a blade. "Better report in before Jade sends the cavalry."

The projection stabilized, revealing Jade in the Imperial City's library, maps pulsing with Souris's unrest reports— vendors guarding holo-chips, artisans scrambling—her scepter glinting with urgency.

Cade stood at her side, green-blue eyes alert, watching Jade with quiet loyalty, their bond flickering faintly on the holo-link, a pulse of warmth Veronica caught.

"Empress," Veronica said, voice steady despite her aching arm. She pulled the talisman from her coat pocket, holding it up, its gold-blue glow flaring on the holo-link, a beacon of triumph, a spark of relief crossing Jade's face. "We secured the Rat Talisman. The test was a thorn maze with riddles—fire, clouds, echo. Omar's strength, Doug's tracking and guesses pulled us through. But we also got a vision—twin figures looming, their chant like a warning bell: 'The knot tightens, betrayal nears.' It seemed deeper than X's schemes, like the Prophecy's weight."

Jade's eyes darkened, red hair catching light like flames. "Well done, Veronica, Omar, Doug—your team's unity is our hope. Your win will help with the riots, which have intensified since you left, markets burning hotter. What do you mean by tied to the Prophecy?"

The holo-link glitched as Doug's nose twitched sharply, his tracker senses prickling like needles.

"Something's coming—sweat and steel, mixed with that market smoke," he whispered, his luck charm thumping, pulsing faintly as if echoing his unease.

Veronica tucked the talisman back into her coat as figures emerged from the pines. Gunshots cracked through the clearing, keen and sudden, her pistol snapping up.

"We've got company!" she snapped, Jade's face freezing in a mask of worry as the link sputtered out, static swallowing her voice.

The air turned intense, a metallic tang of sweat and steel cutting the chill, pines swaying, distant riot echoes faint but ominous, like the disharmony spreading.

Moonlight glinted off daggers and axes as figures emerged—a massive man leading, his leather armor creaking, hardened from skirmishes, machete gleaming wickedly.

His blonde hair was matted with grime, light blue eyes narrowed, determination masking exhaustion etching his brow, as if from relentless battles.

Mercenaries fanned out—wiry Souris locals mixed with black-clad warriors, their axes and blades pulsing with crude zodiac charms, their movements jerky with greed.

"Master X demands the talisman," the leader growled, his voice rough like gravel under boots, exhaustion carving deep lines into his brow.

One mercenary shouted, "Lucas, flank 'em! The boss wants it now!" revealing his name in a hoarse cry.

Veronica's ears caught it, her pistol drawn in a blur, the holo-link's static fading as Jade's image vanished.

"Someone called Lucas and his goons—bad timing," she snapped, her sarcasm a shield for the spike of fear twisting in her gut, her thorn-wounded arm throbbing fresh as she aimed. "Omar, Doug—move!" A blade grazed her coat, tearing fabric, the talisman's glow peeking through, drawing greedy eyes.

Lucas lunged, fingers brushing the talisman—Veronica's blur saved it, blood staining the chill as she stumbled, the near-loss fueling her defiance. A pixiu illusion roared from the mist, dragon jaws snapping, glyphs flaring with Rat Clan fury.

Veronica blurred, tossing her Pine Oath charm into a glyph trap, its gold-blue glow luring the beast. It charged, thorns snaring its form, collapsing in a spectral wail. Doug's sword slashed, shielding her.

"Got you!" he yelled, the maze's hum spiking, her cunning prevailing.

Mercenaries charged, five to one, blades closing in like a tightening noose, Veronica knelt, gasping, arm bleeding, Omar and Doug flanking her, their blades trembling with exhaustion, mercenaries circling like vultures. Steel whistled through the frigid air, shouts drowning pines.

Veronica fired, the shots echoing like thunder, but chill jammed her pistol, a curse escaping as a blade slashed across her arm, hot blood soaking her sleeve and sending venom-like pain shooting through her nerves.

She staggered, grappling a foe to the ground, the world tilting, a mercenary pinning her arm as she struggled.

I'm not Vladimir—I fight fair, she thought, wrestling free, her breath ragged.

Omar roared, shoving enemies back with his bulk, his mace blocking two foes, his Ox Clan strength a wall, mercy tied to honor flashing as he spared a groaning mercenary, his mace poised to strike but held, his dark eyes flickering with conflict, a desperate glance at Veronica sparking strength.

Doug tripped a mercenary with a swift kick, parrying a strike at Veronica's back.

"Got you, Veronica—I'll cover your back!" he panted, tracking senses guiding his blade, sweat mixing with chill, his heart pounding as he fought to keep her safe.

"Thanks, Dougie," Veronica gasped, gratitude raw, reloading with trembling fingers, the recoil jarring her wound. Her arm burned, pain sharpening her focus as she fired, dropping a foe.

Omar shielded her, his massive frame a wall, his glance under pressure sparking strength as he bellowed, "Hold on!" his mace sparking against an axe, glyphs flaring and dying in the cold.

The fight became a frenzy—mercenaries slipping on chill-slick ground, axes clashing with Omar's mace, sparks flying like dying stars, the trio barely holding the line against the overwhelming odds.

At Mara and Lia's camp, soft snow dusted torchlit paths, pines looming like silent guardians, the air carrying faint resin from distant unrest.

Locals chanted zodiac hymns, their voices weaving a shield against the disharmony tearing through Souris's trade hubs—vendors guarding holo-chips with zodiac codes, artisans hiding relic shards in panic.

Mara, the Rat Clan camp leader, stood tall, her ingenuity honed from securing food stores, charting safe paths, and bolstering morale with rhythmic chants. Her axe rested on her shoulder, its blade etched with rat motifs catching the firelight, her voice ringing clear, authority honed from guiding her people through nights of unrest.

Her eyes flicked to her daughter. Lia, who clutched a woven charm tightly, wide-eyed with fear, her small frame trembling in the torchlight.

"Stay strong, Lia," Mara murmured, kneeling to share a Pine Oath tale, "Once, a rat outwitted a storm with cunning and heart," calming Lia's fear as her eyes widened in wonder.

"Will the fighting stop soon?" Lia asked

Mara nodded softly, "Soon, Lia, with their courage," her voice warm.

Mara's runners darted through the pines, delivering bread to weary locals, her chants weaving rat glyphs that glowed faintly, bolstering hope against the distant chaos.

Tate, Sam, Melissa, Alice, and Ryder huddled near the crackling fire, maps spread on a chill-crusted log, planning the next leg to Kusini's plains. Tate's claws tapped impatiently, his voice gruff, "Kusini's plains—speed's our edge."

Sam nodded, her bow resting across her knees, her voice low, "Precision over speed, Tiger. My arrows don't miss."

Ryder's cannon rested against a log, his Rooster Clan bravado gleaming, his grin masking a flicker of doubt in his tightened grip.

"Plains won't know what's coming," he said. Gunshots cracked through the night like distant thunder, keen and urgent, slicing through the rhythmic chants. Sam's bow snapped up instantly, her Snake Clan precision locking on the shadows beyond the camp.

"That's from the clearing—Veronica's team's in trouble," Tate growled, his claws glinting as he flexed, impulsiveness flaring hot in his amber eyes, the Tiger Clan's ferocity bubbling like a storm.

Melissa shot to her feet, axe in hand, her voice keen, "Move! We can't wait—Mara, hold the camp!"

Mara nodded grimly, her voice ringing clear, authority honed from guiding her people. "Guard the perimeter! Guardians, save your friends!" Her eyes lingered on Lia, whose whisper— "Be careful"—faded as the chants faltered, the unrest hitting close to home.

The group raced into the chill-laced woods, pines blurring past as the sounds of battle grew louder—gunshots, steel clashing, shouts echoing—their hearts pounding with a mix of fear and resolve, the talisman's fate pulling them toward the fray.

The holo-link cut off in the Imperial Palace's library, Veronica's "We've got company!" echoing through the chamber. Jade's breath caught, hands trembling on her scepter, heart racing, palms sweating as thoughts spiraled—Am I failing them? Is this X?

Her amethyst eyes darkened, red hair spilling like fire over her sapphire robe, the weight of leadership crushing her chest.

Cade lunged for the holo-panel, fingers fumbling to restore the comms, his green-blue eyes keen with worry yet steadying Jade.

Their bond pulsed with her fear, his fists clenching, longing to fight for her, to wrap her in his arms, but Huan's words— "Know your place, advisor"—rooted him like chains, his Cat Clan doubts gnawing: I'm not enough for her.

"Tate's group is there—they're trained for this," he said, his voice held firm, strained by the urge to do more, his jaw clenched tight.

A memory surged—at seventeen, after her father's death, Jade stood at the throne room's threshold, trembling, the council whispering doubts as their judging eyes waited for her to enter and take the throne. Her father's teachings echoed— "You're ready, Jade." —yet doubt gripped her.

Cade's quiet voice, "You're stronger than you think, Jade," his hand brushing hers, sparked courage then and now. In her mind, his festival touch merged with his pulse, a vision of hands clasped bolstering her will.

She nodded, her trust in her Guardians battling her urge to act, determination hardening, her jaw clenched against the gunfire's distant echo, the talisman's hope a beacon against the dark.

Tate, Sam, Melissa, Alice, and Ryder burst from the tree line into the Souris clearing, chill crunching under their boots as Veronica knelt, gasping, arm bleeding, Omar and Doug flanking her, their blades trembling with exhaustion, mercenaries circling like vultures.

Tate tackled a foe, his claws extending with a metallic snick, raking across armor in a shower of sparks.

"Claws save the day!" he snarled, his Tiger Clan ferocity unleashed, a blade grazing his side but impulsiveness driving him forward. Sam's arrow flew true from the shadows, grazing Lucas's arm, her smirk keen, "Missed me?"

Melissa wove through the melee, her axe chopping aside a blade with Monkey Clan ingenuity, her vine trap snapping shut, tripping attackers.

"Flank left—use the pines!" she called, her voice cutting through the chaos. Ryder punched, yelling, "Take that!" his grin rallying them, his bravado masking doubt as he drew strength from Lia's distant camp chants.

Alice hung back at the edge, tablet blazing as she hacked into glyph wards. "Signals overriding—zodiac pulses disrupting their comms!"

Her projections flared, blinding foes, her Rabbit Clan caution anchoring the team.

The battle intensified: Veronica's breath caught, relief surging as the Guardians arrived, her voice rising, "Push them back!" her wounded arm screaming, but determination unyielding.

Omar's mace crushed a weapon, his determination a fortress, muscles taut as he held the line, his strength anchoring the group.

Doug fought beside Tate, claws and sword in sync, his tracking senses guiding his strikes as he parried a stray axe near Alice's position, shouting, "Stay focused, Alice—I'll cover you!"

Sam and Melissa flanked, arrows and axe relentless, their teamwork a seamless dance. Ryder's laughter cut through grunts, the Guardians' unity overwhelming the mercenaries' faltering ranks, their bond tightened, shared glances and weary nods as they fought.

Lucas bellowed, "Fall back to the forest—regroup!" His men fled.

Veronica's voice rang out, taunting, "Crawl back to X, Lucas!" as she fired another shot, her pain fueling her defiance.

Lucas staggered into the pines, his machete heavy, a memory of a dungeon searing his mind. Chains bit his wrists, traitors' jeers echoing, X's silhouette shattering steel to free him.

"Prove your worth," X had growled. Guilt burned—his treason a shadow, yet X's trust fueled his resolve. The talisman's loss stung, but he vowed to reclaim it, his light blue eyes narrowing in the frost.

The clearing fell silent save for heavy breaths and distant chants; the ground littered with dropped weapons and groans. Veronica's communicator buzzed, intercepting an X scout's signal from the pines.

"Kusini's plains next—Ox Talisman," a voice hissed, rune-etched thorns pulsing green in the dark.

She signaled Omar, her cunning flaring—X's plan loomed, the Prophecy's chaos tightening. Her charm glowed, urging her to guard Sheng Xiao's heart.

Veronica slumped against a pixiu stone, talisman clutched, her arm screaming as she caught her breath. Omar checked her wound, his touch gentle but firm, his gaze sparking warmth, a flicker of something deeper passing between them.

"You okay?" he asked, voice low, his concern anchoring her.

"I'm okay," Veronica murmured, nodding weakly, her gaze meeting Omar's, a shared glance of trust anchoring her spirit.

Doug sheathed his sword, wiping sweat from his brow, his grin shaky but relieved.

"Everyone good? Thanks for the save, Guardians," he said, scanning the group.

"We're beat—let's get to Mara's camp, patch up," Melissa said, her Monkey Clan ingenuity steadying the group.

The team nodded, their bond tightened, shared glances and weary nods as they staggered toward the torchlit paths, chill crunching under their weary steps, their spirits lifted, weary grins breaking through sweat-streaked faces.

Back at the camp, Mara rallied her runners, "Spread word! The Guardians secured the Rat Talisman. It's bringing peace back."

Locals' chants swelled, hope rising as snow fell, markets stabilizing, stalls restocking, unrest fading under the Pine Oath's renewed strength.

Veronica's holo-link buzzed post-fight, reporting, "Empress, talisman secured—riots easing, markets stabilizing."

Mara added, her voice steady, "Our hymns are stronger—your win's a spark for peace."

Jade exhaled, relief flooding her, the balance shifting as Souris's unrest calmed, stalls reopening, chants echoing louder through the pines.

"Well done, all of you—your unity is what will save Sheng Xiao," Jade pressed, her voice ringing firm, newfound determination steadying her as she faced the holo-link. "The talisman strengthens us—Kusini's next. Omar, your Ox Clan strength is vital. Join Tate, Melissa, Alice, Ryder, and Sam for Kusini. The rest return to the palace—we plan the next quests."

In X's fortress in the forbidden wilderness, runic maps glowed with chaotic veins, the Yin Scroll pulsing in a dim, parchment-scented chamber.

Vincent's serpent-shaped scepter flared, tracing forbidden knots for Kusini's plains, his dark blue eyes hiding schemes as he paced, plotting deeper betrayals.

Lucas's holo-link buzzed, his voice strained with fatigue. "X, I failed—the talisman's theirs. Not Jade's army—just a group with different clan insignias, Rat, Ox, Tiger, all mixed."

Vincent's eyes widened, "She called the Guardians?" then narrowed, a smug mask returning. "Lucky move, unworthy empress—we'll need a sharper strategy."

His scepter flared brighter, knots pulsing with venomous intent, his pride stung by Jade's unexpected tactics.

X gripped his love's silver ring, a vision of her lifeless form haunting him, fueling vengeance like magma.

Dolore's lightning flickered, recalling X's rare kindness— a moment he spared her failure in a long-ago raid—her heart aching, her unrequited longing unseen.

X growled, "Lucas, return and get patched up—don't fail again." He turned to Bella, his voice low and keen, "Kusini's yours—take the Ox Talisman, burn their plains if they resist."

Bella smirked, tossing a spark, "They won't know what's coming," her thrill-seeker's edge gleaming amber, her fingers itching for the fight.

Back at the camp, snow fell softly as the Guardians regrouped, their wounds bandaged, their spirits lifted, weary grins breaking through sweat-streaked faces.

Veronica knelt beside Lia, sharing a Pine Oath tale, "My mom's charm saved her from a storm once—kept her cunning keen, like this Rat Talisman."

Lia's fear eased, her eyes wide in wonder as she asked, "Is this a symbol of our clan?"

Veronica smiled, her voice soft, "It's our clan's heart—cunning with honor, not deceit. You'll carry it one day, Lia, and make us proud."

Sam nodded to Tate, "Good claws," their rivalry softening in the firelight.

"Your arrows weren't bad," he grinned, respect flickering in his amber eyes.

Melissa's nod to Veronica, "You led well," steadied her, the Monkey Clan heir's quiet strength a balm.

Ryder teased Lia, "We got your back," his Rooster Clan courage masking doubts, her playful shove sparking warmth in the cold.

Alice synced her tablet, murmuring, "Kusini's plains won't be easy—open fields, no cover." The camp's unity was a fortress, dawn creeping through the pines, the talisman's glow a beacon for Sheng Xiao's fragile harmony as Kusini loomed on the horizon.

Chapter 7: Echoes of Balance

In the Imperial Palace's library, golden fenghuang lanterns cast soft gleams on a zodiac mosaic floor, rats and oxen shimmering like fragile promises under the amber holo-torchlight, the air alive with the map's faint glow.

Jade clutched her scepter, its light pulsing faintly, amethyst eyes clouded as she faced Cade, palms sweating, scepter trembling, the twin figures' vision from Souris— "twin figures looming, their chant like a warning bell: 'The knot tightens, betrayal nears'"—weighing heavy like a storm cloud.

Could they mirror the Yin and Yang Scrolls, their balance hiding betrayal? she wondered, her gut twisting, her heart racing with fear of Guardians lost, Sheng Xiao fractured, her duty a relentless storm pounding her chest.

Her breath hitched, the weight of leadership threatening to crush her, memories of her father's steady voice battling the doubt spiraling in her mind, the Scrolls' ancient power a riddle she couldn't unravel.

She paced, her footsteps echoing on the mosaic, the fenghuang lanterns casting fleeting shadows that seemed to whisper the Prophecy's secrets, her fear of failing her Guardians clawing at her resolve, her pulse quickening as she fought to steady herself, the incense's smoky swirl grounding her.

Cade stepped closer, his hand brushing hers, a fleeting warmth sparking through her like a flame in the dark, his voice steady but laced with strain. "You won't lose them, Jade. You were right about Veronica and the Rat Clan; they proved their strength in Souris. I was wrong to doubt them. Tate and Omar are ready for Kusini, and Omar's Ox Clan loyalty will anchor them."

His heart thudded, longing to hold her, to shield her from the Prophecy's shadow, but duty chained him, his fingers curling into fists, his breath catching as he fought the urge to reach for her again.

Jade's heart flickered, craving his embrace, yet her fingers tightened on the scepter, fear of losing him unspoken, tension simmering like embers beneath their bond.

My throne feels like a cage—what if he sees the weakness beneath? she thought, her chest tightening as she met his gaze, the library's quiet amplifying their unspoken words. She leaned slightly closer, her voice soft, "Cade, if Kusini goes wrong…"

He shook his head, his thumb grazing her knuckle in a subtle reassurance, "It won't. We'll face it together." The moment stretched, their bond humming with unvoiced affection, the air thick with the scent of aged parchment and incense, their unspoken connection growing stronger amid the ancient shelves, the holo-map's hum a soft pulse between them.

Jade stepped toward him then, lips parting as if to confess the depth of her feelings—the way his presence chased away her fears, how she ached for more than stolen glances—but a distant chime from the palace halls shattered the silence.

She froze with a gasp, duty slamming back like a cold wave, her cheeks flushing as she pulled away, the near confession hanging unspoken, her heart pounding with the fear that Hana's bold flirtations might steal him away before she could voice her truth.

A palace guard approached, bowing slightly before speaking. "Excuse me, Empress, —I have an update report."

Jade nodded, gesturing for her to continue. The guard straightened, her voice low but firm. "Listra's ziplines are mending, tourists returning, hope stirring. The Imperial City feels calmer, gardens blooming brighter with roses, though Kusini's plains remain tense, chants not yet full." Her words painted a picture of Sheng Xiao's balance tilting toward good, the Rat Talisman's victory a spark of light in the chaos, yet not fully restored, Kusini's unrest a distant rumble.

Jade's scepter trembled, a memory flashing of Opal at twelve, weaving zodiac threads in the palace garden, wisteria heavy in the air. "Balance holds us, Jade," Opal had smiled, guiding her hands.

Now, duty's weight threatened Cade's loss, her heart torn between love and leadership. The lanterns' glow urged her to lead, her resolve kindling to protect Sheng Xiao and him. Jade exhaled, resolve firming like steel, the scepter warm in her trembling hand, its glow steadying her heart despite the lingering shadows of Kusini's plains, her fear battling her duty to lead.

"Thank you," Jade said, her tone gracious, dismissing the guard with a nod as the report's hope lingered like a fragile bloom.

Patricia's holo-link buzzed, its chime sharp in the quiet library. She was already there with Jade and Cade, having joined them moments earlier after wrapping up a quick check on the training grounds where the other Guardians were honing their skills.

"Veronica and Doug are here!" she said, her Pig Clan warmth cutting through the tension, her smile a balm.

Jade descended to the courtyard, Cade's fleeting touch lingering on her skin, her heart steadying despite the vision's warning echoing in her mind, her steps echoing on the zodiac flagstones as she braced for the Guardians' return.

"I'll tell the others and meet you in the garden," Cade said as she descended, his voice a quiet promise that sent a spark through her.

As noon lit the palace gates, midday sun glinting off intricate fenghuang carvings, Veronica, Doug, and Souris emissaries bearing lore-etched banners strode in, heralding victory, jasmine wafting from the gardens, petals catching the sunlight like scattered stars on the flagstones.

Jade greeted them, red hair swaying, her voice warm but edged with worry.

"Welcome back," she said, her eyes scanning Veronica's bandaged arm, a pang of concern tightening her chest, her fingers gripping the scepter as she fought to mask her fear.

Veronica smirked, tossing her hair, masking her arm's throb with Rat Clan pride, her sarcasm a shield honed in Souris's maze.

"Bagged the first talisman, Empress," she said, her voice steady, pride swelling as she presented the glowing artifact, its gold-blue light flaring in the sunlight.

Her bandage shifted slightly, the wound's ache a reminder of her fight, yet her resolve burned bright, Vladimir's stain fading with each step toward redemption, her smirk hiding the weight of her clan's past.

Doug beamed, Dog Clan spark blazing, his confidence soaring post-Souris, his tracking senses sharper after the maze.

"One down!" he said, grinning, his enthusiasm infectious, his grin lighting the courtyard like the midday sun.

Cade, Patricia, David, Hana, and Gerry joined, along with palace staff bustling with trays of rice wine and glyph-etched sweets, and Lord Huan lingering at the edges, his hawkish gaze appraising the scene with a faint sneer.

Cheers rose under silk lanterns, zodiac cups raised, rice wine gleaming like liquid gold in the midday light.

Jade lifted her cup, her voice ringing, "To the Rat Talisman—eleven more to go."

Veronica grinned, her sarcasm sharp, "Here's to not dying!"

The Guardians exchanged clan sigils—Rat, Ox, Tiger, Rabbit, all zodiac motifs blending in a show of unity—laughter ringing as zodiac cups clinked.

A Souris emissary stepped forward, her banner fluttering, "Our camps bustle again, paper markets thriving with glyph-etched wares and holo-chips—your win sparks hope across Sheng Xiao."

Huan interjected, his tone protective yet challenging, "A solid start, Empress—Listra's floods ease, ziplines humming with tourists. Kusini's chants swell, but tension lingers. Let's ensure it holds."

Jade's jaw tightened, but she nodded, her resolve growing under his scrutiny, appreciating his push to strengthen her rule, the courtyard buzzing with renewed energy from Souris's markets and Kusini's fragile harmony, the midday sun casting long shadows of hope.

Hana raised her cup with a flirtatious, "To the strongest here!"

The group nodded in support, a holo-report flickering with Listra's zipline hum and Imperial City's rose bloom, the zodiac lore of clan unity whispering in their shared strength.

Cade raised his cup, a memory flashing of a palace festival at fourteen, Jade radiant in silks, her laugh bright under fenghuang lanterns.

His non-royal blood felt small beside her, unworthy of her light. Now, her trust sparked his loyalty, the courtyard's jasmine urging him to be her shield, his heart vowing to prove his worth.

Doug stepped forward, gathering the group around a low table as the celebration swelled, his voice animated, hands gesturing wildly to mimic the Souris maze's twists. "The vines were like living traps—resin stung my nose, frost crunched underfoot, thorns scratched my arms raw, but my tracking sniffed out the safe paths. That Rat King? Massive, eyes like onyx, hissing riddles— 'I am not alive, but I grow…' took us forever to crack 'fire'!" He paused, grinning as the group leaned in, captivated, the glyph hums still echoing in his memory.

Veronica quipped, "Took us long enough, pup—my cunning saved your hide," her tone teasing.

David nodded, tactical mind engaged, "Smart move tracking the glyphs. Next time, watch the illusions...they nearly got me at the Dragon Games."

Gerry's eyes widened, "Did the traps shift? How'd you dodge them?"

Doug laughed, "Barely felt the thorns graze my jacket, but I kept us moving!"

Patricia asked, "And the ambush...how did you spot Lucas's men?"

Doug's eyes lit up, "Sweat and steel mixed with market smoke. My nose never lies!"

His confidence shone, laughter bubbling up as he recounted the final shots, Omar's mace crushing a foe, Tate's claws slashing, the Guardians' unity saving the day.

David clapped him on the shoulder, "You've grown, Doug—handled it like a guardian." Veronica smirked, "Told you, pup—you're not half bad."

The story wove them closer, a found family moment, the courtyard alive with their bond, the zodiac lore of Rat cunning and Ox endurance whispering in their shared strength.

Hana leaned toward Patricia, tossing her hair, Horse Clan flair bright.

"David's got muscle," she whispered, her voice teasing, "but Cade's the cutest—those eyes, that body!"

Patricia giggled, her cheeks flushing, "You're smitten!"

Hana smirked, her eyes dancing with mischief as she caught Cade's gaze across the courtyard. She flashed him a playful smile, her flirtatious nature shining through as she tested the waters with the strongest around her. Cade blinked, confused but polite, smiling back awkwardly, his green-blue eyes flickering with uncertainty.

Jade caught the exchange, her heart twisting like a knot, jealousy surging hot in her chest. Her fists clenched at her sides, her chest tightening as she turned away, the celebration's cheer suddenly hollow.

Of course it's him-- he's gorgeous, smart, strong… everything anybody would want. Since childhood, sparring under zodiac banners, his grin was mine alone. But Hana—beautiful, bold—threatens that, a competition I never foresaw. Her pulse raced, awe at Cade's steady stance, his laugh from a past spar echoing, fear of losing him growing, her love crystallizing amid doubt as she watched his strength, her breath catching, the jasmine scent intensifying her turmoil.

After the celebration wound down, Jade pulled Veronica aside under jasmine vines, the scepter dimming in her hand, its faint glow reflecting her worry, the scent of blooms heavy in the air.

"That arm," she said, frowning, her voice soft but firm, "Opal, my sister, was our healer—her salves could mend anything. She'd insist on checking it, and her medics carry her skill."

A memory flashed: Opal kneeling beside her after a childhood fall, chanting softly over a zodiac-etched bowl, a cooling salve glowing as it spread across Jade's scraped knee, her sister's laughter a melody that steadied her heart, their bond a shield against the world's bite.

Veronica scoffed, pride flaring like a spark, tossing her hair, "Just a scratch," wincing as she flexed, Vladimir's stain nagging like a thorn in her mind.

I'm not him, she thought, unease flickering as she recalled Omar wrapping her arm in Souris's frost-dusted camp, his large hands surprisingly gentle as he tied the makeshift bandage, his gruff voice rumbling, "Take care of your wounds," paired with a lingering glance that sent heat rushing to her cheeks.

That moment had ignited a spark, her crush blooming amid the Rat Clan's legacy pressure—Vladimir's betrayal a shadow she fought to outrun, Omar's quiet concern fueling her drive to prove her worth, to redeem her bloodline through cunning and loyalty.

Jade's gaze softened, her sisterly concern echoing Opal's care. "I need you strong, Veronica. Get it checked," she urged, her voice gentle but unyielding.

Veronica's sarcasm faltered, her Rat Clan pride fierce but shaken.

"Fine, for you," she muttered, trudging to the medic bay, her steps heavy, the talisman's weight in her pocket a reminder of her duty, her heart pounding with resolve to honor Jade's and Omar's trust.

Inside, the antiseptic-scented room buzzed with activity—metal tables lined with salves and holo-monitors flickering with vital scans.

A young healer, Opal's apprentice with a nervous smile, wielded a glowing device, its holo-scan projecting a faint zodiac grid over Veronica's arm.

"Infection risk detected," she said, her voice steadying as she applied a cooling salve, the sting sharp but soothing, her hands trembling slightly as she recounted Opal's tales. Veronica frowned, "What about Opal?"

The girl's eyes dimmed, "She died, sadly. I trained under her in Saanp, where she was a top healer. She brought me back to the palace, planning a marriage, but…" Her voice trailed off, the weight of loss lingering.

Veronica nodded, flexing her arm, her internal vow to redeem her clan's honor growing stronger, her jaw tight as she thought, I won't let Jade or Omar down.

At dusk, the courtyard buzzed, flagstones shimmering under holo-torchlight, the zodiac-patterned obstacle course alive with clashing steel and laughter, the air thick with the scent of sweat and steel.

Veronica, Doug, David, Hana, Gerry, and Patricia trained, forging bonds for Sheng Xiao's balance. Veronica coached Doug from the side, her arm resting per the medic's orders, her Rat Clan pride shining as she guided him through a tracking puzzle, her voice sharp but warm. "Focus on the scent trail, Doug—let your instincts lead."

Doug's Dog Clan spark blazed.

"Got it!" he shouted, his confidence soaring post-Souris, his grin wide as he navigated a barrier test, dodging a glyph-etched trap with ease.

David demonstrated a precise katana sweep, guiding Gerry's arm with a firm grip, "Shift your weight forward," his eyes softening with pride as he watched Gerry's progress.

Gerry dodged a drone, "Whoa!" his Goat Clan nervousness easing, "I'll try, Dragon," a quiet bond forming under holo-torchlight, his heart steadying with each move.

Patricia's holo-link buzzed, her voice steady, "Kusini needs tech prep—Alice is syncing signals there with Omar, Tate, Melissa, and Sam, their comms ready for the plains."

A young servant girl, aspiring guardian, struggled with spilled holo-files, her zodiac pendant glinting in the holo-torchlight.

"Got you," Gerry said, scooping them up with steady hands, his Goat Clan heart anchoring him amid the chaos.

As he handed them back, he leaned close, whispering, "Training keeps me steady for her—my mom relies on me back in Ged, her pride in my spear work pushing me through the skittishness."

The faint scent of cliff herbs clung to his tunic, evoking Ged's ocean-sprayed cliffs and botanical gardens, where his creativity bloomed in quiet sketches of rune altars, balancing his role as sole caregiver with the Guardians' demands.

The girl beamed, "I want to be like you! Kusini's challenging—good luck!"

The course pulsed with energy, Guardians' bonds a shield for Sheng Xiao's quests, from Kusini's strengthening chants to the Imperial City's blooming gardens, the balance tilting toward hope under the flickering holo-torchlight.

Hana, still buzzing from the celebration, sidled up to Patricia again during the training.

"Watch this," she whispered, her eyes locking on Cade as he mentored Gerry nearby. With a flirtatious wink at Patricia, she "accidentally" stumbled during a whip drill, tumbling right into Cade's arms.

He caught her instinctively, his strong frame steadying her, confusion flashing in his green-blue eyes before he helped her up with a polite smile.

"Careful there," he said, his voice warm but distant, his thoughts on Jade.

Hana laughed lightly, brushing his arm a moment longer than necessary, her flirtatious energy sparkling like her Horse Clan spirit.

The sudden motion rippled through the spar: David, mid-swing in his katana drill with Gerry, faltered, his blade slipping wide as jealousy flickered in his eyes—Hana's bold move pulling his focus. Gerry dodged nimbly, his spear twisting aside with a quick pivot.

"Close one!" he called, steady despite the near miss. Patricia giggled, caught in the mischief, as Hana winked back at her: Mission accomplished.

Jade, watching from the sidelines, felt a fresh wave of jealousy crash over her. Her chest tightened, scepter quaking in her grip as she fought to mask it.

She clenched her jaw, forcing a neutral smile, her fingers digging into the scepter to still its tremble, her pulse racing with the realization of her deep love for Cade, the fear of losing him to someone like Hana—beautiful, bold, everything she felt she wasn't in her moments of doubt.

"Keep up, Horse!" Veronica quipped, sparring nearby.

Hana retorted, "You're no slouch, Rat!"

David, recovering his stance, gripped his katana tighter.

Her boldness intrigues, but that flirt with Cade stings. he thought, his interest simmering as he adjusted Gerry's form with a hesitant strike, his admiration for Hana growing.

Patricia guided Gerry on a balance beam, "Use your Goat creativity—shift like this," her Pig Clan warmth fostering his confidence, the drill weaving their unity tighter, the steel clanks blending with their laughter.

As Doug navigated a glyph trap, Gerry leaned in, his spear steadying him, a hesitant grin breaking through.

"First time I trained, I tripped over a drone—sprawled flat, spear rolling away," he admitted to Doug, his voice low. "But you all lift me up now."

Doug clapped his back, "You're solid, Goat!" reinforcing their bond.

Meanwhile, Lucas winced as X bandaged his arm, rune-lit walls casting jagged shadows in a dim, antiseptic-scented room, metal tables lined with salves and vials, the sting sharp in the air.

He recalled a raid years ago—flames licking a rival camp, X charging ahead, his blade flashing to deflect a spear aimed at a fallen soldier, pulling the man to safety with a firm grip. The soldier had nodded gratefully, eyes wide with loyalty, as X barked orders to rally the rest.

"Discipline holds," X muttered now, echoing that day, his hands steady as he tied the bandage, the ring glinting faintly, his rare, gruff warmth dulled by loss forging bonds with his team, a stark contrast to Jade's natural empathy.

Lucas nodded, gratitude burning in his chest, the antiseptic scent a stark contrast to the raid's smoke.

In Vincent's chamber, his serpent scepter flared, his dark blue eyes glinting as he paced, plotting Kusini's downfall, the Yin Scroll's silver glow pulsing against rune-carved shelves.

"I can't believe she called the Guardians—no matter, beginner's luck ends now. We'll outmaneuver them in Kusini," he smirked, his mind racing with plans to disrupt the Ox Talisman's balance, his fingers tracing the scepter's serpent coils.

Bella readied to leave, her fire sparking as she turned to Dolore, her amber eyes fierce. "We need a sharper strategy—no more head-on attacks like Lucas's mess in Souris. I'll slip in with stealth, map Kusini's plains on this holo-map, and strike their edges before they sense the danger."

She smirked, studying the flickering map, her thrill gleaming, plotting silent paths through the plains. Dolore glanced at X with longing, her lightning crackling faintly, "Your plan's solid—get the talisman for X."

The words hung ominous, Sheng Xiao's balance trembling as Bella's resolve sharpened, the fortress's gloom amplifying their dark promise.

Chapter 8: The Plains of Kusini

The plains of Kusini unfurled like a golden ocean under a merciless sun, amber grasses whispering secrets in a warm breeze thick with sun-scorched soil, ripening maize, and the distant lowing of oxen trudging through dusty furrows. Endurance pulsed in every swaying stalk, every rutted path carved by generations, but scars marred the land's heart: irrigation ditches choked with debris, rusted gates sagging like broken oaths, trampled fields where eclipse-driven stampedes had crushed lush crops into barren patches.

Omar led his group, his broad frame cutting through the heat like an unyielding anchor, Ox Clan tunic embroidered with bronze motifs glinting, his mace etched with charging horns heavy at his side.

The air shimmered, baked earth seeping into his bones, a jarring shift from Souris's icy thorns.

A memory struck: racing Kofi through these fields as boys, his brother's laughter free, his natural command drawing kids like moths to a flame.

Kofi's ease outshone Omar's stiffness—the heir's mantle pressed like the mace's weight, fists clenching as wistful jealousy twisted his gut, picturing Kofi's effortless grin rallying the plains.

He'd lead without this ache—why me? he thought, jaw tight, the fractured horizon mirroring his doubt. Veronica's smirk flashed from Souris, her "Stay sharp" a warm pulse, stirring a crush that burned like the heat.

Her fire's with me, even here, he mused, heart racing at the thought of her green eyes, her laugh a lifeline amid the thorns.

Tate prowled beside him, claw gloves flexing with a tiger's grace, black hair whipping in the wind, tiger-stitched tunic gleaming like a predator's pelt.

In a Souris camp, post-Rat Talisman, Jade's holo-link flared, her amethyst eyes firm. "Your claws are fierce, Tate, but reckless—Sam's precision can sharpen your lead," she urged, voice steady. Tate's amber gaze flared, impulsiveness stinging.

Jade trusts Sam's shots over my claws? he thought, claws flexing.

Now, Kusini's heat fueled his vow to prove his leadership, Sam's bow a challenge he'd outshine. Amber eyes sparked with a cocky grin, but doubt gnawed.

I'll prove my claws aren't just flash, he seethed, fire hotter than the plains.

"This heat's gonna cook us—let's grab the talisman and bolt before we're roasted," he drawled, voice masking leadership doubts, shooting Sam a challenging glint.

Melissa kept pace, green Monkey Clan tunic clinging with sweat, axe glinting at her hip like a wicked jest.

"Brutal out here," she muttered, swiping her brow, braid swinging as burnout from endless drills chipped her spark. "Hope the Ox Talisman's worth this roast."

Sam trailed, snake-shaped bow poised, orange tunic blending with locals' earth-dyed weaves, proud eyes narrowing at Tate like a coiled viper.

"The Ox Talisman's powerful, but the Buffalo Trial's brutal, I mean, holding a massive stone till the moon peaks? That's endurance, Omar," she said crisply, wisdom veiling envy of Tate's swagger. "You ready, Tiger?"

Alice clutched her tablet, shy eyes darting behind glasses catching the fading light, Rabbit Clan tech whirring as she mapped the grove ahead.

"Data confirms the altar's runes pulse strongest across the river," she whispered, fingers syncing a rune pulse, confidence growing—a quiet defiance against taunts that once silenced her. "It's close, but traps guard the way."

Ryder brought up the rear, Rooster Clan bravado in his jest, cannon slung over his shoulder. "Heavy stone or not, I'll crow it home!" he boasted, laugh cracking.

Tate's grin sharpened atop a hill. "Too heavy for your arrows, Snake? My claws will haul it—watch me."

Sam's eyes slitted, a hiss escaping. "Claws won't outrun my shot, Tate. Keep flexing or it'll bury you."

Rivalry crackled, Tate's boast hiding Jade's doubt, Sam's retort masking her itch for the spotlight.

Omar glanced back, Veronica's smirk a tether in his chest, her "Stay sharp" fueling his crush like a spark in dry grass.

"Cut the egos," he growled, voice gruff but steady. "Kusini's about endurance, not show."

The plains' vastness mirrored the heir weight he'd trade for Kofi's freedom, jealousy of his brother's ease flaring as he eyed the broken fields—once communal pride, now splintered.

At a Kusini harvest festival, years ago, Kofi's charm rallied herders under maize-lit torches, his laugh binding them as Omar's orders faltered.

"Lead with heart," Kofi had grinned, outshining him.

Now, the Buffalo Trial's weight loomed, Omar's doubt burning—could he match Kofi's ease? Veronica's fire sparked his grit, the maize's rustle urging him to endure, his heart vowing to lead for her.

Melissa sidled up, agile step brushing his arm. "Your brooding's slowing us, Ox. Swooning over Veronica's quips?" she teased, burnout edged with spark as she spotted farmers bickering over a hoarded water barrel near a clogged ditch.

Omar's cheeks heated, her jab stirring respect. "She's not the distraction—your chaos is, Monkey," he shot back, a rare smile cracking as her laugh rang out, warm with camaraderie.

He strode to the farmers, their shouts escalating, fists clenched over dwindling water.

"Share it—endurance means lifting each other," he said, voice low but firm, hands parting them like an ox through maize, sweat beading on his brow.

An elder leaned in, voice gravelly: "In the Great Drought, ancestors shared a single maize stalk, binding clans—carry that strength, heir."

His eyes met Omar's with trust, echoing an Ox Clan proverb: "Strength carries all."

A young farmer nodded, adding, "Your father led like that, heir—grit binds stronger than charm." The men froze, then bowed, muttering, "Heir's will endures," their respect a thorny crown.

Tate smirked, leaning close. "Didn't think you had that talk, Ox—almost outshone me." Melissa nodded, eyes glinting. "Less brooding, more leading—nice." Sam watched, bow steady.

"Strategy in action—solid." Omar's breath steadied— Kofi's charm would've won instantly, but their trust sparked pride.

Kofi shines, but my grit binds them too, he thought, a flicker of leadership he could claim.

In the Imperial City's training hall, fenghuang lanterns cast zodiac motifs—rat skittering, dragon coiling, goat leaping— across sweat-slicked tiles, the air sharp with steel and glyph hums.

Veronica paced, pistol holstered, worry knotting her like Souris's thorns.

Omar's facing that heat—his mace saved me, his strength, my rock, she thought, green eyes flashing with Rat Clan pride.

She fired at a holo-drone, bullets ringing like her unspoken fear, each shot a prayer for his quest.

Doug sparred nearby, sword flashing, blue eyes warm with Dog Clan loyalty.

"Omar's tough, V—he pulled us through Souris's traps, he'll conquer Kusini's heat," he said, blade clanging, steadying her.

"Focus, or I'll outshoot you." she said. "Keep up, Dog— his mace saved me, Kusini's trial won't break him."

Hana's whip cracked, teasing David. "Too slow, Dragon—keep up or I'll find a faster partner," she purred, her laugh bright but split, lingering from a spar with Cade.

David's katana faltered, cheeks flushing, heart twisting: *Her smile's for me, then Cade—where do I stand?* he thought

He parried with a strained grin, "Trying, Hana, but you're playing both sides."

While some Guardians sparred like Hana and David, others like Gerry and Patricia rebuilt the palace post-eclipse, mending quake scars to restore balance. Gerry knelt by a cracked mosaic, Goat Clan intuition calming a servant's nerves with a tale of family balance.

"This rat symbol cracked in the quake, so we mend it like kin," he said, his hands steadying tiles, sharing a story of his mother stitching their clan through loss, easing the servant's tension. Patricia directed garden repairs, Pig Clan warmth firm.

"Set boundaries...strength grows there," she told an aide, her voice steady as she guided a sapling's replanting, her calm anchoring the quake-torn grounds. The palace thrummed, unity stitching fractures.

Jade's holo-link had launched the quest after Souris, its memory flickering in Omar's mind as Kusini's heat pressed in. In the library, her projection flared, scepter aglow with fenghuang fire, frost on Omar, Veronica, and Doug's gear, her bandaged arm a badge of their Rat Talisman win.

"Omar, your Ox strength is key—lead Tate, Melissa, Alice, with Sam and Ryder's edge," Jade commanded, voice steady but catching as her fingers brushed Cade's, a spark of tension binding them.

The scrolls' theft threatens all—Omar's strength is our hope, she thought, resolve wavering.

Omar nodded, "On it," duty swelling like the plains' horizon.

Tate nudged him, smirking. "Souris flashbacks, Ox? Are you obsessing over that Rat girl?"

Omar grinned, deflecting. "Planning to outmuscle you, Tiger. Try keeping pace."

Dusk cloaked the plains in starry velvet, a mile from the sacred grove where the Harvest Altar stood. Locals gathered in a clearing, earth-dyed tunics woven with ox motifs fluttering, calloused hands offering roasted maize, its smoky aroma blending with night-cooled soil.

Kweku, an elder and tribe guide with hands scarred from plowing Kusini's stubborn earth, gathered them on woven mats, his ox-embroidered robe swaying like maize under moonlight.

"As tribe guide, I speak for Ox Clan's heart," he said, gesturing to locals chanting a soft hymn of endurance, voices weaving with the altar's distant pulse, a low verse of survival through famine's grip.

Across the river traps, the Harvest Altar—cracked stone etched with stamping hooves, weathered bull horns humming with ancient runes, maize shadows weaving across its surface, faint dust of ancient famines lingering in crevices—pulsed faintly golden, a heartbeat tying Sheng Xiao's bounties to every realm.

"The Harvest Altar anchors harvests across all lands," Kweku rasped, voice rough as drought-parched clay, eyes pinning Omar. "Defile it, and realms suffer—crops wither, rivers dry. To reach it, you face the Buffalo Trial in the grove: under the moon's peak, hold the buffalo stone relic, heavy as an ox's burden, proving endurance as our ancestors did through the Great Drought. Only then can you claim the Ox Talisman to restore balance against the stolen scrolls' chaos."

A herder leaned in, voice weathered, sharing a tale of fields turned to ash, saved by the altar's endurance. "Ancestors held the stone till moon peak, binding clans to survive—endurance claimed the talisman's power, heir." Omar's palms sweated, the altar's glow heavier than his mace.

Kofi's charisma is a better fit. He'd carry that stone without flinching—why me? he thought, his breath shallow with doubt.

Tate smirked, tossing a kernel. "Heavy stone? I'll claw it up quick."

Melissa elbowed him, steadying a herder's spilled basket, her grin warm. "Quick won't outlast an ox, Tiger—endurance rules."

Sam's bow fidgeted, eyes sharp. "Strategy beats brute force—time the moon right, or we're sunk."

Alice's tablet hummed, mapping the grove, voice bolder.

"Data shows the altar's runes spike at midnight—river traps guard the way," she said, syncing a pulse with steely defiance, her tech a shield against taunts that once silenced her.

Banter steadied Omar, Kusini's hymns swelling, the river and grove's trials looming like Souris's maze.

After the chants, Melissa knelt, deft hands untangling a herder's irrigation pipe, admiration flickering as she glanced at Omar, her burnout easing. "Veronica would say you're tougher than this heat, Ox," she teased, her grin sparking.

Omar flushed, Veronica's Souris smirk flashing, his crush a burning ache. "She'd say you're trouble," he muttered, their bond glowing like the maize in his hand.

She'd see me, not Kofi, he thought, heart racing at her imagined nod.

Tate crunched maize, grinning. "I've got speed over your stillness, Ox—top that."

Melissa shot back, "Speed won't budge an ox, Tiger."

Alice's tablet glowed, voice firmer. "The buffalo stone's mass matches a full-grown ox—endurance is everything for the trial." She synced a pulse, bolder now, defiance shining.

Sam nodded, wisdom firm. "Strategy beats brute force—plan the hold, or the moon's peak will break us."

Ryder said, "I'll blast the plan awake!" His laugh faltered, heir pressure stinging.

"This cannon's lighter than my clan's expectations," he muttered, shaking off the weight.

The group huddled by firelight, maize warming hands under stars. Omar stared into flames, Veronica's laugh echoing—her Souris quip a bond like Rat and Ox in sync, her "Stay sharp" fueling his resolve against the looming trial.

Melissa leaned in, eyes mischievous. "Still stuck in Souris, Ox? Veronica would call you a hero for that farmer move."

He flushed, heart racing. "Her edge keeps me sharp."

She laughed, "Admit it—you're smitten!" His blush deepened, her spark bridging their clash into respect.

Sam eyed Tate, arms crossed. "Your speed better match my plans, Tiger."

Tate's glare flared. "Don't need your lectures, Snake—claws outpace arrows." Boast veiled insecurity, rivalry masking doubt.

Sam smirked. "Dream on—precision wins."

Unity held fragile, Kusini's hymns threading the dark, grove's trial looming.

In the palace library, Cade watched Jade pace under fenghuang lanterns, her red hair a defiant flame against cool stone.

Hana's bold laugh and whip-crack skill lingered—her beauty and fearless spark tempting him, as Huan's warning echoed in his mind.

You're the advisor, not a suitor—know your place. She's vibrant, free, a path I could choose, he thought, doubt aching like a bruise, blue-green eyes flickering.

But Jade's voice cut through during the holo-link to Omar. "Kusini's tense—balance must hold, or the realms suffer," she said, her fingers brushing his, lingering longer in the library's quiet.

The scrolls' theft threatens all—Omar's strength is our hope, she thought, resolve wavering. Her throne-weary eyes met his, fierce yet fragile, a spark igniting.

His support's my strength, she thought, heart steadying against the throne's weight.

No, Jade's my true fire—heart and soul, always, he thought, squeezing her hand gently.

"We're in this together, since childhood," she whispered, vulnerability cracking her resolve.

Cade's heart raced, doubt fading. "Always—your courage binds me, Jade." Their eyes locked, a slow-burn promise pulsing like the lanterns above, their childhood bond deepening into something unspoken, her strength his anchor through the chaos.

Kusini's outskirts breathed night-cooled musk, maize rustling like conspirators under dawn's light. Bella crouched in an olive grove, faint fruit scent mingling with dew, crimson scarf a bloodstain in shadow.

Amber eyes blazed as she honed her dagger, fire licking her fingers like eager sparks.

A memory gripped her: village torches blazing, shouts cheering as her flames saved a child, then turning— "Witch! Her fire cursed us!"—stones flying, blaming her for the blaze. X stepped in, blade flashing, "She saved your child—come with me." He took her away, her heart racing, loyalty forged in that rescue, gratitude her chain, tragedy fueling defiance.

He saw value where they saw curse—I'll scorch Kusini for him, she thought, embers warming her chest.

A holo-link buzzed—Lucas's face flickered, wincing as he shifted his bandaged arm, voice cracking with Souris grit. "Blazing ahead, Bella? X patched me, but these scars bite worse than his lectures—missed you before you left, that's why I called." Her fire flickered hesitantly, village rejection echoing in her mind.

"Watch my flames, they'll burn the plains to ash. Get better and we'll celebrate when I snag the talisman," she said, thrill surging, fingers itching for chaos, Kusini's warmth fueling her hunt.

In the Unknown Wilderness fortress, Vincent paced, jagged spires piercing mist, rune-etched arches humming with damp stone. His serpent scepter flared green, a vision of Kusini's plains unfolding.

"The Harvest Altar bends to us," he murmured, picturing its runes disrupted, chaos brewing for X's gain.

In a dark courtyard, X faced Dolore, her lightning dancing in her palms. He gifted a silver dagger, voice soft: "Your storm lights our way."

Her storm aids my revenge for my lost love—my team is family, he thought, eyes warm with care. Her heart raced, loyalty swelling, gaze lingering with unrequited yearning.

He loves a ghost—could I fill that void? she thought, doubt buried.

"For you," she whispered, the runes humming, tying to the Yin Scroll's turmoil.

Dawn gilded the plains, maize waving like persistent tides, herders' hymns swelling as Omar's group trekked toward the grove, maize stalks rustling like ancestral whispers, crimson dawn painting oxen trails with a rune-like glow, the air heavy with earth and hope, a faint rune hum vibrating from the grove's altar.

Omar's thoughts lingered on the buffalo stone, its weight heavier than his mace, a test Kofi's ease would've met with a grin, his own resolve shaky but growing.

Melissa spotted a farmer struggling with a spilled cart, maize scattering across the path. She darted over, Monkey agility fixing the axle, burnout eclipsed.

"You'll hit the market," she winked, farmer's gratitude glowing.

Alice noted, "That's your edge—empathy," glasses catching dawn, her voice steadier.

Melissa shrugged, warmth blooming. "Just doing what's right."

Omar's nod held respect, her spark lingering like Veronica's.

Tate scoffed. "I'd blitz it faster."

Ryder chuckled. "In your dreams, Tiger!"

Banter steadied them, the river shimmering ahead, tied to the altar's balance.

The river surged, banks deceptively calm, water traps lurking with runic sparks like submerged hooves glinting under sunlight, pulsing like the altar's distant hum. Omar halted, mace tightening, the buffalo stone looming, heavier than duty.

"Test of endurance—watch it," he warned, roar thickening air, spray stinging, chill biting through tunics. Veronica's smirk flashed—crush surging as he braced for the trial.

For her, I'll hold steady, he thought, heart pounding.

Tate charged, overconfident. "Easy!"

The bank crumbled, currents yanking him under, churning like a stampede, claws scraping mud. Omar plunged, muscles screaming as he hauled Tate, mace anchoring, fists clenching doubts away.

"We move as one!" he barked, team's reliance steadying him.

Melissa leaped, axe severing reeds, vine securing—her touch lingering on his arm, respect electric.

"Think first!" Omar snapped, soaked.

Melissa grinned. "Slow but solid, Ox." Their eyes locked, a platonic charge echoing Veronica's fire.

Ryder slipped, yelling, "Not cool! This river's heavier than my clan's expectations!"

Alice's tablet redirected flow, syncing runes to divert a trap, her voice firm. "Hold on!" Confidence surged, defying her bullied past.

Sam nearly dragged under, shouted, "Plan the flow, or we sink!"

Omar's rope held, arms bulging, endurance unbreaking as he hauled her across, the current tugging like a stubborn ox, his strength a spark of pride.

A third trap flared—a rune-triggered current surge, currents roaring like stampeding oxen, threatening to swallow them.

Omar anchored a second rope, muscles burning, Veronica's fire driving him, pulling Ryder and Alice free, their gasps fueling his grit. Tate clawed up, Sam's arrow steadying a branch.

"Claws don't need plans—they strike!" he grudged, pride dented, water streaming.

Sam smirked, "Strike wrong, you sink!"

Alice looked up from her pinging tablet. "Grove's near—altar's pulses spiking."

The grove's oaks loomed, rune-carved and glowing, the altar within. A distant fire flared, embers flickering like omens of the scrolls' unraveling chaos, a chill breeze heavy with ash, unseen pursuit closing in.

Omar's Ox tattoo throbbed, Veronica's smirk an anchor, Kusini's plains at stake, their unity a blade against the encroaching dark.

Chapter 9: The Buffalo's Test

The sacred grove stood at Kusini's heart, ancient oaks knitting a cathedral of gnarled branches, their rune-etched bark humming with Ox Clan energy, cradling moonlight that cast dappled gloom across packed earth.

The air pulsed with sunbaked soil, harvest incense curling from braziers like spectral threads, mingling with ancestral hymns, mossy earth vibrating with prayers of survival. Embers flickered in the breeze, a subtle omen of unrest.

Caretakers in earth-dyed tunics chanted an Ox Clan verse— "Endurance binds our runes"—their voices weaving with the altar's pulse, starlit glyphs shimmering unlike the maize-veiled runes of the plains, invoking ancestors who bound clans through the Great Drought's famine.

An elder paused, her voice low, "During the Great Drought, an Ox Clan mother carved a rune with her last strength, guiding her clan to a hidden spring. Her sacrifice bound us, her rune etched in this altar, its cracks a testament to her grit." The story's weight settled over the grove, the altar's cracked stone etched with hooves whispering tales of survival, their faint glow flickering under an ember-laden breeze.

Omar led the group, his broad frame steady, Ox Clan tunic shimmering with bronze embroidery, mace etched with ox horns gripped in his hand, its massive weight a testament to his super strength.

Omar hefted the mace, its heft grounding his resolve, muscles flexing with Ox Clan power.

The Harvest Altar glowed faintly, its oxen glyphs pulsing with a heartbeat of harvests past. An ember-flecked breeze curled through the grove, pricking Omar's instincts, a whisper of chaos beyond the altar's glow, Veronica's cunning wit from Souris a steadying anchor in his chest, her sharp mind a spark fueling his resolve.

Her quick thinking steadies me, he thought, heart racing at her clever quips in Souris's maze, a memory of her outsmarting traps.

The Guardians stepped into the grove, caretakers swarming Omar, their eyes wide with reverence for the Ox Clan heir.

"You'll save us, heir of Kusini!" they urged, hands clasping his tunic. Omar's shoulders tensed, the title filled with the pressure he loathed, the clan's expectations heavier than his mace.

"Just Omar, please—treat me like the team," he said, voice tight.

Melissa caught his gaze, her Monkey Clan heir burden mirrored in her nod. "I get it, Ox—expectations choke you. It is the same for me," she murmured, her parents' drills a shared weight.

Ryder clapped his shoulder, Rooster Clan heir to his own legacy. "You're more than a title, big guy—we've got your back.

It's hard to be heirs." Their empathy eased his unease, grounding him for the trial.

Omar murmured, "Stay sharp," the plains' hum fading as the grove's weight settled, embers dancing in the air.

Melissa smirked, green tunic swirling, Monkey Clan charm sharp as her axe glinted. "Don't choke, Ox—those horns won't lift themselves," she teased, braid bouncing, her spark masking the ache of her parents' relentless drills—endless Mico training, no room for fun, just awards to chase their dreams.

Her mischievous jab hid burnout, a rebellion against their anxieties.

Omar's jaw clenched, "Keep up, Monkey, or you'll be hauling my mace," his tone lighter, catching her spark, easing her guarded edge.

Sam's proud gaze cut through, snake-shaped bow poised, orange tunic blending with grove shadows. "Speed's worthless, Tiger—strategy wins," she snapped at Tate, her aim vowing to outshine his confidence.

Tate muttered, "I'm the leader here," Jade's words in the palace stinging: Be serious, Tate—let Sam's wisdom guide your claws.

I'll prove my claws aren't showy, he seethed, amber eyes glinting.

Ryder's bold grin flashed, Rooster Clan courage blazing. "This grove's no match for my spark—watch me rally this trial!" His laugh eased tension, shaking off the "jokester" sting.

Caretakers tended ritual braziers, their woven ox sashes gleaming as they chanted a hymn of survival, voices weaving with the altar's pulse.

An elder struggled with a toppled brazier, ash and embers spilling across sacred ground. Omar knelt, hands steady, rebuilding the frame, embers flaring anew.

"Your harvest's safe," he said, the elder's face softening.

"You carry us," she murmured, echoing an Ox Clan proverb: "Endurance carries all."

Melissa nodded, "Solid work, Ox—almost outshone my axe, but I'd rather swing." Her grin hid Mico's drills, her parents' voices echoing in her mind: "Win, Melissa, or you're nothing."

Tate scoffed, claws flexing. "I'd have that brazier blazing faster, Ox."

Ryder tossed a pebble, grinning. "My cannon's got more spark than you two!"

Kusini's plains buzzed with a harvest celebration, maize scents mingling with sweet fruits as farmers piled offerings on a zodiac altar, their chants of "Endurance carries all" echoing through the night.

Omar paused, the altar's ox motifs glowing, clansfolk's calloused hands weaving baskets, their voices binding Sheng Xiao's fruit hub to his duty.

Embers drifted in the air, their heat prickling his skin, a faint warning of unrest urging him to stand firm as the heir against the Prophecy's storm, his resolve a shield for Kusini's balance.

In the Imperial City's training hall, Veronica paced, her Rat Clan pistol holstered, sharp wit dulled by worry. Souris's maze—thorny traps, Lucas' attack—had nearly broken her, and now Omar faced Kusini's trial, its weight heavier than any riddle.

His mace pulled me through—he'll endure, she thought, heart racing, her fingers brushing the Rat Talisman's glow in her pocket.

Veronica's fingers tightened on her pistol, her mind racing in the palace's training hall, strategizing Kusini's defenses to aid Omar's trial. Souris's maze had honed her cunning, but her family's shame gnawed, knowing that failure wasn't an option.

He's counting on me, she thought, sketching rune patterns on a holo-pad, plotting ways to shield Kusini's altar from unseen threats. Embers flickered in the air, a faint warning, her resolve hardening to outwit any chaos threatening Omar's victory, her legacy tied to his strength.

"I can't shake this—Omar's out there alone," she muttered, boots scuffing zodiac-clad floors. Doug swung his sword nearby, blue eyes warm, his Dog Clan loyalty a steady pulse.

"Omar's got this, V—he saved me in Souris, he'll conquer Kusini," he said, sweat flashing, their bond a quiet strength.

"He has the other Guardians, too, Veronica," Gerry added.

Patricia parried, Pig Clan calm grounding her.

"Get to Jade—she'll hear you," she urged, nod steady.

Veronica's jaw tightened, worry a live wire, her shots at a holo-drone ringing with unspoken fear for Omar's trial.

The Guardians filled the hall, their voices weaving a lively hum—Gerry leaped, goat-like agility sharp, adjusting holo-targets with a grin, dodging Veronica's playful jab.

"Keep up, Goat, or my pistol's got your name," she teased, her smirk sparking laughter, Omar's resolve her anchor.

Doug and Patricia sparred nearby, their synchronized strikes a steady rhythm, while David's katana flashed, Hana's whip snapping in mock challenge, her grin pulling a chuckle from him.

"Miss Ryder's spark yet, Dragon?" Hana teased, her Horse Clan fire brightening the gloom. "Only if your whip can catch my edge, Horse!" David countered, their banter a flirty spark.

Veronica nodded—Ryder's Rooster vigor would've cut her tension, but Omar's strength burned brighter in her mind.

Veronica burst into the control room, worry etched. "Omar's in deep, Jade."

Jade's scepter flared, sensing Kusini's unrest, embers flickering in the palace air. Cade's green-blue eyes softened, a memory flashing: In Kusini's sun-scorched fields, Commander Calix barked orders, as Cade and Omar sparred, dust swirling.

Calix urged Omar, "Lead like your father—command your clan!" but Omar's stubborn mace swings held firm, outshining the trainees' flair.

Omar's father's presence rallied crowds, his authority binding Kusini, while Omar's grit bore duty's weight. Calix's gaze lingered on the trainees, but Cade saw Omar's resolve— unyielding, raw. A pillar teetered, Omar hoisting it to shield Cade, his strength unyielding.

After practice, Cade grinned, "Dreamed of that redhead again—she's fire."

Omar chuckled, "Don't let her burn you."

"I trained with Omar in Kusini—his strength and stubbornness will carry him," Cade said, steadying Veronica, his glance at Jade warm with trust in her leadership. "He'll pull through, like in Souris. You'll see." The mural's ox flared, a veiled threat coiling.

As embers settled, Omar stepped forward, his resolve firm, ox-stitched tunic catching the light, mace steady with grounded strength.

The earth rumbled, mist swirling as the spectral Buffalo emerged, its bronze hide translucent, crescent horns gleaming with ancient harvest runes shimmering like golden wheat under moonlight, amber eyes radiating timeless wisdom as they glowed with the essence of parched earth revived.

Its hooves cracked the ground, releasing spectral winds laden with echoes of famine-torn fields and whispering droughts, the air thickening with illusions of cracking soil and withering crops that danced around the Guardians, testing their spirit like the Rat King's deceptive riddles but forged in enduring grit and the cycle of the seasons.

"I am the Buffalo of the Great Drought," it bellowed, its voice a deep rumble echoing with the howl of dry winds and the distant thunder of long-lost rains, its form pulsing with ethereal muscle woven from the threads of survived famines. "I bore survival when rains failed. You, child of Ox, seek my talisman. Prove your endurance, or falter under pride."

Tate's grin faltered, glancing at Omar, the Ox Clan Guardian whose tie to this land drew the Buffalo's gaze.

"Your show, Ox—make us proud," he said, voice blending challenge and resolve, stepping back as his rivalry with Sam faded.

Omar squared his shoulders, reverence and determination burning, the altar's oxen glyphs pulsing brighter. A memory flashed—Kusini's ox-pull contest, his siblings' cheers fading as he stumbled under the clan's expectations, the heir's burden heavier than any yoke, his father's commanding presence a warmth he envied but loved.

"Not today," he vowed, Veronica's cunning mind a spark in his chest, her quick wit in Souris's maze a fire that burned now.

The Buffalo gestured, a rune-carved relic materializing—a buffalo-shaped stone thrumming with Ox Clan endurance, its carved hooves sinking into the earth.

"Lift and hold until the moon reaches its peak," it commanded, gaze unyielding. Omar grasped the stone, muscles straining, sweat beading as the trial ignited, the grove holding its breath.

The relic's weight surged, runes pulsing like heartbeats, testing body and mind. The first phase pressed, his knees buckling, visions of ash-choked plains intensifying—Kusini's fields withering, clans starving under a merciless sun, echoes of the Great Drought's desperation clawing at his resolve.

The Buffalo's amber eyes narrowed, a test of spirit woven into the stone's deceptive simplicity, mirroring the Rat King's cunning riddles but forged in unyielding grit.

Omar's breath hitched, the weight doubling as if the plains themselves rested on his shoulders, his mace forgotten at his side. His father's commanding gaze haunted him—his leadership rallying farmers, while the heir's mantle left Omar rigid, a yoke he'd trade for freedom.

I'll fail them all—Kusini, my team, their faith in me, he thought, arms trembling, the altar's glyphs flickering like failing hearts.

Omar's muscles strained under the buffalo stone, Kusini's maize air stirring a memory of an ox-pull contest. His brother, Kofi's grin rallied the crowd, his charisma outshining Omar's stumbles, their father's gaze demanding perfection.

The altar's hum pulsed, Veronica's spark urging his Ox Clan persistence. Doubt clawed deeper—could his grit eclipse Kofi's effortless leadership? The stone pressed harder, famine visions swirling, mirroring his fear of failing Kusini's fields. Veronica's smile in Souris flashed, her fire igniting resolve.

"I'm the anchor," he gritted, pushing through, the moon climbing as his leadership doubts deepened, Kofi's warmth a light he'd never outshine.

"Hold steady, Ox!" Tate barked, his claws digging into the earth, rivalry giving way to urgency as he scanned the shadows, Jade's words fueling a spark of leadership. "We've got your back—use our strength!"

Sam notched an arrow instinctively, her proud eyes calculating the moon's arc. "Endure the pull, Omar—let the rune's rhythm guide you, like a snake coiling before the strike." Her wisdom cut through the haze, a steady anchor against the visions' famine-winds.

Melissa darted closer, her Monkey Clan agility a blur as she adjusted a brazier's angle, redirecting its warmth to ease the chill creeping into Omar's bones. "You're tougher than this rock, Ox—remember Souris? Your mace shattered those thorns. Draw from that."

Her empathy flared, a memory stinging—her parents' drills, "Win or fail us," crushing her spark, her pranks a fleeting escape. Her grin steadied Omar, hiding burnout's ache, her axe a vow to carve her own path.

Alice's fingers flew over her tablet, syncing a rune pulse to map the relic's energy surges. "Three phases detected—first is physical, second mental, third…spiritual. Push through the second since it's peaking now."

Her voice rang with hard-won confidence, glasses fogging slightly from the humid air, her tech defying the ancient magic like a rabbit outwitting a predator.

Ryder pumped his fist, cannon slung over his shoulder. "Strut through it, big guy! If I can crow my way out of a stampede drill, you can lift this hunk of stone!"

His bravado surged, shaking off doubt, as he steadied a brazier with a Rooster's defiant spark, courage a rallying cry.

The Buffalo leaned closer, its spectral form rippling with ethereal muscle, horns casting long shadows that danced like famine spirits. "Endurance is not force alone, heir of Ox—it is the quiet bind that holds clans through starvation's bite."

The words echoed clan tales: the Buffalo's birth in the Great Drought, when skies withheld rain and fields cracked like shattered oaths, the Ox a lone survivor turning its unyielding back to the winds, guiding clans to hidden oases etched with runes of gratitude under parched moons.

Its spirit bound to the talisman after death, a guardian of perseverance, its amber eyes a beacon of resilience—a parallel to Omar's drive to prove his worth despite the heir's burden.

A glyph vision flashed: the Buffalo shielding a child from famine's grasp, its grit a legacy Omar now honored with every strained breath.

The grove's runes pulsed with drought echoes, whispering of rains withheld by the Buffalo's will, resonating with his vow to carry Sheng Xiao's weight.

The presence radiated an oppressive force, the ground quaking faintly under its spectral hooves.

"Not buckling yet, ghost," Omar grunted, his sarcasm a shield for the fire in his veins, Veronica's influence sharpening his edge as he met the Buffalo's gaze with defiant resolve.

Melissa shifted closer, her axe at the ready, a silent pillar of support that sent a warm ember through his aching frame, while Tate edged nearer, claws half-extended, his rivalry fueling a protective stance.

"Let's crush this stone, Ox—don't make my claws do all the work," Tate quipped, earning a rare nod from Sam, "Only if Ryder doesn't blow it into dust first."

The relic pulsed harder, entering the second phase—spectral winds howling like starving wolves, visions of drought-parched rivers testing his will.

Omar's grip faltered, the stone slipping an inch, his father's stern gaze flashing from the ox-pull contest, Kofi's ease binding the crowd while the heir's weight left Omar alone.

I'll fail them all, he thought, sweat stinging his eyes, the altar's hum quickening like a frantic pulse.

A memory surged—Veronica's hand gripping his in Souris's frost, her smirk a flame as she whispered, "You're the anchor, Ox—don't let go." Her fire steadied him now, his heart racing.

"Focus on the team, Omar—our bond's your anchor!" Tate shouted, his voice cutting through, claws carving a shallow rune in the dirt to redirect a wind gust, respect edging out overconfidence.

Sam's arrow whistled harmlessly into the air, dispersing a vision-cloud. "Strategy over brute force—shift your weight like this," she demonstrated, her Snake Clan precision guiding his stance, her eyes glinting with focus.

Melissa leaped onto a low branch, her view spotting a rune weakness. "There! Lean into the left glyph, it'll ease the surge!" Her empathy fueled the call, a platonic charge sparking as their eyes met briefly, her grin a beacon.

Alice's tablet flared, projecting a holo-map of the relic's pulses. "Two minutes to the third phase—your vitals are holding! Push!" Her defiance burned, tech weaving with magic, confidence blazing through her shy exterior.

Ryder's cannon boomed a low warning shot into the earth, scattering debris. "Boom! That's how we shake it off! Keep going, Ox!"

His grin hid the ache of doubt, his Rooster spark flaring brighter as he rallied.

Omar's resolve flared, the buffalo stone's weight easing as he recalled Melissa and Ryder's words in the grove, their shared burdens anchoring his spirit. Their empathy, forged in Mico and Explosivo, mirrored his struggle, their glances during the trial a quiet strength.

Melissa adjusted a brazier, her defiant grin steadying him. Ryder's nod, cannon steady, urged him on.

The altar's runes pulsed, embers swirling, urging him to carry Kusini's legacy not as a title, but as a guardian among equals, his grit fueled by their trust, a bond stronger than any yoke.

Omar's arms burned in the grove, the relic's weight crushing, ox carvings casting a bronze glow across the altar's glyphs.

His knees trembled, childhood doubts crashing—the ox-pull contest, his stumble under his father's stern expectations, the heir's burden heavier than Kofi's warmth.

I must hold on—for them, for Kusini, for her, he thought, the stone slipping, visions of famine intensifying—clans starving, plains ashen, maize fields crumbling to dust. The altar's hum quickened, Kusini's balance teetering, Sheng Xiao's fate in his hands.

Tate's voice pierced the haze. "Claws carve victory, Snake—Omar's got this!" His rivalry softened, respect flickering as he saw Omar's grit, Jade's words echoing: Be serious, Tate.

"Strategy shapes it, Tiger—keep him grounded!" Sam said, her Snake Clan precision calculating rune pulses, guiding Omar's hold, her arrow steadying his focus. "Your claws are all flash—my aim's the real bite!"

Melissa laughed, "Keep steady, Ox—you're tougher than my axe!" Her empathy sparked, burnout fading as she steadied a brazier's base, her nod a quiet anchor.

"Five minutes to moon's peak," Alice said, tablet pinging, her voice bold with defiance, her tech pulsing with resolve.

"My boom seals it, big guy!" Ryder roared, his courage blazing, steadying a brazier with a Rooster's defiant spark. "This stone's got nothing on my cannon's strut!" His grin rallied the team.

The Buffalo's amber gaze bored into him, endurance its sole measure, Omar's resolve fraying as the moon climbed. The relic pulsed harder, a second phase flaring—spectral winds howling, visions of drought-parched rivers testing his will.

For Kusini, for Veronica, he thought, her smirk a fire against the famine's chill.

Omar's knees buckled, the relic slipping, ox carvings dimming as the moon hit its peak. The Buffalo's gaze hardened, a third phase surging—an ash-glow flickering in the altar's runes, a whisper of the scrolls' chaos. The relic's runes flared, weight crushing, testing his soul.

I'm not Kofi, but my grit holds true—Veronica believes in me, he thought, the team's trust anchoring his resolve.

"You're almost there, Ox!" Tate shouted, respect firm, claws steadying a brazier. "Don't let Sam's arrows steal your thunder!"

"Endure!" Sam urged, precision steady, her arrow piercing a vision-cloud. "Your thunder's loud, Tiger, but my aim's sharper!"

Melissa nodded, "Tough as hell, Ox—stronger than my axe!" Her empathy a beacon, steadying the team.

Alice's tablet pinged. "Now!" her tech pulsing, confidence blazing, mapping the final surge.

"Proud of you, big guy!" Ryder grinned, his courage blazing, his cannon a defiant spark. "Take this home, Ox!"

The Buffalo's gaze softened, respect glinting. An ash-tinged breeze stirred the altar's runes, a faint menace tying to the scrolls' chaos. Omar surged, arms firm, relic held high. The talisman emerged, bronze glowing gold-blue, its weight lifting from his soul.

A vision seared Omar's mind—Kusini's fields ablaze, embers swirling in a crimson haze, the altar's runes pulsing with warning. The fire's heat stung, a cryptic omen of chaos looming, urging vigilance beyond his triumph.

Their faith proves my grit, Omar thought, the team's trust anchoring his resolve.

Omar stood in the grove, talisman in hand, its bronze glow warming his chest. The team gathered close, their faith a quiet strength—Melissa's defiant nod, Ryder's steady grin, Tate's firm stance, Sam's focused gaze.

Embers drifted in the Kusini air, catching in the maize-scented breeze, their faint heat a warning of unrest beyond the altar's pulse. Omar's mace felt lighter, the heir's burden eased by their trust, his resolve as a guardian among equals burning brighter.

The embers lingered, a subtle threat urging vigilance, Kusini's balance trembling on the edge of chaos.

Chapter 10: The Stolen Talisman

The sacred grove trembled under a moonlit peak, ancient oaks weaving a cathedral of rune-etched branches, their hum pulsing with Ox Clan endurance. The Ox Talisman glowed in Omar's hands, its gold-blue light tracing ox glyphs that thrummed with the Harvest Altar, cracked stone whispering centuries of survival. A faint ash-scent lingered, braziers flickering with harvest incense, their glow casting outlines of ancient hooves.

Omar exhaled, triumph warming his eyes as he met the Guardians' gazes, Kusini's balance fragile but true.

Tate clapped his shoulder, grinning, "Ox, you crushed it!"

Sam's arrow twirled in her fingers.

Melissa's eyes sparked, "Horns up!"

 Ryder pumped his fist, "Next round's on you if we survive, big guy!"

Alice's tablet pinged, her nod steady.

An ash-tinged breeze pricked Omar's senses, a memory flashing: In Souris's frost-dusted camp, Veronica gripped his hand before he left for Kusini, her green eyes fierce.

"You're the anchor, Ox—hold us steady." Her smirk sparked warmth, her Rat Clan wit a vow he clung to now, her laugh cutting through the frost like a flame.

"We did it," he said, voice low but firm, the altar's oxen glyphs shimmering under silver light.

Chaos erupted as Bella and her mercenaries—X's black-clad warriors and Kusini locals with earth-dyed tunics, axes etched with desperate runes—surged from the gloom, glyph-etched daggers gleaming, leather armor creaking, sweat and steel slicing through Kusini's warmth.

Bella's fire-powered hands sparked wild, flames licking the air like hungry serpents, her sneer twisting the grove's peace.

Her amber eyes blazed, a memory searing: At fifteen, village torches branded her a witch, stones flying as she fled, her fists clenched in terror. X's blade saved her, his voice steady: "You're one of us."

Her loyalty burned, the Ox Talisman's theft a triumph to repay his trust. The altar's glow pulsed, her flames scorching the earth, Jade's Guardians her prey.

Bella's sneer deepened, "Master X claims that talisman, Guardians—hand it over, or burn," a fireball crackling in her palm, embers dancing like malice, the altar's pulse faltering.

Omar dodged a fireball, his mace swinging, sweat dripping as flames singed his tunic, his furrowed brow set with duty. Melissa's axe clashed with a glyph-dagger, her tense shoulders straining, her blade sparking against an oak.

Tate's claws swiped, carving air to block a mercenary's lunge, blood trickling from a grazed arm.

Sam's arrow pierced a cloak, her steady gaze cutting through smoke. Alice's tablet flared, scattering foes, her clenched jaw firm. Ryder's cannon boomed, debris flying, his forced smile hiding pain from a dagger nick.

The grove roared with chaos, steel clanging, flames roaring, attendants swinging rakes, their chants— "Endurance carries all"—echoing amid the fray, spectral winds howling.

Tate's grin flashed, confidence blazing, his tiger-stitched tunic glinting as he spun into a tiger-like flow, low and fluid, claw gloves slashing.

"Get through me first, Fire Girl—your flames can't outshine my claws!" he growled.

Melissa darted, Monkey Clan agility a dancer's grace, tripping a mercenary with a swift leg sweep, her braid whipping, axe glinting.

"Alice, Ryder, Tate—shield Omar!" she shouted, voice piercing the fray, her burnout flaring as sweat stung her eyes— family expectations to gnaw at her mid-fight, a familiar weight pressing like overprotective chains.

Tate muttered, "I've got this, Monkey—save your quips for the victory feast," ignoring her call, charging Bella, leaving Omar exposed.

A net snared his arm, claws grazing a mercenary's blade, blood trickling down his forearm, Jade's warning cutting deeper.

"Flank them, now!" he barked, rallying late, insecurity gnawing as an altar attendant, tunic stained with ash, shouted at a local mercenary, "How could you betray our harvests?" before grabbing a fallen branch to aid the Guardians, swinging it to block a black-clad warrior, his eyes fierce with loyalty.

Other attendants joined, wielding rakes and braziers as weapons, their chants—"Strength carries all"—echoing amid the clash, turning the fight into a desperate defense of Kusini's heart, their tools clashing with glyph blades in a symphony of desperation, invoking Ox ancestors' rune-carved staves from drought legends, spectral echoes whispering endurance through the haze.

Alice's tablet flared, a light burst disorienting two mercenaries, her shy voice firm, "Target the fire-wielder—tech beats fire, watch this glitch her flames!" Her fingers flew, syncing a rune pulse to counter the smoke, confidence blazing through her bullied past—*no more hiding her smarts behind caution*, she thought, as the burst scattered the foes.

Dodging a dagger that grazed her sleeve, she shouted, "Keep the pulse alive!" rerouting runes manually as her tablet glitched from heat, her heart racing with a triumphant spark.

Sam's snake-shaped bow twanged, an arrow piercing a mercenary's cloak, her proud gaze faltering as a fireball singed her hair, the burn searing her arm.

"Omar, keep the talisman safe—my aim won't let my clan fall—clan pride's my steel!" she hissed, orange tunic blending with smoke, her wisdom anchoring the team despite the pain, dodging a glyph-dagger that sparked against an oak, its bite leaving a smoky trail.

Omar clutched the talisman, sweat staining his bronze-embroidered tunic, muscles aching from hours of gripping a buffalo-sized relic, its rune-carved weight grinding his shoulders raw under Kusini's relentless moonrise, until the peak crowned him victor.

Family duty pressed on his chest—could he hold Sheng Xiao steady, or was he just a stubborn heir chasing a fading harvest?

"We can't let them destroy it!" he roared, shielding the Harvest Altar. Bella's eyes narrowed, sneering, "Then watch it burn!"

She hurled a fireball at the Harvest Altar, glyphs charring, flames licking sacred stone, releasing spectral winds like famine spirits howling Sheng Xiao's decay, visions of Ox ancestors binding clans with rune-carved staves flashing in the blaze. Melissa dove to shield it, axe raised, smoke thickening.

A mercenary's glyph-dagger grazed Omar's side, pain flaring like a hot iron, but he swung his mace, toppling the attacker.

Veronica's fire—her smirk, her strength—can't burn out here, he thought, recalling her palace drill quip, "Your horns outshine my shots, Ox," the scent of her leather gloves lingering in his mind, vowing to prove her faith amid the doubt clawing his gut.

Bella hurled another fireball, igniting a brazier, embers raining as Tate dove, his claws singed, grass scorching black, the stench of charred earth choking the grove.

"Split up!" Tate shouted, drawing her fire while Melissa and Alice flanked the altar, teamwork fraying under the haze. A net snared Ryder's leg, his cannon misfiring in the smoke, sparking wildly.

"Not my strut—save the round, Tiger!" he yelled, breaking free, breaking a dagger nicking his shoulder, pain flaring but courage holding as he tackled a mercenary, debris scattering from a cannon blast splintering a branch.

Melissa rallied, "Hold the line!" coordinating a counterattack, her axe slicing nets, Tate redirecting flames with a claw swipe, Omar tackling a local recruit, hesitating at their desperate eyes, his mace swinging.

Sam called shots, "Flames won't stop my aim, fire-witch—your turn's coming!" her arrow severing a net rope, freeing Tate's arm, attendants swinging rakes to block blades.

A horde swarmed, blades flashing with glyph sparks, overwhelming Omar's fading strength—their bites drawing blood. A wiry mercenary lunged, wrenching the talisman free, its gold-blue light fading.

"I got it, Bella—let's move!" he shouted, her sneer triumphant as she hurled a final fireball, igniting a wall of flames that blocked Tate's lunge, embers raining like a curse.

Bella laughed, "Burn with your harvests!" The mercenaries fled into the haze, the altar's blackened glyphs a scar on Sheng Xiao's harvests. Omar's roar echoed as failure sank in, his side throbbing.

"Save the altar!" he shouted, rallying the Guardians and attendants to douse the blaze, Veronica's vow a spark to reclaim later.

Sam fired water-soaked arrows, Melissa shielded glyphs, Tate cleared debris, Alice synced runes despite glitching tech, Ryder hauled buckets, attendants poured water, their chants rising as spectral winds howled, the altar's pulse faltering.

In the Unknown Wilderness's fortress, stone walls pulsed with runes, the Yin Scroll's hum thick with old magic, parchment and smoldering runes tainting the air. X watched Bella's flames in a holo-link, her amber eyes blazing as she raised the ox-shaped talisman, its horns pulsing gold-blue.

A memory flashed: Under Kusini's maize-scented stars, he wove zodiac charms with his love, her laughter warming the night, his trembling hands brushing her cheek before her loss tore his heart.

Vincent's whispers— "Jade's light betrays her"—twisted his grief into vengeance, the altar's glow urging him to break Sheng Xiao's balance.

Bella's voice cut through, "The talisman's ours, Master X," her loyalty a fire forged in his rescue.

X's cold gaze softened, his silver ring glinting, "Bella, your fire surpasses all," his praise warm, the silver ring on his chain glinting, a memory of loss fueling vengeance.

Dolore's lightning dimmed, Bella's radiant beauty stealing X's gaze, her own sharp features paling in comparison.

My lightning will eclipse her fire—next talisman's mine, she thought, unrequited longing burning, fingers sparking faintly. Vincent's shadow loomed, his serpent scepter pulsing, a sly grin flashing at the talisman's capture.

"X's triumph begins," he murmured, his voice low with cryptic intent, "The talisman's just the start," green runes twisting through Vincent's spellbook, bound to his serpent scepter, pages writhing under his veiled control, glowing unnaturally with a sickly hue.

Lucas tensed, bandaged arm aching, Vincent's glee chilling him—X's eyes too blank, flickering unnaturally, his will bent like a puppet's strings, Vincent's ambition overshadowing X's. As Vincent's gaze flicked to him, Lucas averted his eyes, feigning loyalty, his gut twisting with unspoken doubt.

Something's off—feels less like vengeance, more like a shadow pulling strings, he thought.

Should he warn Bella or Dolore? The idea twisted like a dagger, but loyalty held his tongue.

Kusini stirred under dawn's haze, smoke curling from the grove, the air heavy with ash and despair, cracked earth swallowing wilting maize fields, farmers' chants faltering. Omar hauled water, dousing the altar, flames searing glyphs, braziers collapsing, the acrid burn stinging his lungs.

The runes flickered, farmers' desperate chants trembling as a threat of famine crept beyond the grove.

Attendants hauled debris, their voices a tense hush, hands shaking as they etched new runes, praying for Ox ancestors' strength. Omar's clenched fists tightened, his side throbbing—Kusini's heart hangs by a thread, but we'll forge it anew.

Melissa's axe cleared charred roots, her tense shoulders unyielding, inspiring a farmer's resolve.

Sam stood in the grove, her grip tightening, steady gaze fixed on the smoldering altar. Her Snake Clan wisdom battled envy—Tate's flair had cost them, but her aim could've steadied the team.

I should've called the shots sooner, she thought, vowing to outshine his bravado in the next fight, her bow steady as she planned Kusini's defense, her resolve anchoring the Guardians.

Alice knelt in the grove, steady hands syncing altar runes, her tablet glitching under the heat, her clenched jaw defying her bullied past.

No more "Glitch girl," she thought, rerouting pulses to stabilize Kusini's balance, her Rabbit Clan caution guiding farmers to brace glyphs. Her confidence blazing, a spark against the ash, proving her tech could outwit chaos.

Tate hauled debris in Kusini, his softened gaze on a farmer's child. His ego had flared, leaving Omar exposed, but now he aided locals, claws steadying a crumbling brazier.

I'll protect them, not just shine, he vowed, his resolve binding Kusini's heart, ash stinging his lungs. Ryder dragged buckets in the grove, his forced smile masking a shoulder wound, Rooster Clan courage holding as he rallied attendants.

No jests this time, he thought, his parents' scolding—"Courage, not jest"—guiding his hands to brace runes, embers swirling as a warning. His spark steadied farmers, proving his grit beyond bravado.

Omar stood by the altar, ash coating his tunic, his trembling hands gripping his mace, doubt clawing—*Am I enough to lead them back?*

The grove's charred earth mirrored his fear of failing Sheng Xiao, but the Guardians' nods ignited his duty. *Veronica's faith burns brighter than this blaze,* he thought, vowing to reclaim the talisman, Kusini's balance his anchor.

Sam pinned debris with arrows, bandaging her arm with an Ox Clan sash, its runes a faint spark.

"Endurance binds—my wisdom forged this resilience," she winced, her steady gaze directing locals to brace runes.

We should've seen this coming, like Souris—too cocky to brace for X's fangs, she thought, her voice a quiet vow.

Ryder pulled a caretaker from debris, his shoulder aching, courage masking doubt as he steadied a child. Tate saved a girl from a brazier, his claws trembling, insecurity raw as Jade's warning cut: *My flash cost us.*

Melissa's agility darted, slicing roots to free a farmer, her forced grimace unyielding, inspiring a mother who etched runes on a stave, whispering prayers for strength.

"Your claws saved that kid—build on that," the mother said, voice thick with ash. Tate's gaze softened, "Thanks, Snake—next time, prepared."

My flash cost them the talisman, he thought, jaw tightening.

Sam's voice was firm: "Not just you, Tiger—we rise together." Their rivalry softened into a pact.

Melissa stepped beside Omar, tunic torn, Monkey Clan charm subdued.

"You steadied me at the river, Ox," she said, her hand on his shoulder, respect replacing their clash. "You held the talisman—the team faltered, not you."

Omar nodded, "Your agility saved the altar, Monkey— now we fight together." Their eyes locked, her forced grimace sparking hope. "Your axe saved my horns—next time, we lead as one,"

Alice's tablet pinged, her clenched jaw steady. "Runes fading—harvests could fail if we don't etch more."

Ryder's forced smile faltered, "There's no strutting through famine..." his cannon heavy as he steadied a farmer. "If this smoke's my cologne, Fire Girl's paying!"

Tate clapped his shoulder, "Your grit's tougher than my claws, Rooster," forging a bond. Ryder admitted, "Pain's real, but we're not done," their loyalty a spark.

Omar's holo-link buzzed, his voice rough, "Empress, we lost the Ox Talisman—Bella torched the altar. We're etching runes to stop the harvests failing."

Jade's voice cut through, "Your endurance holds us—reclaim it, Omar. Sheng Xiao needs your strength. Patricia, sync your hammer to Alice's tablet."

Jade paced the palace, her scepter trembling, her furrowed brow showing the vision's echo—altar in flames, Sheng Xiao fraying. Her duty to the empire weighed heavy, Cade's report of crumbling realms fueling her resolve.

I must hold the balance, she thought, her amethyst eyes steadying, force-field magic humming to shield Sheng Xiao's heart.

Veronica's face flickered on the link, her pacing steps trembling. "I felt your pain, Ox—fight for me," she said, her shaky breath pulsing with relief.

"I'll reclaim it for you," Omar replied, her eyes softening.

He's my anchor too, she thought, fingers brushing the Rat Talisman, their Souris victory a fleeting warmth. Patricia's holo-link buzzed, connecting to Alice in Kusini.

"Sync your tablet to my hammer's runes," Patricia urged, her Pig Clan tattoo pulsing pink-gold, joined by Veronica, Doug, Hana, and Gerry's zodiac tattoos humming in the palace.

Veronica's resolve sharp, Doug's loyalty steady, Hana's spark bold, Gerry's agility fierce. Alice nodded, her Rabbit tattoo glowing, as Omar's Ox, Tate's Tiger, Sam's Snake, Melissa's Monkey, and Ryder's Rooster united the pulse, merging into a golden light stabilizing the altar.

The palace throne room glowed under fenghuang lanterns, clan glyphs—dragon, rabbit, horse—shimmering on the Great Race mural, its ox pulsing wildly, cracks spiderwebbing as Kusini's altar burned. Patricia's hammer glowed, her calm unwavering.

"The ox glyph's tied to Kusini's altar," she said, leading a chant, pendants humming, slowing the realm's decay. "It's holding—for now."

Jade paced in a side chamber, scepter trembling, the vision's echo—altar in flames, Sheng Xiao fraying—chilling her, her bond with Cade sensing "betrayal burns." She turned to Cade, her voice tight.

"Cade, scout the realms—Kusini's loss is spreading," she whispered, scepter aglow, force-field magic humming, her amethyst eyes meeting his with desperate trust, fear of loss raw. "Be careful, Cade—come back to me,"

Cade winked, his mismatched eyes sparkling, "Always, for you," drawing a fleeting smile from her. His shadows swirled like elegant silk, enveloping him.

Kusini's chaos spreads—harvests tie Sheng Xiao's realms, and the next talismans loom, he thought, choosing Cochan, Ged, and Listra. In Cochan, silos crumbled in ashen heaps, wheat dust choking the air like a suffocating fog, farmers' wails piercing the cracked fields, sour rot stinging his nose, tying to Kusini's scorched altar.

In Ged, cliffs rotted in slimy decay, vines wilting like defeated limbs under a cursed tide, damp rot heavy in his lungs, panic's tang mingling with the Prophecy's whispers.

In Listra, rainforests drowned in torrents, vines twisting in flooded valleys like strangled serpents, ash-scent heavy in the humid deluge, chaos rippling from the altar's wound.

He reappeared, breath ragged, samples of crumbling wheat, rotting vines, twisted roots in hand, shadows fraying from fatigue, doubts gnawing—*How can I protect her?* Jade's voice sparked in his mind, "You're my strength", steadying his edges.

"Cochan's silos crumble, Ged's cliffs rot, Listra floods—but we'll hold, Jade," he said, her hand steadying his, her concern deepening, "Your shadows shield my heart—don't fade," their bond pulsing.

Cade vowed, "For you, I'll endure," their eyes locking, a silent vow.

The Guardians staggered, wiping blood from scrapes—Sam hissed as she bound her singed arm, Tate flexed his singed claws with a grunt. Attendants hauled debris, their chants fading to a tense hush.

Omar's chest tightened, his side throbbing.

My team's fire lifts Kusini, but am I enough to lead them back? he wondered, fingers brushing the gash.

"Next time, Snake, your bow better outshoot my claws," Tate teased, earning a smirk from Sam.

"Only if you keep up, Tiger—my aim's still sharp." Their rivalry softened into a pact. Melissa gripped her axe, her forced grimace meeting Omar's.

"Your horns held us—my burnout won't break me again," she vowed, sparking hope. A fierce resolve seized him—Kusini's heartbeat through their scars, and he'd forge it anew.

"We reclaim it," Omar growled, "for Sheng Xiao's balance." The Guardians' nods hardened, their bonds tempered in the dawn's ash-streaked light, ready to chase the next fight.

Chapter 11: Echoes of Loss

The Imperial City's throne room shimmered under the warm glow of evening lanterns, their silk shades rippling with fenghuang patterns across towering marble pillars, the air thick with the smoky tang of sandalwood incense and the distant hum of palace chants drifting from the courtyards below.

The Great Race mural loomed overhead, its ox glyph dimmed to a faint, mournful throb, a golden scar against obsidian that whispered Kusini's defeat, the throne room's hush broken only by the soft crackle of rune-lit braziers casting flickering shadows.

Jade stood before the Fenghuang Throne, her red hair a fiery banner against the golden wood, amethyst eyes swirling with a storm of worry that threatened to crack her regal mask.

Her scepter's light flickered like a guttering flame, each erratic throb mirroring her racing heart, a fragile rhythm battered by the Prophecy's crushing weight—twelve talismans to anchor Sheng Xiao's fate, and now one ripped away by X's merciless fire.

The holo-link crackled alive, Omar's broad frame flickering into view, his voice rough and weary, ash streaking his bronze-embroidered tunic like war paint from the grove's blaze. "Empress, we're on our way back—Kusini's a smoking ruin, the Harvest Altar's a charred wound, but we're dragging ourselves home with what fight we've got left."

Behind him, Tate's amber eyes flashed with unspent fury, Melissa's braid hung frayed and soot-dusted, Alice clutched her glitching tablet like a lifeline, Sam's bow bore fresh scorch marks, and Ryder's grin was a weary shadow.

The transmission glitched as Tate's growl sliced through, "We lost the Ox Talisman. Bella's forces crushed us—she turned the grove into an inferno."

Omar's steady rumble followed, "She stole it in a blaze of hellfire, her flames scorching everything we fought to protect." The words hit like a dagger to Jade's gut, the Harvest Altar's blackened scar flashing in her mind, its pain bleeding across Sheng Xiao's harvests, failure sinking into her bones like a cold, creeping fog.

Doubt clawed at her—had her call to arms sent her Guardians to slaughter? The throne room's silence pressed down, heavy with the scent of polished stone and her own sweat, resolve snapping like a taut bowstring as she clutched the scepter.

A memory surged—her father's gentle voice during a childhood lesson, the scent of jasmine from the open window mingling with the warm glow of bedside lanterns as he tucked her in, his hand brushing her hair, "An empress finds strength in her heart, my pearl—trust its light to guide you through the dark."

She remembered the way his violet eyes, so like her own, sparkled with quiet pride, his stories of the Great Race weaving dreams of balance and courage, a shield against the night's shadows that now seemed so fragile. His painted eyes in the portrait above glowed with that same warmth, now a bittersweet anchor.

"Can we win this?" she whispered, voice cracking, tears stinging as the talisman's loss gnawed at her—X's power swelling like a tide, her Guardians hurt, Sheng Xiao's balance teetering on a razor's edge.

The famine's rot crept beyond Kusini: Cochan's silos crumbled to ash, farmers' wails piercing dust, Ged's vines blackened, and Listra's jungles drowned.

How could they beat X now? His forces struck like shadows, always one step ahead, the Yin Scroll's chaos amplifying his vengeance.

Jade's mind raced. *X's team grows stronger with each talisman...our Guardians are wounded, our realms wilting. Father trained me, but was it enough? Percy's lessons on countering dark runes, Huan's strategies for clan unity—they prepared us, but X adapts. If we falter again, the Prophecy crumbles—how do we outmaneuver an enemy who's already claimed a piece of our soul?*

The worry choked her, a storm of self-doubt threatening to drown her resolve, visions of Sheng Xiao's fall flashing like shattered glyphs.

Cade lingered at her side, his presence a quiet bulwark, green and blue eyes soft with concern, dark hair mussed from the day's strain, knives at his belt a silent promise.

A flashback surged—Percy standing tall during a storm that battered the palace, rain lashing the windows in relentless sheets, thunder rumbling like a beast as a young Jade trembled, her scepter sparking wild in her small hands.

Percy's voice, calm and sure, cut through the chaos: "Breathe, little phoenix—your will is the anchor that holds us," his green eyes twinkling with that mischievous glint as he grinned, his hand steady on her shoulder, guiding her to focus the rune-light until the tempest eased, the air clearing to reveal stars peeking through, his laughter a shield against the lingering thunder.

Cade ached for Percy's wisdom now, lost to the emperor's fall. What would he say to lift her? Their telepathic bond thrummed, a lifeline beneath her panic.

"They fought with everything, Jade," he said, voice a gentle tide, stepping closer to wrap her in his warmth. "We'll take it back—your heart's our guide."

The zodiac glyphs flared briefly, witnessing their fragile hope. Jade leaned into him, the scent of his leather cloak grounding her.

"Your words echo Percy's, Cade," she murmured, fingers tracing his knife hilt. "But this loss... it's unraveling everything. How do we mend what's breaking?"

His arm tightened, a silent vow, as the mural's ox glyph throbbed like a fading heartbeat. "You were trained by the best— your father, Percy, even Huan. We researched the Guardians, mapped ways to counter X's schemes. We never give up, Jade. We train more, fight harder—the Prophecy demands it, and so do our clans."

The throne room stirred with the heavy tread of the Kusini Guardians' return, their ash-streaked tunics and bloodied limbs a grim testament to their resolve, the air thick with smoke and sweat, armor clinking against marble.

Veronica's eyes lit with fierce joy, her Rat Clan agility propelling her to Omar, who met her with a warm embrace, his bronze ox tunic reeking of charred earth, his frame trembling from exhaustion.

"You're back—horns still kicking, Ox? Thought I'd have to raid Kusini myself!" she said, hands brushing his ash-smudged face with tenderness, her green eyes searching for unspoken wounds.

Omar's arms tightened, a shy grin breaking through. "Missed you, Rat—your fire pulled me through that inferno," his voice hoarse from shouting orders.

Her fingers lingered on a fresh scar, sarcasm fading. "This one's new. You carried too much alone. Let me share it now."

Omar's brown eyes softened, his callused hand covering hers. "Your spark kept me standing, Veronica. In the blaze, I saw Souris—your hand pulling me from thorns. I don't want to face this without you." Their foreheads touched, a brief kiss sparking, sealing a bond forged in scars.

"Then don't, Ox. We're together—cunning and strength, no holding back. But don't get used to me playing soft—this rat's still got bite," she teased, drawing a low chuckle. They shuffled to the healers' wing, where soft chants and herbal salves filled the air, a caretaker weaving a Rat Clan healing verse— "By cunning's grace, mend the brave"—as she anointed Omar's wounds with zodiac salve, the sting drawing a hiss Veronica mirrored.

"Your strength's my anchor, Veronica," he murmured, gripping her hand, their love flickering like a warm glyph in the dim light.

"Then I'll tether you, Ox—always," she replied, fingers lingering on his palm, etching their shared vow.

Doug clapped Omar's shoulder with a loyal grin, his Dog Clan warmth pulling a weary chuckle from the group, their laughter weaving a zodiac-threaded bond, each scar a rune etching their shared vow. "You two—Veronica's been a pacing terror without you!"

The Kusini team debriefed—Tate's voice rough with guilt, "My flash got us burned—should've clocked Bella's trap," his claws flexing, Jade's warning about seriousness a thorn in his pride.

"We should've expected it—after Souris's ambush, we knew X's forces strike fast. For Listra, we stay mindful, prepared—no more surprises. In Souris, we barely escaped Lucas's mercenaries, in Kusini, Bella's fire caught us off guard. For Listra, we scout ahead, map traps, expect the worst." Jade said.

"Jade's right—claws alone won't cut it for Listra. Sam, your wisdom guides this time," he added, amber eyes humbled.

Omar's shoulders sagged, "I failed as heir, let the altar fall," his voice cracking, the weight of Kusini's loss heavy. "And that vision from Souris—it's sharpening. Those twin figures chanting 'the knot tightens, betrayal nears'... it's tied to X's ranks, like the knot's unraveling now with the altar burned."

Tate nodded, "The shadows looked like twin emblems."

Jade's eyes darkened, "We've seen echoes before...it's undeciphered, but I've wondered if it's the Yin and Yang Scrolls, their balance hiding betrayal. Discuss it with the caretakers—it hints at deeper fractures."

Patricia's calm steadied them, "We all carried that weight since Kusini's pain is ours. We'll rise as one."

Gerry clasped Ryder's arm in a Goat Clan gesture of solidarity, the group's weary eyes meeting in silent resolve, Ged's wilting cliffs a shared tremor in their hearts.

Later in the healers' wing, Cade approached Omar and the others to check on their wounds, his green-blue eyes reflecting concern.

"You all holding up?" he asked, clasping forearms with Tate and Melissa.

As the group dispersed for salves, Omar pulled Cade aside, the herbal scents and soft chants a balm against his churning guilt. "Cade, old friend—from those Kusini training days, you know me. I led them into that blaze, failed to protect the altar. As heir, it's on me—Kofi would've rallied them better. He's always been the natural leader, charming the clans with ease, while I'm just the stubborn one holding the line."

Cade clasped his shoulder, shadows flickering in his eyes. "You're the strength of your people, Omar—Kofi's charm is great, but your endurance anchors Kusini. Tate's right—we should've seen the ambush coming after Souris. But you fought like an ox—your strength held the line."

Tate nodded from nearby, "Yeah, Ox—you led us through the flames. For Listra, we'll be ready, watchful."

Sam added, "Your resolve inspires—we'll fight harder, wiser."

Melissa grinned, "Horns held high—we've got this."

Alice and Ryder nodded, their encouragement lifting Omar's burden, a reminder that leadership wasn't perfection, but unity.

Omar exhaled, guilt easing, Veronica's fire and the Guardians' trust a beacon. I led them through flames, not perfectly, but truly—Kusini's heart beats in me, and I'll fight to reclaim it. "Thanks... it means a lot."

Veronica overheard, stepping close, her eyes fierce with pride. "Ox, you led like a champ—those horns held us through flames. Don't doubt yourself, we need you for Listra." Her hand squeezed his, a spark of love bolstering his resolve, their bond a shield against the altar's loss.

He paused, confiding softer to Cade, "Veronica's my light now—her fire keeps me going, like that red head you always rambled about in Kusini drills."

Omar's eyes widened. "Wait... that red head—it was Jade all along?"

Cade's cheeks flushed, shadows deepening. "Yeah... always her. Duty's held me back, but she's everything."

Omar grinned, "Then fight for her, like I do for Veronica. We train harder, never give up—the realms depend on it." Their talk forged a deeper bond, Kusini's lessons echoing in the healers' wing.

Omar stood in the healers' wing, ash from Kusini still clinging to his tunic like stubborn war paint, the holo-link humming softly with Veronica's face flickering in the dim light, her green eyes steady as she checked in from the throne room.

Leading the recovery, directing farmers to etch new runes on the scorched altar, stabilizing the fading glyphs with his unyielding grip, rallying attendants to haul debris amid the maize-scented haze, had proved his grit stronger than Kofi's effortless charisma.

A memory of stumbling in the childhood ox-pull contest under his father's stern gaze faded, replaced by the Guardians' nods of respect in the blaze.

Tate's humbled claws, Sam's precise arrows, Melissa's defiant axe—they'd followed his steady commands, not charm, but endurance. The zodiac carvings on the healers' walls pulsed faintly, echoing Kusini's agricultural heart, his mace feeling lighter as pride ignited.

Kofi's light shines bright, but my grit binds the team through famine's shadow—proving I'm heir enough, Omar thought, a triumphant resolve grounding him, the holo-link's hum weaving Veronica's voice like a warm anchor: "You held us, Ox—now heal and fight on."

Jade surveyed the Guardians, scepter dimming, voice steady. "Rest and heal for two days with the healers—let the salves mend you. In two days' time, Tate, Melissa, Alice—head to Listra for the Tiger Talisman, with David, Hana, and Sam. Tate, you lead. The rest—Omar, Veronica, Doug, Patricia, Gerry, Ryder—aid the Imperial City and clan lands. The Harvest Altar's burn has wilted the cherry blossoms here, their petals browning under a blight, lotus ponds clouding with decay."

A snowstorm battered X's fortress spires, flurries swirling like vengeful spirits, the ox talisman flickering in Bella's hand, its gold-blue pulse jagged, shaking the war room's runes, frost creeping over stone, a zodiac backlash whispering famine's spread, Bella's fingers tightening as dread chilled her triumph.

In the war room, runes glowed under starlight, casting an eerie green hue, the Yin Scroll's hum a predator's growl, winds carrying scorched parchment's bitter scent.

Bella presented the ox-shaped talisman, its horns pulsing gold-blue, her smirk taunting. "The Guardians crumbled under my flames—Omar's endurance was no match, his mace useless as the altar burned." Her thrill gleamed, but unease flickered—village torches accusing her as a witch, X's rescue forging loyalty, yet the destruction's rush left a hollow ache.

Bella handed the talisman to X, who clutched it, linking it to the Yin Scroll's chaotic veins, a surge of power pulsing as Vincent watched with narrowed eyes, subtly draining a fraction of its energy into his scepter.

X raised a rune-etched goblet, "To Bella's fire—our first talisman!" The war room erupted, a wiry Cochan mercenary with dark braids toasting Bella, her earth-tuned axe etched with zodiac runes. Dolore's lightning crackled in envy, her smile strained as Bella's radiance stole X's gaze.

Lucas joked gruffly, "My scars from Souris ache worse than your lectures, boss—Bella's flames beat my machete!"

He pulled Bella aside later, his voice low and careful, glancing over his shoulder at Vincent. "I saw him earlier—Vincent's scepter glowing sickly, twisting runes in his spellbook while X stood blank-eyed, like a puppet. We gotta watch him...something's off, and if he catches us--"

Bella's eyes narrowed, suspicion sharpening as she clutched the talisman, her thrill tempered by wariness. They were witnessing dark manipulations that could unravel everything if Vincent discovered their suspicions.

Vincent's scarred hand twitched, memory searing—a moonlit duel when the emperor fell, Percy's Cat Clan shadows coiling like whips, his knives flashing with green-eyed fury, carving deep scars across Vincent's arm as he snarled, "How could you?"

Vincent's rune scepter flared green, a blast felling Percy, his lifeless form crumpling as Vincent's ambition bound him to the Yin Scroll's chaos.

He smirked, his overconfidence swelling as he channeled the talisman's power, its gold-blue energy merging with his scepter's green runes, amplifying his schemes with a surge that made the storm outside rage fiercer.

X's eyes flickered unnaturally, a blank glaze as Vincent's scepter pulsed, a shadow pulling strings behind his vengeance.

Lucas whispered to Bella again, "Vincent's scepter twists his spellbook—it's wrong, glowing sickly." Her mistrust glinted, the storm's howl amplifying their dread, X's veiled design coiling with Sheng Xiao's doom.

The palace control room buzzed, clan banners fluttering—tiger, dragon, snake—over relic maps, tiles etched with Sheng Xiao's past.

Patricia's holo-link flared with a call from Kusini, the caretakers' faces urgent amid the altar's charred ruins. "The famine spreads—crops wilting, plains cracking. We need aid to boost the runes, or the balance shatters."

The holo-link showed Kusini's altar, blackened ox glyphs pulsing faintly, scorched earth reeking of ash, caretakers' hands trembling as they traced fading runes.

Patricia nodded, "We'll link now—hold the chant." She raised her hammer, its pink-gold runes flaring as she channeled

Pig Clan resilience, amplifying Kusini's fading glyphs via holo-link.

Caretakers' faces flickered, grim but hopeful, their chant— "Strength carries all"—weaving with her effort, their voices weaving ox motifs, runes flaring like fading embers, sweat beading as her growth shone, boundaries set against burnout, the remote synergy pulsing like a shared heartbeat across realms.

"This buys time for Listra's quest, but we'll need all the talismans to heal the core," she vowed, anchoring the room, the mural's cracks a warning of betrayal.

As the glyphs stabilized and the chant faded, Hana pulled Patricia aside, whispering, "Cade's mismatched eyes are so cute!"

Patricia countered, "He's Jade's, Hana—you see their spark."

Hana scoffed, "Jade's Empress—she'll marry a prince. I'm bold, beautiful—he'd choose me!"

Her smirk hid a pang—*Father's betrothal chains taught me to seize my own spark, but does Cade see me?*

Jade froze, overhearing, heart racing, Cade's silence a riddle. *Is my crown the wall between us? Hana's free, skilled, unburdened—could he choose her spark over mine?*

David flushed, Hana's glance at Cade stinging, her spark draws me, but Cade—where do I stand?

"Your plans too stiff, Horse, or is Cade your target?"

Hana's whip cracked, "Keep up, Dragon—my spark's for anyone!"

Sam snapped, "X's flank's mine—Monkey's too slow!"

Melissa retorted, "Sneaky Snake wishes!"

Alice's fingers flew over her tablet, syncing Listra's traps, defiance flashing—No more hiding from taunts. Ryder grinned, his cannon a shield against 'jokester' jabs.

I'll prove my spark in Listra. he thought.

"Gonna roast X's traps like festival skewers!" Ryder said.

Tate traced tiger maps, humility sharpening his focus, "No flash—claws strike smart." War drums echoed their resolve, Listra's perils steeling their hearts.

Jade slipped into the palace gardens, moonlight glinting off lotus pools, their sweet scent mingling with night-bloom jasmine, zodiac statues' jewel eyes looming like sentinels. Her heart raw from Hana's words.

What if Cade sees her as his match? She'd only ever seen Cade, his green-blue eyes her anchor since childhood—festivals, training, lessons, and play—but now doubt gnawed. Cade followed, his shadow silent, sensing her turmoil through their bond's thrum.

"You're here," Jade whispered, voice trembling, "but do you see me, not the empress?"

Cade's heart pounded, his love for her burning since their youth, her laugh in festival dances a spark he'd carried.

"You're the light that guides me, Jade—always have been, since we were kids," he said, voice raw, hand lingering on hers, then pulling back. "Duty binds us both."

You're my everything, his mind thrummed, unspoken, a spark promising more

Her breath caught, a thorn of doubt piercing her. Hana's spark could steal him—my crown binds me, but does it dim his light?

"Then stay close," she urged, stepping closer, but a priest's chant— "By zodiac's grace, mend the brave"—echoed, pulling them apart.

Cade stayed by her side, his presence a steady shadow, as Jade clutched her scepter, Hana's words lingering, Sheng Xiao's fragile hope trembling in the wilted blooms.

Chapter 12: Listra's Flooded Jungles

The torrents of Listra crashed like the roar of a thousand untamed spirits, transforming the once-vibrant rainforest into a labyrinth of swollen rivers and treacherous mudslides. Vines, thick as pythons and etched with faint, glowing Tiger Clan runes, dangled from the canopy like forgotten nooses, swaying in the relentless downpour that had swallowed the realm whole.

The air hung heavy with the scent of sodden earth, crushed orchids, and the sharp tang of ozone—a storm not born of nature, but of the festering wound in Kusini's Harvest Altar, where the stolen Ox Talisman had unleashed chaos across Sheng Xiao's veins. Maize fields withered in distant plains, rivers cracked in Cochan's silos, and here in Listra, the jungles drowned under floods that clawed at the roots of ancient trees, threatening to uproot the very balance of the zodiac realms.

Tate led the Guardians through the deluge, his claw gloves flexing instinctively against the slick bark of a fallen log, water sluicing off his tiger-stitched tunic like blood from a fresh wound. The fabric clung to his frame, heavy and sodden, mirroring the weight of Kusini's failure that still burned in his chest.

The Ox Talisman's theft—Bella's flames scorching the sacred grove, Omar's endurance crumbling under a hail of fireballs—had left scars deeper than any claw mark. Tate's amber eyes narrowed against the rain, his usual cocky grin subdued into a tight line.

Jade saw leadership in me, he thought, replaying her words from the palace tattoo ceremony, the fresh ink on his arm still stinging like a brand. But be serious—let Sam's wisdom guide your claws. she had said.

Kusini had been his chance to prove it, and instead, it had been a blaze of overconfidence, his flashy strikes leaving gaps Bella exploited. *No more flash. Listra's mine to lead—prove the claws cut deep, not wide.*

A memory flickered: before the Prophecy's shadows loomed, the jungles had been a paradise of sun-dappled canopies, rivers gentle and teeming with iridescent fish, villagers laughing as they swung from vines in playful games. Treehouses buzzed with celebrations, the air alive with tropical fruits and rhythmic drums, joy as abundant as the orchids blooming in every nook.

Now, the floods had twisted it all—rivers raged like beasts, swallowing paths and homes, yet the people's spirit endured, rising above the waters like unyielding vines. *If they can find joy in this ruin, so can we,* Tate vowed, his resolve hardening.

Beside him, Melissa matched his pace with Monkey Clan agility, her braid whipping like a live wire in the wind, green tunic darkened by the rain, but her sharp grin undimmed.

"This jungle's got more bite than your ego, Tiger," she teased, vaulting over a root with effortless grace, her axe glinting at her hip like a promise of chaos. Burnout from home's grueling training drills and Kusini's battle against Bella's flames lingered, but Listra's wild energy sparked defiance—a reminder survival was dancing through the storm.

Gerry bounded ahead, his Goat Clan leaps defying the mud's greedy pull, landing with a splash that sprayed the group. "Come on, slowpokes! If I can outdance this flood, you lot can keep up!" His cheeky smirk flashed, eyes twinkling with that irrepressible mischief.

Alice's fever had hit hard back in the palace—a sudden chill after Kusini's ash-tinged return, her Rabbit Clan tech whirring faintly as she synced data from her tablet, only to collapse mid-ping. Jade had debated with Omar in the throne room: "Alice needs rest, but Listra demands agility. Gerry's leaps rival Melissa's, he's our spark against the floods," she'd decided, clapping his shoulder firmly.

Gerry's skittish flair, often dismissed as reckless creativity, burned brighter under the honor: a chance to prove his leaps carried strength for his mother's sake.

I'll make you proud, Ma, he thought, her smile flashing in his mind.

David strode with purposeful fury, his Dragon Clan fists clenched at his sides, katana sheathed but humming with restrained power. The rain plastered his dark hair to his forehead, and his temper simmered just below the surface, honor demanding he channel it into vigilance rather than outburst. Kusini's betrayal by local mercenaries had hit him hard—how could kin turn on their own glyphs?

Discipline holds the fire, he reminded himself, eyes scanning the canopy for threats.

Hana's whip coiled at her hip like a serpent ready to strike, her Horse Clan energy crackling even in the downpour, her hijab framing her face with quiet strength as rain beaded on the fabric. She shot David a playful wink, her smirk bold against the gloom. "Loosen those scales, Dragon, this isn't a drill. Listra's got rhythm, let's find it before the floods do."

Her tease drew a reluctant twitch from David's lips, a flush creeping up his neck despite the chill. Their banter was a spark in the storm, but beneath it, Hana's eyes flicked toward the path ahead, her mind wandering to bolder pursuits—like Cade back in the palace, his mismatched eyes a puzzle she itched to solve.

Sam brought up the rear, her Snake Clan bow taut and ready, orange tunic blending seamlessly with the locals' earth-dyed weaves she'd adopted for camouflage. Her proud gaze clashed with Tate's every few steps, their rivalry a low, electric hum that had softened since Kusini's ashes.

"Eyes on the traps, Tiger," she said crisply, her voice cutting through the rain like an arrow.

"No charging ahead like last time. Strategy over swagger." Tate shot her a glance, half-grin returning. "Learned that the hard way, Snake. Lead on—your aim's the bite we need."

Faint violet sparks flickered in the distant sky, a thrum of unnatural lightning that set Tate's instincts prickling. The group pressed on, the jungle path narrowing into a torchlit clearing that burst with defiant life.

Listra's heart pulsed here, unbowed by the chaos: massive treehouses loomed overhead, their vine-woven platforms bustling with locals and hardy tourists braving the rain, lanterns swaying like fireflies in the canopy. The humid air thickened with the aroma of damp earth, wild orchids, and simmering spices—curries bubbling in communal pots, their heat a rebellion against the flood's chill.

Before the disaster, Listra had been Sheng Xiao's jewel of joy: sunlit rivers hosted floating markets where vendors bartered exotic fruits and rune-carved jewelry, celebrations lit the nights with bioluminescent vines, and communities thrived in harmony, their laughter echoing like eternal drums.

The floods had changed everything—waters rose, swallowing lowlands, forcing villagers to rebuild higher, rationing supplies scavenged from submerged groves. Yet, they rose above it: dances adapted to platforms, songs turned floods into tales of triumph, their spirit a beacon proving chaos could be met with unyielding happiness.

Locals swarmed the newcomers, their tiger-stitched tunics vibrant splashes of gold and black despite the deluge, melodic cadences rising in warm greeting.

"Guardians of the zodiac! The White Tiger welcomes kin who dance through storms!" An elder woman with silver hair braided in vine beads and glowing orchid petals—Elder Zuri—stepped forward, her eyes crinkling with timeless wisdom.

She clasped Tate's hand, her grip surprisingly firm, then gathered the whole group under the shelter of a massive banyan tree, its roots forming natural arches etched with Pixiu carvings—

winged lion-beasts guarding Sheng Xiao's edges. "Joy rises above floods, young Guardians," she intoned, her voice a melodic anchor carrying Listra's unyielding soul. "We choose happiness, no matter the rains—our spirit dances on. Before the altar's scar, our rivers flowed gentle, markets afloat with laughter and trade. Now, waters rage, but we rise—building higher, weaving vines into bridges, turning loss into lessons of unity. The floods teach us: scatter, and drown, unite, and thrive."

To bring her words alive, Zuri signaled the start of a ritual, torches flaring brighter as dancers swirled into motion under the banyan, their tiger-stitched tunics whipping like flames.

Vines in their hands glowed faintly, weaving patterns that summoned a spectral White Tiger—its silver fur shimmering ethereally, emerald eyes glinting with fierce wisdom.

The apparition prowled the circle, tail lashing as Zuri continued her tale, voice rising with the drums: ancestors dancing through ancient deluges, vines guiding their steps to hidden grottos where the White Tiger revealed its secrets.

"The Tiger guards Sheng Xiao's agility—move as one streak, or the floods claim you as scattered leaves," she warned, her gaze sweeping them all as the spectral form split into shadows, testing the dancers' unity before reforming in a burst of light. "Long ago, during the Great Eclipse, the White Tiger bound the realms' speeds when chaos scattered the winds. "It's spectral form split into fleeting streaks, testing clans to reunite as a streak—fierce, agile, unbreakable. Lose its talisman, and Listra's rivers rage eternal, drowning Sheng Xiao's paths in endless storm."

Tate's jaw tightened, the weight of the quest settling like the rain, his mind flashing to Kusini's divided fields. Unity. No solo strikes.

Sam nodded subtly, her wisdom aligning with Zuri's without a word. Melissa leaned in, eyes bright.

Gerry fidgeted with excitement as David's honor stirred at the grit.

Hana's energy synced with the rhythm of the tale.

In the heart of the treehouse hotel that swayed above the clearing, the ritual deepened into a display of Listra's enduring tourism culture.

Dancers wove intricate vine motifs under rain-soaked canopies, their movements a hypnotic blend of grace and power, the patter of droplets on broad leaves syncing with the drumbeats like a natural orchestra. Tourists huddled under woven awnings, wide-eyed as the vines glowed with rune-light, forming ephemeral bridges between platforms—symbols of how Listra turned peril into spectacle. Orchid scents mingled with the rain, the air alive with chants of "Unity rises above floods," the performers' tiger-stitched tunics shimmering as they leaped between levels, drawing gasps from visitors who clutched rune-carved souvenirs.

This wasn't mere performance, it was a living testament to the realm's spirit, where even in chaos, joy invited outsiders to witness and heal, steadying Tate's claws as he absorbed the lesson of unbreakable bonds.

The village enveloped them in ritual warmth. Under the banyan, locals offered steaming bowls of jungle boar curry searing the tongue.

One dancer, a young woman named Moira with tiger-claw tattoos snaking up her arms, pulled Tate into the fray after the spectral tiger faded.

Her eyes held a quiet fire, shadowed by loss—her family's floating market stall swallowed by the floods weeks ago, fruits and jewelry lost to the depths.

"We dance to remember the joy, not mourn it," she said, her voice steady as she shared a quick sip of curry with him. "Before the scar, our stalls bobbed like stars on the river—now we rebuild on vines, trading stories instead of goods."

Tate nodded, the contrast hitting hard, and as the drums pulsed, he guided her step, claws retracted, whispering, "Lead the rhythm—show me how your streak moves unbroken."

Moira's laugh rang out, her hips twisting in fluid arcs, and Tate stumbled at first but soon found the beat—his tiger-like flow syncing, a grin breaking free. This is leadership? Not commands, but joining the dance? Moira pulled Sam in next, their shared precision sparking as vines whipped.

"They always picked flash over aim in my old games," Sam murmured, a memory surging: Snake Clan training fields, her arrows true but overlooked for bolder shots, pride sharpening her resolve like a whetted blade.

Moira nodded fiercely. "Keep shooting true—they'll see your streak." Melissa joined seamlessly, her Monkey agility turning flips into the routine, while Gerry leaped in with goatish flair, drawing cheers. Even David cracked a smile, his rigid stance loosening as Hana twirled him into a spin, her whip cracking overhead like thunderous applause.

As night deepened, the jungle path reclaimed them, mud sucking at boots like greedy mouths, swollen rivers roaring like beasts unchained.

Sam took point, bow steady, eyes scanning for traps—rune-etched vines that could snare like whips, submerged pitfalls pulsing with faint glows.

"Focus, Tiger," she said, voice crisp over the din. "No ego trips. The floods don't care for claws." Tate paused, double-checking a suspicious root, the altar's char flaring in his mind—smoke and screams, Bella's sneer. "I'm focused, Snake. We cross as one."

Gerry vaulted a root with a whoop, "Keep up, or I'll outdance the floods!"

Melissa laughed, matching his pace. "Dream on, Goat—my flips win every time."

David's fists tightened as a branch snapped overhead, temper flaring. "Stay sharp— this storm's no accident."

Hana's whip cracked near him, smirk bold. "Loosen up, Dragon—Listra's got rhythm enough for both of us!"

David's glare softened into a flush, her tease a welcome spark. The river loomed, its current a snarling beast, vines dangling like snares from overhanging branches.

Sam traced the bank. "We cross—carefully. Melissa, scout the vines."

Melissa moved first, agility defying slick rocks, but a surge yanked Hana's footing, her whip tangling in the current.

"Got you!" Melissa shouted, arm snagging Hana's with Monkey grace, pulling her to a protruding root with a grunt.

Their grins flashed amid the spray. "Nice save, Monkey—thought I'd be fish food."

Gerry dodged a tumbling boulder, spear jabbing to redirect it: "Watch above—the canopy's shedding tears!"

Melissa laughed. "Good call, Goat—don't want to get hit from above."

Hana's whip cracked across Listra's river, spray stinging as she steadied David, a memory of Fahal Alkhayl's festival flashing. Her whip snapped a suitor's blade aside, saffron grounding her rebellion.

"I choose my spark," she declared, Cade's mystery a thrill.

David's honor felt like home, his katana shielding her. The river's roar echoed her heart, vowing trust. David's hand gripped hers tighter, his temper cooled by her fire, their steps syncing like a dance born of storm.

"You're the rhythm I needed," he murmured, eyes locking as they cleared the bank, the commitment shift burning like rune-light in her chest.

Gerry's spear trembled in Listra's rain, a memory of Ged's cliffs flashing. At fifteen, his hesitation on a stormy ledge nearly cost his mom, her cry echoing as he froze, skittishness overshadowing his Goat Clan creativity.

"Leap, Gerry!" she urged.

Now, the White Tiger's lair loomed, his spear ready but doubt lingered—could he act decisively? The vine-scented air pulsed, urging his resolve. He thrust forward, jabbing a snapping vine mid-air, the tension breaking as he landed firm, Melissa's nod a spark.

"That's the Goat I see," she said, his skittishness yielding to creative fire.

David's fists tightened as a branch snapped overhead, temper flaring. "Stay sharp—remember to be vigilant." The river surged higher, a rune-trap flaring—a submerged glow yanking at David's ankle like a spectral claw.

He slammed his fist free, roaring, "Keep moving!" Hana's wink steadied him, her hand brushing his arm. Honor in the pull—don't let it drag you under.

A third peril erupted: the current birthed a whirlpool, vines whipping like tentacles, dragging Gerry under for a heartbeat—then surging toward David, pulling him into the churning depths with a roar of water.

Panic flashed: Doragon's misty peaks, Kenta, his Doragon mentor, barking during a river drill, "Channel fear into focus—discipline pulls you through!"

David had nearly drowned then, lungs burning, but honor had anchored him, fists cleaving the current until safety.

Now, he twisted free with a katana slash, surfacing gasping as Tate's claws hauled him out, Sam's arrow pinning the thrashing vines.

"Got you, Dragon—dry land's that way," Tate grunted.

Gasping, Gerry coughed water beside him. "Remind me... to stick to dry land."

Their laughter cut the tension, bonds tightening like woven vines. The jungle deepened, rain hammering relentlessly, a distant roar—the White Tiger's lair—echoing promises of trial.

Tate's claws flexed at Listra's cavern, rain soaking his tunic, a memory of Jade's tattoo ceremony stinging.

"Be serious," she'd warned, her amethyst eyes piercing his pride, ink burning. Kusini's flames exposed his ego—claws leaving gaps Bella exploited.

The White Tiger's lair loomed, Zuri's words urging unity. The vine-scented air steadied him; Sam's aim a spark. He envisioned the talisman's glow, his strikes precise, not flashy—unity the blade that cuts through storms.

Resolve hardened, he nodded to the team. "We enter as one streak."

Far from the flood's fury, in the Imperial Palace's moonlit chambers, Jade paced Alice's recovery room, tapestries glowing with Rabbit Clan motifs under soft cedar-scented air, healing herbs lingering like whispered prayers.

"You're looking better," she said to Alice, amethyst eyes warm as she clasped Alice's hand, scepter pulsing faintly.

Alice smiled shyly, glasses catching the light. "Thanks to you, Empress—and the fever's no match for Rabbit resilience."

Jade crossed to the balcony, her gaze drifting to the training yard below, where Cade sparred with Doug and Patricia under the stars.

Doug's Dog Clan sword clashed with fierce loyalty, light blue eyes blazing as he parried. Patricia's Pig Clan hammer countered with calm precision, pink-gold runes flaring like dawn. She paused, hammer pulsing, sensing the Great Race mural's tiger glyph flicker overhead.

"Listra's floods worsen," she warned, glancing up at Jade. "The altar's scar feeds the deluge—we must send zodiac charms to Tate's team."

Omar nodded from the sidelines, Veronica at his side, her Rat Clan eyes sharp. "Strength carries them, but charms will bind the runes."

Jade's heart stirred, memories flooding like Listra's rivers: At ten, childhood games of hide-and-seek in the palace gardens, Cade's laughter echoing as he shadow-traveled behind tapestries, her giggles free and unburdened. At twelve, her father's diplomatic travels tore her to distant realms—Coinin's tech spires, Saanp's scorching dunes—leaving Cade behind, summoned by Calix for royal training.

They'd been too busy for letters—Jade buried in lessons on force-field magic and Prophecy lore, Cade honing his knives in Doragon's misty peaks, Saanp's endless dunes, Ged's crashing shores.

But Percy had bridged the gap: shadow-traveling updates to Jade during her rare palace visits, his green eyes twinkling as he shared tales of Cade's parries and triumphs. "He's dreaming of a red-haired beauty, little phoenix —your spark keeps him sharp." Her heart had soared, a secret anchor through the separation.

At fifteen, his return—taller, shadows deeper—had ignited a crush that bloomed into unspoken love, his mismatched eyes her anchor.

Now, watching him below, knives flashing in swift arcs, Hana's shadow loomed from reports: her bold flirts, unburdened by crowns. *Does he see her spark over mine? Father taught me an empress's heart guides the Prophecy yet if I falter here, chaining duty over desire, how can I lead Sheng Xiao?* The scepter's pulse urged a bolder decision—perhaps confiding in Cade, risking the crown's weight for their shared fire.

In the Unknown Wilderness's fortress, jagged spires pierced the mist, rune-etched arches humming with damp stone.

X paced the war room, his blade flashing in the dim light, a holo-vision of Sheng Xiao's realms unfolding: Kusini's plains cracked and barren, Listra's jungles drowning in unrest that Vincent's gaze lingered on with a cryptic glance, even their own hideout battered by unnatural blizzards spilling over from Souris's lingering frost. Vincent's serpent scepter flared green subtly, his sly grin hiding frustration.

"The altar's burn ripples back. Our stores from Souris raids dwindle, rations tight against these storms," he murmured, eyes glinting toward the flickering Listra feed.

Bella nodded, amber eyes sharp, her fire flickering weakly against the chill as Lucas winced, bandaged arm aching in the cold drafts.

Dolore's absence left a gap, her lightning needed for defenses.

X's fist clenched, his vengeance for lost love fueling resolve, but consequences bit deep—stolen grains from Kusini now rationed, Souris's frozen caches thawing unevenly, the team huddled around sparse fires.

"Our chaos returns to us," X admitted, voice low, a rare crack in his armor. "But it steels us—press on, for the scrolls demand it." Vincent's shadow loomed, ambition coiling in that knowing glance, as the fortress groaned under snow-laden winds, their actions' echoes a harsh teacher.

Deep in Listra's shadowed ridges, Dolore crouched, lightning-charged fingers crackling with violet fury, her brown eyes tracking the Guardians' distant torches like prey. Mercenaries shadowed her, black-etched tunics blending with night, their steps masked by the rain's symphony.

"They're close. Stay sharp," she hissed, heart burning with ambition's fire. Bella's radiant theft in Kusini taunted her—X's praise for the Ox Talisman a dagger to her pride. *My storm will eclipse her flames.*

A memory surged, vivid as lightning: Years ago, in a collapsing shrine in a forsaken realm, crumbling stone and howling winds closing in, bandits' blades glinting with greed. Dolore's power faltered, bolts fizzling against the onslaught, her body crumpling under a fallen beam. Then X appeared, a silhouette of vengeance, blade flashing in a crescent arc—elegant, precise, carving foes like silk through storm. Blood sprayed, bodies fell, and he knelt, sorrowful eyes meeting hers.

"You're worth more than this ruin," he murmured, pulling her from the rubble, his touch a spark that ignited devotion.

His sword danced with graceful legacy, a master's poise that drew her heart, her vow to outshine Bella forged in that mercy. *For you, X—I'll claim the Tiger and your gaze.* Ambition flared, recklessness summoning another bolt as she advanced, the storm her ally.

Back in the canopy-shielded hollow, the Guardians camped, fire sputtering against the damp, jungle roars a lullaby of warning.

Sam aided a stranded local villager, her bow guiding him to higher ground, her voice gentle: "Stay with the village—the floods spare no stragglers." The man nodded gratefully, vanishing into the gloom. Tate sat by the flames, the altar's char scarring his thoughts like embers on skin.

"I won't fail them again," he murmured, eyes shadowed, resolve hardening into steel.

David met his gaze, a nod of respect. "Not bad, Tiger—honor sees your grit."

Gerry tossed a twig into the fire, smirking. "Stealing my moves now, huh?"

Tate chuckled, grin softer. "Keep dreaming, Goat."

Hana leaned against a trunk, sharing a damp ration with David. "Careful, Dragon—you're almost smiling." Her tease drew his rare warmth, their bond a quiet glow.

Melissa's laugh flared as Gerry nudged her. "Bet I outdance you first in the village!"

Their banter wove through the night, Listra's spirit lifting weary souls. But lightning roared closer, violet pulses sharpening the air, an unseen threat coiling like a vine.

The White Tiger's roar echoed faintly from the depths, its test waiting—a trial of unity in the heart of the tempest, the talisman's emerald glow pulsing like a beacon through the storm, hinting at the agility that could bind Sheng Xiao's fraying realms.

Chapter 13: The White Tiger's Trial

The jungle's roar pulsed like a living heartbeat, its torrents clawing at Listra's heart as the Guardians pressed toward the White Tiger's lair, violet lightning cracking overhead like a warning of Dolore's pursuit. Rain lashed their faces, the canopy's vines writhing with glowing Tiger Clan runes, their faint hum drowned by the churn of swollen rivers below. The air stung with ozone and crushed orchids, a storm fueled by Kusini's scorched altar, where the stolen Ox Talisman had torn Sheng Xiao's balance, flooding Listra's paths and forcing villagers to weave defiant bridges high above.

Tate led the way, his tiger-stitched tunic sodden, claw gloves glinting under flickering torchlight, the memory of their campfire's resolve—*I won't fail them again*—burning fiercer than the distant jaguar cries. Zuri's words echoed: "Joy rises above floods, dancing through storms." The team moved as one, their steps steady despite the mud's greedy pull, the cavern's glow a beacon through the tempest.

Deep in this flooded chaos, Dolore navigated a treacherous ridge slick with relentless rain, her lightning-charged fingers crackling arcs that lit the canopy like fleeting storms. Her brown eyes locked on the cavern's distant, eerie glow, ambition burning hotter than the ozone-scented air.

Mercenaries trailed her: a mix of X's hardened warriors in black-etched tunics and local Tiger Clan turncoats in gold-black weaves stained with mud, their eyes sharp with betrayal, curved daggers glinting under sporadic torchlight, boots sinking into swollen rivers. A vine-trap snared one subordinate, its thorny coils tightening like a living snare, pulling him toward the churning waters below.

"Keep up or we're lost," she hissed, slicing him free with a dagger humming from her electric touch, her recklessness a searing flame.

The mercenary grumbled, wiping mud from his face, voice low with doubt: "This storm's unnatural, boss—Kusini's burned altar is flooding everything, bleeding disasters across the realms. Are we pushing too hard?"

Dolore's eyes narrowed, lightning flickering in her palms as she rounded on him, air crackling with tension. "Question me again, and you'll feel the storm firsthand. X demands the talisman—failure's not an option."

Her words silenced him, but stirred her own buried doubts, the ridge collapsing nearby in a cascade of rocks and mud, forcing the group to brace against the surge.

She pressed on, daydreaming of X's praise, his sorrowful eyes softening as he cupped her face, a kiss sealing her victory over Bella's radiant fire, her heart soaring past the eclipse's fleeting streaks.

Memories of his mercy in that ruined shrine fueled her— his blade's crescent arc carving through bandits, pulling her from rubble, his voice a vow. Yet doubt crept in like the floods: Bella's flames claimed Kusini's talisman, earning X's warm gaze—could her lightning ever eclipse that? The Ox scar's fallout slowed them, rivers rising like vengeful spirits, linking to the altar's wound.

A minor peril erupted—a rune-triggered flood wave crashing from a hidden gully, violet sparks dancing on the water's surface.

Dolore unleashed a bolt to shatter the wave, steam hissing as it parted, her mercenaries scrambling through the mist. Rain lashed her face, Listra's jungles testing her resolve, vines coiling like wraiths, their whispers urging her onward.

The cavern's glow pulled her closer, her ambition a firestorm, X's silhouette her unyielding guide.

In the Imperial Palace's training yard, Cade stood atop a balcony under a canopy of wilting cherry blossoms, their petals browning from Kusini's spreading blight, the air thick with the faint rot of lotus ponds below.

He watched Doug's Dog Clan sword clash with Patricia's Pig Clan hammer, the ring of steel echoing like a heartbeat, their unity sparking memories of shared drills. Patricia's hammer glowed with pink-gold runes, her calm precision grounding Doug's loyal swings, while Omar coached from the sidelines, his Ox Clan strength a steady anchor, Veronica's Rat Clan spark adding quick jabs and teasing quips: "Faster, Dog—don't let her hog the glory!"

Their laughter rang out, a brief light against the Prophecy's shadows, Omar's arm brushing Veronica's in a quiet moment of affection that made Cade's chest tighten with longing.

He was happy for Omar's bond, yet yearned for Jade's presence, her amethyst eyes his anchor.

At twelve, Cade sought Jade to announce his call-up, summoned by Calix's decree for royal duty, but her father's diplomatic travels whisked her to Coinin's tech spires and Saanp's scorching dunes.

Percy shadow-traveled to him instead, green eyes twinkling as he relayed her message: "Jade was crushed—she said, 'Tell him to sharpen those knives. I'll need his shadows when I return.'"

The words eased Cade's guilt, Percy's hand on his shoulder a brotherly anchor: "She sees your spark, little bro—don't let duty dim it."

Doragon's misty peaks honed his precision, fog-shrouded dojos testing knife throws amid howling winds, the chill seeping into his bones like doubt.

Saanp's dunes taught resilience, endless sands shifting underfoot during endurance runs, heat mirages blurring his vision as he parried invisible foes. Ged's shores sharpened footwork, crashing waves demanding agile dodges on slick rocks, salt spray stinging his eyes. Coinin's tech labs challenged his mind, holo-puzzles syncing with his shadows, circuits humming like the Prophecy's pulse.

Under Calix's stern gaze, Cade perfected a spinning parry, the commander's sword guiding his form, knives twirling in swift arcs that mirrored his growing affection for Jade. Muscles hardened through relentless drills, skills adapted not just for survival, but for her protection—visions of her red hair a flame in his thoughts.

Around a campfire in Doragon's valleys, troops resting under starlit skies, Calix gazed upward, dreamy.

Cade teased, "Dreaming of Opal, Commander?"

Calix smiled softly: "Love demands courage, lad—more than any blade." Nervously,

Cade confessed, "Could an Empress-to-be, so far above, choose me? Her crown dwarfs my hopes."

Calix's eyes clouded with understanding. "Courage bridges any gap: love finds a way, even through thrones."

Their bond deepened that night, Calix's heart mirroring Cade's quiet yearning for a royal girl, his advice a lantern against the doubt.

At fifteen, Jade's return stirred hope, her amethyst eyes igniting a love that burned steady, his parry vowed to protect her forever. Yet Hana's bold spark lingered—her whip cracks and fearless laughs during recent spars, a reminder that someone like her might be more fitting for his station, unburdened by crowns.

No, Jade's my anchor—heart and soul, always, but am I worthy of her throne? Listra's jungles hone Tate's claws—my knives must match them. His hope flared, Listra's call echoing through the realms, the palace's pulse uniting them amid the blight.

Jade watched from a shadowed alcove, her scepter humming faintly, sensing the Tiger glyph flicker on the Great Race mural overhead—a distant echo of Listra's trials. Cade's form below moved with graceful precision, knives flashing like extensions of his shadows, but her heart twisted with unspoken fears.

Hana's words from the gardens haunted her: "Jade's Empress—she'll marry a prince. I'm bold, beautiful—he'd choose me!" The doubt gnawed, her crown a barrier to the simple joys Hana flaunted—whip in hand, flirting freely without the Prophecy's weight.

Does duty chain him more than my heart's fire? A memory surfaced: Percy's shadow-travel updates during her travels, his grin easing her loneliness: "Cade's knives are sharper than ever—he dreams of a red-haired phoenix pulling him from the dunes." Her telepathic bond with Cade thrummed now, a warm pulse, but she held back, fearing rejection.

Veronica's teasing banter below drew a smile—her spark with Omar a mirror of what Jade craved. *Perhaps it's time to risk it,* she thought, stepping into the light, her voice carrying: "Cade, a word?"

His eyes met hers, mismatched and soft, a silent promise amid the yard's clamor. Their bond sparked: You're my strength, always, she sent, his response a gentle echo: And you're mine.

Listra's jungle thrummed with relentless torrents, vines twisting like Sheng Xiao's Guardians under storm-lit cliffs, the air heavy with the musk of sodden orchids, crushed leaves, and the distant rumble of thunder.

Tate led the Guardians down a narrowing path, claw gloves glinting under sputtering torchlight, tiger-stitched tunic sodden and clinging like a second skin. The White Tiger's lair loomed ahead, a cavern carved into a limestone cliff, its vine-framed entrance shimmering with an eerie, rune-pulsed glow. Pixiu carvings—winged lion-beasts with fierce emerald eyes—guarded the threshold, Sheng Xiao's protectors entwined in eternal vigilance.

Kusini's Ox Talisman loss tightened his jaw, the altar's burn a scar that fueled these floods, but Elder Zuri's words echoed like a mantra: "Joy rises above floods, dancing through the storms to claim our strength." Her tales of villagers weaving vines into bridges amid deluges steadied him, Listra's vibrant spirit—its songs and dances—pulsing in his heart like a defiant drum.

A flashback hit: the village dance under Listra's swaying lanterns, rhythms syncing, his claws hesitant but finding flow with Sam's guidance—her calm aim taming his fire, unity born from rivalry. We'll dance through this too, he vowed. He scanned the team, fear of failure a silent pulse, the jungle's roars blending with the rain's symphony, a reminder that unity was their only shield.

Tate's claws flexed at Listra's cavern, rain soaking his tunic, a memory of a Tiger Clan test at ten stinging sharply. His flashy strikes faltered, missing a holo-target as the crowd's laughter cut deep, Jade's warning— "Be serious"—burning like fresh ink.

His rivalry with Sam blinded him then, his ego chasing cheers over strategy. The White Tiger's lair loomed, Zuri's words urging unity over swagger.

The rune-hum vibrated, Sam's steady aim a spark that grounded his fire. Kusini's flames taught me—claws alone fail. We strike as one. He envisioned the talisman's glow, his strikes precise, not showy—unity the blade to carve victory. Resolve hardened, he nodded to Sam, her bow a silent promise.

"We move together," he said, voice firm, the jungle's pulse syncing with his heart, ready for the trial's test.

Melissa's braid swung wildly, Monkey Clan agility primed as she vaulted over a flooded root, her grin sharp despite the burnout gnawing at her edges—family pressures to excel in endless drills, amplified by Kusini's flames. "This jungle's got teeth—stay light, team!"

Gerry leapt over roots with Goat Clan nimbleness, his smirk daring as he dodged a mudslide, the honor of replacing Alice fueling his leaps: "Ma would love this—proving my hops carry us all!"

David's fists clenched, Dragon Clan honor firm, his temper low but simmering, Kusini's betrayal by locals a fresh wound: "No mistakes—honor demands we hold."

Hana's whip swayed, Horse Clan energy crackling, winking at David despite her mind wandering to Cade's eyes. "Show this flood some rhythm, Dragon—keep up or I'll lead the dance!"

Sam trailed, Snake Clan bow taut, her proud gaze meeting Tate's, their rivalry softened by Listra's trials into grudging respect: "Together, Tiger—your claws, my aim." Lightning's threat haunted their steps, violet arcs flickering closer, an unseen menace weaving through the jungle's heart, the air thick with ozone and impending peril.

The cavern's path twisted into treacherous gullies carved by the floods, a low growl blending with the jungle's roars, vines writhing on the cliff like living motifs of Sheng Xiao's legacy. Tate paused, torchlight catching the carvings' hum, a faint warmth pulsing from the stone.

"This is it," he said, claws flexing, Zuri's wisdom steadying his cockiness into focus.

Sam gripped his arm firmly: "Stay tight, Tiger—lead with more than claws."

Gerry smirked at Melissa: "Ready to dance with danger, Monkey?"

She nudged him back: "Save your leaps, Goat—let's not trip into the abyss."

Their grins steadied the team, a playful echo of the village's defiance. David's gaze sharpened: "No room for slips— honor binds us."

Hana's smirk flashed: "Then let's give this beast a show, Dragon—your fire with my spark."

A mini-trap flared—a gully flooding suddenly, Hana's whip lashing out to save Gerry from the surge, her pull yanking him to safety as water roared below.

Tate's heart thumped, a quick flashback to Kusini's guilt hitting him—the altar's flames claiming the talisman, his overconfidence a spark that fed the blaze. No more failures—unity first. The cavern's glow pulsed, vines parting like a curtain, beckoning the trial ahead.

The cavern opened into a vast arena, walls etched with tiger motifs shimmering under rune-light, the floor slick with rain pooling in jagged cracks. Clan etchings adorned the stone—tiger claws intertwined with Pixiu wings, glowing faintly with Listra's lore, whispers of ancient guardians echoing like distant drums.

The air hummed with humid glow, the scent of moss and ozone thick, Pixiu carvings humming a low vibration tied to Sheng Xiao's protectors. A spectral White Tiger emerged from the mist, its translucent fur radiant silver, emerald eyes blazing with agility and ferocity, a guardian born of Listra's wild heart.

Its tail lashed like a whip, massive form coiling with spectral winds, its voice a quake rattling the walls: "I am Listra's White Tiger, guardian of Sheng Xiao's jungle heart. You seek my talisman, zodiac children. Prove unity in a duel or falter amid the storms."

Team reactions rippled as Melissa's empathy flared, sensing the beast's ancient sorrow while David's honor vowed to match its ferocity.

Hana cheered softly, "Let's dance!"

Tate's grin flared, Kusini's lesson tempering his cockiness.

"We're ready," he said, claws poised.

Sam's eyes narrowed, bow aimed. "Together, Tate—not your solo show."

Vines parted, revealing a narrow path suspended over a yawning chasm, its edges jagged with rune-traps, leading to a stone pedestal where the Tiger Talisman glowed gold-blue, a Tiger-Pixiu motif shimmering, Listra's winged protectors entwined in eternal guard.

Fleeting streaks flickered on the walls, foreshadowing visions of loss, the air pulsing with Prophecy's cryptic hum. The Tiger leapt, a silver blur, claws glinting like moonlight on water.

"Begin," it growled, the arena quaking as the first phase ignited.

Tate and Sam stepped forward, their rivalry crackling like the storm outside, Tate's tiger-like flow fluid and instinctive, Sam's archery poised and calculated.

The Tiger lunged, its tail knocking Tate off balance, claws scraping stone as he skidded toward the chasm's edge, winds howling up from the depths.

Melissa shouted, "You've got this—dance through it!"

Sam fired, her arrow grazing the Tiger's flank, voice urgent: "Get up, Tate—sync with me!"

Their rhythm clashed at first, the Tiger's growl taunting: "You fight as foes, not allies."

"Stay sharp!" David urged, his fists ready.

Tate's grin faded, Kusini's lesson sinking deeper, Sam's earlier jab in the floods echoing its sting: "You're right—lead, Snake."

She shook her head: "You're part of the Tiger Clan—call the shots, but listen."

Tate nodded: "Left, now!" Sam's arrow flew, missing narrowly as the Tiger advanced, but their moves began aligning.

"Right, strike!" Tate urged, Sam adjusting her aim, their strikes weaving through the relentless attacks.

Gerry yelled, "Nail it—leaps like mine!"

Hana cheered, "Go—rhythm's key!"

Tate's claws synced with Sam's shots, a dance honed through errors, the path quaking as vines erupted in a second phase, whipping like tentacles from the walls, spectral winds howling with visions of Tate's Kusini failure—the altar burning, talisman slipping away in flames.

The Tiger split into fleeting streaks, one lunging at Tate, the other at Sam, emerald eyes glinting with judgment.

Winds nearly pulled Sam over, her bow slipping, but Tate dove, claws anchoring her: "Hold on—unity pulls us through!"

She nodded, arrow piercing a streak as he raked the other, the illusions dissolving into mist.

A third phase surged—rune-triggered floods cascading from the ceiling, waters churning with visions of Sam's overlooked pride, her envy in the wake of Tate's swagger. Gerry leapt in, his Goat agility snagging a vine to steady the path. David's temper flared as vines struck, his katana slicing with honor-fueled precision, channeling fury into focus.

Hana's whip cracked, severing a whipping tendril: "We've got your back—keep dancing!"

The true Tiger reappeared at the pedestal, its growl a final test: "Prove unity, or drown in division."

Tate drew its focus: "Now, Snake!" Sam's arrows struck true, the Tiger fading with a reluctant nod, its emerald eyes softening to approval.

As Tate grasped the talisman, fleeting streaks flickered on the walls—a couple's forms, the girl dissolving into mist, the male reaching in vain, his voice breaking: "No... come back!"

Sheng Xiao's balance twisted in the vision, a cryptic riddle of loss tied to the Prophecy's scrolls, grief heavy in the humid air.

Tate flinched, the talisman's tiger-shaped warmth pulsing like a vow, its gold-blue light a beacon against the chaos.

"What does it mean?" he questioned aloud, the warmth steadying him as the vision faded, a whisper of betrayal lingering like Kusini's scar.

The cavern's glow softened, vines revealing a safe path, the jungle's roar calling them deeper. Tate clutched the talisman, its pulse a vow to evolve Zuri's wisdom: "We danced through the storm—joy claims victory."

Sam's voice softened: "Good work, Tiger." Tate spun her in a brief, triumphant hug, their laughter echoing, bond sealed, joy surging like a flood receded.

Melissa cheered, "That's our team—burnout be damned!"

David nodded, honor satisfied: "Well fought—your unity honors us all."

Gerry grinned: "Bet I outleap you next, Horse!"

Hana flirted back: "Got the spark for it, Dragon?" As she spotted movement, her whip flew, tripping a figure in a black-etched tunic like those from Souris and Kusini.

Tate frowned: "X's mercenaries again?"

Sam nodded: "They're tracking us—be ready, they'll attack like in Souris and Kusini."

Melissa's eyes narrowed: "How many more? A full force?"

Playful taunts faded as suspicion tightened their resolve, the scout whispering ominously, "The storm comes—faster than you know." Lightning pulsed outside, violet arcs sharpening, hope surging amid danger, the talisman's light a beacon in the tempest.

Back at X's fortress, Vincent paced the war room, his serpent scepter flaring green, a holo-vision of Listra's floods unfolding like a chaotic tapestry. He clutched the Ox Talisman, hoping to use its power.

"The Tiger Talisman slips closer to their grasp," he murmured, ambition coiling as he subtly drained energy from the stolen Ox Talisman into his scepter, its sickly glow twisting unnaturally, a scar from Percy's final duel throbbing faintly on his arm—a reminder of that moonlit betrayal.

X stood nearby, eyes blank and flickering for a moment, his will bent like puppet strings under Vincent's veiled control, then snapping back with a shake of his head. Bella leaned against a rune-carved pillar, amber eyes sharp: "Dolore's lightning will claim it—her storm outshines my flames this time."

Lucas leaned in, his bandaged arm healing steadily but tender: "As long as Vincent doesn't twist it first—his scepter's glow feels wrong, draining something from the talisman. And X... he zoned out again."

Bella's mistrust glinted, her thrill tempered by wariness: "We watch him close—if he catches on..."

Their whispers hung heavy, suspicion brewing like the storms outside, Sheng Xiao's balance teetering under their schemes.

Back in the cavern's fading glow, the Guardians emerged into the jungle's embrace, but violet lightning cracked overhead, Dolore's bolt grazing Tate's shoulder in a searing arc.

"They're here!" he roared, team readying for the fight, the talisman's warmth a defiant pulse against the encroaching storm.

Chapter 14: Lightning's Reckoning

Violet lightning cracked overhead, Dolore's bolt grazing Tate's shoulder in a searing arc. "They're here!" he roared, team readying for the fight, the talisman's warmth a defiant pulse against the encroaching storm. Pain lanced through his arm like fire, his grip loosening on the artifact—it slipped from his hip, tumbling toward the mud-slick ground. But Tate's Tiger Clan agility surged; he twisted mid-fall, claws extending to snatch it mid-air, securing it firmly as he rolled to his feet.

"Not losing this—not after Kusini!" he growled, the memory of Bella's flames stealing the Ox Talisman fueling his resolve. *No more failures; this light stays with us.*

"For X!" Dolore hissed from the ridge, her charged fingers weaving arcs of searing energy. "Your quests stirred the storms—X promises real balance!"

The initial assault hit like a thunderclap—bolts lancing through the rain, igniting vines into sparking snares that coiled around the Guardians' ankles, rune-traps humming with unnatural energy drawn from the storm's fury. Tate's instincts fired; he rolled aside, claws raking the earth to free himself, but a mercenary's dagger grazed his other shoulder, drawing a hot line of blood.

"Flank them—don't let the sparks divide us!" he barked, his voice cutting through the chaos, rallying the group as guilt from Kusini flared in his mind.

In that scorched grove, his overconfident strikes had left gaps Bella exploited, the Ox Talisman slipping away in flames. *Not here—not with Listra's heart at stake.* He lunged, claws slashing a mercenary's tunic, the fabric ripping like thunder, his redemption burning hotter than the ozone-scented air, the sharp tang biting his lungs amid the crushed orchids' sweet rot.

Dolore's lightning cracked in Listra's jungle, rain soaking her, a memory of a ruined shrine flashing vividly. X's blade carved through bandits, pulling her from rubble, his sorrowful eyes whispering, "You're worth more."

Her unrequited love burned, a storm fiercer than Vincent's cold whispers urging chaos. Bella's Kusini triumph—X's warm praise—stung like a fresh scar, but her heart clung to X, vowing to claim his gaze. Her bolts seared vines, the Tiger Talisman's glow a prize to eclipse Bella's fire. The jungle's pulse thrummed, her ambition a reckless blaze—she'd win his heart, not just his cause. Each strike fueled her loyalty, her lightning a vow to prove her worth, X's touch an imagined anchor in the chaos, her resolve unyielding despite the storm's wrath, the talisman's light a beacon she'd seize for him alone.

The Guardians rallied, their preparedness a shield— Hana's discovery of the scout had given them moments to brace, drills in the palace yard echoing in their minds.

"Remember how we trained—unity over chaos!" Sam shouted, her Snake Clan bow drawn taut, orange tunic shimmering faintly under wavering torchlight, her keen eyes tracing the attackers' paths with unyielding focus.

Melissa's braid swayed with each poised step, her Monkey Clan agility primed, her sharp grin a bold challenge to the deluge's fury. "Form up—like Jade's simulations!"

Gerry bounded over gnarled roots with Goat Clan nimbleness, flashing a daring smirk, his spirit undaunted by the mire's grasp. David's katana, a sleek blade of Dragon Clan honor, gleamed with quiet menace, his temper held in check by iron discipline honed through years of rigorous training, honor guiding his strike.

Hana's whip coiled at her side, Horse Clan energy crackling like the storm itself, her playful wink sparking a fleeting warmth in David's stoic gaze, a moment of levity amidst the tension: "Time to dance, Dragon—show them our rhythm!"

Sam's arrow, swift and true, pierced the air, but a jagged bolt seared her arm, a white-hot agony rendering it useless, her cry swallowed by the deluge's roar as pain surged through her veins. She dropped to one knee, bow clattering against slick stone, but her pride refused to yield—Kusini's lessons echoing: strategy over pain.

Gritting her teeth, she snatched the bow with her good hand, firing a wild shot that pinned a mercenary's cloak to a tree, buying precious seconds. "I'm not out—cover me!" The wound burned like venom, visions of her clan's overlooked wisdom flashing—envy of Tate's swagger now forged into alliance. She forced another arrow, nocking it awkwardly, her shot grazing a mercenary's thigh, driving him back into the mud.

"Sam!" Melissa shouted, her agile flips weaving through crackling bolts with Monkey Clan grace, outmaneuvering mercenaries' strikes, her defiance a radiant spark in the chaos. She vaulted over a sparking vine, axe cleaving through another trap that threatened to ensnare Gerry, her burnout from endless drills forgotten in the adrenaline surge. Rain plastered her green tunic, mud splattering her face, but her movements were a blur—dodging a bolt that charred the branch she'd just left, her axe embedding in a mercenary's shield, splintering it with a crack that echoed like breaking bones.

Gerry's nimble spins taunted foes, his spear jabbing, laughter defiant: "Missed me again, you fools!" He dodged a bolt that charred the ground where he'd stood, his leaps turning the mire into an ally, but a mercenary's boot caught his leg, sending him sprawling—only for Hana's whip to lash out, coiling around the attacker's wrist and yanking him off balance. Gerry rolled up, spear thrusting to disarm another, his Goat Clan intuition guiding him through the slick footing, each evade a testament to his mother's tales of leaping through adversity.

Hana's whip cracked with unerring accuracy, disrupting Dolore's aim, her voice fierce: "Back off, now!" She spun, whip severing a vine-trap mid-coil, her Horse Clan spark fueling a burst of speed that shielded David from a flanking strike. The rain stung her eyes, but her hijab held firm, rain beading on the fabric, her movements a whirlwind that cracked like thunder, pulling a mercenary into the mud where David's katana could finish the threat.

David's katana carved a relentless path through mercenaries, his honor blazing like a forge stoked by righteous fury. Each swing was disciplined precision, honed in Doragon's misty peaks, his temper channeling into arcs that felled two assailants in quick succession, their blades clanging uselessly against his guard.

Blood mixed with rain on his blade, his Dragon Clan resolve unyielding—echoes of Souris's and Kusini's betrayals, kin turning on their glyphs, now vivid as he parried a local traitor's strike, eyes widening: "Not again—how do floods twist loyalty so quick?"

The turncoat muttered through gritted teeth, "Lost my grove to your 'balance'—X rebuilds what you drown!"

Tate's ferocity flashed, his claws a whirlwind; Sam's defiant arrows, despite her searing pain, struck, their unity a bold rebuke that mocked Dolore's ambition. But Dolore pressed on, her violet eyes narrowing as the Guardians' coordination tightened. A holo-call from Kusini replayed in her mind—Bella's triumphant face flickering, X's voice warm: "Your flames light our path, Bella—victory suits you." The praise stung like a fresh scar, fueling her desperation. She couldn't fail X, not after his mercy in that ruined shrine, pulling her from rubble with sorrowful eyes.

Her unrequited yearning twisted into resolve—she'd eclipse Bella's radiance, claim X's gaze, his heart, as her own. To win his affection, she needed this triumph; Bella's fire had stolen his warmth, but her storm would bind him forever.

Recklessness surged; she overextended, channeling her power to summon natural lightning from the storm's core, violet arcs amplifying into a blinding web that lit the jungle like day.

"Burn with your precious talisman!" she snarled, bolts lancing toward Tate, who shielded the glowing artifact at his hip. The Guardians scattered, locals drawn by the cataclysmic noise emerging from the underbrush, their tiger-stitched tunics vibrant against the gloom, gasping: "Vines charred, earth scarred!" Their voices trembled with sorrow yet kindled with courage, rushing forward to shield the talisman with woven vine-shields, their unity a defiant stand against the devastation—contrasting sharply with the turncoats' fractured loyalty, proving Listra's true spirit rose above the floods.

Tate seized the moment: "Locals, cover the flanks— Guardians, push back!" His claws raked a mercenary's arm, drawing blood, while Sam's one-handed shot grazed Dolore's shoulder, forcing her to falter. Melissa flipped onto a low branch, axe severing a bolt mid-arc, steam hissing as it dissipated. Gerry's spear impaled a trap-vine, pinning it harmlessly, and Hana's whip coiled around Dolore's leg, yanking her off balance.

David charged, katana clashing with a mercenary's blade in a shower of sparks, his honor refusing to let the line break.

The locals formed a human barrier, their chants invoking the White Tiger's protection, vine-shields absorbing stray bolts that crackled harmlessly against rune-etched weaves, their defiance a beacon: "Floods rage, but we rise—unity weaves our strength!"

Dolore's overload peaked—the amplified lightning recoiled, a rogue bolt slamming into her chest like a hammer. Ribs cracked under the impact, agony exploding through her like shattered glass, breath faltering as vision dimmed to black spots. She collapsed, gasping, the storm's wrath turning inward.

Mercenaries, their resolve crumbling like ash, dragged her faltering form into the shadows, retreating in frantic disarray—one pausing to stabilize her with a makeshift bandage, whispering, "Hold on, boss—we'll get you to X."

As Dolore's forces fled, the rain softened to a gentle drizzle, rivers still churning with untamed might, yet the locals' spirits soared, the Tiger Talisman secure, Tate's leadership anchoring its glow, Listra's pride surging.

In the haze of pain, Dolore vowed silently: *I'll heal, eclipse Bella's flames—X will see my storm as his light, his heart mine at last,* imagining his hand on her cheek, a whisper of "Your storm saved me once—now claim your due."

In an abandoned treehouse hotel, its vine-choked platforms creaking under Listra's relentless embrace, mercenaries huddled, their hope strangled by the hideout's shroud, as they activated a holo-link to X, his sword glinting like a shard of midnight in a sleek, holo-lit war room pulsing with strategic control.

"Dolore's collapsed, the talisman lost—she combined her lightning with the natural storm, and it backfired, no escape," one of the assassins stammered, heads bowed under his piercing gaze, his voice trembling with defeat.

X's fist clenched, Dolore's failure a wound to the promise of protection he'd vowed in a ruined shrine, her loss stinging as deeply as Lucas's past injury, when X's pledge to shield his loyal follower had bound them through shared trials.

A flashback gripped him: the shrine's collapse, stones tumbling like judgment, bandits' blades raised over Dolore's crumpled form. His crescent arc had carved through them, pulling her free with steady hands: "I won't let chaos claim you."

Now, her defeat mirrored that vulnerability, his honor demanding action despite the setback. She'd pushed too far, her storm's ambition a mirror of his own vengeance—worry knotted his chest for her safety.

"Lucas, extract them," he ordered, his voice a blade of steel, loyalty binding his command. Lucas gripped his machete in X's fortress, frost biting his bandaged arm, a memory of Souris's frost-dusted campaign searing vividly. His orders faltered, allies lost to thorn traps, honor stripped as screams echoed through icy paths.

X's vow— "Redeem your blade"—ignited his duty. Dolore's failure stung; her extraction was his chance to prove his worth. The rune-etched stone pulsed, Vincent's sickly scepter glow taunting his resolve. He'd save her, counter Jade's Guardians, and reclaim his edge. His machete gleamed, vowing to carve redemption through Listra's chaos. Lucas nodded, his departure swift, driven by a loyalty forged in past wounds.

Before leaving, Lucas pulled Bella aside in the fortress's dim corridor, his voice low: "Watch Vincent close while I'm gone—his scepter's glow... it's poisoning X's edge. If he zones out again, signal me—be careful; we can't get caught."

Bella nodded, fire flickering warily in her amber eyes: "Get Dolore safe; her storm's too fierce to lose. We'll hold here—

we need her lightning to counter Vincent's schemes if he turns on us."

Bella's suspicion sharpened, Vincent's shadow deepening her doubt. Vincent's eyes glinted, plotting anew, his cold resolve masking a frustration that Jade's victory had thwarted his schemes, his plans burning brighter, undeterred. The scepter's sickly glow pulsed faintly, a subtle drain on the stolen Ox Talisman hidden in his chambers, ambition coiling as he envisioned the next strike—perhaps Coinin's tech traps bent to his will.

Anger flashed in his eyes, his scarred hands clenching—Percy's final duel a thorn: "Jade wins again—her light dims our schemes. No more setbacks; Coinin falls next, or I twist harder." Outside, the fortress's unnatural blizzards eased, winds slowing to a whisper, faint sunlight piercing the mists—a reluctant respite from Sheng Xiao's mending balance, fueling Vincent's rage further, his fist slamming the rune-etched table, cracks spiderwebbing like his fractured plans.

In the palace's grand hall, its marble columns shimmering under holo-lights, the Great Race mural pulsing faintly, Jade paced with Cade, her scepter humming faintly. She pulled him into a shadowed alcove, Hana's brazen flirtations a persistent thorn.

"Cade, Hana's spark—unburdened, bold—does it draw you? My crown weighs us both, chains my heart... what if I'm not enough without it?" Her amethyst eyes searched his mismatched gaze, telepathic bond thrumming, "You're my strength—don't let her steal it."

Vulnerability cracked her regal mask, tears stinging as memories surged—childhood festivals where his laughter had been her light, travels tearing them apart, Percy's updates her lifeline. "I've hidden behind duty too long—tell me, is there us beyond the throne? My heart's yours, but fear whispers I'm just the empress to you, while Hana offers freedom without the weight."

Cade's heart ached, his love unspoken since those days, yearning to confess: "Jade, you're my only light—duty chains us, but not my heart. I've loved you since we were kids, your laugh my anchor through every shadow. You're more than the crown— you're everything. Hana's spark is nothing compared—"

Their hands brushed, a spark igniting, lips nearing in the dim light, breaths mingling in a promise of vulnerability shared, but Tate's holo-link flickered alive, interrupting. "Empress, we've got it—the talisman's secure, glowing strong against my hip. Here, see its light."

He held it up, gold-blue radiance pulsing through the hologram, Jade leaning in with wide eyes, Cade murmuring, "Its light... it's mending already."

Tate continued: "We triumphed over Dolore; her storm broke before ours did. But that vision in the cavern... fleeting streaks of a couple, the girl dissolving into mist, him reaching— 'No... come back!'—it twisted Sheng Xiao like a knot tightening. And the rains? Down to a drizzle now; Listra's sighing relief."

Jade nodded, relief flooding her, the moment's intimacy lingering like a promise deferred. "Well done, Tate—respite comes. Guardians, check your clans; report improvements."

Omar holo-linked Kusini: "Plains mending—crops sprouting faint green, irrigation ditches flowing clear."

Veronica pinged Souris: "Frost thawing; thorns receding, icy grip loosening on the paths."

Doug checked Ged: "Vines blooming anew, coastal cliffs vibrant with herbal scents." Patricia scanned Cochan: "Silos stabilizing; dust settling, wheat dust turning to golden promise."

Gerry beamed via link: "Listra's platforms hold strong, orchids blooming brighter!"

Alice's Rabbit Clan tablet hummed, tracking signals: "Realms easing—balance stirs, Coinin's tech humming steadier."

Ryder grinned. "Cheer about it—victory's ours!"

In the Imperial City, wilted cherry blossoms stirred, petals unfurling with fresh color, lotus ponds clearing as the blight receded—a tangible sigh from Sheng Xiao's wounds.

Back in Listra's scorched clearing, amid the easing drizzle, the Guardians regrouped, the talisman's light unyielding, a radiant vow of their hard-won triumph. Sam's arm throbbed with relentless pain, yet her resolve had burned fiercer through the fight, a fire no wound could quench until now, her collapse dramatic in Tate's arms, spirit tempered by the crucible of Listra's trials.

Locals, their faces etched with grief yet alight with defiance, brought bandages woven with ancient herbs, cleared debris with steady hands, and meticulously rebuilt ritual platforms flanking the cave shrine, sacred for White Tiger dances that honored the talisman's legacy, their resilience a radiant beacon that pulsed through the jungle's heart. Chants rose softly, invoking Pixiu guardians, vines woven into fresh motifs that hummed with renewed energy, the drizzle's patter a gentle accompaniment to their unyielding joy.

An elder shared a flood legend mid-rebuild: "Our ancestors danced vines into bridges, turning rage to rhythm— rising above adversity, as you did today."

Tate nodded, reflecting: "Their spirit... it's what pulled us through, weaving chaos into strength."

Melissa, her voice calm yet commanding, guided the effort, "Treat Sam, clear the platforms," her Monkey Clan leadership anchoring the recovery, her steady guidance rallying locals who offered healing salves, their spirits unbowed by the devastation, their hands weaving tradition into every restored plank.

A treetop hotel, its platforms swaying gently above the jungle's lush embrace, welcomed them with steaming curries, their spices mingling with the scent of rain-soaked orchids, the treehouses glowing with Listra's indomitable spirit, winding paths framed by vibrant ferns pulsing with the land's enduring heartbeat. Locals danced, their vine-dances weaving intricate stories of triumph and resilience, curries simmering with communal warmth, their tiger-stitched tunics vibrant against the drizzle's gentle caress. Healers patched wounds—Sam's arm bound in herb-soaked wraps, her collapse eased by salves that cooled the venomous burn, Tate's grazes mended with orchid poultices that numbed the sting, each application a ritual of gratitude.

Tate, his presence a steady anchor, supported Sam, his voice soft but resolute: "You held us together, Snake," their bond forged in the fire of Listra's trials, unbreakable as the talisman's glow. Resilience forged Tate and Sam's unity, Zuri's wisdom anchoring their spirit, their bond defying the storm.

In the treehouse's quiet nook, Tate clutched the talisman, vowing silently: *Kusini's failure won't repeat in Coinin—I'll protect this light, lead without ego.* Sam stirred weakly, her proud eyes meeting his: "We did it—your claws, my aim... unbreakable."

As they prepared to depart, Listra's drizzle a gentle caress, its rivers swollen but no longer raging, Sam and Tate stood shoulder to shoulder, their reflections woven with quiet pride.

"We're stronger together, forged in this jungle's heart," he said.

Nearby, locals discussed the captured turncoats—bound with vines, their false promises exposed: "X vowed balance, but these Guardians delivered it—the rains ease because of them, not his schemes." Tate nodded: "We'll report this to Jade; her light mends what betrayal breaks."

Hana leaned closer to David, sharing a steaming bowl of curry, their eyes locking in a moment of shared warmth, her playful grin drawing a rare smile from his guarded heart. She traced a finger along his arm, voice soft: "That katana

swing...saved me back there. You're more than honor, Dragon—
you're my spark in the storm."

David's flush deepened, his hand covering hers: "And
you're the rhythm that steadies my fire, Hana. Let's face Coinin
together."

"Are you smiling now, Dragon?" she teased, her voice a
melody that softened his stoic guard, their bond glowing gently.

Gerry, his Goat Clan mischief undimmed, taunted Melissa
with a playful grin.

"Leading us now, Monkey, or just stealing my spotlight?"
he asked.

Her sharp retort, laced with a grin, echoed through the
clearing, their banter a vibrant thread in Listra's tapestry. Tate's
vow carried the talisman's radiant light, uniting them as Listra's
spirit guided their path to the Rabbit Talisman, their journey
turning to Coinin, its trials beckoning.

Chapter 15: Tensions and Bonds

Jade stood in the palace's grand hall, marble columns etched with Sheng Xiao's zodiac beasts—dragons curling, tigers prowling, rats scurrying—gleaming under soft holo-lights. The air carried jasmine, heavy with anticipation, mingling with the faint metallic hum of holo-projectors casting ethereal zodiac motifs across polished floors.

Her holo-link flickered to life, summoning Listra's Guardians: Tate, Sam, Melissa, Gerry, David, and Hana.

"Guardians, your triumph over the White Tiger's trial is a beacon for Sheng Xiao," Jade said, her voice steady and warm, eyes alight with pride as she addressed the flickering images. "Tate, your leadership turned the jungle's fury into unity, Sam, your precision pierced the storm, Melissa, your agility wove through chaos, Gerry, your leaps defied the floods, David, your honor held the line, Hana, your spark rallied the dance. The talisman's golden glow in Tate's claws restores hope. Well done. Return to the palace swiftly and we'll celebrate your victory here. Sam, get that arm treated upon arrival," she urged, concern etching her amethyst eyes as she studied the bandaged wound on the holo-feed.

Memories of Listra's orchid paths and tiger-stitched tunics warmed her mind, a vibrant echo of resilience amid the floods that had nearly drowned the realm.

The next day, the hall's polished floor shook as the Guardians arrived from Listra, their footsteps echoing like a triumphant drumbeat. Palace guards roared in salute, their zodiac-emblazoned armor clinking as they parted to allow entry.

Sam led the way, her arm freshly bandaged but her orange tunic worn and mud-flecked, Snake Clan spirit unbroken despite the limp in her step from exhaustion.

Tate followed, his grin wide, Tiger Clan pride gleaming in his amber eyes as he held the talisman aloft, its gold-blue radiance bathing the hall in a warm light that seemed to chase away lingering echoes of doubt.

The full ensemble of Guardians converged—Tate's group joining Omar, Veronica, Doug, Patricia, Alice, Ryder, and the others already in the palace.

Cheers erupted, a tapestry of bonds reforming: Melissa clapped Alice on the back, Monkey and Rabbit Clans sharing a laugh over tech tweaks that could've aided Listra's traps, Alice's glasses fogging slightly from the humid Listra air still clinging to their clothes, Gerry bounded toward Ryder, Goat and Rooster Clans trading jests about "strutting through floods," their laughter booming like Ryder's cannon.

Doug's loyal embrace pulled Sam into a steady hug, his Dog Clan warmth a balm for her weary frame.

Omar's broad frame enveloped Tate in a brotherly clasp, while Veronica's Rat Clan wit sparked with a quip to Hana: "Back from the jungle, Horse? Your whip must've tamed more than vines."

The air thrummed with camaraderie, the talisman's glow symbolizing not just victory, but the weaving of their fates tighter against X's unraveling chaos, mud-caked boots leaving faint trails on the marble as they gathered, the scent of Listra's orchids still faint on their tunics.

Patricia welcomed Melissa with Pig Clan calm, sharing a quick strategy tip on Coinin's illusions, her pink-gold runes glinting as she adjusted a gauntlet on Melissa's arm.

Doug nodded to Gerry, their Dog and Goat Clans bonding over tales of leaping through adversity, while Alice eagerly examined the talisman with Ryder, Rabbit and Rooster Clans speculating on how its energy could sync with Coinin's tech, the group's energy a vibrant mosaic of zodiac harmonies.

"Zuri said, 'Joy rises above floods,'" Tate told Jade, his voice warm as he presented the talisman, placing it reverently on a rune-etched pedestal where it hummed in sync with the Great Race mural overhead, its gold-blue light merging with the Rat Talisman's steady pulse and the Yang Scroll's golden veins.

The harmony rippled through the room, a soft vibration that Jade felt in her chest, easing the altar's burning scars from Kusini and tilting Sheng Xiao's balance further toward the light, realms sighing as rivers calmed and crops stirred anew.

As the group settled around a massive oak table laden with fresh fruits and zodiac-etched platters, Jade raised a goblet filled with sparkling nectar, her voice ringing out: "To Listra's Guardians—your triumph mirrors the Rat Talisman's victory, weaving Sheng Xiao's balance stronger. May the Tiger's roar guide us forward!"

The Guardians lifted their goblets—Snake, Tiger, Monkey, Goat, Dragon, Horse motifs glinting in the light—cheers echoing through the hall, a moment of pure joy before the conversation turned grave, the clink of glasses like a seal on their unity. Omar raised his Ox goblet high, Veronica's Rat one clinking against it, their smiles reflecting the group's shared victory.

Tate leaned forward, claws tapping the wood. "X's influence is spreading—those local turncoats in Listra, they weren't just mercenaries. Floods destroyed their groves, and X's whispers promised 'real balance,' turning kin against us."

Sam nodded, her bandaged arm resting on the table. "Like Souris and Kusini—betrayals from within. He preys on desperation, offering power where we bring trials."

David's fist clenched, his Dragon Clan honor flaring: "It twists loyalty...we saw it firsthand, locals fighting their own for a false promise."

Melissa chimed in, her wit sharp: "And his lieutenants...Bella's flames in Kusini scorched the altar before we could react, Lucas's machete in Souris nearly cleaved our team, now Dolore's lightning... she overextended, but next time?"

Gerry nodded, tossing a pebble idly: "We were ready in Listra, scouted, trained. That's why we held the talisman."

Jade's eyes darkened, the weight of the crown pressing. "We can't let divisions fester. I'll increase communications by sending holo-broadcasts to all clans, envoys sharing our quests' purpose. Transparency mends what fear breaks. We'll show

Sheng Xiao's true balance lies in unity, not X's schemes. And for his agents, we prepare: study their patterns, counter their elements. Bella's fire meets our water strategies, Lucas's brute force our cunning dodges, Dolore's storms our grounded endurance."

The Guardians murmured agreement, Alice syncing notes on her tablet: "I'll map influence patterns—predict where he strikes next, and profile those lieutenants for weak spots."

Their resolve hardened, a plan forged amid the hall's jasmine-scented air, the two talismans' light casting long silhouettes that seemed to retreat under their collective will.

In the palace library, Patricia studied Cochan's festival records, the scent of parchment dust and candle flickers stirring a memory of betrayal at fourteen.

Her generosity—sharing rare wine at a festival—led to a friend stealing her family's recipe, naivety stinging her Pig Clan heart.

"Trust wisely," her mother urged, her words a lesson in boundaries. Now, the Guardians' unity sparked hope—could she balance generosity with caution in Coinin's tech traps?

The library's glow pulsed, her resolve hardening to protect her team, not just give blindly. Her gauntlet's pink-gold runes flared, a vow to weave trust with strength, the candlelight a beacon for the Rabbit Talisman's challenge, her naivety tempered by Sheng Xiao's growing balance.

Omar and Veronica lingered by a relic pedestal nearby, their Ox and Rat Clan strengths aligning in quiet harmony. Their fingers brushed as Veronica traced a rune, her green eyes meeting his with a soft smile.

"Your mace pulled us through Souris—now Listra's safe because of Tate's claws. We're unbreakable, Ox." Omar's hand steadied hers, his voice low: "And your spark lights the way, Rat. Souris's thorns couldn't dim it."

Their bond sparked hope against Jade's quiet doubts, a tender kiss sealing their vow amid the hall's hum, reminding all that love endured Sheng Xiao's trials, their embrace a brief sanctuary before the next quest called.

In the palace armory, Tate polished his claw gloves, the scent of oil and steel grounding him as Listra's unity flashed in his mind. His claws had synced with Sam's arrows, their rivalry forging a bond that turned the jungle's storm.

A childhood test—flashy strikes missing a holo-target— stung, the crowd's laughter echoing Jade's warning: "Be serious." Sam's wisdom had guided him in Listra, her aim steadying his fire.

"We're stronger together," she'd said, her words a spark in the cavern's glow.

The armory's clangs echoed, his heart realizing bravery shone through teamwork, not ego. The Tiger Talisman's warmth pulsed, a vow to lead without swagger in Coinin, its tech traps no match for their unity. He nodded to himself, claws gleaming, ready to face the Rabbit's illusions with a team forged in Listra's crucible.

Gerry tossed a pebble at Tate, smirking: "Still boasting, Tiger?"

Tate laughed, clapping his shoulder, their banter filling the hall like a lively echo of Listra's dances. Holo-lights pulsed, zodiac beasts watching from the columns as if approving the Guardians' unbreakable spirit.

Jade's resolve deepened, Zuri's words a guiding star, her heart steady despite love's uncertainty, the talismans' glow a beacon for the quests ahead.

The next day, Jade entered the training courtyard, stone tiles scarred by drills, ivy swaying in the warm breeze carrying hints of blooming cherry blossoms—Sheng Xiao's mending touch. She set her ceremonial scepter aside, its golden glow fading, and drew a slender blade, its edge flashing in the midday sun.

Cade stood ready, his knives gleaming, their swift strikes echoing Percy's old training cuts, a memory flickering as blades clashed.

Sweat beaded on Jade's brow, her grip tightening as Hana's flirtation burned in her memory—Hana's hand grazing Cade's arm at their arrival, her teasing purr, "Miss me, Cade?" echoing like a taunt.

Fear of losing him to Hana's charm drove Jade's blade wild. Her strikes veered, slicing air near Cade's chest, his stumble a flinch, eyes clouded with hurt. The unfinished conversation from the alcove haunted her—her vulnerability laid bare, words of love interrupted by Tate's call, leaving her heart exposed and aching. *What if Hana's freedom won him over?*

The jealousy surged, a storm she channeled into her swings, but it only fueled the wildness, her mind racing with doubts: *Duty chains me, but does it dim his light for her bold spark?* She paused, blade trembling, the courtyard's breeze doing little to cool the fire of her fears.

"What's wrong, Jade?" he asked, voice low, concern etching his mismatched gaze.

Just then, Hana sauntered into the courtyard, pausing to bow respectfully to Jade with a graceful dip, her Horse Clan energy momentarily subdued before she turned, tugging Cade to "help" Sam with a training drill, her smirk sharp as a blade, bold but laced with uncertainty after Patricia's words.

Cade glanced at Jade, seeking permission, but she waved him off, eyes cold, her hurt stinging deeper—a storm of jealousy raging unchecked. The interruption gnawed at Jade, her unfinished confession hanging like an unresolved rune—words left unsaid, vulnerability exposed but unreciprocated in that moment, the alcove's intimacy now a distant ache as Hana's laugh rang out, twisting the knife of her fears.

She gripped her blade tighter, channeling the pain into a solitary strike against a training dummy, the wood splintering under her force, duty her only shield.

David's katana clashed in the courtyard, Hana's whip snapping nearby, her grin sparking a Listra jungle memory.

Her whip cracked through rain, saving him from the flood, her Horse Clan fire igniting admiration. Her flirtation with Cade stung, his Dragon Clan honor warring with yearning for her spark. The scent of sweat and steel grounded him, vowing to prove his worth in Coinin's tech traps, his katana a blade of trust and discipline.

Her boldness drew him, but Cade's presence loomed—could he claim her heart without losing his honor? His strikes sharpened, each cut a vow to rise above pain, the courtyard's clangs echoing his resolve to face the Rabbit Talisman's illusions with a steady heart.

David stood nearby, his katana clinking as he turned from Hana's glance, Dragon Clan honor hiding a quiet sting deepened by her pursuit of Cade, his temper simmering like a coiled dragon ready to unleash with the flirtation a dagger to his pride.

"Hana's games end here," he muttered, channeling the hurt into his strikes, katana whistling through the air with renewed ferocity.

Patricia noticed, pulling him aside later: "Let honor guide your heart, Dragon—not pain." But the wound lingered, his quiet resolve hardening for Coinin's trials.

Jade turned, her mind fleeing Hana's shadow, her holo-link humming as she assigned Alice, Melissa, David, Patricia, and Ryder to Coinin's Rabbit Talisman quest, duty masking her pain.

Their faces flickered on the screen, Coinin's quest a challenge looming ahead—holo-puzzles and tech illusions that would test wit over brawn. The courtyard's jasmine breeze stirred, Listra's spirit lifting her resolve, her heart fighting love's weight amid the unresolved tension.

By the palace gardens, Sam, Melissa, and Patricia wove zodiac charms from jasmine petals, the vines' rustle soothing as a gentle breeze carried floral scents.

Sam's voice softened, "My pride almost broke us in Listra—Tate's claws outshone my arrows, but we managed to work together."

Melissa nodded, "Mico's drills burned me out, but Listra taught me to lead through chaos."

Patricia's gauntlet glowed pink-gold, "Cochan's fields taught patience—trust takes time."

Their laughter mingled, charms glowing—snake, monkey, pig—a bond forged against Coinin's looming illusions.

Sam's bandaged arm steadied, Melissa's grin defied burnout, and Patricia's calm anchored their fears, the jasmine's perfume a vow to face the next quest as sisters, their unity a shield against X's divisive whispers, the gardens' bloom a mirror of Sheng Xiao's mending heart

In X's fortress, a sterile medical room glowed with faint runes, the antiseptic air sharp against Dolore's skin, mingling with the metallic tang of healing salves.

X knelt beside her, binding her scorched chest, his hands steady as he wrapped splintered ribs, consulting a mysterious healer who applied rune-etched poultices to knit bone and soothe burns.

Memories of a lost love softened his resolve, his duty to his troops firm, but worry creased his brow—Dolore's storm had been his edge, and her injury a blow to their cause.

"We'll get you back. Ged's vines hold rare herbs. I'll send scouts if needed," he murmured, his voice laced with concern, planning her recovery as carefully as a battle strategy.

Dolore's brown eyes flickered, her whisper frail, "You're here."

Her fingers brushed his wrist, love surging, fierce despite pain. She clung to his presence, her heart tethered to his quiet strength, visions of his sorrowful eyes in the shrine fueling her will to heal.

X's voice was low: "Rest, Dolore, your lightning will strike again." His concern deepened their bond, a leader's care masking his own vulnerabilities.

In a shadowed war room, Vincent paced, his spellbook's green runes casting light across the stone.

"I'll crush Coinin's tech with my magic," he declared, his eyes glinting with ambition, plotting chaos for the Festival of Lanterns, where holo-floats and pulsing circuits would dance, Listra's tiger-stitched legacy a distant thorn. "Jade's victories mock us—Coinin will be her downfall, my scepter twisting her precious balance, sabotaging the festival with corrupted runes that turn illusions against her Guardians."

Rage boiled as he slammed his fist on the table, cracks forming.

Turning to X, Vincent pressed: "Let me lead the Rabbit hunt. Lucas, Bella, Dolore had their shots. With remote support from them, my magic will outdo Jade's light."

X nodded, his trust firm: "I trust you, Vincent—win this, and they'll support remotely. Bring the talisman...our cause depends on it."

In a dim corridor, Lucas gripped Bella's shoulder: "Have you noticed something weird about Vincent, Bella? It's wrong…"

They peeked from shadows, their whispers hiding fear, as Vincent's scepter pulsed, green runes flaring, X's spellbook writhing.

Bella's eyes narrowed, mistrust glinting: "He's twisting X—zoned eyes, blank commands. When Dolore heals, she'll see it too." Starlight cast Vincent's shadow long, the balcony's runes humming, X's veiled design coiling with Sheng Xiao's doom, their worry a seed of potential rebellion.

Cade stood in the palace's training hall, its holo-screens flickering with Coinin's schematics, holo-floats glowing for the Festival of Lanterns, their Rabbit motifs pulsing with Sheng Xiao's spark. The air was sharp with sweat and steel, the montage of preparation unfolding like a symphony of resolve.

Alice's Rabbit Clan precision calibrated a training drone, her fingers swift on a holo-pad, its Rabbit runes flickering as she tweaked its settings, her focus unyielding, glasses catching the light as she simulated Coinin's illusion traps, solving a mid-air puzzle while dodging simulated bolts.

Melissa's Monkey Clan agility weaved through laser grids, her braid swinging, a blur of motion that dodged holographic snares with flips and rolls, her axe gleaming as she cleaved virtual targets.

David's Dragon Clan katana sliced through targets, his strikes precise, each cut a testament to his discipline, channeling his hurt over Hana into focused fury that shattered drone after drone. Patricia's Pig Clan calm steadied a mended gauntlet, her hands gentle but sure, reinforcing shields with pink-gold runes that hummed against simulated attacks.

Ryder's Rooster Clan boldness taunted a sparring bot, his laughter echoing as his cannon boomed low-warning shots, testing defenses with defiant crows. Their unity forged strength for Coinin's quest, a challenge looming on the horizon, its trials a test of their bond.

Hana leaned close to David, tossing her hair, her voice teasing: "Miss me, Dragon?"

Her grin faltered as he glared.

"Focus, Hana!" he said, his katana striking harder, eyes distant, Dragon Clan honor masking a quiet pain deepened by her pursuit of Cade.

Patricia pulled Hana aside, her voice gentle but firm: "Stop chasing two hearts, Hana! David values honor, not games. Reflect on what you truly want: bold sparks fade if built on shifting sands."

Hana's eyes narrowed, her Horse Clan energy dimming as she reconsidered, crossing her arms, uncertainty flickering amid her bold facade, Patricia's words echoing like a wake-up call.

In that moment, Hana's mind raced: Cade's enigma tempted with mystery, but David's steady honor offered a foundation she craved—could she build with either, or was her boldness a mask for indecision?

Melissa nudged David, grinning: "Lighten up, we're a team!"

David's lips twitched, a rare smile breaking through, her warmth easing his guarded heart. Jade's holo-link buzzed from the throne room, her voice cutting through: "The realm's future rests on our next move."

Cade's thoughts drifted to his reunion with Jade at fifteen, a flashback surging: The palace gardens bloomed with jasmine, petals drifting like soft rain as she stepped from the carriage, her red hair a vibrant flame against the green foliage. His heart had raced, the years of separation melting away in her smile.

"You're back," he'd stammered, mismatched eyes locking on her amethyst gaze, her laugh a melody that anchored him through every trial of training and duty.

"I missed this," she'd said, her hand brushing his, igniting a love that burned steady, unspoken until now. Now, that jasmine scent lingered in the hall's chaos, a reminder of unspoken bonds.

In the palace's dining hall, holo-schematics of Coinin's tech-laden spires glowed with Rabbit motifs, Sheng Xiao's pulse guiding their next move.

Tate clutched the Tiger Talisman, its gold-blue glow steady, as he and Sam reviewed mission plans, their Tiger-Snake unity sharpened by Listra's trials, Sam's bandaged arm steady as she nodded: "Coinin's ready for us, Tiger."

Melissa's wit blazed, tracing holo-routes, her strategy rallying Alice and Patricia, their eyes bright with purpose.

Hana faced David in the corner, her whip snapping with Horse Clan boldness, voice teasing yet uncertain: "Still mad, Dragon?" David's katana sliced with Dragon Clan precision, eyes cold.

"Honor doesn't play games, Hana."

Gerry tossed a twig, Goat Clan mischief sparking: "Melissa, planning or just bossing us?"

She laughed: "Watch and learn, Goat!"

Doug's Dog Clan sword clashed nearby, his loyalty anchoring the team, a quiet vow for Coinin's trials. Alice's tablet flickered with Rabbit runes, her tweaks sharpening their tech edge.

Jade's holo-link buzzed, her voice resolute: "The Rabbit Talisman awaits—bring it home."

The Guardians' resolve flared, Coinin's challenge beckoning, Sheng Xiao's spirit uniting them. As plates cleared, a group reflection stirred: Tate leaned back, "Listra taught us— adversity bends, but joy straightens. Those floods... we rose above, just like Zuri's ancestors."

Sam nodded: "And with Coinin's illusions ahead, we weave that resilience into our plans—unity against the tricks." Their words wove a tapestry of hope, Listra's lessons a shield for the trials to come.

Later, from the throne room, Jade broadcasted a realm-wide message, her image flickering on holo-screens across Sheng Xiao.

"People of the realms, our Guardians have secured the Rat and Tiger Talismans, easing the floods and mending our balance. As Coinin's Festival of Lanterns approaches, know we support its lights—envoys will share our quests, fostering unity. Together, we rise above chaos."

The message echoed, a call to harmony, the talismans' light amplifying her words. Across the realms, villagers in Listra cheered as rivers calmed, farmers in Kusini watched crops sprout, elders in Souris saw thorns recede—hope stirring like a gentle wind.

Chapter 16: Coinin's Festival

Coinin's tech-city thrummed with an electric vitality that seemed to pulse straight from Sheng Xiao's heart, its neon spires piercing the twilight sky like glowing circuit-veins etched into the heavens. Drones zipped through the air in synchronized swarms, their sleek metallic bodies weaving intricate patterns that cast shimmering digital shadows across the sealed streets below.

The Festival of Lanterns had transformed the city into a living tapestry of light and sound: zodiac holo-lanterns floated overhead, their holographic forms shifting between rabbits darting through starry fields and tigers prowling with ethereal grace, all infused with the subtle hum of Sheng Xiao's ancient pulse.

Circuit-shrines dotted the avenues, where clans gathered to offer coded prayers to the Moon Rabbit, their screens flickering with rune-infused algorithms that promised good fortune and technological harmony.

The air was thick with the tantalizing scents of festival fare—circuit-fried dumplings with golden crusts etched in glowing zodiac patterns, sizzling zodiac skewers threaded with spiced meats and vegetables that popped with tech-infused flavors, and holo-spiced tea steaming from circuit-etched cups, its tangy aroma blending citrus and synthetic ozone in a way that made the tongue tingle with innovation.

AI-synthesized flutes played melodies that wove Sheng Xiao's ancient notes into modern harmonies, their sounds echoing off the spires and mingling with the laughter of revelers. Holo-dancers in silver tunics spun across elevated platforms, their movements a hypnotic tribute to the Moon Rabbit's legend—graceful leaps that left trails of digital stardust in the air.

Clans from across the realms crowded the booths, raffling AI drones and competing in holo-games, their cheers broadcast realm-wide on massive holo-screens, fostering a sense of unity that had been sorely needed after the chaos of recent weeks.

The festival wasn't just a celebration: it was a testament to Coinin's ingenuity, where every booth and shrine told a story of innovation born from necessity. Vendors hawked glowing trinkets—tiny holo-amulets that projected personalized fortunes, or circuit-woven scarves that shifted colors based on the wearer's mood, drawing from Sheng Xiao's emotional pulse.

Children darted between legs, chasing after floating drone-balloons shaped like playful rabbits, their laughter a bright counterpoint to the deeper hum of the city's grid. Elders from distant realms like Kusini and Listra shared tales around communal holo-fires, their voices blending with the AI flutes in rhythmic harmony.

One such group, clad in mud-flecked tunics from Listra's recovering jungles, marveled at the tech, whispering how the Tiger Talisman's glow had finally calmed their floods, allowing them to travel here for the first time in years.

The energy was palpable, a vibrant mosaic of lights, sounds, and scents that wrapped around the Guardians like a digital embrace, reminding them that Sheng Xiao's realms were interconnected threads in a grand tapestry.

At Coinin's School of Technology, a towering spire of glass and circuits pulsing with neon veins, students gathered in a ritual chamber under a dome etched with lunar grids. They synced holo-pads to the glowing arrays, circuits humming like a symphony as zodiac rabbit motifs flickered to life.

Clansfolk chanted in unison, "Code weaves harmony," their voices echoing off the walls lined with Sheng Xiao's electronics hubs—massive servers whirring with data streams that powered the realms.

Alice observed from the edge, her own pad glowing in sync, the ritual's energy sparking her resolve. Neon glows danced across faces, honing skills forged in innovation's forge, a testament to Coinin's role as Sheng Xiao's tech heart. The chamber thrummed with promise, circuits aligning under the moon's gaze, fueling Alice for the Moon Rabbit's riddle ahead.

Since the Guardians had claimed the Tiger Talisman in Listra's flooded jungles, Sheng Xiao's energy had begun to stabilize. Power outages that once plagued Coinin's grids had faded to mere flickers, harvests in Kusini swelled with renewed vigor, and even the lingering scars from Souris's frost and Kusini's altar burn seemed to heal under the talisman's gold-blue glow.

But tonight, the festival's climax—the Moon Rabbit's midnight riddle—would test that fragile balance. Sparked by the Guardians' calling and Empress Jade's summons, the riddle was no mere tradition: it was a talisman challenge, one that only Alice, the Rabbit Clan guardian, could face this year. The weight of it hung in the air like an unspoken prophecy, drawing eyes from every corner of Sheng Xiao.

Whispers rippled through the crowd: Would Alice's code hold against the Moon Rabbit's cunning? Or would threats from X's schemes—echoes of Bella's flames or Dolore's lightning—disrupt the harmony?

Alice gripped her holo-pad tightly, its screen displaying a detailed map of Coinin's grid, her Rabbit Clan precision cutting through the festival's bustling chaos with unerring focus. She stood at the edge of a crowded booth, the neon lights reflecting off her glasses as she adjusted a flickering algorithm.

Her heart raced, a familiar knot of shyness twisting in her stomach—why did crowds always make her feel so exposed, like a glitch in the system?

Memories of her holo-grid trial flashed unbidden: the arena aglow with pulsing circuits, her fingers flying over the pad as she outmaneuvered Lillith's sluggish loops and Kai's crashing arrays, the crowd's roar crowning her as guardian.

But that victory had come with a price—envy from her peers that still lingered like a bad code. Tonight, with the Rabbit Talisman at stake, she couldn't afford doubt. Sheng Xiao's tech heart depended on her. What if her code faltered under the Moon Rabbit's gaze, unraveling the stability they'd fought so hard for in Souris, Kusini, and Listra?

As if summoned by her thoughts, Lillith and Kai emerged from the throng of revelers, their silver tunics glinting under the circuit-beacons like sharpened blades. Lillith's eyes narrowed, her posture rigid with the same resentment that had simmered since that fateful trial.

"Look who's playing guardian tonight," she sneered, her voice slicing through the festival's hum like a corrupted signal. "You don't belong up there, Alice. That trial was a fluke since your code barely held together."

Kai crossed his arms, his sneer matching hers, jealousy burning in his gaze like a live wire short-circuiting. "Coinin needs a real guardian. We should be the ones facing the Moon Rabbit. Your 'precision' crashed us out last time, remember?"

Alice's cheeks flushed, her grip on the holo-pad tightening until her knuckles whitened. The memory surged clearer now: the holo-grid arena, a vast dome of swirling code under Coinin's central spire, the air thick with the ozone scent of overclocked processors. She had entered as an underdog, her family's quiet lab in the outer districts far from the elite clans' polished academies.

Lillith had started strong, her loops elegant but predictable, weaving a digital web that Alice unraveled with a clever subroutine. Kai's arrays had been aggressive, crashing against her defenses like waves on Ged's shores, but she'd anticipated the flaws—overloaded variables, unchecked recursions—and turned them against him.

The crowd's roar had drowned out their protests as the judges declared her victor, but their glares had followed her ever since, whispers of "lucky glitch" echoing in clan halls. Now, under the festival's glaring lights, those old wounds reopened.

"That trial was fair," Alice said, her voice steadier than she felt, pushing back against the shyness that threatened to silence her. "I earned this—just like we'll earn the talisman tonight."

Lillith laughed, a sharp, cruel bark. "Prove it, then. Or watch your code crumble like Kai's did."

The confrontation drew stares from nearby clans, tension crackling like a pending glitch, but Alice held her ground, her resolve hardening.

This wasn't just about the riddle, it was about proving she belonged, not just to them, but to herself.

Melissa bounded forward beside her, her Monkey Clan braid bouncing wildly as she eyed a nearby holo-game duel booth, its virtual targets flashing in vibrant neon arcs.

"Alice, let's duel! Come on, it'll loosen you up before the big riddle!" Her grin was wide and infectious, her green tunic catching the festival lights in a way that made her seem like part of the spectacle.

This was Melissa's first Festival of Lanterns—a thrill she'd missed during years of grueling jungle training in Mico's wilds, where Monkey Clan duties had kept her swinging from vines rather than dancing under neon spires. The energy here was intoxicating, a far cry from the burnout she'd felt after Kusini's fiery battles and Listra's floods. "Look at all this! Holo-dancers, drones everywhere—it's like the whole realm's alive!"

Spotting Patricia nearby, Melissa waved her over, the two girls converging amid the bustling booth. Patricia, with her Pig Clan calm, handed Melissa a steaming cup of holo-spiced tea, the tangy vapor curling between them like a shared secret.

"First time here? It's overwhelming at first, but let it fuel you," Patricia said, her voice a soothing anchor, pink-gold runes on her gauntlet glowing faintly.

Melissa sipped, the spice zinging through her, and leaned in. "Back in Mico, training was endless—vaulting through data-vines, dodging sim-traps that mimicked real threats. No festivals, just survival drills. Remember Kusini? That fire nearly broke me, but your calm kept us grounded."

Patricia nodded, her eyes softening with memory. "Cochan's fields taught me endurance—harvesting under dust storms, mending silos with steady hands. We balance each other, Monkey. Your agility, my strength—it's what'll get Alice through tonight."

Their conversation wove through the crowd's hum, a moment of female solidarity that bolstered Melissa's spark, reminding her that guardianship wasn't solitary; it was a web of support, much like the zodiac's interconnected clans.

As they laughed over a shared skewer, the bond deepened, a quiet empowerment amid the festival's chaos.

Ryder crunched into a skewer nearby, the crispy spice bursting on his tongue as he savored the tech-infused heat. His Rooster Clan swagger was in full force; his tunic embroidered with explosive motifs that seemed to glow with his bold energy.

"You'll crash and burn in that duel, Monkey," he teased, flicking a burnt tip from the skewer with a smirk. But his eyes softened as he turned to Alice, setting down his half-eaten snack. "Don't overthink the riddle, Rabbit. You've got the smarts—we all saw how you synced those traps in Souris. Just trust your code."

Ryder's cannon hummed faintly at his side in Coinin's bustling plaza, neon glows stirring a memory from Explosivo's dusty forges.

At fifteen, his boastful prank had backfired spectacularly: rigging a cannon to fire confetti for a festival show, but overloading the charge turned it into a chaotic blast that scorched the blacksmith shop's roof and scattered tools like shrapnel. Laughter from the crowd had twisted into gasps, his parents' glares stinging his Rooster Clan pride as they hauled him aside.

"Courage isn't showmanship, Ryder—it's knowing when to hold back," his father had growled, disappointment heavy in his eyes.

The facade of the jokester had cracked then, revealing the vulnerability beneath: a fear that his bravado masked true strength, born from years of Explosivo's weapon-forging expectations. Now, with Coinin's festival chaos looming and the Rabbit Talisman at stake, doubt lingered—could he channel real courage without the bluster? The circuit arches pulsed around him, urging his resolve to rise above the past, transforming boastfulness into reliable valor for the team's sake.

David stood tall a few paces away, his katana gleaming faintly under the holo-lanterns, his Dragon Clan gaze sweeping the crowd with vigilant honor. He'd always been the steady one, channeling his temper into disciplined precision, much like in Doragon's misty peaks where he'd honed his blade against howling winds.

"You've trained for this, Alice," he said, his voice a calm anchor amid the chaos. "Remember Listra—the White Tiger tested our unity, but you'll face this riddle with the same resolve." His words carried the weight of their shared trials, from Souris's icy betrayals to Kusini's scorching flames.

Patricia, ever the grounding force, adjusted a crooked neon sign for a nearby vendor with her gentle hands, her Pig Clan calm radiating like a soft pink-gold rune. The vendor's grateful nod warmed her, a small victory in the festival's whirlwind.

"Thank you, guardian," he said, his smile as bright as the sign flaring back to life.

Turning to Alice, Patricia offered a reassuring smile. "You're our champion, Alice. Take a breath—the Moon Rabbit will recognize your heart."

Alice paused at a dumpling stall, the vendor's eyes gleaming with pride as he handed her a circuit-fried dumpling, its golden crust etched with intricate patterns that hummed faintly. "Taste Coinin's soul!" he urged.

She bit in, the spice bursting on her tongue—a crisp delight that blended traditional flavors with the subtle zap of embedded tech, rooted in Coinin's age-old fusion of magic and machinery. It grounded her, reminding her of home: late nights in the clan labs, coding under the glow of zodiac screens, her family's quiet encouragement pushing her through self-doubt.

As the flavor lingered, the vendor leaned in, his voice dropping to a storyteller's timbre. "You know the legend of the Moon Rabbit, young guardian? Long before Sheng Xiao's talismans, the Rabbit wove code into harmony, guarding secrets in the digital veil. But a code thief—much like those whispers of X—tried to corrupt its algorithms. The Rabbit didn't fight with force, it danced through illusions, turning chaos into clarity."

Alice's eyes widened, the tale resonating like a prophecy echo. It tied to the talismans they'd claimed—the Rat's cunning in Souris, the Ox's endurance in Kusini, the Tiger's unity in Listra.

"How does it connect to the Prophecy?" she asked, her shyness easing. The vendor smiled mysteriously. "The scrolls say the Rabbit's light mends the veil between tech and spirit. Fail, and chaos engulfs. Succeed, and Sheng Xiao shines eternal." The story lingered in her mind, a thematic thread weaving doubt into determination, fueling her for the challenge ahead.

But as she swallowed, her holo-pad buzzed sharply, a green pulse spiking through its zodiac rabbit display, jagged bursts disrupting the serene image. Alice's fingers flew to quell it, the Rabbit runes glowing faintly as the anomaly faded. She leaned toward David, her voice low and laced with uncertainty. "This isn't a glitch—not any tech I've seen…feels like magic?"

Her shy heart raced: what if this was a sign, a shadow from X's schemes creeping into Coinin's light?

Melissa, still buzzing from the festival's novelty, nudged her shoulder with a grin. "Chill, Rabbit! We've got time before the riddle, let's enjoy this!"

But Ryder's eyes narrowed at the pad, his bravado momentarily subdued. "She's right. Something's off."

Patricia frowned, glancing at a nearby circuit-shrine where a similar green flicker danced across the runes. "This isn't normal…"

David scanned the crowd, his hand instinctively resting on his katana's hilt, sensing an unseen threat lurking beneath the revelry.

The team plunged deeper into the festival, Ryder challenging David to a holo-game duel at a nearby booth, his taunts brash and full of Rooster fire.

"Bet you miss that virtual target, Dragon!" he called, tossing a skewer bit into the air and catching it with a flourish.

David's eyeroll was stoic, but he humored the challenge, stepping into the holographic arena where virtual foes materialized—zodiac beasts woven from code, roaring with digital ferocity. Ryder fired first, his cannon booming a low-warning shot that shattered a holographic rooster illusion, drawing cheers.

But as David swung his katana, slicing through a dragon mirage with precision, a green surge ripped through the booth's grid. The holograms warped, the dragon foe glitching into a corrupted apparition that lunged unpredictably, its claws phasing through barriers.

"What the—" Ryder yelped, dodging as the glitch spread, a nearby drone swarm buzzing erratically overhead, their paths disrupted.

David parried the aberrant form, his honor flaring into action, but the anomaly hinted at darker forces—X's influence, perhaps, echoing the mercenaries' ambushes in Listra.

Alice rushed in, her holo-pad flaring as she coded a patch, quelling the surge just in time.

"That wasn't random," she muttered, the mini-chaos a foreshadowing thrill that quickened their pulses, revealing the festival's fragility.

The crowd applauded, mistaking it for part of the show, but the Guardians exchanged wary glances, the action sharpening their vigilance.

Patricia slipped a holo-coin to the vendor, her calm presence steadying the group's excitement even as she kept an eye on the subtle glitches.

A holo-lantern above flickered with another green surge, its rabbit motif glitching briefly, a shadow creeping over Coinin's pulse. The festival's drums—blending circuits and ancient beats—echoed louder, urging Alice toward the Moon Rabbit's midnight challenge, her determination flaring like a neon spark amid the growing unease.

In the Imperial Palace's training hall, far from Coinin's neon glow, a massive holo-screen flickered with the festival's vibrant scenes—booths alive with dumplings and clans raffling drones under the starry sky. The air here was cooler, scented with polished stone and the faint ozone of active holo-projectors, but the tension was palpable.

Hana entered with her usual Horse Clan crackle; her whip coiled at her hip like a promise of bold action. Her eyes locked onto Cade, who sat polishing his knives across the room, his jaw tight from Jade's earlier cold dismissal in the throne room.

The memory stung him: her sharp words about focusing on duty, pushing him away when all he'd wanted was to share the burden of the Prophecy. Now, he kept his distance, mismatched eyes fixed on the screen.

"Rooting for Alice, Cade?" Hana asked, tossing her hair with a grin that was sharp yet playful, a spark in her hazel eyes.

She kept her distance this time, sensing the rift—no bold flirtations, just genuine concern. But inside, her heart twisted. David's steady honor called to her more each day, yet Cade's enigma lingered like an unsolved puzzle. Cade looked up, a tired smile tugging at his lips despite the hurt.

"Yeah, tough day," he said softly, his Cat Clan aura flickering faintly around him.

Hana leaned against a pillar, her tone light but probing. "Cheer up, hero! Save that frown for X's lackeys!"

Cade chuckled, the sound warming the space between them, a playful edge softening his tension.

"You're fun, Hana," he admitted, the words slipping out before he could catch them, igniting a flicker of guilt as he glanced toward where Jade might enter.

Jade entered just then, gripping her scepter tightly, her amethyst eyes blazing with a mix of leadership resolve and unspoken jealousy. *Why's my heart racing like a glitched drone?* she thought, her composure fraying at the sight of Hana's easy banter with Cade.

The Prophecy demanded her focus—the talismans, the realms' balance—but her heart tugged toward him, memories of childhood gardens and stolen moments clashing with the crown's weight. Those days in the palace gardens, petals drifting like soft rain as Cade shadow-traveled behind tapestries, his laughter her light amid duty's burdens.

Separations had torn them apart—her diplomatic travels, his trainings—but Percy's updates had kept the flame alive. Now, seeing Hana's spark, fear whispered: *What if he chooses freedom over the throne?*

"Focus on training," she snapped, her voice cutting like glass, eyes darting to the holo-screen where Coinin's festival glowed, silver-tunicked dancers twirling in rhythmic grace. But the words tasted bitter, regret blooming as Cade's face fell. Hana stepped back, her own confusion swirling—David's reliability versus Cade's mystery.

"Jade, I didn't mean—" she started, but Jade waved it off, forcing a regal mask.

"The quest comes first. Alice needs our support." The exchange hung heavy, the triangle's tension a microcosm of Sheng Xiao's divisions, urging Jade to confront her vulnerabilities before they unraveled like Kusini's altar.

Tate stood in the hall's center, drilling Doug's sword forms with Tiger Clan intensity, the Dog Clan guardian's blade arcing with loyal grit.

"Swing harder, Doug!" Tate growled, his claws flashing as he demonstrated, leadership anchoring the room like it had in Listra's trials. Sam coached nearby, her bandaged arm from Dolore's lightning steady as she guided Gerry's staff against a training drone, her Snake Clan wit sharp.

"Block higher, Gerry," she urged, eyes tracking his moves with the precision that had pierced the White Tiger's illusions. Gerry smirked, his Goat Clan mischief dancing as he parried the drone's buzz.

"Sam's too fierce!" he teased, dodging a laser with a nimble leap, their banter sparking warmth amid the hall's tension.

Omar and Veronica huddled close, their Ox and Rat Clan strengths aligning in quiet harmony, hands brushing as they watched the screen.

"Your endurance pulled us through Kusini," Veronica whispered, her green eyes meeting his with a soft smile.

"And your spark lit the way in Souris," Omar replied, their bond a steady anchor forged in betrayal's fires.

Jade's grip tightened on her scepter, the festival's glow reflecting her inner turmoil, the dancers' silver tunics shimmering like Coinin's resilient heart.

The festival's energy, fueled by the Tiger Talisman's restorative power, thrummed through the screen, stirring Jade's thoughts toward Alice's team and the Rabbit Talisman's quest. Hana's smirk faded, her flirtation a flame threatening Jade's restraint, but the holo-screen's dancers caught her eye, their spins a call to action.

Neon signs flashed, urging Jade toward the quest shaping Sheng Xiao's future, her resolve burning brighter than the festival's glow.

Meanwhile, at X's fortress, a holo-screen glowed with Coinin's festival, silver-dressed dancers twirling, a beacon for Sheng Xiao's clans. Another screen displayed Coinin's grid schematic, circuit-veins pulsing, vulnerable hubs marked in red.

Bella's amber gaze scanned the holo-grid, her fingers tracing circuit weak points, pinpointing festival hubs ripe for disruption—memories of her Kusini triumph fueling her precision, X's praise a lingering warmth. Lucas mapped drone paths, his steady hands marking gaps in Coinin's defenses, his focus as sharp as his machete, bandaged arm a reminder of Souris's close calls.

Dolore rested nearby, her breathing soft, brown eyes closed as she recovered from Listra's wounds, her quiet strength a shadow in the room, ambition simmering for her next strike.

X stood at the schematic's core, his voice cold as steel, relaying plans to Vincent in Coinin.

"Target the holo-grids," he ordered, eyes fixed on the pulsing lines, his mind flashing to the stolen Ox Talisman, its power a twisted vow. Vincent's scarred hands gripped his serpent scepter, runes flaring with green pulses, spreading across Coinin's festival, ready to unravel its energy.

Bella's holo-scan pinpointed a central hub, circuits exposed.

"Strike here," she said, voice sharp, fingers steady as she relayed coordinates.

Lucas nodded, his map highlighting a drone swarm's path to amplify chaos.

"The grids will fall," Vincent hissed, runes primed, a shadow poised to strike Coinin's pulse. The festival thrummed on the holo-screen, its vibrancy teetering under Vincent's magic.

The schematic glowed, Coinin's circuit-veins exposed, Vincent's green pulses surging, ready to plunge the festival into chaos and unravel Sheng Xiao's unity at the Rabbit Talisman's midnight challenge.

Chapter 17: The Moon Rabbit's Riddle

As midnight deepened over Coinin's central plaza, the lunar-veil screens intensified their starry dance, weaving a cosmic tapestry that heightened the Festival of Lanterns' climax. Starlit banners pulsed with Sheng Xiao's energy, lunar runes glowing silver and gold in tribute to the Moon Rabbit's lore.

Towering rune totems flanked the square, their holographic glyphs humming in sync with the city's grid, while holo-puzzle stages cast neon arcs, challenging clans with twisting digital mazes that burst with confetti for victors. The air thrummed with anticipation; every breath held in collective suspense as the moment of the talisman trial drew near.

The plaza itself had transformed into a living circuit, its cobblestones etched with glowing pathways that pulsed in time with the city's heartbeat.

Clans stood shoulder-to-shoulder in a sea of zodiac tunics, their faces illuminated by the shifting light of holo-lanterns that floated overhead like captive stars. The scent of holo-spiced tea and circuit-fried dumplings lingered in the air, now mixed with the sharp tang of ozone from overworked processors.

Children ran, chasing the last floating drone-balloons shaped like playful rabbits, their laughter a fragile counterpoint to the tension that thickened the night like storm clouds gathering on the horizon.

The hum of the city's grid vibrated through the ground, a constant reminder of Coinin's role as Sheng Xiao's tech heart, where every circuit and rune carried the weight of the realms' interconnected fates.

Before the riddle commenced, clans gathered at a central circuit-shrine for Coinin's coded prayer ceremony, a ritual showcasing the realm's electronic ingenuity.

Holographic interfaces invited participants to sync their holo-pads with riddle-sync drones—sleek, Rabbit-shaped gadgets with circuit-etched casings amplifying code inputs—into a collective algorithm surging with Sheng Xiao's energy.

The drones hovered in perfect formation, their ears twitching in sync with the plaza's pulse, their eyes glowing with soft lunar light that seemed to hold ancient secrets.

Alice joined the Guardians at the shrine's edge, her Rabbit precision aligning seamlessly, code flowing like a harmonious stream that made the drones respond with gentle chimes.

Melissa synced beside her, her Monkey agility turning the process into a playful dance that drew smiles from nearby children, her braid whipping through the air as she spun on one foot. Ryder's Rooster boldness added a flourish to his input, his fingers moving in sharp, confident strokes that made a drone chirp in approval.

David's Dragon honor grounded the ritual with precise taps, each keystroke a reflection of discipline honed in misty dojos. Patricia's Pig calm radiated outward, her pink-gold gauntlet glowing softly as she stabilized the energy fluctuations.

"Link your essence to the Rabbit's veil," the shrine elder intoned, his voice amplified through the arches, resonating in every chest. The plaza unified in the glow, farmers in Cochan toasting with wine that caught the light like liquid gold, fishers in Dingo pausing their nets to watch the pillar rise, as the prayer promised clarity and protection.

But midway through, a green spike disrupted the veil, runes flickering erratically, drones sparking as their casings crackled with unnatural energy. Gasps rippled through the crowd like waves across a pond, Alice's holo-pad vibrating in protest as she patched it quickly, her fingers flying across the interface to isolate the corruption.

"That's no standard error," she muttered, the anomaly tying to earlier glitches—dumpling stall surges that had made flavors glitch into bitter ash, shrine flickers that had silenced prayers mid-chant, warped lantern that had twisted rabbit motifs into serpentine coils—quickening her pulse for the riddle's trials.

The green spike left a lingering chill in the air, a shadow that made the lunar light feel colder, the plaza's hum slightly off-key.

Alice stood with Melissa, David, Patricia, and Ryder on the sidelines, her holo-pad gripped tight in trembling hands, Rabbit Clan precision warring with the nerves that knotted her stomach like tangled code.

The plaza's glow reflected in her glasses, casting fractured rainbows across her focused expression, but her mind was elsewhere, breath shallow as doubt crept in like frost across a window.

Why's my code glitching? What if I falter and unravel everything we've fought for? she thought, the crowd's pressure amplifying her shyness into a system overload. The trial's victory—outcoding Lillith and Kai amid boos—had earned her this stage, but envy still lingered like corrupted data. Tonight, the Rabbit Talisman at stake, one mistake could crash Sheng Xiao's fragile harmony.

She vowed to embrace her smarts openly, transforming past pain into fuel for victory, her identity as Guardian no longer hidden but wielded with quiet courage for Sheng Xiao's sake, the weight of every realm resting on her trembling shoulders.

Melissa clapped her shoulder, braid swinging wildly, her grin infectious from the thrill of the moment, a holo-flute's notes catching her ear like a siren call amid the tension that made the air feel charged.

"You're a coding genius, Alice! You'll nail it!" she said, excitement infectious, her green tunic shimmering under the neon arcs like leaves in sunlight.

The energy coursed through her, a stark contrast to the burnout of past trials, where endless challenges had left her yearning for moments like this—unbridled possibility under Coinin's spires that made her heart race with joy.

Pulling Alice and Patricia aside for a quick huddle, Melissa's eyes sparkled with Monkey Clan fire. "This is our moment. Your smarts got us through the worst—trust that here, let it flow like data-vines in the wind."

Patricia nodded, her Pig Clan warmth grounding, pink-gold runes on her gauntlet glowing softly as she placed a steady hand on Alice's arm. "You've got endurance and spark. We're in this together—let's weave your code like the Rabbit's legend, thread by thread until it holds."

Alice's heart eased, their words a shield against old doubts that had once made her shrink, her voice steadier as shyness yielded to quiet courage, their bond echoing the unity of the Guardians, empowering her as the riddle neared and the plaza's energy surged like a wave about to break.

Ryder nudged Melissa, grinning as he set down his cup of steaming tea that sent curls of citrus-ozone vapor into the air, eyes warm despite his Rooster Clan bravado that made his tunic's explosive motifs seem to spark.

"Humming flutes again, Monkey? Save it for the next puzzle!" he teased, his voice carrying the easy confidence of someone who had faced fire and come out laughing. Turning to Alice, his tone softened, the bravado giving way to genuine faith. "Don't overthink it, Alice. You've got the smarts—we all saw how you handled the traps, turning chaos into order with a flick of your wrist. Just trust your code, let it sing."

David stood close, his Dragon Clan resolve a steady pillar amid the swirling crowd, katana glinting subtly at his side like a promise of protection. He'd channeled his temper into unyielding discipline, honed against volcanic winds that howled like angry spirits in Doragon's peaks.

"You've trained for this," he said, his calm voice lifting her spirit like a guiding rune etched in stone, steady and unbreakable.

Patricia handed a circuit-carved mochi to a wide-eyed child nearby, her Pig Clan warmth earning a delighted smile that lit the child's face like sunrise.

"You're our champion, Alice," she said, voice firm and reassuring, easing the knot in Alice's stomach with her grounding presence that felt like earth after rain.

But the doubts lingered, amplified by the plaza's hum that seemed to vibrate in her bones. A holo-puzzle booth's screen flickered erratically, a green pulse spiking through its zodiac rabbit display, jagged bursts twisting the image into something unnatural that made nearby clans step back in unease.

Alice's fingers trembled as she tapped her holo-pad to quell it, the Rabbit runes glowing faintly in response like a heartbeat fighting to stay steady.

Her mind raced back to the earlier anomalies—green surges in the dumpling stall that had made flavors glitch into bitter ash on tongues, the flickering circuit-shrine during Melissa's holo-coin toss that had silenced a prayer mid-chant, the warped lantern above their heads that had twisted rabbit motifs into serpentine coils that seemed to watch with malevolent eyes.

"This isn't tech I know…something else?" she whispered to David, her shy heart racing with doubt that made her palms sweat, the pattern too deliberate, too foreign, like a virus infiltrating Coinin's core and spreading through every circuit like poison in bloodstream.

Ryder squinted at a nearby stall, spotting a similar green shimmer dancing across its display like corrupted fireflies.

"She's right. Something's off," he said, his bravado fading into cautious alertness, Rooster Clan vigilance kicking in as he scanned the crowd for threats.

Patricia frowned at a circuit-shrine's flicker, its runes glitching green in a pattern that defied standard diagnostics and made the air around it feel heavier.

"This isn't normal…" she murmured, her calm sharpening into concern that tightened her grip on her gauntlet.

David scanned the crowd, his hand resting instinctively on his katana's hilt, sensing a hidden threat lurking beneath the revelry, much like the mercenary ambushes that had tested them in Listra's flooded jungles where shadows hid blades.

Melissa, still caught in the thrill of the moment, hummed along to a holo-flute's notes that floated through the air like silver threads, shrugging off their doubts with a toss of her braid that caught the light.

"It's new tech for the festival—relax!" she called, tossing a holo-coin to a vendor with playful flair, her Monkey Clan agility making light of the unease that had begun to ripple through the crowd like static.

The announcer's voice rang out across the plaza, amplified by the circuit-woven arches, cutting through the din like a digital clarion that silenced even the wind. "Tonight's Moon Rabbit riddle, a talisman challenge sparked by Empress Jade's summons, calls our Rabbit guardian, Alice!"

The crowd erupted, cheers echoing realm-wide through the broadcast, a tradition that every year unveiled Coinin's cutting-edge innovations—holo-devices for enhanced zodiac abilities that made warriors faster and farmers more precise, algorithms for optimized harvests that turned barren fields fertile, drones for secure trade routes that connected realms like never before—engaging clans from Explosivo's forges where fire met code to Dingo's beaches where waves carried data streams.

But this year, Jade's decree had streamlined the event, channeling all focus into the Moon Rabbit's trial, with Alice at its heart, transforming the festival into a realm-unifying spectacle of prophecy and progress where every clan's fate hung on one girl's code.

Across Sheng Xiao, Kusini farmers paused their labors under starlit skies, Doragon miners halted their digs in volcanic depths, Fahal Alkhayl traders silenced their markets where spices and circuits mingled, Cochan vintners stilled their presses as wine fermented in silence, and Ged herbalists quieted their workshops where potions bubbled with forgotten magic, their eyes fixed on Alice's challenge through screens that flickered with lunar light.

The Moon Rabbit's golden silhouette loomed in Coinin's plaza, a majestic spectral form with twitching ears and luminous eyes channeling lunar energy that made the air itself feel charged with ancient power, its fur etched with intricate circuit patterns that glowed in rhythmic pulses, blending ancient magic with Coinin's tech ingenuity in a fusion that took Alice's breath away.

Distinct from the silver-clad dancers honoring its myth with graceful leaps that left trails of digital stardust, the Rabbit stood as a beacon of Sheng Xiao's tech heart, its golden hues shifting like flowing data streams that carried the weight of centuries.

The announcer's voice boomed, weaving lore into the moment with words that resonated in every heart: "Behold the Moon Rabbit, guardian of secrets since Sheng Xiao's dawn! Legend tells of its code woven into harmony, safeguarding the digital veil against corrupters who sought to twist its algorithms with dark intent. It danced through illusions, turning chaos into clarity—a test of heart and wit that mends the veil between tech and spirit, between past and future. Tonight, Alice faces this legacy!"

Alice's mind flashed to the vendor's words from earlier, his mysterious smile echoing the tale as he leaned in close, his voice a storyteller's timbre that had made the legend feel alive, reinforcing her determination amid the crowd's gasps that rose like a wave.

Starlit banners flickered with increasing urgency, circuit-woven arches humming with holo-puzzle games that tested wits in escalating complexity—digital webs that shifted like living entities with minds of their own, rewarding solvers with bursts of light that lit faces in wonder and drew cheers from clans who had traveled realms to witness Coinin's ingenuity.

The Moon Rabbit spoke its riddle, projecting a holo-circuit maze pulsing with code that hovered before Alice like a living challenge, asking in a voice that vibrated through her bones, "What weaves light but holds darkness, guards secrets yet speaks to all?"

Alice's hands shook as she raised her holo-pad, Rabbit runes surging across the screen in waves of silver and gold, the device growing warm in her grip as she faced the golden rabbit, its glow towering like a judgmental sentinel that seemed to see into her soul.

She traced lunar circuit patterns with careful precision, her holo-pad's runes flaring brighter as a lunar energy surge lit the plaza in brilliant white, clans gasping as the maze warped under green shimmers that slithered through the code like venom. Lillith and Kai stood in the crowd, eyes sharp with envy that had festered since the trial, their boos cutting through the cheers like corrupted signals.

"You'll crash, Alice!" Lillith jeered, her past trial loss raw, the wound from Alice's outcoding still festering like an open circuit.

"Coinin needs a real guardian!" Kai taunted, his voice drowned by the crowd's roar but stinging nonetheless, a reminder of the resentment that had followed her victory.

David overheard their taunts, his glare sharp as his katana that glinted with lethal promise.

"Ignore them, Alice," he said, voice unyielding, his Dragon honor a shield against their barbs that would have crushed a lesser spirit.

Melissa, eyes wide from the festival's electric atmosphere, guessed wildly with Monkey Clan zeal, "The answer's in the code!" rallying from the sidelines as her braid bounced with every enthusiastic gesture.

Ryder nodded, spotting green flashes on a booth's screen that made his cannon hum in warning, his Rooster boldness tempered by caution that tightened his grip.

"Feels like magic," he said, tone shifting as the anomalies escalated, his eyes scanning the shadows for threats.

Patricia, her Pig Clan intuition flaring like a warning light, pointed to a cloaked figure slipping through the shadows with unnatural grace.

"That figure's suspicious," she said, calm sharpening into vigilance that made her gauntlet glow brighter.

David mused, his mind racing through Sheng Xiao's lore for riddle possibilities, "Maybe it's a circuit pattern—echo, or fire?" watching Alice with unyielding support that felt like a steady hand on her shoulder.

Alice's fingers flew across her holo-pad, decoding patterns with Rabbit precision that made the maze respond with chimes and flashes, her heart pounding as she tested solutions one by one.

First, "echo"—she wove the word into the maze's code with careful keystrokes, runes aligning briefly in perfect harmony before collapsing in a digital ripple of failure, the structure tightening like a constricting noose around her code, sweat beading on her forehead as the crowd's murmurs pressed in, amplifying her nerves until they felt like static in her ears.

"Fire," she tried next, inputting the sequence with careful precision, the holo-pad heating under her touch as flames flickered in the projection like golden dancers, but the green shimmers surged with malevolent force, extinguishing the attempt and warping the paths further into impossible knots.

"Not that," she muttered, breath ragged as her shyness gave way to focused determination that burned in her chest.

The Moon Rabbit's eyes seemed to watch with ancient judgment, its circuit patterns pulsing expectantly, the lunar energy amplifying her doubts until they threatened to drown her. She recalled the vendor's legend, the Rabbit dancing through illusions with grace and wit—perhaps the answer lay in harmony, not force, in connection rather than conquest.

Tracing a new pattern with trembling fingers, she experimented with "web," the maze responding with a tentative glow that made hope flare in her chest, edges stabilizing before a green pulse disrupted it with violent force, booths sparking as riddle-sync drones buzzed erratically, their Rabbit-shaped casings crackling with green static that made children cry.

Clans panicked, scattering as the drones veered dangerously close, the broadcast capturing the chaos realm-wide in flickering feeds. Alice patched the grid with desperate speed, hands steadying as the vendor's words echoed in her mind: harmony, not force, connection over isolation.

"Circuit," she tried, runes pulsing as the maze aligned briefly in perfect symmetry, but green shimmers intensified with malicious intent, her holo-pad overheating until it burned her palms.

One last attempt—"veil"—the maze flared with brilliant light, nearly locking as its patterns wove light and darkness in perfect balance, the talisman's power shimmering at the core like a promise about to be fulfilled, but a drone sparked violently overhead, sending clans scrambling in terror, screams echoing across Sheng Xiao as the broadcast amplified her struggle to every corner of the realms.

The crowd gasped louder, their cheers turning to worried murmurs, the riddle's glow intensified to blinding levels, Guardians cheering with desperate hope, their voices a lifeline as Coinin's energy teetered on the edge of collapse, Alice fighting for the Rabbit Talisman to protect Sheng Xiao's balance with every ounce of her being.

Chapter 18: Vincent's Escape

As Coinin's plaza reeled from the Moon Rabbit's unsolved riddle, Alice's holo-pad flared with the maze's final pulse, its "veil" attempt collapsing in a shower of green sparks. Drones crackled, clans screamed, and her courage surged, Rabbit Clan caution hardening into resolve to protect Sheng Xiao's tech heart. The spectral Moon Rabbit's glow flickered sickly green, its ears twitching in pain, the festival's harmony teetering under an unseen assault.

Alice's heart pounded—*I won't falter now*—her trial's victory over Lillith and Kai fueling her, their past jeers no longer a weight but a spark to fight the chaos erupting around her.

The Moon Rabbit's golden silhouette towered over Coinin's central plaza, its circuit-etched fur pulsing with frantic desperation, luminous eyes flickering like dying stars under a midnight sky torn by unnatural gales.

Starlit banners whipped violently above, their edges fraying with corrupted energy, while lunar rune totems screeched with discordant static, their holographic glyphs splintering into jagged fragments that rained like shattered code. The Festival of Lanterns, once a vibrant mosaic of light and sound, shuddered in chaos, the air thick with the acrid stench of smoldering holo-panels, the sour tang of spilled holo-spiced tea, and the metallic bite of ozone from overloaded grids.

Shattered zodiac displays sparked erratically, their rabbit motifs twisting into serpentine coils, while panicked clans—Kusini farmers clutching children, Ged elders chanting Sheng Xiao hymns—wove defiance through the pandemonium. Coinin's self-repairing grids flickered, their circuits humming faintly, struggling to mend, a testament to the realm's tech ingenuity pushed to its brink.

Alice's holo-pad vibrated violently, its screen a maelstrom of corrupted data streams, green warnings flashing like venomous eyes.

"Not again!" she gasped, Rabbit Clan precision clashing with panic knotting her stomach.

Her glasses fogged in the humid air, but she swiped them clear, fingers darting across the interface. The green anomalies she'd battled all night—spikes in dumpling stalls, flickering shrine screens, warped zodiac lanterns—had erupted into a full-scale assault on Coinin's tech-magic heart. The vendor's words echoed: harmony, not force. But force slithered toward her—Vincent, emerging like a serpent uncoiling in the night.

His cloak billowed in the gusts, serpent scepter raised, its emerald runes blazing with sickly light, casting jagged shadows across the plaza. His scarred hands, etched from Percy's moonlit duel, gripped the scepter, scars pulsing with fury.

"The talisman's mine!" he hissed, voice a venomous slash through the crowd's gasps.

A flashback surged—Jade's crowning, her amethyst eyes radiant as she united Sheng Xiao's clans, "Unity is our strength," she'd declared.

I'll unravel her balance, he vowed, ambition burning to eclipse Jade's light. He thrust the scepter forward, unleashing serpentine runes that coiled toward the Moon Rabbit, their green tendrils wrapping its golden form, twisting its glow into sickly verdigris. The Moon Rabbit wailed digitally, ears twitching erratically as the holo-circuit maze fractured, paths collapsing into pixelated shards like broken stars.

Vincent's scepter flared green in Coinin's plaza, a memory of an Ogham grove's mossy shadows surging. His scarred hands traced cryptic runes on ancient stones, their glow whispering dominion—Sheng Xiao kneeling, Jade's light dimmed under his command. A crest-like rune sparked resentment, her privileged crown mocking his struggles.

Percy's duel flashed, knives carving his arm, betrayal fueling fury.

"I'll seize this realm's power," he vowed, the runes' pulses igniting ambition to dominate through chaos.

Alice's breath caught, doubt clawing.

Can my code match his magic? she thought, but Rabbit Clan grit surged like a firewall.

Sheng Xiao's tech harmony rested on her, and with the Guardians, she wouldn't falter, not after Souris's thorns, Kusini's flames, or Listra's floods. Her mind flashed to the holo-grid trial, her fingers outcoding Lillith's loops and Kai's arrays, their jeers fading under the crowd's roar.

That victory had come with a price: envy from her peers that still lingered like a bad code. Tonight, with the Rabbit Talisman at stake, she couldn't afford doubt.

"This is magic!" she shouted, her voice steadier than she felt, pushing back against the shyness that threatened to silence her.

Her code clashed with Vincent's runes in a digital tempest, sparks arcing from her holo-pad like misfired fireworks, weaving a protective algorithm from Coinin School's lunar circuit drills.

A shimmering veil shielded the Moon Rabbit, deflecting Vincent's runes with a hum vibrating through the plaza's circuit-woven arches, Coinin's self-repairing grids pulsing faintly.

Vincent sneered, his scepter twisting like a living serpent, summoning rune-eyed drones—Rabbit-shaped gadgets corrupted by his magic, their circuit casings crackling with green static.

"Your tech is child's play—Jade's light dims under my power!" he taunted, dodging a collapsing holo-puzzle stage, its maze exploding in virtual confetti that stung like digital hail.

He channeled emerald energy into the Moon Rabbit's core, runes burrowing like venomous worms, twisting its silhouette with agonizing pulses. The Rabbit writhed, its wails echoing, circuit patterns fracturing as the green sickness spread, eyes dimming to a pained glimmer.

Alice's heart wrenched, her holo-pad sparking as she screamed, "Stop, you're hurting it!"

The Guardians froze, horror on their faces—Melissa's axe lowering, Ryder's cannon trembling. Vincent's eyes gleamed, scarred hands tightening as the Rabbit convulsed, expelling the Rabbit Talisman in a burst of lunar light.

The rune-etched artifact fell into his grasp, thrumming faintly, while the Rabbit collapsed, flickering sickly green, ears limp, shuddering like a glitched hologram.

"This proves I'm better than her," he hissed, tucking the gold-blue talisman into his cloak, sprinting into the crowd amid scattering clans and sparking debris.

Melissa vaulted over a sparking booth, Monkey Clan braid whipping, green tunic shimmering under neon arcs. Her first festival's thrill ignited leadership, honed in Mico's jungle drills where dodging data-vines taught her to dance through chaos.

"Alice, keep coding—we've got the crowd!" she yelled, pulling a Kusini farmer from a toppled skewer stall, meats sizzling.

Burnout flickered, but she reflected, Mico's drills forged me for this—lead or lose, spinning her axe in a whirlwind to cleave a drone swarm, their green cores bursting in violet flashes that lit her determined grin.

She flipped over a holo-panel, its serpentine runes flaring, and rallied civilians, "To the arches—move!" Spotting Vincent's fleeing form, she signaled Ryder, "Flank him—use Dingo's fishing drones!"

She swung her axe to smash a festival drone, its net-like fragments tangling a rune barrier deployed by Lucas, her leadership a beacon in the chaos.

A collapsing holo-shield maze loomed, Coinin's cutting-edge tech flickering with green corruption, its translucent walls shifting like liquid glass.

"Ryder, hit the maze's core—break those shields!" she shouted, her axe slicing through glyph-activated traps that erupted from the plaza's floor, their emerald tendrils snapping like whips. Sparks flew as she carved a path, dodging a collapsing festival booth that spilled circuit-carved mochi across the debris-strewn ground, her voice rallying David and Patricia, "Keep the path clear—that magic user is not getting away!"

Her heart pounded, the weight of Mico's endless drills fueling her resolve to outmaneuver Vincent's chaos, proving her leadership wasn't just agility but a spark that could guide Sheng Xiao through the storm.

Ryder charged beside her, Rooster Clan boldness blazing, cannon slung over his shoulder like a defiant crow.

A flicker of fear crossed his mind—What if I fail Explosivo's forges again? —his parents' disappointment in his "jokester" facade a lingering sting that echoed their stern voices: "You're more than quips, Ryder."

He shoved it aside, tackling a Ged elder from a glitching holo-puzzle stage, where digital webs twisted into rune traps, their green pulses snapping at his heels.

"Stay down!" he roared, smashing a drone with a gauntleted fist, its fragments scattering across the plaza like metallic hail.

He grabbed a floating zodiac lantern, its holographic stardust trailing like a comet, and hurled it into a drone swarm, the explosion disorienting the machines in a burst of shimmering light.

"These pests won't quit!" he bellowed, his cannon booming a low-warning shot that dispersed another swarm, the recoil jolting his frame but not his spirit. In the holo-shield maze, he faltered, the shifting walls closing in, his fear surging—I can't let Explosivo down again.

Melissa's shout cut through, "Ryder, hit the arch's core—unleash Explosivo's fire!" Her words ignited his resolve, and he aimed his cannon at the maze's pulsing green core, a rune-etched crystal suspended in the air.

The blast shattered the shields, their translucent walls collapsing in a cascade of digital shards, clearing a path.

He grinned at Melissa, "Bet my cannon hits harder than your axe!"

She smirked, "Keep dreaming, Rooster!" as they sprinted forward, dodging a glyph-activated trap that erupted in a burst of green sparks, the debris of a fallen festival booth—its skewers smoldering—crunching under their boots.

David and Patricia joined the chase, their teamwork a defiant pulse against Vincent's schemes, Ryder's heart pounding with the need to prove his worth not just to his clan but to himself.

David's katana carved through rune traps erupting like emerald vines from the plaza's floor, their tendrils coiling toward civilians with malicious intent. His Dragon Clan honor burned like a forge, each strike precise, channeling discipline honed in Doragon's misty dojos against volcanic winds.

"Form a line—protect the weak!" he commanded, his temper simmering but controlled, fury at Vincent's betrayal fueling his blade.

A drone swooped low, its green pulse grazing his shoulder, singeing his tunic with a hiss of scorched fabric, but he spun, his katana slicing it in half with a crack that echoed like breaking stone. He lunged toward Vincent, his blade grazing the villain's cloak, forcing him to stagger, a thin line of blood seeping from a shallow cut.

"You won't escape!" David roared, his honor a shield against the chaos, his eyes locked on Vincent's fleeing form as he pushed through the maze's remnants, the air thick with the ozone of corrupted tech.

Patricia moved beside him, her Pig Clan calm grounding the pandemonium, pink-gold runes glowing softly on her gauntlet as she yanked a Cochan child from beneath a shattered mochi stall, its circuit-carved treats sparking faintly in the debris.

"You're safe," she murmured, her voice a steady anchor, her hammer disabling a ground trap with a resonant thud, its runes flaring to neutralize the green pulse.

Alice knelt amid the debris, her holo-pad rebooting with a faint hum, fingers steadying despite the chaos. Lillith and Kai emerged from the scattering crowd, their silver tunics torn, their past envy forgotten in the face of Coinin's crisis.

Lillith approached first, her eyes wide with the plaza's devastation, her voice earnest, "Alice, we were wrong...your code saved us in the trial. You're the guardian, lead us now."

Kai nodded, his usual sneer replaced with determination, "Yeah, tell us what to do since Coinin's our home too."

Alice's shyness melted under their words, a rare confidence blooming as she took charge, her glasses catching the neon glow of a nearby totem.

"Sync your pads to mine," she directed, her voice steady, sketching a strategy on her holo-pad's glowing interface. "Lillith, handle the totem links—reroute their power to the central hub to bolster the grids. Kai, stabilize the drone frequencies to disrupt the magic user's swarm. We'll start a lunar rune dance to sync the totems—it's an old Coinin ritual to harmonize the tech-magic weave."

Lillith nodded, her fingers flying over her pad, "Got it— rerouting the totems now," her loops aligning seamlessly with Alice's algorithms, their code surging like a harmonious stream.

Kai's arrays reinforced the shields, his voice low, "Hacking the drones—let's ground those pests."

Together, they initiated the rune dance, their silver tunics swirling under the flickering totems, their steps tracing ancient patterns that pulsed with lunar energy, the plaza's grids stabilizing inch by inch.

Lillith muttered, "We underestimated you, Alice, should've listened sooner," as Kai added, "This dance...it's syncing everything."

Their teamwork, guided by Alice's leadership, sparked hope, the spectral Moon Rabbit's sickly green fading, a faint yellow struggling against lingering corruption, circuit patterns stuttering, lunar energy faltering under green taint, its ears twitching faintly in recovery as the ritual's rhythm countered Vincent's chaos.

Meanwhile, a holo-screen flickering with the festival's ruins—clans fleeing as lunar-pulse grids sparked erratically. Bella's amber gaze scanned the grid, her fingers tracing weak points with sharp precision, memories of Kusini's flames fueling her ambition.

"Vincent, path's clear—north alleys, avoid the central arches," she said, voice sharp as a dagger, relaying coordinates via holo-comm. "I'm sending a drone swarm to block the Guardians—use the darkened alleys near the circuit-shrines."

Lucas's steady hands danced over stealth-grid consoles, coding rune-eyed drones with green pulses to swarm Coinin's plaza.

"Target the lunar grids—disrupt their tech, create openings," he smirked, his bandaged arm aching faintly from Souris's betrayals, muttering, "He's too reckless—hope he doesn't botch this." His holo-comm buzzed with Vincent's updates, "I've deployed obstacles—rune barriers on the east flank, exploding glyphs in the side streets to slow Jade's lapdogs."

Dolore tracked signal patterns, her brown eyes sharp, strength returning from Listra's wounds, lightning simmering in her palms.

"Signals falter across Sheng Xiao with outages spreading like wildfire," she said, fingers tracing a data stream that lit her face in eerie green. "Vincent, watch for self-repairing grids, I'm amplifying the disruptions with a lightning spike—head for the north hub, I'll cover your exit with a storm veil."

X stood at the schematic's core, his voice cold as forged steel. "Vincent, escape through the north alleys—drones will cover you. Bring the talisman! Our vengeance demands it," he ordered, eyes fixed on the pulsing lines, his sorrow for lost love twisting with the stolen Ox Talisman's power. "Prove you're better than Jade—unravel her light."

Vincent reached Coinin's edge, his serpent scepter flaring with emerald runes, corrupting the final hub in a cascade of green sparks, festival booths collapsing in his wake like dominoes, their zodiac displays reduced to smoldering heaps.

"North hub's down," he hissed into his communicator, cloak brushing past startled clans who scattered like leaves in a storm, the talisman's weight a triumphant burden in his grip.

Drones swarmed overhead, their green pulses scattering pursuers, Sheng Xiao's unity unraveling as his magic surged, a triumph over Jade's radiant light.

In the Imperial Palace's training hall, holo-screens blazed with Coinin's chaos—shattered stalls, clans fleeing like leaves in a storm, grids glitching with green venom. Lights flickered out, screens crackling as outages swept Sheng Xiao.

Hana's whip twitched, mind on David, doubt faltering—David's honor or Cade's mystery?

Patricia's words echoed: "Stop chasing two hearts." She tightened her grip, resolve hardening.

Cade lunged, shielding Jade from a falling circuit-panel sparking green, halting it inches away.

"Stay back!" he shouted, mismatched eyes blazing, hurt from Jade's dismissal fading. Jade's scepter trembled, amethyst eyes wide with gratitude, her hand brushing his, electric.

"Thank you, Cade," she whispered, trust reigniting, their bond a quiet flame.

Jade's voice cut through: "Guardians, check your clans!"

Omar, Veronica, Tate, Sam, and Gerry huddled, sharing a vivid montage of chaos: Kusini's altars flared green, harvests faltering, Souris blackened, thorns encroaching, Listra's vine-nets trapped dancers, floods stirring, Saanp's serum-vaults corrupted, medicines failing, and Ged's cliffs rumbled, comms faltering, Gerry's mother hurt in the outages from a fallen comm-shrine.

Gerry's spear trembled, his mischief hardening into duty: "I'll get to her," he vowed, activating a holo-link to Ged locals. "Please—check on her, she's injured in the outages," he pleaded.

A Ged elder's face appeared, "We'll take care of her, Gerry—she's family. Focus on the quest."

They agreed, their assurance easing his worry, his resolve a spark for Ged.

Jade pulled Cade aside to the library, its circuit-lit shelves glowing faintly, holo-tomes flickering with archived lore, the air heavy with the scent of aged paper and ozone from overtaxed systems.

"Please scout the clan lands of our Guardians in Coinin— Doragon for David, Mico for Melissa, Explosivo for Ryder, Cochan for Patricia," she said, pulling on his cloak with a flutter of shadow wisps, her hand lingering, her amethyst eyes clouded with unease. "Cade, the magic user's power —it's not Saanp's venomous precision, nor any clan's weave. It's darker, jagged, like a forgotten power tearing at Coinin's grids." Her scepter trembled in her grip, its runes dimming as if sensing the threat, her voice dropping to a whisper. "I studied Saanp's runes in their desert archives, years ago, under starlit dunes—scrolls etched with serpent strikes, fluid and precise, like a dance of venom. This is different—chaotic, ancient, pulsing with a malice that doesn't belong to Sheng Xiao's lore."

A flashback surged: Jade in Saanp's archives, her fingers tracing runes that flowed like sand, their elegance stark against Vincent's jagged pulses that seemed to writhe with unnatural hunger.

"It terrifies me, Cade—what if this power is beyond our talismans, something we can't counter?" Her voice cracked, fear etching her regal mask, her hand tightening on his. Cade's mismatched eyes narrowed, his shadow wisps coiling protectively around her. "It's not Sheng Xiao's, but it's not unstoppable. His voice was steady, a vow forged in their shared history, his resolve a spark against her fear.

"We'll face it together," he added, his hand brushing hers, the touch grounding her as the holo-tomes flickered, casting eerie shadows across the library's walls.

Jade nodded, her leadership reigniting. His shadow wisps enveloped him, leaving Jade alone, her scepter pulsing faintly, her resolve burning to mend Sheng Xiao's fragile balance.

Cade strode back into the training hall, cloak fluttering, fatigue etching his mismatched eyes as he met Jade's knowing glance.

"Doragon's holo-temples flicker with static, but dojos hold, Mico's data-vines stutter, yet jungles endure, Explosivo's signal-towers spark, forges dim but safe, and Cochan's comm-shrines falter, but plains rally," he reported, his voice steady despite the weariness of shadow-travel.

Jade urged, "Rest, Cade," her voice soft with care, hands brushing in a moment that deepened their bond, trust rebuilt like mended code.

Omar and Veronica stood close, their eyes locked, Ox and Rat Clan bond tense with unspoken words amid the reports.

"We'll rebuild," Veronica said, her voice firm, Omar nodding as he pulled her into a steady embrace, their vow tightening like woven fates.

The Guardians' efforts steadied Coinin, Alice's code stabilizing the grid inch by inch, the Moon Rabbit's glow partly restored to dull yellow, Sheng Xiao's balance hanging fragile like a glitching lantern.

Signal disruptions lingered as a rune-tinged echo of Vincent's victory, but their courage burned brighter, a promise to reclaim the talisman and mend the zodiac weave.

Chapter 19: Shifting Bonds

As Coinin's chaos lingered, the palace's relic hall thrummed under flickering lunar-glow arches, ancient holo-relics stuttering with zodiac lore, their static hum echoing Sheng Xiao's waning energy.

Backup power cast dim light across zodiac sigils etched into marble walls, their patterns flickering like fading stars. Jade stood near a cracked holo-screen, its shattered relays showing Coinin's unrest—battered streets strewn with scattered grain cakes, broken booths, Rat Clan hauling lumber, Kusini farmers sharing harvests, faces etched with defiance despite faltering tech under Vincent's signal disruptions.

Her scepter trembled, amethyst eyes scanning reports, leadership steady as Sheng Xiao's fragile balance pressed heavy. A guard rushed in, calling for an update. Jade nodded, resolve firm, the hall's relays humming with tension, her mind racing to rally the Guardians against the growing threat.

The holo-comm flared, glitching with static, Melissa's face flickering from Coinin, her Monkey Clan braid frayed, voice strained over the crackling connection.

"Jade, the cloaked figure took the Rabbit Talisman," she reported, eyes shadowed with exhaustion. Patricia's voice broke through, heavy with guilt, Pig Clan calm strained from Coinin's chaos.

"Alice feels awful—she tried everything," she said, warmth tinged with sorrow.

David's katana gleamed faintly, Dragon Clan resolve firm despite the loss.

"It was magic, Jade—his runes, not tech. We weren't ready," he said, words sharp, the team's defeat cutting deep.

Jade nodded, leadership steadying.

"You saved countless lives—magic blindsided us, not your fault. Wrap up Coinin and return," she said, rallying, lifting their spirits.

The glitching holo-comm flickered, Coinin's unrest darkening Sheng Xiao, the villains' hold on two talismans—Ox and Rabbit—a dire threat, Jade's resolve burning to reclaim them, the palace's shattered relays humming with tension.

Back in X's fortress, shadow-grid screens pulsed with Coinin's grid, shattered relays marked in red, a holo-screen flickering with the festival's ruins—battered streets, lunar-glow arches dimmed by Vincent's victory.

Vincent staggered in, serpent scepter glowing faintly but erratically, Rabbit Talisman clutched in scarred hands, its dull yellow light pulsing weakly under his grip.

His breaths came ragged, cloak dusted with Coinin's debris and torn from the escape, his face pale and slick with sweat, the toll of weaving runes through the chaotic festival and dodging Guardians leaving him drained, magic's cost biting deep like a venomous recoil that left his limbs heavy and vision blurred.

"We did it," he rasped, voice hoarse from exertion, leaning against a console to steady himself as fatigue clawed at his edges.

X stood at the schematic's core, cold eyes gleaming as he took the talisman, holding both Ox and Rabbit Talismans, Vincent's runes in scepter and book flaring brighter, green glyphs pulsing wildly across etched metal and pages, power surging with Sheng Xiao's stolen energy.

The air in the war room thickened, the Yin scroll and the stolen talismans' combined essence rippling outward like a venomous wave.

Across Sheng Xiao, the effects were immediate and insidious: Coinin's grids, already fragile from Vincent's assault, sputtered into rolling blackouts, plunging entire districts into darkness where holo-lanterns had once danced.

Souris's thawing thorns encroached anew, frost creeping over Rat Clan paths like a recurring nightmare, forcing villagers to huddle in lumber camps for warmth.

Kusini's harvests wilted at the edges, the Ox Talisman's scar reopening with faint cracks in the earth, threatening the sturdy farmlands and harvest altars that had just begun to recover.

Listra's rivers swelled subtly, vines twisting unnaturally as if sensing the imbalance, flooding the treehouse hotels and dancer clans' platforms once more. Doragon's volcanoes rumbled ominously, spewing ash that darkened the crater lake, pagodas trembling as tech-magic relays sparked.

The Rabbit Talisman's tech-magic essence fueled Vincent's runes to unprecedented heights—a dark evolution that made him feel invincible, his ambition coiling tighter than ever, craving X's praise and the talismans' might.

X clasped Vincent's shoulder, his voice a low rumble of approval, eyes flickering with a rare spark of genuine pride amid the blank haze that seemed to cloud X's eyes more often lately.

"Vincent, you've outdone yourself. Coinin's festival was their beacon of hope, and you shattered it like fragile code. The Rabbit Talisman...its power surges through us now, twisting their tech against them. With the Ox amplifying our endurance and this one corrupting their harmony, Sheng Xiao bends to our will. Bella's flames scorched Kusini, Dolore's lightning cracked Listra, Lucas's brute force cleaved Souris—but your cunning? It strikes at their core, invisible and unrelenting. You've proven why you're indispensable." he said.

Vincent's scarred hands tightened on his scepter, the praise igniting a fire in his chest despite the exhaustion weighing him down like chains, his body protesting the magic's drain but his mind sharp with vindication, cementing his place at X's side.

Lucas's sharp gaze caught it, military precision alert, posture rigid.

"The runes—they're stronger," he said, glancing at Bella, voice low with unease.

She nodded, amber eyes narrowing.

"Something's shifting," she said, instincts humming with the anomaly's weight.

Dolore scoffed, strength restored from Listra's battles, dismissal sharp as she leaned against a console.

"It's just Sheng Xiao's power—nothing more," she said, tone cutting, brushing off their concern.

But as X turned away to study the holo-screens, Lucas pulled Bella and Dolore into a shadowed alcove, the damp stone walls pressing close, the faint hum of the talismans echoing like a distant heartbeat.

His bandaged arm from Souris ached faintly, a reminder of the costs they'd paid, but his military focus was unyielding. "Dolore, listen, we're heading for the Dragon Talisman, but Vincent's scepter...it's not right. The way it drains the talismans, the green pulses growing wilder—it's like it's feeding on X, zoning him out more often. If you love X, protect him while we're gone. Watch Vincent close...his ambition's twisting everything. He's not just serving, he's scheming, pulling strings we can't see."

Bella nodded, her amber eyes fierce, flames flickering faintly in her palms as she recalled Kusini's triumph and the praise it earned her—praise Vincent now craved like a starving wolf. "X pulled you from that shrine rubble, Dolore—his mercy forged your devotion. Don't let Vincent unravel it. Those zoned-out moments X has? They started after Souris, when Vincent first touched the spellbook. If those runes surge again, strike first. We've seen him glance at the talismans like they're his crown.

We're counting on you since our cause crumbles if X falls to his own lieutenant."

Dolore's brown eyes flashed with lightning, her unrequited love for X a storm within, but doubt crept in like Listra's floods, memories of X's sorrowful gaze in that ruined shrine, his blade carving through bandits to save her.

She nodded curtly, fingers crackling with restrained power. "I'm worth more than this ruin. For X, I'll guard him like my own storm. But if Vincent crosses the line...his runes won't save him from my bolt." The alcove's shadows deepened with unspoken tension, a seed of rebellion planted amid their loyalty, the group's fractures widening as the talismans' power amplified their suspicions.

X raised the talismans, voice cold as steel.

"Lucas, Bella, target the Dragon Talisman—they're vulnerable now," he ordered, disruptions weakening their defenses.

As X turned, Bella whispered to Dolore once more, "If you love X, protect him while we're gone..." voice urgent, Dolore nodding, duty-bound.

Lucas gulped, concern lingering in his sharp eyes. The fortress thrummed, rune glow intensifying, Sheng Xiao's balance unraveling further, the villains' celebration a spark of triumph, their plans for the Dragon Talisman sharpening, the shattered relays on the holo-screen a testament to their growing power.

Coinin's streets lay battered, food scattered across cracked pavement, booths broken into jagged heaps, Dingo fishers clearing debris with nets, Cochan bakers distributing grain cakes, their hands steadying the weary under dim lunar-glow arches, shattered relays sparking erratically in the cloaked figure's chaos.

Alice stood amidst the wreckage, holo-pad pulsing with code, Rabbit Clan precision steady despite raw guilt over the talisman's loss.

"For Coinin's Rabbit Clan!" she shouted, voice firm, shyness burned away by resolve, rallying the community with a fire she hadn't known she possessed.

Lillith nodded, former envy replaced by determination, Kai following, their respect earned as they worked holo-pads to steady the tech, algorithms syncing seamlessly.

"We've got this, Alice," Lillith said, tone earnest, Kai's quiet focus reinforcing their effort.

Alice's code flared, weaving through the realm-wide grid, signals stabilizing but fragile, a delicate thread holding Sheng Xiao's tech together.

"Blackouts might rotate—stay vigilant," she warned, eyes scanning glitching relays, mind racing to prevent collapse.

Her thoughts drifted to how far she'd come: from the isolated coder in the holo-grid trial, outsmarting Lillith and Kai amid boos and isolation, to this moment—leading her clan through chaos. Souris's thorns had tested her caution, Kusini's flames her cleverness, Coinin's chaos her endurance.

The Rabbit Talisman's loss stung, but it forged her into a true guardian, her shyness yielding to a quiet fire that now rallied her peers, tying into the Rabbit's caution versus her bullying past, where hiding her intelligence from peers like Lillith and Kai had once isolated her, but now united them.

Melissa cleared debris, guiding civilians to safety, Monkey Clan agility swift as she navigated chaos.

"Keep moving!" she called, leadership sharp, voice cutting through the din. She reflected on her journey: Mico's jungle drills burning her out, but Kusini's battles igniting her defiance, Listra's floods teaching her to lead with empathy.

Coinin's festival had been her first taste of joy beyond duty, and though chaos stole it, her spark endured, weaving agility into strategy as she directed Dingo fishers to secure loose drones, her Monkey's cleverness shining against mischievous burnout from overprotective parents.

Ryder distributed food, Rooster Clan strength steady as he handed skewers to weary clans.

"Take this," he said, gruff tone softened by care. His mind wandered to Explosivo's forges, where his parents' disappointment in his "jokester" ways had pushed him to prove more—Kusini's endurance building his grit, Listra's unity tempering his fear of failure, Coinin's chaos honing his boldness.

The Rabbit's loss hit hard, but it fueled his resolve, his cannon now a symbol of protective fire rather than flashy crows, embodying the Rooster's courage versus boastfulness.

David tended to the injured, Dragon Clan calm firm, bandaging a clan member's arm.

"You'll be okay, I promise..." he assured, steady hands a calm pillar. Doragon's misty dojos had forged his discipline, channeling temper into honor—Listra's storms his bond with Hana, Coinin's chaos his vigilance.

The magic's blindsiding defeat gnawed at him, but it sharpened his katana's edge, ready for the Dragon quest in his homeland, where volcanoes and mining hubs awaited, his Dragon's power clashing with temper from high family expectations.

Patricia offered drinks, Pig Clan warmth soothing as she passed water to exhausted workers.

"Stay hydrated!" she said, calm steadying the chaos.

Cochan's fields had taught her patience, harvesting strength from adversity—Coinin's chaos her empathy and quiet leadership. The talisman's theft weighed on her, but her gauntlet's pink-gold runes glowed with renewed purpose, a balm for the weary, reflecting the Pig's generosity versus naivety, learning boundaries from over-trusting.

The Coinin Guardians, battered but united, pushed through the cleanup, their efforts a lifeline against unrest, Alice's resolve anchoring the streets, blackouts looming, Sheng Xiao's energy fragile as lunar-glow arches flickered, their fight a spark against the cloaked figure's victory.

The palace's training hall thrummed, glitching holo-comms casting jagged light, realm-wide recovery reports from Kusini, Souris, Listra, and Ged flickering on shattered screens, Gerry's mom's injury heavy in the air.

Tate hauled debris, Tiger Clan claws steady, his mind heavy with Kusini's failure, where his claws scraped ash, ego leaving gaps Bella exploited.

Listra's storms tempered him, his bravery now a honed roar, vowing no more lapses in Doragon's volcanic trials. Sam coordinated supplies, Snake Clan bow at rest, pride once rivaling Tate's now allied, her wisdom trumping envy, arrows aiding Coinin's recovery.

Doug anchored the effort, Dog Clan sword steady, Souris's betrayals teaching him to anchor, his blade steadying Coinin's chaos, loyalty trumping abandonment fears forged in Dingo's coastal losses, his strength a quiet pillar.

The Coinin Guardians returned, faces etched with exhaustion, demoralized by chaos. Alice's shoulders slumped, guilt raw over the talisman's loss. Melissa's braid was frayed, spark dimmed. Ryder's swagger faltered, Rooster Clan grit worn. David's katana hung heavy, Dragon Clan resolve strained. Patricia's calm was taut, Pig Clan warmth battling fatigue.

Jade stepped forward, voice ringing with conviction.

"You reduced casualties in Coinin—hundreds are safe because of you," she said, lifting spirits.

She met each guardian's eyes, acknowledging their growth: Alice's transformation from shy coder to rally leader, her Rabbit's caution overcoming bullying, Melissa's burnout yielding to empathetic command, her Monkey's cleverness triumphing, Ryder's jokes masking a deepening courage, his Rooster's boastfulness forged into true valor, David's temper forged into unyielding honor, his Dragon's power controlled, Patricia's calm becoming a grounding force, her Pig's generosity wiser, Tate's ego tempered into focused bravery, Sam's pride into strategic alliance, and Doug's loyalty overcoming fear.

Their trials in Souris, Kusini, Listra, and now Coinin had woven them tighter, scars into strengths, preparing for Doragon's volcanic trials and beyond.

She pulled Cade close, scepter trembling, amethyst eyes clouded. The library's dim glow enveloped them, holo-tomes flickering with lore, scent of aged paper mingling with ozone from glitching systems.

"Hana's spark scared me, Cade...I-I thought you'd choose her," she whispered, heart bare, fear of losing him heavy.

Memories flooded: childhood gardens blooming with jasmine, Cade's laughter her anchor during separations—her diplomatic travels tearing her to Coinin's spires and Saanp's dunes, his trainings in Doragon's peaks and Ged's shores. Percy's shadow-traveled updates bridged the gap, his green eyes twinkling: "He's dreaming of your spark, little phoenix."

At fifteen, Cade's return ignited her crush into love, his mismatched eyes her secret flame. But duty chained her, Hana's boldness a mirror to her burdens. "My crown... it weighs us. Do you see me or the crown?" Tears stung, vulnerability cracking her regal mask.

Cade's hand squeezed hers, Cat Clan warmth grounding her, mismatched eyes steady, a vow unspoken to stand by her through Doragon's trials.

"It's always been you, Jade," he said, voice low, sparking hope. "Your light guides me, crown or not."

Hana watched from the hall's edge, her heart shifting, David's resolve now her focus. Patricia's words echoed: "Stop chasing two hearts—reflect on what you want."

Hana's Horse Clan energy had danced through flirts, but Listra's storms and Coinin's chaos revealed David's steady honor as her true rhythm.

She pulled Patricia aside, voice low amid the glitching lights. "I see it now. Jade and Cade—they're an item, aren't they? How could I not notice? The way he looks at her, those mismatched eyes softening...I feel awful, chasing him like that, ignoring David's quiet strength. He saved me in Listra, his katana a shield, and in Coinin, his temper held for the team. I was blind, Patricia—overconfident, rebelling against my parents' marriage pressures by flirting wildly. But David's honor...it's what I need, not mystery."

Patricia's Pig Clan warmth shone, her hand on Hana's shoulder. "You see it now—that's growth. Jade and Cade's bond is deep, rooted in years of separation and duty. Forgive yourself, boldness is your strength, but channeled right, it'll steady you with David."

Hana nodded, eyes misting with regret but resolve, her headscarf framing a determined face.

Approaching David, her whip coiled at her hip, she said softly, "Your katana saved us in Coinin—let's face Doragon together."

David's flush deepened, a rare smile breaking, their banter evolving into something deeper, hands brushing in promise, tying into Hana's free-spirited nature versus overconfidence.

Sam placed a hand on Gerry's shoulder; Snake Clan resolve steady.

"We'll help your mom," she said, calm grounding his worry, their bond a quiet strength.

Gerry's Goat Clan mischief had lightened Listra's floods, but Ged's outages and his mom's injury weighed heavy—Souris's traps testing his leaps, Kusini's endurance his creativity, Coinin's chaos his family ties. Sam's pride, once rivaling Tate's, had softened into alliance, her arrows aiding Coinin's recovery, her Snake's wisdom overcoming envy.

Jade rallied, assigning the Dragon Talisman team, saying, "Rest first, then pursue the Dragon Talisman. David, lead— Dragon Clan lands are your domain, with volcanoes, mines, and crater lakes testing your honor. Patricia, Ryder, Hana, Gerry, Omar, prepare,"

The group nodded, converging for their next move: Tate's leadership tempered by Kusini's failure, Sam's strategy sharpened by Listra's unity, Omar's endurance forged in Souris and Kusini,

Veronica's wit a spark against doubt, Doug's loyalty anchoring all, the Coinin team's fresh scars fueling vengeance, all building toward Saanp's desert ruins and beyond.

Before departing, Veronica pulled Omar close, her Rat Clan heart racing, fear flaring from the Ox Talisman's loss and Coinin's chaos. The hall's glitching lights cast flickering shadows on their faces, amplifying the tension.

"Omar, Souris's thorns scarred you, Coinin's chaos threatens us—I can't lose you," she whispered, voice trembling, hands clutching his tunic.

Memories surged: their first spark in Souris's frost-dusted forests, navigating glyph traps side by side, her cunning solving riddles while his strength held the maze's illusions at bay and Souris's thorn maze, where his mace cleared her path, their bond deepening amid the frost. "Come back safe—I need your steady heart."

Her lips met his in a fierce, urgent kiss, hands trembling as she clung to him, haunted by the Rat Talisman's traps and Bella's betrayal, the kiss lingering with desperation and love, a vow sealed in the chaos.

Omar's Ox Clan strength steadied her, his arms wrapping around her, his nod firm, eyes locked with hers. "Your spark lights my path, Veronica. Souris taught us cunning endures. I'll return; our bond's unbreakable." Their foreheads touched, breaths syncing, the moment a blazing vow against the Dragon quest's dangers in Doragon's misty peaks.

Gerry turned to Sam as he said, "Keep me updated on Mom," worry raw, Sam nodding, supportive.

The Guardians' resolve burned, Coinin's unrest lingering, their courage a flame against shattered tech, ready to pursue the Dragon Talisman, their unity a spark against the looming threat.

As the holo-screens flickered with reports of rotating blackouts and encroaching thorns, Jade felt Sheng Xiao's pulse quicken—a warning that the villains' grip tightened, but so did the Guardians' unbreakable weave, foreshadowing the battles in Saanp's deserts, Fahal Alkhayl's trade routes, and beyond.

Chapter 20: Doragon's Peaks

David's memories of Doragon shimmered like fragments of a half-forgotten dream, pulling him back to a time when the realm pulsed with unyielding harmony. He could almost feel the cool mist rolling off the serene crater lakes, their glassy surfaces mirroring the disciplined dojos perched on misty peaks, where Dragon Clan warriors drilled in precise formations under the watchful eyes of mentors like Kenta.

The pagoda roofs had gleamed under clear, azure skies, their curved eaves etched with ancient dragon motifs that seemed to breathe with Sheng Xiao's vital energy. The air had been crisp, carrying the faint, sweet scent of wisteria blossoms from distant gardens.

Honor had been a steady pulse, binding the clan like an unbreakable chain—warriors moving as one, their shouts echoing off volcanic cliffs, forging bonds that withstood any storm. David had been a boy then, his small hands gripping a wooden sword, Kenta's voice guiding him: "Honor is not glory, David. It is the quiet strength that holds when all else crumbles." Those lessons had shaped him, turning his youthful temper into disciplined resolve, preparing him for the guardianship he now bore.

But now, as David led Patricia, Ryder, Hana, Gerry, and Omar through the ash-choked streets of Doragon's main city, that dream had twisted into a nightmare. The sky hung heavy with a crimson haze, volcanoes spewing plumes of dark ash that blotted out the sun, casting an eerie, blood-red glow over everything.

Molten lava snaked through cracked cobblestone streets like glowing veins of fire, hissing and bubbling as it devoured wooden carts and market stalls. Steam curled upward in thick, sulfurous clouds, stinging David's eyes and throat with every breath, making his lungs burn as if he'd inhaled embers. The ground trembled faintly underfoot, a constant reminder of the unrest below, and the air tasted bitter with ash that coated his tongue like fine grit.

Miners, their faces etched with strain and soot-streaked sweat, dug frantic channels with obsidian shovels, diverting the lava flows before they could engulf the pagodas. One such structure loomed ahead, its once-elegant roof sagging under the weight of accumulated ash, its dragon carvings charred and cracked.

David gripped his katana tightly, the hilt familiar and grounding in his calloused hand, his shoulders squared against the chaos. The sulfurous air clawed at his nostrils, a far cry from the fresh mountain breezes of his youth, and his jaw clenched with determination.

Honor demanded he protect his clan's land, but the contrast between memory and reality seared his heart like a fresh wound. David's pulse quickened, his Dragon Clan honor—forged in the arena's fire, where he'd bested a gauntlet of fire-dancers in the Dragon Games, dodging their blazing assaults and volcanic illusions with precise katana forms honed through grueling trials—urging him to restore balance.

"We need to reach Kenta's dojo," he said, his voice steady despite the knot in his chest, urging the group forward through the choking haze.

The shattered relays sparked erratically along the streets, their tech-magic cores flickering like dying stars, a direct consequence of the Rabbit Talisman's loss in Coinin. Without its stabilizing influence, Sheng Xiao's interconnected grids had faltered realm-wide, but here in Doragon, the disruption amplified the volcanic fury, turning the once-orderly city into a molten ruin. Holo-screens that had once broadcast clan announcements now glitched with static, projecting fragmented images of erupting peaks.

David's boots crunched over cooled lava shards, each step a reminder of the fragile balance they fought to restore. Patricia walked beside him, her Pig Clan gauntlet glowing faintly with pink-gold runes, her calm demeanor an anchor in the turmoil.

"The miners are holding, but barely," she observed, her voice warm yet practical, nodding toward a group hauling boulders to reinforce a barrier.

Ryder, ever the Rooster Clan firecracker, adjusted his cannon strap with a grin that didn't quite reach his eyes, his mind flashing to Explosivo's forges where his jokes had masked failures. "This place looks like Explosivo after a bad forge day—minus the fun explosions."

Hana trailed a step behind, her whip coiled at her hip, her Horse Clan energy simmering beneath a layer of quiet focus, though David caught her glancing at him with an unspoken tension that stirred his own doubts.

Gerry gripped his spear tightly, his Goat Clan mischief subdued by the gravity of the scene, his thoughts drifting to his mom's injury in Ged's outages, fueling a quiet resolve to push harder. Omar's massive frame cut a path ahead, his Ox Clan strength ready to shove aside any obstacle, his mind lingering on Veronica's fierce kiss before departure.

They reached Kenta's dojo at the city's edge, a sturdy structure of dark wood and stone that had withstood centuries of Doragon's volcanic fury. Kenta, David's mentor since boyhood, emerged from the haze like a ghost from the mist, his gray eyes sharp with the unyielding wisdom of the Dragon Clan.

His obsidian blade was sheathed at his side, its hilt wrapped in weathered leather, and his hands were smudged with ash and dirt from digging channels alongside the miners. His tunic, once pristine, was torn and sweat-stained, but his posture remained ramrod straight, a testament to the discipline he'd instilled in David.

"David," he greeted, his voice warm yet laced with the weight of command, clapping a firm hand on his protégé's shoulder. The touch grounded David, pulling him back from the edge of doubt.

Kenta invited them inside the dojo's dim interior, where wooden beams etched with intricate dragon motifs arched overhead, and the faint scent of incense lingered despite the sulfur infiltrating from outside.

Over steaming cups of green tea—bitter with ash that had settled in the water—and bowls of simple rice porridge, Kenta recounted Doragon's ruin in measured tones, his words painting a vivid picture of the catastrophe.

"The altar's burning in Kusini woke the volcanoes from their slumber," Kenta explained, his gaze heavy as he stirred his tea, the steam rising like volcanic plumes in miniature. "Eruptions that were once rare now rage unchecked, lava flooding the valleys and ash choking the skies. The Rabbit Talisman's loss has crippled our tech-magic relays—holo-comms glitch, drones falter, and even the simplest grids overheat. But the Tiger Talisman's recovery has eased the worst of it. The flows slow slightly, giving us time to dig, but still, the spectral dragon at the crater lake stirs, its test awaiting a true guardian."

He fixed his eyes on David, the weight of expectation pressing like a physical force. "It's up to you, David, to restore balance. Honor binds the clan—navigate the mine tunnels to the crater lake, face the spectral dragon's test with dragon-claw slashes and wind gusts in the misty peaks. Prove your discipline, or Doragon falls."

David nodded, Kenta's words igniting a fire in his chest, a blend of pride and resolve that battled the sting of Hana's lingering gaze.

Her shift toward him after Coinin had been a spark, but doubts about her past flirtation with Cade still cast a shadow on his focus, a quiet jealousy he pushed down like an unwelcome intruder. He couldn't afford distractions—not when Sheng Xiao's fate hung in the balance.

Vowing silently to unite the team, David drew strength from Kenta's teachings, the mentor's steady presence a reminder of the boy he'd been and the guardian he'd become.

As they finished their meal, the Guardians stepped out into Doragon's ash-choked streets once more, the air thicker now with the acrid bite of cooling lava.

They aided miners along the way, Patricia organizing supply lines with her compassionate efficiency, directing weary workers to safer routes.

"Stay low and keep your masks on," she urged, her voice a soothing counterpoint to the chaos, earning grateful nods from the soot-covered clansfolk.

Omar scouted ahead, his mace swinging easily as he cleared a path through debris, his Ox Clan endurance unyielding.

Gerry signaled miners to safety with quick gestures, his spear raised like a beacon, his focus sharp despite the worry for his mom gnawing at him like a persistent thorn—news from Ged had been spotty since the glitches began.

Ryder, trying to lighten the mood, quipped as he helped haul a boulder, "More fire to dodge? Should be easy! Explosivo's forges make this look like a cozy campfire."

His Rooster Clan grit eased the tension, drawing a few chuckles from the miners, but David caught the underlying strain in his friend's voice, a hint of the insecurities Ryder hid behind humor.

Hana stepped closer to David as they walked, her whip coiled tightly, her voice soft amid the rumbling earth.

"David, I'm here for you—no matter what," she offered, her eyes searching his with a warmth that made his heart twist. He met her gaze briefly, doubts flickering—could he trust this shift, or was it just the quest's pressure?

"We need to focus now," he replied, his tone gentler than before but still guarded, "but... I appreciate you being here." The words hung between them, a small bridge over the gap, her nod understanding as she fell back a step, determination hardening her features.

David's katana gleamed amid Doragon's ash-choked hills, sulfur stinging his eyes, the weight of duty pressing like molten rock on his shoulders.

A memory surged from a dojo spar at fifteen, the mist chilling his skin as katanas clanged in rhythmic fury. His temper had flared then, a rival's taunt igniting rage like a volcano's core—blade swinging wildly, missing Kenta's precise target and clashing harmlessly against stone. The dojo echoed with his frustrated roar, shame burning hotter than the obsidian forges below.

Kenta's steady gaze pierced him: "Honor, not anger, David. Power unchecked is a dragon without scales—vulnerable, destructive."

The crater lake loomed ahead now, Hana's budding trust a fragile spark in his chest, but his temper simmered, threatening to erupt and fracture their leadership.

The zodiac carvings on the tunnel walls pulsed faintly, as if urging him to harness his Dragon Clan might, forging duty into unyielding discipline before the spectral test consumed them all. He clenched his fist, vowing to temper the fire within, for Sheng Xiao's sake—and his own redemption.

Kenta's voice echoed in his mind: "The dragon's heart cracks when honor falters—yours won't."

The words grounded him, a reminder from boyhood drills where Kenta's steady gaze had tempered his rage. The crater lake loomed, Hana's trust a fragile spark, but his temper simmered beneath. He clenched his fist again, vowing to lead with discipline, not fury—for Sheng Xiao, for the team.

The city's unrest pulsed through him, Doragon's honor teetering on the brink, his leadership burning to reclaim the talisman and mend the wounds inflicted by X's schemes.

In X's fortress, Dolore slipped into Vincent's chamber, the air thick with the residue of his magic—faint green sparks lingering on his serpent scepter, propped against a console. She gulped nervously.

Vincent lay on a cot, his face pale and drawn, breaths shallow from the exhaustion of unleashing his runes in Coinin. His scarred hands twitched faintly, as if still channeling the power that had drained him like venom from a wound.

Dolore's brown eyes softened with concern, her unrequited love for X warring with her suspicion of Vincent's growing ambition.

"You pushed too hard," she said, her voice low and probing, sitting on the edge of the cot.

Vincent's eyes cracked open, irritation flashing as he waved her off weakly. "It was necessary. Jade's Guardians crumble under my strikes. The talismans feed my runes now...soon, even X will see my true worth."

His words carried a sly edge, his gaze drifting to the stolen Ox and Rabbit Talismans on a nearby pedestal, their pulses syncing with his scepter. Dolore's lightning crackled faintly in her fingers, doubt stirring like Listra's floods.

"Rest, then. X needs you sharp for Doragon." She left, her mind churning with Lucas and Bella's warnings—Vincent's fatigue masked something darker, a scheme coiling tighter.

Deep in Doragon's mines, Lucas and Bella crept through the damp, echoing tunnels, their footsteps muffled by the thick layer of volcanic dust underfoot. The air was heavy with sulfur, condensation dripping from the jagged stone ceilings, and obsidian veins glinted ominously under the faint glow of their rune-torches.

They plotted flame snares and rockfalls with ruthless precision, their men hauling massive boulders to block key paths, sweat beading on their brows despite the chill.

Bella's fire flared across narrow routes, her amber eyes glinting as she wove intricate dragon-scale traps that mimicked Doragon's lava flows, the heat singeing the air and casting flickering shadows on the walls, her Kusini triumph fueling a hunger for more praise from X.

Lucas's fingers flew over rune-grid consoles, syncing rune-eyed drones to the Ox and Rabbit Talismans' pulses, their green glows priming to disrupt the crater lake's sacred energies.

"These Guardians think honor will save them," Bella sneered, her voice echoing faintly, amber eyes narrowed with precision. "We'll bury them in their own mountains."

In their fortress briefing earlier, X had ordered with cold authority, "Strike after the Guardians claim the talisman—use the mines to your advantage, target the crater lake as Vincent suggested."

Vincent's sly grin had lingered in Lucas's mind, the magic user's ambition coiling like his serpent scepter.

Now, as their team set the traps, a scout stumbled into a sudden lava surge, his screams echoing through the tunnels as the molten rock claimed him, the acrid smell of burning flesh mingling with the sulfur. Bella's eyes scanned the slopes, her instincts humming with alertness.

"Keep moving—you don't want to end up like him," Lucas barked, his voice chilling the air, his military precision masking the unease gnawing at him. Their traps poised to strike, the mines blocking holo-comms with deliberate interference, the tunnels thrumming with danger, their plan sharp as obsidian blades. The Guardians' path would be perilous, Sheng Xiao's balance fragile under the weight of their malice.

Back in the Imperial Palace's command chamber, cherry blossom petals drifted lazily outside Jade's arched window, their delicate pink hues glowing softly in the moonlight that filtered through.

Her scepter rested on an ornate stand, pulsing faintly with amethyst light, while stained-glass windows cast Sheng Xiao's storied history in muted, colorful hues across the room—dragons coiling around zodiac symbols, guardians of old standing defiant against chaos.

The Rabbit Talisman's glitches caused the chamber's lights to flicker erratically, casting jagged shadows over the holo-screens displaying realm-wide reports. Cade stood close to her, their recent confession hanging between them like a lingering fire, her heart racing at his proximity, his mismatched eyes a silent vow of protection.

"I'm worried—I need to help them," Jade whispered, her voice laced with the fear of the magic user's growing threat, Vincent's green runes haunting her thoughts like a venomous shadow.

She paced slightly, her mind replaying the Guardians' brutal encounters: Bella's flames scorching Kusini's altar, Dolore's lightning cracking Listra's vines, Vincent's chaos unraveling Coinin's festival. "They've faced magic at every turn, and I'm the only one with power to counter it. If I don't go, Doragon could fall like the others."

Cade's eyes darkened, worry creasing his brow as he stepped closer, his hand brushing hers in a tentative touch that sent a spark through her.

"You're the empress—it's too dangerous," he countered, his voice raw with concern, the image of the Guardians' scars flashing through his mind.

"Only my magic can match his," she urged, her gaze steady and unyielding, the weight of the crown pressing on her shoulders, her fingers lingering on his for a moment longer than necessary.

"I can't bear to see you hurt, Jade," he said, his voice softening, the intensity in his eyes making her pulse quicken.

"You'll protect me, together, we're unstoppable," she pressed, her determination igniting like a spark, their shared history—childhood gardens, separations, Percy's updates— fueling the unspoken pull between them. Cade hesitated, his Cat Clan instincts warring with his love for her, but he nodded finally.

"I'll protect you, but stay close—no risks," he agreed, their bond deepening in that moment, the plan solidifying like forged steel, a promise of more to come. The palace buzzed with activity below, but in this chamber, their focus sharpened, Jade's resolve burning brightly to aid the Guardians in Doragon.

David led the Guardians through the ash-choked hills beyond the city, where sparse pagodas dotted the rugged countryside like ancient sentinels, their roofs sagging under layers of volcanic dust.

Lava flows cast an eerie, pulsating glow across the landscape, steam curling upward in thick tendrils, and miners forged obsidian barriers with disciplined strikes, their hammers ringing against stone despite the exhaustion etched on their faces.

The earth cracked ominously underfoot, and a sudden rumble shook the ground, sending a small lava surge bubbling toward them.

David reacted instantly, his katana flashing as he directed the group. "Omar, block it—everyone, to the ridge!"

Omar swung his mace, shattering a boulder to divert the flow, while the others scrambled up the incline, hearts pounding from the near miss. David gripped his katana, jaw clenched against the sulfur stinging his eyes, honor driving him forward like an unquenchable flame.

Kenta's teaching echoed in his mind— "Honor binds the clan"—guiding his resolve to unite the team, even as Hana's presence stirred unresolved tension.

Patricia strategized evasion routes, her Pig Clan compassion directing miners to safer paths, her voice firm and reassuring.

"Stay low and follow the ridges," she urged, earning nods of gratitude as she handed out water skins from their packs.

Ryder looked around at the glowing flows and quipped, "Nice barbecue spot... if you like your meat extra charred."

His Rooster Clan grit was sharp, but it masked the flicker of doubt in his eyes—memories of Explosivo's forges, where his jokes had hidden deeper insecurities.

Hana stepped closer to David again, her whip coiled at her side, her voice soft amid the rumbling earth. "David, that was quick thinking—I'm glad we're in this together."

He met her gaze, doubts flickering, but softened slightly.

"We do need to focus... but your insight helps," he admitted, a small step toward trust.

A miner approached them at a precarious barrier, her face ashen and desperate, recognizing David from afar. "You're the one who won the Dragon Games—your victory in the gauntlet, dodging blazing assaults and volcanic illusions with precise katana forms honed through grueling trials, inspired my family during the last period of calm before the volcanoes awakened. Please, Guardians, my comrades are trapped deeper in the mines. Save them if you can."

Her plea fueled his resolve like a fresh wind, tying into a quick flashback: the arena's roar as he bested fire-dancers with precise katana forms, Kenta's proud nod crowning him guardian, temper forged into honor.

Omar scouted ahead, his Ox Clan strength clearing fallen rocks with ease, while Gerry gripped his spear tightly, his focus wavering as thoughts of his mom in Ged's outages deepened his determination—he couldn't let her down by faltering here. Kenta's words echoed louder now, urging David to prioritize unity over personal glory.

The poison air thickened as they climbed, but the Guardians pressed forward, carving paths through the haze toward the mine tunnels. The countryside thrumming with volcanic menace, the trial's mine tunnels looming like dark maws ahead, Sheng Xiao's balance fragile under the weight of imbalance.

As they neared the entrance, the miner who had pleaded for help paused at a small shrine nestled against the rocky outcrop, its obsidian altar etched with dragon motifs and wreathed in faded wisteria vines. She gestured for the Guardians to join her in a brief ritual, her voice low and reverent as she led a chant of dragon-scale verses, sulfur scents mingling with the faint, lingering fragrance of the wilted blooms.

The Guardians echoed her words, their voices rising in unison: "Honor binds the clan, forged in fire and depth." The chant mimicked mining strikes—hammers to stone echoing the realm's economy of Sheng Xiao's obsidian veins—the altar's surface quivering like molten glass under the crimson haze.

David felt the ritual's pulse steady his katana grip, urging him to embrace its ancient power, honoring Doragon's mining heritage as he prepared for the spectral dragon's test. The Guardians united, their courage a defiant spark against the cloaked figure's insidious malice—Vincent's venomous schemes—and David's leadership burning fiercely to face the spectral dragon and reclaim what was rightfully theirs.

In the palace, Sam shared good news about Gerry's mom, her recovery lifting the spirits of the Guardians gathered in the command chamber—Veronica, Sam, Doug, Tate, Melissa, and Alice—where glitches cast jagged light across strategy maps.

"She's mending well in Ged's clinics," Sam announced, her Snake Clan resolve evident in her steady tone.

Melissa asked, "Have you told Gerry? He's been worried sick."

Alice replied, adjusting her glasses as her holo-pad glowed, "We've restored most holo-comms, but the mines block Doragon's signals."

Doug examined a tactical display, his Dog Clan loyalty sharpening his focus. "They're likely inside by now—deep in the tunnels."

Jade gathered the Guardians, her voice firm and commanding.

"Aid the clans and repair Imperial City's tech—I must handle a critical task," she said, her eyes guarded, not revealing her plan to join the Doragon team

After Jade had slipped away following her announcement, the Guardians wondered about her task.

Tate added with a shrug, "Jade's maybe seeking tech-mages for allies in the spires."

Veronica whispered to the group, "Is she rallying clans in the cherry gardens?"

Alice's holo-pad flared brighter, countering Rabbit Talisman glitches in the Imperial City's spires, her Rabbit Clan focus fierce and unwavering.

Melissa aided refugees with calm resolve, organizing food distributions in the plazas below, their efforts unwavering amid the flickering lights. The palace buzzed with purpose, their unity a spark in the darkness, Sheng Xiao's balance teetering as their courage burned brightly against the encroaching storm.

329

Chapter 21: Tunnels of Peril

David led Patricia, Ryder, Hana, Gerry, and Omar into the mine tunnels of Doragon, the damp stone walls slick with condensation that glistened like dark tears under the stuttering glow of holo-torches. Obsidian veins snaked through the rock, catching the flickering light and casting jagged shadows that danced across scarred surfaces, as if the mountain itself pulsed with unease.

Moisture dripped in slow, rhythmic rivulets, their echoes mingling with the howling wind that tore through jagged cracks like a ghostly wail, carrying the acrid bite of sulfur that burned David's throat with every breath.

The tunnels twisted unpredictably, their rough surfaces snagging at cloaks and scraping against skin, while pebbles crunched underfoot, a constant reminder of the unstable ground.

The Rabbit Talisman's glitches—its loss still raw from Coinin's chaos—caused the holo-torches to flicker erratically, their light weaving through the dank air, barely holding back the encroaching darkness. David steadied his stance, his katana gleaming faintly in the dim glow, the sulfur clawing at his lungs as he drew on memories of his Dragon Games victory.

He could still hear the roar of the arena, feel the weight of his blade as he perfected swordplay forms against fire-dancers, their flames licking at his heels under a crimson sky, earning his title as clan champion before Empress Jade's recent summons crowned him guardian. Kenta's voice had anchored him then, as it did now: "Honor binds the clan."

That lesson urged unity, a fire in his chest as he led the Guardians toward the crater lake, their path fraught with unseen threats.

Before entering deeper, David paused at the tunnel's mouth, where a carved dragon altar stood, its scales pulsing with faint tech-magic, etched with zodiac runes that shimmered like molten glass.

A Dragon Scale Relic—a jagged shard of tech-magic crystal said to channel the spectral dragon's power—rested at its center, glowing with the hues of Sheng Xiao's zodiac symbols, sparking faintly as if kissed by dragon's breath.

"Let's honor the clan," David said, his voice steady despite the sulfur's sting, leading a call-and-response chant taught by Kenta. "Through fire and stone, honor binds us," he intoned, the Guardians echoing, "The dragon's breath guides our blades."

Their voices rose in unison: "In zodiac harmony, we find our path."

The Guardians bowed to the altar, a gesture of respect, as the carvings flared brighter, projecting a holographic zodiac wheel that spun above, its symbols—tiger, rabbit, ox—pulsing with ancient power, casting a soft glow across their faces.

A faint mist rose from the altar, carrying visions of the spectral dragon's creation: a celestial beast, scales glinting like molten stars, forging Doragon's peaks from volcanic fire, its breath weaving tech and magic into Sheng Xiao's balance, its roar shaping the crater lake as a heart to guard against chaos.

David's mind flashed to a boyhood memory by Kenta's dojo fire, the mentor's voice low: "The dragon bound the realms, David, its spirit in every stone, but only honor can restore its harmony when chaos rises."

The relic's spark warmed his hand as he touched it, a surge of resolve pulsing through him, the altar's hum resonating like a heartbeat, the faint scent of ancient incense cutting through the sulfur, grounding them.

"Long chant, David—trying to outdo Explosivo's bards?" Ryder quipped, tossing a pebble at Gerry, who smirked.

"You'd trip over your own lyrics, Rooster," Gerry shot back, their banter easing the tension as the altar's glow faded, a low rumble signaling the dangers ahead.

The ground shook, the vibrations rattling loose stones and causing spiked nets—barbed traps strung across narrow passages—to sway ominously, their glinting barbs catching the torchlight like predatory teeth. The altar's light dimmed as if in warning, seamlessly blending ritual into peril.

David's eyes narrowed, his katana flashing as he slashed through a net with precise strokes, the metal snapping with a sharp twang. "Stay sharp," he called, his voice resolute despite the raw sting in his throat, his heart set on the trial ahead, the spectral dragon's test looming like a storm on the horizon.

His leadership was a spark against the imbalance threatening Sheng Xiao, but doubts lingered—could he fully trust Hana, with her past flirtation with Cade still a quiet thorn in his focus?

The miner they'd met in Doragon's hills, her face ashen from the volcanic chaos, guided them deeper, her voice hoarse as she clutched a worn pickaxe.

"Others are trapped further in—follow me," she urged, her eyes reflecting gratitude for David's earlier aid, her son inspired by his Dragon Games triumph that marked him as clan champion before Jade's summons.

"My brother was lost to these tunnels last season," she whispered, her voice breaking, "but you give us hope." They reached a collapsed tunnel, the air thick with dust and the faint scent of charred stone, the ground trembling again.

Omar heaved massive rocks with his Ox Clan strength, muscles straining as he cleared a path, his thoughts drifting to Veronica's fierce kiss in the palace, her Rat Clan wit a light in his mind that steadied him like an anchor.

Hana passed debris to Gerry and Patricia in a swift line, her hands trembling but steady, her Horse Clan agility turning the labor into a dance of precision. Ryder tossed rubble aside with a quick spin, his Rooster Clan grin flashing despite the strain, his mind flickering to Explosivo's forges where his parents' stern voices— "You're more than quips, Ryder"—still stung.

"This dragon's got bad decorators," he quipped, dodging a falling pebble, his humor masking fear of failure.

Patricia piled stones to mark safe paths, her Pig Clan compassion grounding the team as she steadied a wavering miner with a gentle touch, her pink-gold gauntlet glowing faintly.

"Keep steady," she urged, her voice warm, earning nods of trust from the soot-streaked clansfolk.

They freed the trapped miners, who embraced their comrade with dust-streaked faces, relief heavy in the air like a lifted burden.

"Head to the surface—warn others of the strange green lights we've seen," David instructed, his voice firm but kind. The miners nodded, their leader grasping his arm.

"You've given us hope, guardian. Your Dragon Games victory inspired my son, and now you save us. May the spectral dragon watch you," she said, her voice thick with emotion, the tale of her lost brother adding weight to their mission.

They hurried away, their footsteps echoing in the darkening passages, leaving the Guardians to face the looming traps alone, the warning about "green lights" lingering like a foreboding omen, hinting at the cloaked figure's malevolent runes.

Lucas and Bella's traps escalated—a rune-etched floor glowed green, triggering a collapsing ceiling, its dragon carvings fracturing with a deafening crack that echoed like a dying beast. Hana's Snake Clan instincts flared, spotting the rune first.

"Hold!" she shouted, her whip cracking to disable the glowing sigil, saving David from falling rocks that would have crushed him.

"Thanks," he said, eyes softening, a flicker of trust sparking. "I need you out here, Hana,"

She nodded, asserting, "I'm proving it," her voice firm, her rebellion from past quests giving way to purpose, their bond mending like a circuit reconnecting.

David leaped over a spiked pit, his katana slashing another net, its barbs clattering to the ground.

A second trap surged—a rune-activated cave-in, green-glowing rocks tumbling from above, their edges sharp as dragon claws. Hana led again, her whip snapping to deflect shards, guiding the team.

"Veer right!" she called, dispersing a poison cloud hissing from a vent, its green shimmer echoing the miner's warning, a clear mark of the cloaked figure's style. David slashed a boulder, their movements syncing.

"You're quick," he said, a rare smile breaking through. "I was wrong to doubt you,"

"I'm here for the team—and you," she replied, her eyes steady, their trust solidifying like forged steel.

A third trap erupted—a rune-etched floor pulsed green, unleashing a flood of volcanic ash that roared through the tunnel like a gray torrent, choking the air with heat and grit.

David shouted, "Brace!" as Hana's whip lashed a rune to slow the flow, her quick-thinking buying time.

Ryder fired his cannon, blasting ash to clear a path, the recoil jolting him.

"This dragon's got too much flair," he quipped, coughing, tossing a pebble at Gerry, who grinned.

"Aim better, Rooster!" Gerry teased, propping a barrier with his spear to shield the team, his worry for his mom in Ged's outages fueling his resolve.

Omar diverted the ash flow with his mace, his strength unyielding, his heart aching for Veronica's embrace, her kiss a steady anchor. Patricia guided the team, piling stones to mark a safe path, her calm unshaken.

"Stay close!" she called, her gauntlet glowing brighter, a beacon in the chaos.

A trio of Lucas's mercenary scouts lunged from the shadows, blades gleaming with malicious intent, their boots echoing in the tight passage. Hana's whip cracked, disarming one in a swift arc, while David tackled another, pinning him against the wall, his katana at the scout's throat.

"Who sent you?" he demanded, his voice a low growl.

The scout rasped, "Vincent's orders—" before a rune-arrow from a fellow scout exploded in a burst of green light, killing him instantly, the acrid smell of magic choking the air.

The remaining scouts bolted, and the Guardians gave chase through the narrow tunnel, dodging falling debris from the ash flood's aftermath.

Hana, crouched near a crevice, overheard Bella's voice ahead: "Vincent's plan will finish them at the lake."

David's eyes met hers, the name "Vincent"—the cloaked figure—fueling their resolve, a spark of urgency driving them forward.

"He's not here, but his traps are," Hana whispered, her voice tense, the mystery deepening.

Ryder's cannon dispersed a drone swarm buzzing from a hidden alcove, their green cores bursting in violet flashes.

"Nice shot, for once," Gerry quipped, pulling David and Hana from debris, his movements quick despite the weight of his mom's injury, her recovery a distant hope.

The group caught their breath, the crater lake's glow faintly visible, pulsing with menace, the air thick with the promise of the spectral dragon's test.

In Jade's private quarters in the Imperial Palace, lacquered walls etched with zodiac constellations glimmered under the soft glow of amethyst crystals from a small shrine, their light casting starry patterns across a balcony overlooking cherry blossom gardens, the air scented with lotus incense.

Cade stood there for the first time, his heart racing at the intimacy of the space—vases of jasmine flowers, zodiac tapestries shimmering with starry threads, her amethyst scepter glowing on a lacquered stand.

Her strength, her beauty, the way her amethyst eyes caught the light, drew him like a magnet, his Cat Clan warmth urging him to hold her, to kiss her, but respect for her empress role held him back, his love a fire he kept banked.

Jade felt the electricity, no man ever in her chambers, Cade's strong form and mismatched eyes igniting her love, her nerves tingling with the thrill of his presence, her heart torn between duty and the desire to close the distance.

"I'm scared, Cade," she whispered, her voice trembling with vulnerability, stepping closer until their hands brushed, sending sparks through her veins. "The cloaked figure's magic—Coinin's fall, Kusini's flames, Listra's floods—it's tearing us apart. I must stop him."

Cade's breath caught, his hand lingering on hers, his desire to pull her close warring with restraint.

"You're the heart of Sheng Xiao, Jade," he said, his voice husky, eyes locked on hers. "I'd face any darkness for you—always will."

Their faces drew close, a near-kiss moment charged with longing, the air shimmering with their shared love. Jade took a breath, her resolve hardening.

"We can't let the Guardians face this alone," she said, her voice steadying.

Cade nodded, his hand tightening on hers.

"Then we go—together," he replied, their partnership a vow against the storm.

"We're shadow-traveling to Doragon," Jade said, her tone firm.

"Hold me tight—it's like sinking into a dream," Cade replied, his voice soft but intense. "I've never brought anyone," he admitted, concern flickering, "It might unsteady you."

She pressed against him, her pulse racing, the air electric with their love.

"I trust you, Cade," she murmured, their eyes locked, the moment magical as velvet shadow tendrils swirled around them, a starry dance of darkness and light, her heartbeat syncing with his as they vanished, the chamber silent, the scent of lotus lingering like a whisper of their love.

They emerged outside Doragon's tunnels, the starlight casting a faint glow over the volcanic slopes, the crater lake's waters shimmering faintly below, its surface rippling with an eerie promise. Jade swayed slightly, the shadow-travel's pull lingering, her head spinning from the void's embrace. Cade steadied her, his hands gentle on her arms, worry creasing his brow.

"You, okay? That was rough," he said, his voice soft, checking for dizziness, his touch lingering as he searched her face, his heart pounding with fear for her safety.

She smiled, her hand brushing his, reassuring, "I'm good—your strength carried me through."

They paused under the starlight, their hands still clasped, a quiet vow forming.

"We'll face X's threat together," Jade whispered, her eyes steady.

Cade nodded, his gaze fierce.

"No matter what, I'm with you," he said, their bond electric with warmth, a promise to stand united.

They crouched at the tunnel entrance, shadows cloaking their steps, hearts pounding as they slipped into the mines, spying on Bella and Lucas setting traps near the lake's entrance.

Cade whispered, "Just Bella and Lucas—no cloaked figure in charge."

Jade's eyes narrowed, scanning the gloom.

"That's Bella—she burned Kusini's altar," she said, her voice tight with memory of the fiery scars.

"And Lucas fought in Souris," Cade added, his knives ready, their blades glinting faintly.

They disabled lone scouts silently, Cade's shadows cloaking their strikes like a silken tide, Jade's magic flaring to collapse a spiked pit, the tension crackling in the damp, sulfurous air.

As they eavesdropped, Lucas muttered, "Vincent will be pleased—we strike after they claim the talisman," and Jade's breath caught—the cloaked figure's name was Vincent, a revelation that hardened their resolve, their hands tightening in silent agreement.

The palace war room buzzed with urgency, holo-screens flickering with reports from Sheng Xiao's clans—Coinin's grids stabilizing slowly, Ged's clinics mending, Kusini's harvests holding despite cracks, Listra's floods easing. Stone pillars carved with dragon motifs stood sentinel, their shadows dancing under humming holo-screens sparked by Rabbit Talisman glitches.

Veronica rallied Rat Clan scouts to aid Ged's clinics for Gerry's mom, her commands sharp, her heart racing for Omar's safe return, his steady Ox Clan strength a beacon in her thoughts, their kiss in Souris's frost a lingering warmth that steadied her.

Alice decoded glitch patterns, her holo-pad glowing with Rabbit Clan focus, her glasses fogging slightly, her mind flashing to Coinin's chaos where her code had held the grid together, a quiet pride fueling her as she tweaked a new fix.

Sam trained medics for Coinin's recovery, her Snake Clan voice steady, recalling her Listra alliance with Tate, their pride now a shared strength.

Doug and Tate fortified the spires, weaving through cherry gardens where blossoms drifted like hope. Melissa rallied refugees, her Monkey Clan resolve ironclad, a flashback to Mico's jungle drills—dodging data-vines under starlit canopies—fueling her pep talk to inspire hope.

"Where's Cade?" Doug asked, examining a tactical display.

Tate shrugged, his Tiger Clan claws gleaming. "Not in training."

Veronica grinned, her Rat Clan wit sharp. "Jade's gone too—together?"

Sam teased, her bow resting nearby. "Secret mission?"

Melissa laughed, adjusting a holo-grid. "Maybe seeking temple allies."

Alice smirked, tweaking her holo-pad. "Or spires strategy—Jade's sneaky like my code."

Tate chuckled, "Like when I botched Kusini's altar? Sam's arrows bailed me out."

Sam grinned, "You owe me, Tiger!"

Their banter warmed the room, a spark of unity in the chaos, Sheng Xiao's balance fragile but bolstered by their efforts, Coinin's recovery a testament to their resilience.

Back at X's fortress, X stood before a holographic map of Sheng Xiao's realms, its blue glow casting stark shadows across his cold, angular features as he gritted his teeth.

The Ox and Rabbit Talismans rested on a pedestal, their pulses faint but menacing, amplifying his vendetta—a wound from a lost love that drove him to shatter Jade's radiant harmony.

Reports of the Guardians arriving in Doragon, relayed through glitching holo-feeds showing David's team cutting through the hills, stirred a rare unease in his chest, a crack in his steely resolve.

"They're more persistent than I thought," he muttered, fingers drumming on the console, his mind flashing to a distant memory of a lover's smile, now ashes in his heart, pushing him to tighten his grip on the realms.

Vincent entered, his serpent scepter sparking with green runes, his face pale from Coinin's exertion but his eyes burning with ambition. He approached a forbidden scroll, its Snake Talisman runes etched in shimmering ink, guiding his strategy to enhance his scepter's power, promising control over the mystical serpent guardian, its power a shadow of the Moon Rabbit's defeat.

"The Snake Talisman's next," he said, his voice sharp, almost feverish.

Dolore leaned forward, her brown eyes narrowing, her loyalty to X clashing with doubt seeded in Listra's ruins.

"Can your scepter bind the serpent guardian, like it did the Moon Rabbit?" she asked, her lightning crackling faintly in her fingers, the scroll's pulsing runes hinting at danger.

Vincent sneered, gripping the scepter tighter, sparks flaring like a vow. "It's not Sheng Xiao's power...my scepter will tame it, make it mine, stronger than their pathetic Guardians." X's voice cut through, cold as steel.

"Do it, Vincent, or answer to me. The Guardians' arrival in Doragon threatens us, strike where it hurts most."

Dolore's gaze lingered on X, her unrequited love a storm within, but Vincent's ambition coiled like a venomous threat, his hunger for power growing reckless, the scroll's glow a warning of chaos to come.

"Lucas and Bella are ready," X said, his smirk masking unease, "though comms are lost in the tunnels."

Vincent retreated to his chamber, the scroll's runes pulsing in his mind, visions of the Snake Talisman and the Guardians' defeat fueling his fury, his scepter humming with dark, perilous energy.

David's team pressed through the tunnels, their chant echoing faintly: "Through fire and stone, honor binds us."

The lake's glow grew brighter, its waters shimmering under starlight, rippling with the spectral dragon's promise. Ryder dodged a collapsing beam, his cannon ready, fear of Explosivo's failures buried beneath his quip.

"Okay, maybe I was wrong—this dragon's got flair," he said, tossing another pebble at Gerry, who grinned, his spear steady despite his mom's distant recovery fueling his duty.

"Keep up, Rooster!" Gerry teased, his mischief a spark against the gloom.

Omar's thoughts held Veronica's kiss, his Ox Clan strength a pillar. Hana's whip snapped again, guiding them past a final trap, her eyes meeting David's with quiet hope, the green runes echoing Vincent's style, a mystery deepening.

The Guardians emerged at the tunnel's end, the crater lake's glowing waters pulsing with menace, David's honor surging as he recalled his Dragon Games swordplay—dragon-claw slashes and wind gusts that had crowned him guardian. The spectral dragon's test loomed, Sheng Xiao's balance teetering, his leadership blazing like a beacon for the talisman.

Chapter 22: The Dragon's Trial

The Guardians approached the crater lake's edge, waves crashing against obsidian cliffs with a thunderous roar that echoed like Sheng Xiao's heartbeat, lava flows bubbling with crimson heat, casting flickering shadows across a sky bruised with ash. Volcanic tremors rattled the ground, the Dragon Talisman's faint throb glowing beneath the water, a beacon of Doragon's legacy. Holo-torches stuttered from the Rabbit Talisman's glitches, their erratic light dancing across jagged rocks, steam swirling in sulfur-scented wind that stung David's eyes.

Zodiac symbols—dragon, tiger, rabbit, ox—etched in the lava flows shimmered ominously, carved eons ago by the spectral dragon, Sheng Xiao's guardian spirit, its scales forging tech and magic into equilibrium. The cliffs bore intricate reliefs: dragons entwining tiger stripes, rabbit circuits, and ox horns, their rhythms once harmonized, now fractured by the talismans' theft, flickering like a faltering grid.

The lake was a living archive, its depths holding the dragon's first breath, a spark that bound Sheng Xiao's realms, now trembling with imbalance, the carvings surging faintly as if mourning their lost kin.

David's pulse quickened, his Dragon Clan honor—forged in the arena's fire, where he'd bested a gauntlet of fire-dancers in the Dragon Games, dodging their blazing assaults and volcanic illusions with precise katana forms honed through grueling trials—urging him to restore balance.

Memories of serene dojos by this lake, their waters mirroring disciplined harmony under azure skies, clashed with the chaotic scene, his jaw clenching as doubts crept in—could he lead through this tempest? His breath caught, the weight of Kenta's expectations pressing like molten stone, the arena's roar echoing in his ears as he recalled the fire-dancers' taunts igniting his rage, their flames scorching his skin and nearly shattering his resolve in that grueling gauntlet. His katana's hilt grounded him, sulfur burning his throat as he scanned the steaming horizon.

In the mist-shrouded cliffs, Bella and Lucas crouched with their mercenaries, rune-enhanced blades sparking green, armor glinting.

A rogue scout, jittery from tales of the Guardians' victories in Coinin and Listra, muttered, "They're too close—we can't wait!" His voice trembled, eyes darting to the lake's glow, sweat beading despite the chill.

Bella hissed, "Hold, fool!" her amber eyes flashing with frustration, her Kusini triumph—stealing the Ox Talisman under a blazing altar—fueling her need for control.

Lucas barked, "Maintain ranks!" his military precision strained, but the scout's blade gleamed as he charged prematurely, igniting a chaotic brawl, forcing Bella and Lucas to join, their curses— "Reckless idiot! You've ruined the plan!"—echoing as their disciplined strategy unraveled.

David countered, katana whistling, "Form up!" his command slicing the tension, his mind locked on the spectral dragon's challenge but forced to face the immediate threat.

Bella and Lucas's forces swarmed from the cliffs, a disciplined wave weaving through steam, their rune-enhanced blades sparking green, armor clanging against obsidian. A second wave surged, rune-drones buzzing overhead, their lasers cutting through the haze, chaos intensifying.

A third wave faltered, jittery from unseen shadows haunting their flanks—one mercenary stumbled, blade swinging wildly, hissing, "Something's out there!"

Their own rune-traps misfired, green explosions scattering debris, claiming four of their own as shards pelted allies, the acrid scent of scorched rune-metal mingling with sulfur. David's katana carved a path, slashing a mercenary's sword in two, the metal ringing as it fell, his Dragon Clan forms flowing like a river of steel, the blade's hum vibrating through his arms, sweat stinging his eyes as embers singed his sleeves.

His mind flashed to Kenta's lessons: "Honor over glory." He spun, deflecting a drone swarm's lasers, the heat singeing his tunic, then slashed upward, cleaving three drones in half, sparks raining like dying stars.

Hana led a flank, her whip cracking to save Ryder from a blade's arc, "Circle right!" she shouted, her Horse Clan agility a blur as she disarmed a squad, her whip coiling around a mercenary's ankle, yanking him toward a lava pool's edge, his scream echoing as he scrambled back singed. "Push them back—we've got this!"

Her leadership empowered the team, her whip coiling to down two drones, their green cores bursting in violet flashes.

Patricia coordinated, her Pig Clan compassion steadying the chaos, redirecting a faltering drone's path with her gauntlet, pink-gold runes radiating to knock a mercenary back, toppling three others and breaking their formation with a resonant hum.

"These fools rushed the party!" Ryder quipped, dodging a swing and landing a precise kick, Rooster Clan agility shining as he blasted a rune-trap with his cannon, the explosion scattering foes in a shower of glowing embers. "Guess they didn't get the dragon's invite!"

He fired again, the recoil jolting him, clearing a path through the third wave, his grin masking a flicker of doubt from Explosivo's forges.

Gerry scouted, his spear parrying a rune-blade, his mom's resilience fueling his focus as he leaped over a lava stream, "Your cannon's got no finesse, Rooster!"

He jabbed a shield, triggering a trap that erupted in green sparks, knocking out three foes, the blast reverberating.

Omar shattered a mercenary's weapon with his mace, Veronica's kiss burning in his heart, his roar scattering enemies, Ox Clan power surging as he smashed a rune-barrier, its green coils snapping, opening a path.

Hana rallied, "Hold the line!" her whip snapping to yank a drone from the sky, her voice a beacon.

A hand-to-hand brawl erupted, David and Hana tag-teaming a mercenary, their strikes syncing, Ryder's cannon blasting a path, Gerry disarming a trap with his spear, their unity a shield against the onslaught, the mercenaries' ranks thinning to a dozen as their traps backfired.

From the fringes, Jade and Cade struck. Cade's velvet shadows cloaked his crescent-moon strikes—knives arcing in curves honed under a mentor's eye—felling a mercenary silently, his body crumpling without a sound.

Jade's amethyst blasts roared, visible bursts shaking the ground, claiming four foes in a blaze that lit the lake like dawn, their armor sizzling, the steam parting to reveal her regal figure, her scepter glowing with zodiac might.

They pursued through the cliffs, Jade's power seeming boundless, her visible blasts drawing all eyes while Cade's unseen shadows amplified the chaos without detection.

"The empress's wrath—it's everywhere!" one mercenary cried, his voice cracking as he fled, Jade's power seeming to command even the darkness alone.

Bella's face paled, amber eyes wide, startled by Jade's might, a specter shaking her confidence, her flames flickering weakly in her palms as she whispered, "How can she wield such power alone?"

Lucas's strategic mind faltered, "Run!" he snapped, ordering a retreat as survivors scrambled, his armor charred from a near-miss, leading survivors through the tunnels to the ash-choked countryside. Jade and Cade paused at the tunnel exit, seeing the villains escape, then turned back to aid the Guardians at the lake, their steps swift, resolve burning.

Doragon's volcanic roars yielded to the ash-choked countryside, where Bella, Lucas, and four surviving mercenaries stumbled over hills, lava flows hissing like serpents, breaths ragged, boots slipping on gravel, starlit sky offering no solace, volcanoes rumbling.

Bella activated her holo-comm, voice trembling, "Jade's magic crushed us! Her amethyst blasts tore through the steam—she's unstoppable! Shadows swallowed our men, but it was her power alone—or was there something else in the dark?" Her hands shook, the memory of Kusini's blazing altar flickering in her mind, its flames a pale echo compared to Jade's radiant fury.

In the forbidden wilderness, X growled in his fortress, teeth gritted, "Regroup—how did she ambush you?" His vendetta—a lost love's wound—flared, his mind flashing to a distant memory of a lover's smile now ashes, pushing him to tighten his grip on the realms.

Vincent's anger surged, serpent scepter sparking green, "Her magic overshadows mine—impossible!" he spat, pacing furiously, gripping a scroll, its runes throbbing ominously, whispering secrets of ancient power. "I'll find a way to outwit her, X—I need a plan to break her light and their cursed spirit!"

His ambition coiled, visions of Guardians kneeling fueling a reckless hunger, his eyes gleaming with defiance as he dreamed of eclipsing Jade's reign.

Dolore watched, brown eyes narrowing, doubt deepening from Listra's ruins, her loyalty to X clashing with Vincent's hunger, her lightning crackling as she muttered, "You'll unravel us, Vincent—your ambition blinds you. Stay focused, or you'll lose everything."

Her fingers twitched, the air humming with her suppressed storm, memories of X's rescue in a crumbling shrine fueling her resolve to guard him from Vincent's recklessness.

X's voice cut through, "Devise a plan to shatter their spirit, Vincent. Their victories grow bold. Break their hope, or you'll you answer to me." Vincent retreated, the scroll's runes fueling visions of Guardians' defeat, his scepter humming with dark energy, his mind racing with schemes to eclipse Jade's radiance.

X turned to him, voice low: "Jade's crown blinds her—strike her, for the one we lost."

The words hit like a blade. Vincent's scar throbbed—Percy's last gasp, "How could you?"

The memory burned: Percy's knives carving his arm, his own runes striking true. Percy fell. X's grief had forged their pact, but Vincent's ambition coiled tighter. The talismans would be his key. Jade's light would dim.

"I'll bury them," Vincent hissed, vanishing into the mist.

Jade and Cade stopped before exiting the tunnel, their bond electric, Cade's hand brushing Jade's.

"You were brilliant," he whispered, mismatched eyes shining with admiration. Jade smiled, her hand covering his, the warmth spreading through her like a gentle current, the

Guardians' silhouettes visible against the glowing waters of the lake's edge.

Far from the Unknown Wilderness's mists, in the Imperial Palace's control room, Veronica, Alice, Sam, Doug, Tate, and Melissa gathered around flickering holo-screens, stone pillars carved with dragon motifs sparking from Rabbit Talisman glitches. Coinin's grids sputtered into blackouts.

Alice's holo-pad glowing as she coded fixes, rallying clans to rebuild shattered booths, her Rabbit Clan focus fierce, glasses fogging as she muttered, "Hold together, circuits!" Her efforts in Coinin—patching grids amid debris-strewn streets, uniting clans under dim arches—fueled a quiet pride.

Ged's clinics flickered, Veronica aiding with Rat Clan scouts, her heart racing for Omar, their kiss in Souris's frost a lingering warmth, her voice sharp, "Get those lights back—Gerry's mom needs them!"

Souris's thorns crept anew, Sam organizing defenses, her Snake Clan resolve steady, bow resting as she directed villagers, "Barricade the paths!"

Kusini's harvests wilted, cracks reopening. Listra's rivers swelled, vines twisting unnaturally.

Tate fortified spires, his Tiger Clan intensity sharp, claws gleaming as he directed repairs, his mind heavy with Kusini's lessons, channeling ego into leadership, "Keep those beams steady—we're holding Sheng Xiao together!"

Doug anchored Coinin's defenses, his Dog Clan loyalty overcoming past abandonment fears from Dingo's coasts, aiding refugees with steady hands, "Stay strong—help's coming!"

Melissa rallied, her Monkey Clan resolve ironclad, her Mico drills fueling a pep talk, "They're united, like Coinin! Keep the realms strong—they'll bring that talisman home!"

Cherry blossoms drifted like snow outside, their delicate scent a fleeting hope against the flickering screens.

"No word from Doragon—comms are dead," Veronica said, voice tense, her hands trembling as she checked a holo-feed.

Alice tweaked her holo-pad, "Grids are stabilizing, but we need that talisman."

Sam nodded, "They'll pull through—like in Listra, when Tate and I held the vines."

Doug examined a display, "Gerry's mom's recovering—clinics hold, but barely."

Tate grinned, "Ryder's dodging storms, I bet, clawing through like Kusini."

Veronica paused, frowning, "Where's Jade? And Cade? No one's seen them since the spires."

Sam smirked, adjusting her bow, "Probably off sparking that romance—those glances in the hall weren't subtle."

Alice chuckled, tweaking her holo-pad, "Maybe a secret mission, but I bet it's love."

Tate grinned, "Cade's moves with her light—hope they're safe."

Doug nodded, "They're unstoppable together."

Melissa laughed, "Bet they're saving Doragon!"

Their banter and worry fueled resolve, hands fidgeting with holo-pads, a beacon of unity.

As palace lights flickered, Doragon's lake pulsed anew, waters churning, lava flows hissing, the spectral dragon's voice thundering, "Unite as one, or falter," vibrating through obsidian cliffs like Sheng Xiao's core.

David guided the Guardians along the shore, jagged paths demanding collaboration, steam clouding vision, the ground trembling.

"Coordinate now," he ordered, katana ready, senses alert, his jaw clenched against doubts of leadership.

A lava surge roared, Hana mapping the flow, "Divert it left with barriers!" pointing to weak rocks, her eyes scanning patterns like Doragon's wind gusts.

Patricia organized, her compassion steadying the team, piling rune-enhanced stones, her gauntlet radiating pink-gold to reinforce barriers, sweat beading on her brow.

"Together—we hold it!" she urged, her calm bolstering trembling Guardians, her voice a warm anchor.

Ryder quipped, "This dragon's playing hardball!" heaving rocks, dodging embers, his cannon blasting a boulder to clear the path, his agility key. "Your spear's no match for my boom, Gerry!" he teased, grinning despite the heat.

Omar shattered stones, passing them to Gerry and Patricia, his mind on Veronica's kiss, muscles rippling as he grunted through the strain, stabilizing a collapsing path with his mace.

Gerry scouted safe paths, spear steady, duty driving him, his mom's resilience fueling his heart as he wedged his spear to lever a rock, "Keep up, Rooster!"

Patricia chimed in, "Both of you need better aim!" her rare humor lightening the mood.

Their efforts shifted the surge, paths reuniting, the lake's glow throbbing stronger, its zodiac carvings flaring briefly as if acknowledging their unity. Hana's insight complemented David's command, their eyes meeting with trust, Cade's memory fading, their bond deepening as her fingers brushed his arm, warmth spreading like zodiac fire.

The lake's heart boiled, waves pounding, steam shrouding. The dragon's voice thundered, "Sacrifice for all, or perish," reverberating like Sheng Xiao's judgment.

David guided the Guardians across a treacherous path, a whirlpool pulling Hana toward the talisman's glow. She fought, her whip slipping, the vortex trapping her, water churning like a living force. David hesitated, Dragon Clan glory tempting, but Kenta's words flashed: "True strength is sacrifice."

High expectations from Kenta, from the clan—could he measure up without cracking? The arena's fire-dancers loomed in his mind, their taunts once sparking rage that cost him a spar, his blade faltering under pressure, Kenta's stern gaze a reminder to channel fury into focus.

He dove in, "Hold on!" battling currents, grasping her arm as her strength waned, kicking upward with her help, the cold stinging his skin.

Gerry threw a rope, "Grab it!" anchoring it against a rock, his duty etched on his face, his mom's resilience inspiring him.

Ryder and Omar hauled, Ryder's pull quick, Omar's grip powerful, their strength dragging the pair from the depths. Patricia helped them ashore, cloaking Hana, her calm reinforcing unity, her gentle touch steadying trembling hands.

Hana gasped, "You could've taken it," gratitude trembling, their eyes locking, trust solidifying.

David shook his head, "The team comes first," his voice rough, the sacrifice forging their bond, his clenched jaw softening as her hand lingered.

The dragon rumbled, "Sacrifice proven," the whirlpool calming, steam parting.

"That was close," Ryder said, wiping sweat, his humor lightening the mood. Omar's thoughts drifted to Veronica, his strength unwavering. Patricia nodded, reinforcing unity. Hana brushed David's arm, a quiet thanks, their bond deepening as her fingers trembled against his, warmth spreading like zodiac fire.

The lake thrashed, lava erupting, steam shrouding, the zodiac carvings throbbing with ancient energy. The spectral dragon materialized, its scales shimmering with zodiac constellations—dragon, tiger, rabbit, ox—etched in molten glass, eyes blazing with molten fire that cast crimson glows across the cliffs, claws crackling with tech-magic energy that sparked like miniature stars, tail whipping up volcanic winds that howled with Sheng Xiao's fury, the air heavy with ozone and searing heat.

"Fight or perish, Doragon guardian!" it bellowed, fire arcing in a blazing torrent, claws slicing with lethal precision, tail smashing rocks into glowing shards, the lake's waters boiling with its wrath.

Patricia called, "Hold the line!" raising pink-gold barriers to deflect embers, her compassion steadying the team.

"Show it who's boss," Ryder said, firing his cannon to disrupt gusts, the recoil jolting him, "This dragon's got style!"

Hana said, "You can do this," her whip diverting the tail's arc, her trust deepening.

Gerry yelled, "You are the dragon!" hurling a rock to distract the beast, his spear steady.

Omar said, "Remember your training!" smashing a claw's descent, his mace a pillar.

David's katana flashed, evading a fire burst that scorched the shore, the heat searing his skin, blocking a claw-slash with a precise twist, the impact jarring, deflecting a tail-lash, wind testing his footing.

The dragon cornered him, jaws snapping with a roar that shook the cliffs, but his blade struck home, glowing with the relic's surge from the earlier ritual.

"For the team," he muttered, forms honed through years of training. The dragon vanished, nodding approval, the lake calming, Sheng Xiao's balance shifting.

David dove, retrieving the Dragon Talisman, its light bursting.

A vision struck—flames roaring through crowded streets, shadowy figures striking with rune-etched blades glinting in firelight, screams piercing smoke-choked air, spires crumbling under relentless assaults, the ground trembling as chaos reigned, a warning of battles to come that chilled the Guardians' hearts.

David gripped the talisman, voice low, "This looks like a new enemy—something darker."

Hana frowned, "Like Kusini's altar, burning again?"

Ryder chuckled nervously, "Hope it's not my Explosivo forges going up in flames!"

Patricia urged, "Stay focused—it's a warning, not here yet."

Omar growled, "Reminds me of Souris's traps—treachery."

The Guardians clustered, chanting, "Through fire and stone, honor binds us," voices a shield grounding the chaos, hands gripping weapons tightly. Hana steadied David's shoulder, eyes bright with trust.

Ryder quipped, "Nice swim, champ!" tossing a pebble, lightening the mood. Patricia's calm anchored them, gauntlet glowing faintly. Omar's nod was firm, mace steady, sparks crackling.

Jade and Cade emerged, witnessing the celebration.

"David secured the talisman," Cade murmured, smiling at Jade, her amethyst eyes sparkling.

Under the starry sky, her heart raced, relief washing over her like the lake's waves. A flashback stirred—palace gardens, cherry petals falling, Percy's visits sharing Cade's training tales in Doragon's dojos or Ged's cliffs, his mismatched eyes sparking love through separations, their bond deepening at fifteen in jasmine-scented nights, duty pulling them apart, fate drawing them closer.

With the talisman won, Jade stepped closer, eyes locked, the talisman's glow throbbing, zodiac symbols—dragon, tiger, rabbit—shimmering in a celestial dance, enveloping them in a starry veil, sparks crackling like a cosmic vow. Her heart trembled, vulnerability breaking her regal mask.

"Cade, I've loved you since those garden nights," she whispered, voice trembling, "your shadow steadied me through every storm, every separation. I feared the crown would tear us apart, but you're my heart's truth."

The jasmine scent from her quarters lingered in his mind, pulling him closer. She kissed him boldly, lips soft but passionate, hands clasped, her amethyst magic radiating, mingling with his velvet shadows in a radiant dance, sparks crackling like a cosmic vow. Cade's surprise melted, his arms wrapping her, returning the kiss with fierce passion.

"Jade, you're my light, crown or not—I've never felt worthy, but I'll be your shadow forever, guarding your heart through every storm," he vowed, eyes shining, voice trembling with devotion.

"You're more than worthy. I love you," Jade replied, tears glistening, fingers tracing his jaw.

"And I love you, Jade—always," Cade said, their magic entwining in a radiant embrace, a beacon of their long-kindled love. They kissed again, deeply, magically.

As their lips parted, the Guardians' cheers broke the spell, Ryder leading the celebration.

Ryder cheered, "Talisman's ours!"

Patricia nodded, "Victory earned."

Omar and Gerry high-fived, stars mirroring in the lake, David's determination blazing, Jade's kiss a radiant spark against the chaos.

Chapter 23: Gathering Storm

Jade and Cade emerged from the shadowed mouth of the tunnels, the crater lake's waters rippling under a canopy of starlight that pierced the ash-veiled sky like scattered diamonds. Waves lapped gently against the obsidian cliffs, their rhythmic hush a soothing counterpoint to the distant, fading rumble of Doragon's volcanoes. Lava flows, once raging torrents of crimson fury, now cooled to faint, ember-like glimmers along the rugged slopes, their heat dissipating into wisps of steam that curled lazily into the night air.

The volcanic hum that had shaken the earth like Sheng Xiao's unsettled heartbeat softened to a low, distant murmur, as if the realm exhaled in relief.

The Dragon Talisman's recovery wove its restorative magic through the land: green shoots pushed through ash-blanketed soil in Doragon's valleys, Ged's clinics glowed with steady holo-lights as outages ceased, Cochan's fields bloomed with vibrant harvests under renewed vigor, Fahal Alkhayl's trade routes cleared of sandstorms that had buried caravans, Mico's hydroelectric jungles hummed with stabilized data-vines no longer glitching, and Souris's thorns retreated into thawed earth, while Listra's rivers calmed to gentle streams, allowing treehouse hotels to reopen their vine-nets to dancers.

Even Explosivo's forges sparked brighter without overheating, and Dingo's coastal nets pulled in bountiful catches free from erratic tides.

Jade's heart leaped at the signs, her amethyst eyes reflecting the lake's ethereal radiance, a surge of hope mingling with the exhaustion etched into her bones.

"We made it back," she whispered to Cade, their hands intertwined, his Cat Clan warmth grounding her amid the quiet triumph. His mismatched eyes met hers, a silent promise forged in the tunnels they'd navigated together, his velvet tendrils faintly coiling around their clasped fingers like protective vines. The Guardians clustered near the shore, David holding the Dragon Talisman high, its light surging like a living heartbeat, casting golden hues across their dust-streaked faces and illuminating the subtle shifts in the landscape—the lava's retreat, the stars emerging brighter overhead.

The team turned at their approach, surprise lighting their expressions like the talisman's radiance. Patricia's eyes widened in warm recognition, her Pig Clan gauntlet shimmering faintly with pink-gold runes as she stepped forward.

"Jade? Cade?" David exclaimed, lowering the talisman, its radiant energy reflecting in his steady gaze, his Dragon Clan honor radiating like a quiet flame. "You helped us—from the tunnels? Those amethyst blasts... the traps collapsing just in time—it was you two, wasn't it?"

Patricia nodded, her calm voice infused with gratitude, her hand brushing a strand of hair from her face. "We felt it—the magic guiding us through the chaos, your strikes turning the tide. It was like Sheng Xiao itself watched over us."

Ryder's grin spread wide, his Rooster Clan boldness shining through his weary posture as he clapped Cade on the back with a hearty thump. "Not bad for an advisor—you and Jade strike like a storm. Explosivo's forges could use that kind of firepower!"

Hana's gaze softened with relief, her Horse Clan fire blazing with quiet pride, though a flicker of wariness crossed her features as she noticed Jade and Cade's intertwined hands—their closeness a new spark that tugged at her heart, stirring reflections on her past flirtations with Cade.

She pushed the thought aside, her focus settling on David, his steady honor anchoring her.

Gerry beamed, his Goat Clan mischief returning in a relieved laugh, "This changes everything for the clans—Ged's clinics are lighting up, Mom's recovery stronger!" Omar fist-bumped Ryder, his Ox Clan strength evident in the solid clap, "Honor won—pure and simple. Doragon's peaks are calming already."

The group erupted in cheers, embracing tightly amid the lapping waves, the volcanic hum fading further as relief washed over them like the lake's cool embrace. They gathered by the shore, sharing quick stories of the skirmish and trials, the talisman's radiance illuminating their faces and weaving a tapestry of camaraderie.

David recounted the spectral dragon's fierce test, his katana's clash against molten claws echoing in his words, his mind flashing to Kenta's dojo lessons that had tempered his youthful rage into disciplined precision, a growth that now anchored the team. Patricia described diverting lava surges with rune-enhanced barriers, her compassion shining as she praised the team's unity, recalling Cochan's patient harvests that taught her to nurture strength in others.

Ryder quipped about his cannon blasts shattering rune-traps, his humor lightening the mood, "Those mercenaries didn't stand a chance—boom, and they're running like scared chickens!"—his Explosivo doubts fading as he embraced his role beyond jokes.

Hana shared her whip's precise deflections, her voice steady but her eyes darting to Jade and Cade, their evident bond stirring a subtle introspection. Gerry spoke of scouting safe paths, his spear's jabs against green-glowing obstacles, his worry for his mom easing with the talisman's promise, his Ged roots fueling a deeper duty.

Omar's deep voice rumbled as he described smashing through barriers, his thoughts drifting to Veronica's kiss, fueling his endurance, his Ox Clan power a pillar forged in Souris's betrayals and Kusini's flames.

The Dragon Talisman's influence rippled outward, visible even in this remote spot: ash clouds thinned, revealing a starlit canopy and distant pagodas' holo-lights flickered back to life, their tech-magic relays stabilizing and a harmonious hum resonated from the zodiac carvings on the cliffs, as if Sheng Xiao's essence mended itself thread by thread.

Jade activated a holo-link to the palace, the device stabilizing without glitches, Veronica's face appearing first amid the control room's flickering screens, shifting from worry to joy. "You all okay? The relays are holding—Doragon's volcanoes are quieting on our maps!"

Cade's shadows flickered by the lake's edge, Jade's eyes a radiant spark in the night, a memory of saving her from Doragon's traps flashing vividly—his knives arcing through the gloom, felling scouts silently as her amethyst blasts lit the tunnels like dawn.

His Cat Clan loyalty surged then, but doubt lingered like the ash-scented wind: an advisor from humble roots, worthy of an empress? Percy's brotherly spars echoed— "Protect her, always"—yet the crown's prestige mocked his place, his mismatched eyes reflecting unworthiness in the lake's glow.

Jade's kiss burned in his mind, her confession a flame that warmed his heart, but fear tugged—could he stand beside her without dimming her light? The talisman's radiance hummed, shadows coiling protectively around his fingers, a vow forming: his loyalty would prove him enough, guarding her through every storm, his love a shadow that strengthened, not shaded.

The starry sky above seemed to nod, sparks of zodiac magic affirming his resolve, the realm's restored balance a mirror to his own.

Jade smiled, her voice carrying leadership laced with warmth, "David got the talisman, so we're on our way back. The realms are feeling it...the balance is tipping our way."

Sam leaned into the frame, her Snake Clan bow slung over her shoulder, "Yes! Kusini's harvests are swelling, no more wilting edges—Listra's floods are receding, and Coinin's grids hum steady."

Doug and Tate high-fived in the background, their Tiger and Dog Clan strengths a visible anchor, while Melissa clapped enthusiastically, her Monkey Clan energy bubbling from her refugee work. "The blackouts are gone—holo-lanterns hum steady again!"

Alice nodded with a rare, triumphant smile, adjusting her glasses as her holo-pad beeped, "Clan relays are stabilizing across Sheng Xiao: Souris's thorns are retreating, and Cochan's plains bloom anew. The Dragon Talisman's power syncs with the Tiger's—the zodiac weave is knitting together."

Veronica's eyes locked on Omar, her Rat Clan wit softened by longing, "Hurry home—I've got stories too, and a hug waiting."

David stood by the crater lake, the Dragon Talisman's radiance warming his palm, Hana's trust a lingering spark in his chest. Saving her from the whirlpool had tempered his anger, Kenta's "Honor binds" echoing through the steam as he recalled his sacrifice—diving into the vortex, currents pulling like his inner rage, but discipline holding firm.

A dojo memory surged—temper costing a spar against a rival, his blade wild, Kenta's stern gaze urging control: "Power unchecked destroys."

That lesson had forged him, his youthful fury now a harnessed flame, the spectral dragon's test proving his growth. Hana's gaze stirred a new warmth, her Horse Clan fire a rhythm tugging at his heart, the coming quests in Saanp's dunes calling for their shared strength.

The lake's ripples mirrored his resolve, steam parting like doubts retreating, the talisman's light a beacon—his temper no longer a threat, but a tempered blade ready for Saanp's trials, romance blooming like Doragon's restored valleys.

The link ended on shared laughter, the Doragon Guardians packing up with vigor, the lake's edge buzzing with victory and anticipation.

Hana pulled David aside near a cooling lava vein, her voice low amid the waves, "Thanks for the save back there—it means a lot. Your honor... it's what pulled us through." Her fingers tightened on her whip, its leather warm against her palm, as David's steady gaze anchored her. Her heart flickered, no longer chasing Cade's elusive charm.

A memory of her parents' stern voices—demanding a suitor—faded against the lake's cool breeze, David's honor a new rhythm pulsing through her Horse Clan fire. David nodded, their tension easing, his hand tightening on his katana.

"We're stronger together, Hana," he said, a step toward trust. The palace's cherry blossoms seemed closer, Sheng Xiao's equilibrium shifting toward stability, Jade's magic tingling with hope.

At X's fortress, dim lights flickered over cold stone walls etched with jagged runes, holographic maps projecting Sheng Xiao's realms in an eerie blue glow, casting menacing shadows from ornate scepters and ancient artifacts. The air hung heavy with smoldering scrolls and metallic tang, the arches humming with malice.

Bella and Lucas stumbled in, bruised and breathless, their armor charred, the absence of their mercenaries a bitter defeat.

X leaned forward from his throne-like chair, his angular features sharpened by the blue light, eyes piercing as he gritted his teeth, "Report—every detail. How did the Dragon Talisman slip through?"

Bella panted, her amber eyes wide with shock, flames flickering weakly in her palms as she steadied herself. "The Guardians got the talisman—Jade's magic wiped out our team. She was unstoppable, blasts shaking the tunnels like zodiac thunder. Her amethyst surges pierced the steam, collapsing our traps and felling our men."

Lucas nodded, fear in his military-sharp gaze, his bandaged arm throbbing, "Her power crushed us—we barely escaped. It was like she anticipated every move, her light everywhere, halving our force with a single strike."

X's fingers clenched the throne's armrest, knuckles whitening, his cold gaze flickering as if haunted by a distant memory—a lover's smile turned to ashes—fueling his venomous resolve. "Jade's that strong? She's a bigger threat than we thought. Her crown's light blinds them to our schemes, but we'll eclipse it."

Vincent, pacing with his serpent scepter sparking dark energy, froze, rage surging like a tempest.

"Her magic dares challenge my dominion? I'll shatter her!" he snarled, the scepter flaring with green pulses, casting venomous shadows, his pride wounded, mind racing with visions of Jade's defeat—her scepter crumbling, her eyes dimming.

X turned to him, voice a low rumble, "You called her weak, Vincent. Prove your words—forge a plan to crush her and this realm."

Vincent's voice thundered, "I'm forging it now, a devastation that exploits their every weakness. She'll beg for mercy before I end her light."

X nodded slowly, gaze lingering on the Ox and Rabbit Talismans pulsing on their pedestal, "Make it devastating. The Snake Talisman next—strike where it hurts most."

Dolore smirked from the shadows, her brown eyes crackling, "Snake Talisman now? Or strike while their victory blinds them?"

Vincent waved it off, "Patience—we'll hit where it hurts most, twisting their hope into despair."

Vincent retreated to his chamber, iron-barred windows casting jagged shadows in dim torchlight, his scepter humming with dark energy as he spread forbidden scrolls across a rune-etched table. His scarred hands flipped through serpent-skin bindings, their pages whispering ancient curses.

The scepter's green pulses flared as he tested unstable glyphs, weaving stolen talisman essence—Ox's endurance, Rabbit's tech corruption—into a spell crackling with venomous potential.

Memories of Coinin's triumph fueled him, his runes unraveling the Moon Rabbit's veil, but Jade's amethyst blasts mocked his supremacy. Muttering, "Her light will break," he scrawled chaotic patterns, hours vanishing in a frenzy of research, his rage forging a devastating plan to twist Sheng Xiao's harmony into despair.

Bella, Lucas, and Dolore lingered in the hall, their whispers adding to the malice—Bella's flames flaring as she recounted Jade's blasts in detail, "She turned the tunnels against us, like the zodiac bent to her will,"

Lucas nodding grimly, "We need to strike her weaknesses—family, crown, all that she cares about."

Dolore's lightning crackled, her loyalty to X steady, "Vincent's plan will break her. X commands it, and we execute. No more failures."

In the hall, Bella whispered to Lucas, "Vincent's furious since we struck a nerve with Jade's power."

Lucas scoffed, glancing at Dolore nearby, her lightning fingers tracing a console. "Good, let him handle her and we'll reap the rewards. But Dolore, what about X and Vincent? You were here. Did X seem zoned out?"

Dolore's brown eyes flashed, her hand on the console steady. "X was in control, Vincent following like a whipped serpent. No haze, so our doubts are unfounded. X leads; Vincent serves." Her tone reassured, though a faint doubt lingered.

Bella nodded, flames flickering, "Then we press on—the Snake Talisman will be ours." The fortress thrummed with malice, Sheng Xiao's equilibrium shifting dangerously, Vincent's rage a storm brewing.

The palace buzzed, cherry blossoms drifting outside arched windows like pink whispers, their petals catching morning light through stained-glass zodiac guardians. Holo-screens flickered with clan reports—Kusini's harvests swelling, Souris's thorns retreating, Listra's floods easing, Coinin's grids humming, Doragon's volcanoes slumbering, Cochan's plains blooming, Ged's clinics radiant.

Incense from Sheng Xiao shrines scented the air with jasmine and sandalwood, guards patrolling fountain-lined plazas, refugees sharing hopeful stories. Veronica paced the control room, Guardians gathered—Sam, Doug, Tate, Melissa, Alice—discussing Jade and Cade's mission with animated gestures, the Dragon Talisman's influence evident in stable holo-displays.

"They went alone?" Sam asked, brow furrowed, leaning on a zodiac-etched table.

Doug examined a tactical display, "Risky, but Jade's speeches rally us—maybe she's more than words. Ged's clinics are fully powered, no outages."

Tate nodded, claws retracted, "Cade's knife work wins battles, like our holo-grid surge—Sam's thinking, my strength."

Melissa's braid bounced as she grinned, "Jade and Cade are glowing—about time!"

Tate grunted, claws retracted, "Good for 'em—Jade needs that spark."

Their banter warmed the control room, a beacon against the Prophecy's storms. They fortified tech grids, sparks flying, lights steady thanks to the Dragon Talisman.

"Clans aided, repairs progressing," Alice reported, her Rabbit Clan precision guiding tools. "Imperial City's walls strengthen, but Saanp's dunes show subtle shifts."

Sam added, "No surges—balance returns, but we stay vigilant." Doug directed guards to weak points, Melissa rallied refugees, their hope mirroring Coinin's recovery. The palace towers gleamed, Sheng Xiao's equilibrium shifting toward stability.

The palace gates swung open, cherry gardens blooming vibrantly, petals carpeting paths like a triumphant welcome. Plazas bustled with refugees, guards waving as the Doragon Guardians arrived, dusty but triumphant.

"Welcome back!" Veronica cried, rushing to Omar, hugging him tightly, hands clutching his tunic.

"I missed you—your strength kept me going through every glitch." Omar wrapped his arms around her, his Ox Clan endurance melting into tenderness, "Your kiss was my anchor in those tunnels, Veronica. Souris's frost, Kusini's flames—nothing compared to being away from you."

Their lips met in a fervent kiss, hands tracing familiar lines, a Souris memory flashing—her cunning solving glyph traps, his mace clearing their path, their bond sealed in frost amid the thorns, her spark igniting his heart through the cold.

The moment lingered with passion, a vow renewed amid the blooming sanctuary—her Rat Clan wit complementing his steady determination, their love a quiet flame against the looming quests.

Gerry asked nervously, "What about my mom?"

Melissa smiled, hugging him, "She's recovering strong in Ged's clinics, full of stories for you. Sent a holo-message praising your bravery."

Gerry sighed, high-fiving Ryder, "Best news—let's celebrate!"

David showed the talisman, its power humming, "For the realm—we all earned this."

Patricia nodded, inspiring, while Hana and David shared a moment by a fountain, tension eased, bond solidified. Tate and Sam exchanged a glance, their teamwork unspoken but strong.

As the celebrations continued in the grand hall, Huan's Monkey Clan tunic gleamed under the hall's holo-lights, his jaw tightening as he eyed Cade's hand in Jade's.

Raised beside her in the palace, he'd watched Percy's brother climb to advisor—yet his unknown roots grated against the crown's prestige. His fingers twitched, itching to challenge Cade's place, his protective glare a silent warning of duty's weight.

"Empress," Huan said, his voice low but edged with concern, stepping closer with a bow that didn't hide his furrowed brow. "The talisman's victory is joyous, but... this closeness with your advisor—does it befit the crown? Cade's worth is in his blade, not beside the throne. Your parents would caution against such distractions. The realms need your undivided focus, not whispers of favoritism."

Jade's cheeks flushed, her hand tightening on Cade's, a flicker of doubt crossing her amethyst eyes—Huan's words echoing her own buried fears of duty clashing with heart.

"Huan, your protection is valued, but my heart chooses its path. Cade has proven himself through every storm—Souris, Kusini, now Doragon."

Cade met Huan's gaze steadily, his mismatched eyes unyielding, "I serve the empress, not the throne's expectations. My loyalty is to her, as it always has been."

Huan hesitated, his pushiness tempered by Jade's resolve, but he nodded curtly, "As you wish, but remember—the crown demands sacrifices. I'll watch the horizons for threats."

The exchange hung briefly, adding a layer of tension to the triumph, Huan's protectiveness a reminder of the external pressures on their bond, yet strengthening Jade's determination to balance love and duty.

Huan turned away, his Monkey Clan tunic disappearing into the shadows.

Jade's heart raced, his words echoing like a warning bell: "The crown demands sacrifices."

She pulled Cade into the garden alcove, cherry blossoms drifting like soft tears around the marble fountain. Her fenghuang-shaped scepter rested against a stone bench; its amethyst glow dimmed to a weary pulse.

She traced the carved dragon motif on the rim, her fingers trembling. *He shadow-traveled through Doragon's traps to shield me...But Huan's right—duty feels like a chain.* she thought, her chest tightening.

Cade stepped from the shadows, his Cat Clan grace silent despite the ash still clinging to his cloak. His mismatched eyes— one green, one blue—caught the moonlight, reflecting the same storm that churned in her heart.

"Jade," he said softly, his voice rough from the sulfur-choked tunnels, "you've been avoiding me since we returned."

She turned, her red hair spilling over her shoulders like a defiant flame, amethyst eyes glistening.

"Huan's right," she whispered, the words bitter. "The crown demands sacrifices. I confessed my love by the lake, Cade—under those stars, with the talisman's light binding us. But here, in the palace, duty tears at me. My travels tore us apart once—Coinin's spires, Saanp's dunes—while you trained in Doragon's peaks and Ged's shores. Percy bridged us with his visits, his green eyes twinkling with your stories. Now...I fear I'll lose you to the throne's weight, or to someone freer, like Hana." Her voice cracked, vulnerability breaking her regal mask, her hand reaching for his but hesitating, the fountain's mist cool against her skin.

Cade closed the distance, his calloused hand gently cupping hers, his touch grounding her like the lake's steady waves.

"Jade, you're my only light," he said, his voice low and fierce, eyes locking on hers. "I doubted my worth—an advisor from humble roots, never fit for an empress. But in those tunnels, shadow-traveling to shield you from X's traps, I knew: my shadows exist to protect your fire. The crown doesn't chain me— it elevates us. I love you, beyond duty, beyond fear." His thumb brushed her cheek, wiping away a tear, his warmth chasing the chill of her doubts.

Their lips met in a kiss deeper than the lake's, passionate and urgent, her amethyst magic flaring in radiant pulses that mingled with his velvet shadows in a starry dance, sparks crackling like a cosmic vow. Her scepter pulsed brighter on the bench, the garden's jasmine scent enveloping them, their hands entwined as the world faded to just this moment.

"You're my heart, Cade," she murmured against his lips, her fingers tracing his jaw, "Always."

He pulled her closer, his voice a vow, "And you're mine, Jade—forever."

Huan watched from the shadows of an archway, his jaw tight with unspoken conflict. She chooses him...he thought, his protective instincts warring with duty, a flicker of respect for

Cade mingling with his fear for the crown's stability. He turned away, the moment a quiet seed of tension for the trials ahead.

After steaming baths scented with healing herbs and a meal of zodiac-etched dumplings and spiced teas, the group gathered in the training hall, swords clashing, Jade addressing them, "Prepare for the Snake Talisman—stay sharp, train hard. Saanp's dunes await, but our unity will prevail."

By the palace fountain, Omar, David, and Ryder tossed zodiac coins, laughter echoing under blooming cherry trees, petals drifting like fragrant confetti.

Omar's ox coin splashed, rippling the surface as he chuckled, "I thought I'd fail Veronica—Kofi's charm outshone me in those palace drills, making me doubt my place by her side."

His massive frame leaned against the fountain's edge, the cool stone grounding his Ox Clan strength, memories of Souris's frost and Kusini's flames flashing—times when his endurance held, but his heart wavered.

David flipped a dragon coin, watching it arc and sink, "My temper almost broke us in the tunnels—rage bubbling like Doragon's lava, nearly costing Hana." He gripped his katana's hilt, the metal cool against his palm, Kenta's dojo echoes urging discipline over fury.

Ryder grinned, tossing a rooster coin with a flourish, "My cannon saved your hide in that ash flood—boom, and the path cleared! But Explosivo's forges taught me jokes hide doubts, my parents always said I was too boastful to lead."

The coins glinted in the fountain's radiance, their chuckles echoing like a shield, brotherhood forged in shared battles—a defiant spark for Saanp's dunes, where loyalty would temper their fears.

Jade and Cade slipped to a garden alcove, cherry blossoms falling like confetti, fragrant air heavy with jasmine and fountain trickles. Moonlight glinted off Jade's scepter, propped against a tree, as their hands intertwined.

"I couldn't stop thinking of you in Doragon," Jade confessed, voice trembling, her hand locking onto his. "Your strength, your heart—they complete me, Cade. I love you, truly, beyond the crown's burdens."

Cade pulled her into a tight embrace, his warmth enveloping her. "You're my everything, Jade—I've loved you since we were kids, but I doubted my worth, just a Cat Clan protector bound to your side. Now I know—I love you beyond doubt, forever, through every storm and talisman."

They kissed deeply, passion surging, her magic flaring in radiant pulses, his tendrils swirling in a starry embrace, her scepter sparking with imperial fire. The kiss deepened, their bond celebrated in the blooming sanctuary, a beacon against the gathering storm, Huan's caution a distant echo that only fueled their conviction.

The palace hummed with unity, Sheng Xiao's equilibrium shifting toward stability, their love and the Guardians' resolve a defiant spark against Vincent's brewing malice, foreshadowing the venomous trials in Saanp's shifting dunes.

Chapter 24: Clash of Shadows

The Imperial City stood radiant under the noon sun, cherry gardens blooming vibrantly with petals drifting like pink snow in the gentle breeze, fountain-lined plazas teeming with citizens enjoying the hard-won peace, their laughter mingling with the throb of stabilized tech grids. Modern towers blended seamlessly with ancient spires carved with zodiac guardians, Sheng Xiao shrines radiating harmonious energy that pulsed through the city like a revitalized heartbeat.

David patrolled the outer walls, his katana at his side, the Dragon Talisman's power throbbing warmly in his pocket—a beacon of Doragon's victory that had begun mending the realms. The air carried the sweet scent of blossoms, a stark contrast to the volcanic sulfur of his clan lands, and he allowed himself a rare smile, watching children chase drone-balloons shaped like playful dragons.

His thoughts drifted to Hana, her recent shift toward him a quiet warmth amid the chaos they'd endured, her Horse Clan fire complementing his steady honor in ways he hadn't expected. He glanced at her nearby, her whip coiled as she scanned the horizon, and felt a surge of protectiveness—not just for the city, but for the bond they were forging.

Patricia strolled nearby, her Pig Clan gauntlet catching the light as she helped a vendor repair a glitching holo-cart, her calm compassion drawing grateful nods from passersby.

"The talisman's working wonders—Cochan's fields are thriving again," she said to David, her voice a grounding anchor, her mind flashing to the patient endurance that had seen her through Kusini's flames and Listra's floods.

Ryder leaned against the wall, cannon slung over his shoulder, quipping to Gerry, "Bet those kids could use a real boom—Explosivo style!"

Gerry laughed, spear twirling idly, his Goat Clan mischief lightening the patrol, though his mind lingered on his mom's full recovery in Ged, a relief that fueled his vigilance. "As long as it's not aimed at us, Rooster," he shot back, their banter a spark of normalcy.

Hana joined David at the parapet, her whip coiled at her hip, a soft smile playing on her lips as she brushed his arm.

"The city's alive again—thanks to you," she said, her eyes meeting his with a spark that spoke of their growing bond, forged in Doragon's trials and Coinin's chaos.

David's heart quickened, his hand briefly covering hers. "We did it together, Hana. And we'll keep doing it."

Omar nodded from his post, mace ready, his thoughts on Veronica's kiss waiting inside, his Ox Clan endurance a silent vow to protect this fragile peace. "All quiet so far," he rumbled, his deep voice steady.

A deep rumble quaked the earth, alarms piercing the air like shattered glass, jolting David from his reverie. The ground shook violently, citizens below freezing in terror as cracks spiderwebbed through the plazas.

X, his sword slashing through the outer defenses with ruthless precision, the blade gleaming with stolen talisman energy, and Dolore, her violet lightning scorching the gates with electric fury that arced like living storms, led a wave of mercenaries storming the walls. Catapults hurled flaming projectiles that arced through the sky like falling stars, setting gardens ablaze and igniting cherry trees in bursts of orange blazes, the sweet scent twisting into acrid smoke that stung the eyes and choked the lungs.

Walls cracked under the assault, stone crumbling like ancient relics giving way to chaos, debris raining down on fleeing crowds below.

David sprinted toward a towering catapult, katana flashing, dodging a flaming projectile, its heat searing his cheek as embers grazed his hair. Ryder flanked, cannon slung low, sweat stinging his eyes as he aimed at the creaking frame.

"Cover me!" Ryder shouted, the ground quaking. David's blade slashed a mercenary's shield, metal screeching, his arm burning from the strain. Hana's whip cracked, snaring a rope to destabilize the arm, her Horse Clan agility a blur.

Patricia hammered a support beam, pink-gold runes crackling, her grunts echoing as wood splintered.

Gerry jabbed his spear at the base, piercing taut cords, "Take that!"

Omar's mace smashed the foundation, muscles screaming as stone dust clouded the air. Ryder fired, the cannon's boom splintering the arm into fiery shards, a shockwave singeing their cloaks.

"Nice teamwork!" David roared, yanking Ryder from a collapsing beam's path, their fists bumping amid soot-choked chaos, hearts pounding with defiance as another catapult loomed, suspense gripping them—could they hold the line?

"To the gates—defend the palace!" David shouted, his voice steady despite the erupting pandemonium, rallying imperial soldiers alongside Hana, Patricia, Ryder, and Gerry. "Omar, head inside—protect the control room and Veronica!" He drew his katana in a fluid motion, the blade glinting as he charged forward, heart pounding with the weight of protection. "Hana, cover the left flank—Patricia, reinforce the barriers! Ryder, take out those catapults!"

Hana and Gerry surged forward, weaving through the plaza's chaos, smoke stinging their lungs. Hana's whip snared a rune-drone buzzing overhead, its green core pulsing ominously.

"Nice aim, Goat!" she shouted, yanking it down with a crack, sparks erupting as it crashed.

Gerry's spear pierced its core, violet flashes bursting, "Better than your lasso!" he grinned, dodging a mercenary's blade, his pulse racing as another drone whirred close, suspense building—would it strike before they could react?

Their teamwork held, Hana's lash deflecting a second drone, Gerry's spear finishing it, their banter a spark against the inferno, grounding the team as the plaza burned.

Hana sprinted beside David, her whip snapping to entangle a mercenary's legs, yanking him down with a thud amid the smoke.

"They're hitting the weak repairs from Coinin's surges!" she called, her Horse Clan agility a blur as she dodged a flaming arrow, the heat singeing her tunic, her breath quickening with suspense—would the next strike find its mark? She lashed out again, her whip coiling around another foe's weapon, pulling him off balance. "David, behind you!"

Patricia swung her hammer with Pig Clan calm, smashing debris to clear paths for archers, her gauntlet's pink-gold runes crackling as she shouted encouragements. "Hold steady—archers, fire!"

She smashed another catapult projectile mid-air, shards raining like fiery hail, her compassion fueling a protective fury for the innocents below, her swings precise but her heart racing as a throb nearly toppled her, the ground heaving like a beast awakening.

"Time to crash their party!" Ryder yelled, his cannon booming a deafening shot that splintered a catapult into wooden fragments, the recoil jolting him back as he dodged a counterattack, his Rooster Clan boldness masking the adrenaline-fueled fear, his quip a defiant spark amid the roar. "Take that, you fiery pests! Who's next?"

But suspense built as a mercenary closed in, sword raised—Ryder rolled aside just in time, the blade embedding in the stone where he'd stood.

Gerry scouted enemy movements from a wall perch, his spear jabbing at vulnerabilities, driven by his family legacy to protect the city—memories of Ged's outages spurring him to leap down and impale a climbing mercenary, the impact vibrating through his arms.

"Gotcha—stay down!" he taunted, his Goat Clan mischief turning lethal in the heat of battle, though his pulse raced as another foe lunged, forcing him to parry with a desperate thrust.

Chaos erupted as mercenaries breached a section, blazes consuming cherry blossoms in roaring infernos, fountains running with soot-blackened water, tech grids sparking as imbalance throbs flickered the shrines, casting erratic, dancing shadows across the battlefield.

Civilians screamed, fleeing through debris-choked streets, while holo-screens glitched with warnings, barriers failing in showers of electric sparks. The ground heaved with another throb, cracking open fissures that swallowed a group of attackers, the air thick with the scent of burned wood and ozone, suspense hanging like a blade—would the next fissure claim one of their own?

David's katana sliced through attackers with precise strikes, sweat beading on his brow as he parried a blade, the clang echoing like thunder. A mercenary's sword grazed his arm, drawing blood that stung like fire, but he spun, countering with a dragon-claw slash that felled the foe, his mind racing—We can't let them reach the shrine!

"Hold the line!" he commanded, his voice cutting through the din, as another throb rocked the ground, cracking the wall beneath him, forcing him to leap to safety, his heart pounding with the fear of collapse.

The city's power hub—the central shrine—faltered, throbs causing holo-screens to glitch wildly and barriers to collapse, civilians panicking as lights flickered like dying stars. Hana's whip entangled another weapon, her shout piercing, "Flank from the towers—cut them off!"

Patricia's hammer pounded obstacles, directing reinforcements with swift swings amid rising smoke. Ryder's cannon fired another blast, Gerry's spear targeted gaps, Sheng Xiao's equilibrium teetering as the city's heart pulsed with danger, David's determination blazing like a beacon against the encroaching storm. Suspense built as a massive catapult shot hurtled toward them—David shoved Hana aside just in time, the projectile exploding nearby in a shower of flames that singed his cloak, the heat wave knocking Gerry back, his spear skidding across the stone, Ryder coughing through the smoke, "Close one—keep firing!"

Amid the plaza's chaos, Jade directed evacuations, her fenghuang-shaped scepter glowing to shield civilians from fiery meteors, her voice straining, "To the shelters!"

Cade fought nearby, his knives arcing to deflect a rune-bolt, their eyes locking through the smoke.

"Jade, I love you—stay strong!" he vowed, his voice raw with passion, her hand gripping his arm.

"Cade, take the children to safety—I'll hold the line here!" she urged, her heart aching as he nodded, dashing to guide the kids, their bond pulsing like the talisman, a romantic anchor as debris rained, suspense gripping her—would they reunite amid this storm? Her scepter throbbed, guiding a child to safety, her heart tethered to Cade's fierce gaze, their love a defiant spark against the inferno.

Inside the palace's training area, spacious and weapon-lined with training mats underfoot, alarms blared, holo-screens flashing red warnings, guards scrambling through chaotic halls as explosions rocked the foundations, dust sifting from the ceiling. Veronica clutched the Rat Talisman, its radiance struggling to stabilize tech grids, her pistol drawn as Bella spotted the talisman's gold-blue light seeping through her cloak. Bella and Lucas burst in, their eyes blazing with vengeance for their Souris defeat, joined by X, his sword slashing a guard aside with a grunt, the blade dripping blood, and Dolore, her lightning blasting mats with electric sparks that ignited the edges, the air crackling with ozone.

"Hand it over, or die!" Bella snarled, flames scorching the floor in a wave of heat, her fire relentless as she lunged forward, the air shimmering with intensity, her amber eyes locked on Veronica with Kusini-fueled rage.

Veronica fired her pistol, bullets grazing Bella's armor with sparks, "Not today!" her speed guiding her aim as she rolled aside, dodging a fiery bolt that charred the mat, her mind flashing to Souris where she'd outwitted Lucas after the thorn maze, claiming the talisman from his grasp, her Rat Clan wit sharpening her resolve. "You won't take it again!"

Omar charged with his mace, swinging at Lucas, "You'll face us both!" his voice a roar as he connected with Lucas's shield, the impact jarring his arms, his Ox Clan strength surging with memories of Veronica's kiss before Doragon, fueling his protective fury. "Get away from her!"

Sam's arrows pierced a mercenary's armor with Snake Clan precision, "Take that!" she quipped, her bowstring twanging as she nocked another, recalling Listra's illusions where her wit had pierced through deception, her arrow whistling past Dolore's lightning. "Missed me!"

Doug's sword slashed a shield in loyal Dog Clan grit, "Not on my watch!" he grunted, his blade clanging as he defended Sam's flank, his Dingo roots driving him to anchor the line against abandonment, parrying X's sword with a clash that sparked metal.

Melissa's axe cleaved a weapon with Monkey Clan agility, "Swing and a miss—for you!" she teased, her braid whipping as she flipped over a foe, her Mico training turning the fight into a chaotic dance, her axe glancing off Bella's flames with a hiss.

Alice's tablet hacked enemy comms to sow confusion, her fingers flying across the screen.

"Signals jammed—your turn to glitch!" she said, her Rabbit Clan precision disrupting Dolore's lightning patterns, causing a bolt to misfire and scorch the wall.

Tate's claws raked a foe with Tiger Clan fury.

"Claws out, intruders!" he growled, his slashes leaving trails of blood, his Kusini ego tempered into focused rage from Listra's alliances, lunging at X with a roar that shook the air.

Dolore's lightning scorched the palace mats, her brown eyes blazing as she hurled bolts, a memory of a ruined shrine flashing—X's blade carving through bandits, pulling her from rubble, his voice low, "You're worth more."

Her unrequited love for him burned hotter than her sparks, Vincent's whispers urging chaos, but her heart clung to X's command, his strength a beacon through her doubt. The Rat Talisman's theft was her vow to prove devotion, her bolts crackling fiercer as she blasted a guard, the air thick with ozone and her resolve.

X's trust was all she craved, even as Vincent's ambition loomed, her loyalty a storm against the Guardians' light, her fingers trembling as she recalled his hand lifting her from ruin.

Lucas, fueled by his Souris grudge for losing the Rat Talisman to Veronica—memories of her cunning outwitting him after the thorn maze, his pride stung as she claimed it—tackled Omar in a brutal clash, hurling him against a wall with bone-rattling force, the stone cracking under the impact.

"You stole it from me—now pay!" he bellowed, his bandaged arm throbbing but unyielding as he pinned Omar, mace clattering away, the suspense thick as Omar struggled, his breath ragged.

Veronica's eyes widened, firing another shot that grazed Lucas's shoulder, drawing blood that soaked his sleeve. But he pressed on, his machete clashing against her pistol in a flurry of sparks and grunts, the training mats tearing under their feet.

"Give it up—you're outmatched!" he taunted, disarming her with a swift twist that sent the pistol skidding, his free hand snatching the Rat Talisman from her cloak as she staggered back, the radiance transferring to his grasp with a throb that made him grin triumphantly.

Bella seized the moment, her fiery bolt stunning Veronica's aim further, scorching the air with a wave of heat that forced Sam and Doug to shield their eyes, the flames licking at Melissa's axe.

"Got it!" Lucas roared, retreating through smoke-filled halls as X and Dolore covered them with sword slashes that cleaved through guards and lightning bolts that shattered holo-screens, the room filling with acrid ozone and screams, the suspense peaking as a bolt nearly struck Tate, forcing him to roll aside.

The scale tipped immediately, imbalance throbs exploding like thunder, lights flickering wildly across the palace, tech grids failing in cascades of sparks, the palace quaking like an earthquake as barriers collapsed in showers of debris, dust choking the air and mats igniting in spots.

"They've broken the balance!" Veronica cried, rushing to Omar's side, helping him up, his breathing ragged but resolute, "We'll get it back," she vowed, her hand in his amid the chaos, their eyes meeting in a tender moment—her Rat Clan spark igniting his resolve, a quick kiss sealing their bond before she helped him stand.

"I love you—stay with me," she whispered, her voice trembling with fear for him, his wound bleeding through his tunic.

The city center descended into a maelstrom, spires crumbling under bombardment from catapults and magic, crowds fleeing through debris-choked streets choked with tattered banners, Sheng Xiao shrines cracking as throbs sparked tech grids into chaos, fountains overflowing with boiling water that scalded the unwary. Jade directed evacuations from a central plaza, her fenghuang-shaped scepter radiating to shield civilians from fiery meteors raining down like vengeful stars, the impacts shaking the ground and sending cracks spiderwebbing through pavement, suspense building as a meteor nearly breached her shield, the heat wave forcing her to grit her teeth.

"This way—to the shelters!" she called, her voice straining over screams and crumbling stone, her heart aching for the innocent as a child clutched her robe, wide-eyed in terror, Jade's free hand gently guiding them while her scepter pulsed with protective light, her thoughts on Cade, his absence a void amid the storm.

Vincent emerged from a side alley cloaked in smoke, serpent scepter humming with dark energy, his sneer twisting as he stepped into the plaza.

"Your reign ends, Empress—time to fall!" he hissed, launching a barrage of dark magic bolts, the air crackling with malice, the ground quaking as green pulses snaked toward her like venomous serpents, corroding stone and igniting banners in their path, the suspense thickening as one pulse grazed a civilian, eliciting a scream.

Jade countered with a magnetic pulse, her scepter radiating amethyst light that clashed against Vincent's in a burst of light and darkness, sparks flying like shattered stars. The force pushed her back, her boots scraping stone, but she held firm, channeling Sheng Xiao's essence into a shield that absorbed the next strike, the force vibrating through her arms like a storm. "You won't break us!" she shouted, sweat beading on her brow as the Guardians converged—David's katana slashing at Vincent's runes with dragon-claw precision, "Take this, serpent!" the blade whistling through the air.

Hana's whip coiling around his scepter to disrupt a spell, "Not so fast!" her lash cracking like thunder.

Patricia's hammer smashing ground traps he summoned, "Stay down!" the impact sending shockwaves.

Ryder's cannon blasting a dark energy wave, "Boom—eat that!" the recoil nearly toppling him.

Gerry's spear jabbing at his defenses, "For Ged—for everything!" the point grazing Vincent's cloak.

Vincent laughed, dodging with sly grace, his scepter summoning illusions of coiling serpents that lashed at the Guardians, forcing David to parry shadows that felt all too real, the illusions hissing with venomous intent, one striking Gerry's shoulder and drawing blood. "Fools—your talismans can't match my power!" He unleashed a venomous bolt at Jade, the air hissing with toxic fumes that burned the lungs, the bolt streaking like green lightning, suspense peaking as it hurtled toward her heart.

From afar, Cade spotted the attack, his mismatched eyes widening in horror—Jade exposed, Vincent's bolt closing in.

"No!" he roared, shadow-traveling through the chaos, his Cat Clan speed a blur as he materialized between Jade and the blast, knives arcing in crescent-moon strikes to deflect the edges, the blades glowing with ethereal light.

"I love you, Jade—always!" he cried, his voice raw with desperate passion, eyes locked on hers as he intercepted the lethal core with his body, a final vow before collapsing.

The force slammed into his chest, Cade screaming in agony as his shadows fractured into claw-like tendrils, screeching like a chorus of enraged cats—ancestral Cat Clan spirits, awakened by the curse--hissing and yowling, splitting the air with unnatural light, writhing as if alive, their forms twisting in tormented agony, lashing out wildly and scorching nearby debris, the noise a haunting wail that chilled the blood.

The sight froze everyone—Guardians gasped in horror, David shouting, "Cade—no!" mistaking the shadows for Vincent's curse, his katana dropping slack, fear gripping him as the tendrils snapped at the air.

Hana's whip fell from her hand, "It's... possessing him!" her voice trembling.

Patricia recoiled, hammer trembling, "That sound—it's like tormented souls!"

Ryder's cannon lowered, "Get back—it's going wild!"

Gerry stared, spear frozen, "Like a beast unleashed!"

The villains recoiled: Vincent's scepter faltered, his eyes widening in terror at the "demonic" display, the hissing shadows lunging toward him, forcing him to stumble back.

"What abomination is this? It's not human!" Bella's flames dimmed, her face pale, "It's cursed—those screams!"

Lucas clutched the talisman tighter, "We're outmatched—retreat!"

Dolore's lightning sputtered, "That power... it's unholy!"

X, unnerved by the shadows' ferocity, his vendetta shaken by the unnatural force that seemed to claw at reality itself, barked, "Retreat—now! We have the talisman!"

The villains fled into the smoke, Vincent casting one last venomous glance, his plan disrupted but malice intact, the shadows' hissing echoing in his ears like a warning, fear gnawing at his ambition for the first time.

Huan, arriving mid-battle from the walls, witnessed the save from afar—his eyes widening as Cade's sacrifice unfolded, the shadows' display cracking his skepticism, a flicker of respect dawning amid the chaos, hinting at a future shift in his view of the "unworthy" advisor.

Perhaps I was wrong, he thought, his pushiness tempered by the heroic act.

Jade dropped to Cade's side amid the rubble, cradling him as tears streamed, her scepter pulsing golden light into his wound. Her tears soaked his tunic, fingers trembling on the fracture as memories of their childhood garden flashed—Cade's laughter under cherry trees, their hands entwined in jasmine-scented nights, now fading like a dying star.

"Healers—now!" she screamed, voice raw with desperation, her free hand pressing against the fracture, feeling the shadows writhe under her touch like living entities, the hissing fading but the tendrils still twitching.

The fracture resisted, claw-like tendrils lashing at her magic, screeching faintly.

"Don't leave me, Cade—not now," she pleaded, her heart fracturing as his breath weakened, eyes fluttering shut, his hand going limp in hers, her romantic dreams shattering in the moment.

"Guardians—secure the city, evacuate the citizens, protect the shrines!" she ordered through sobs, her leadership shining even in grief, before turning fully to Cade, her world narrowing to him as healers arrived, their hands glowing with restorative energy.

The city's power hub failed completely, throbs shaking the ground like aftershocks, Sheng Xiao's equilibrium shattered, darkness closing in like a suffocating veil as fires raged unchecked, spires toppling with deafening crashes, shrines fracturing with green cracks, their zodiac carvings dimming as imbalance throbs sparked city-wide blackouts, a distant dune storm flickering on a glitching holo-screen, Saanp's sands stirring ominously.

The air filled with the cries of the wounded and the crackle of collapsing tech.

The palace garden lay in ruins, ash-covered blossoms trampled, survivors huddling amid charred debris and fallen statues, the air thick with smoke, cries, and burned cherry wood, the once-vibrant space a testament to the attack's devastation.

Jade cradled Cade, his chest bandaged hastily, shadows flickering faintly as healers applied healing salves. Her fenghuang-shaped scepter pulsed weakly, her magic helping calm Cade's shadows.

Healers' faces darkened, monitors beeping erratically as his body convulsed faintly, the fractured shadows writhing unpredictably, resisting their salves, suspense gripping Jade— would he survive, or would the shadows consume him?

Shrines across the city fractured with green cracks, their zodiac carvings dimming as surges sparked city-wide blackouts, a distant dune storm flickering on a glitching holo-screen, Saanp's sands stirring ominously.

In X's fortress, Vincent gripped his serpent scepter, the Rat Talisman's energy surging within it, his sneer cold.

"Jade's empire crumbles—the Snake Talisman's guardian will bow to my scepter, twisting Saanp's sands against them," he muttered, a holo-map highlighting a desert shrine, its dunes pulsing with ominous green light, his plan to shatter Sheng Xiao's harmony sharpening with venomous intent, a personal strike against Jade's hope looming like a storm.

Plotting the Snake Talisman's capture, its spectral guardian under his sway, his ambition burned brighter, fear from Cade's shadows fading against his hunger for dominance.

In the palace infirmary, Jade knelt by Cade's cot, his chest bandaged, shadows flickering faintly as healers adjusted glowing monitors. Her fenghuang-shaped scepter pulsed weakly, her magic spent.

The knot tightens—betrayal coils in the dark.

A vision struck her: green cracks spiderwebbing a holo-screen, Ogham knots twisting like living vines. The air hummed with forbidden power, a whisper from banished crafters. Sheng Xiao's balance teetered, the Guardians' resolve the only light.

"Hold on, Cade," she whispered, tears falling.

In the control room, David, Hana, and Sam stood over a holo-map, her whip coiled, his katana sheathed, Sam's bow gleaming, Snake Clan ready for Saanp's trials.

"We strike for the Snake Talisman," David vowed, their bond a spark against the darkness. Sheng Xiao teetered, but the Guardians' resolve burned, a defiant flame for the battles ahead.

Epilogue: The Cat's Wail

Felidae's golden temples gleamed under a blazing sun, their onyx veins surging like veins of night, tranquil pools reflecting towering cat statues with sapphire and emerald eyes shimmering with Li Shou's grace. Orchards heavy with figs and pomegranates rustled in the breeze, their sweet aroma weaving through a vibrant market where silken shadow-cloaks glowed like liquid starlight.

Elders haggled, hands deft among woven threads, children darted through blooming groves, their shadow-charms dancing like fireflies, laughter echoing off golden stones. An oasis district of Dendera hummed with life, a sanctuary of Cat Clan honor, its silken shadows a testament to Tai's legacy, forged in the Great Race's blood and trust.

Lira, Head Priestess and Healer of Felidae, stood at the shrine's heart, her vivid green eyes catching starlight like emerald pools, raven hair gleaming like starlit waters. Her fingers wove midnight veils with sacred precision, the threads pulsing with Li Shou's grace.

A shy smile faded as she glanced at Kael, her protector, his panther-like muscles rippling under moonlit skin, daggers gleaming, unaware of her heart pounding at his nearness, her hand lingering on his arm, a flare igniting in the desert air.

Lira clutched her crescent-moon healer's amulet, a pang piercing her chest as Cade's fading essence tugged like a waning star, stirring a childhood memory in Felidae's orchards. At ten, under fig trees, she'd woven shadow-charms, their silken glow surging with a sacred tie woven by Li Shou—Cade's pulse, binding her as Felidae's destined healer to the Cat Clan guardian in the west.

"Your hands will mend his light," the elders had vowed, placing the amulet in her palms, its runes flaring with starlit duty.

"We're tied," she'd whispered then, charms flaring like starlight.

Now, his pulse dimmed, weakening the clan's protective threads, her determination surging—she'd heal him, mending Sheng Xiao's balance. Her vivid green eyes flared, sensing his fading essence, her hands trembling as fig scents mingled with the shrine's mystic surge.

A searing pain stabbed the clan, silken shadows flickering like frayed threads, their protective glow faltering across souls. Elders dropped baskets, figs spilling, clutching hearts in silent agony. Children froze, charms falling, trembling, their cries rising like mournful cat wails, echoing across realms to the Imperial City's palace, chilling the air where Cade lay broken.

Cade's pulse fades—a cat's wail crosses realms.

Lira gasped, shadow-threads scorching her palms, her vivid green eyes flaring, sensing Cade's fading essence tied to Li Shou's grace.

Her heart raced, vision blurring with his dying light, breath hitching as she staggered, the shrine's emerald core dimming, quaking as if mourning Cade's pulse, suspense gripping—would she reach him before his essence vanished? She pressed the amulet to her lips, whispering, "I choose this path— not duty, but love for the light he carries."

Kael rushed to her, panther-fierce grace blurring, his hand catching her arm, a flare igniting as her heart skipped, longing unspoken.

"Lira!" he growled, daggers drawn, protectiveness burning as rogue surges twisted the clan's shadows, coiling like disrupted silk. A memory flashed—Felidae's market, a thief lunging for her charm, its threads glowing. Kael had pinned the thief's sleeve with a dagger, its weight heavy in his grip, pomegranate scents mingling with her relieved smile.

"Stay back," he'd snarled, her eyes sparking his heart. Now, his blades sliced through the surges, scattering distortions with a snarl, his duty to Lira a fire against the chaos, her nearness warming his conviction.

"Hold them off!" he roared, shielding her, his breath hitching as their eyes locked, her warmth stirring his resolve.

The square erupted in chaos, cat statues flickering ominously, tech grids glitching as shadows quaked, glowing protectively yet trembling under the surge's weight. A catastrophic throb shook the ground, shadows flickering like wounded guardians, threatening the shrine's emerald core.

Market stalls toppled, figs scattering as elders screamed, their voices trembling but defiant, weaving protective threads, children clutched charms, eyes wide as sparks sputtered futilely, the oasis quaking as Sheng Xiao's heart faltered.

A distant desert's malice pulsed, green light flickering in the shrine's core, threatening the clan's hope, suspense heavy as Saanp's sands loomed in Lira's mind, their venomous stir a shadow of coming peril.

Clansfolk gathered under the cat statues, weaving shadow-charms, their sapphire and emerald eyes glowing as silken threads surged with Li Shou's grace, fig scents mingling with chants of "Light and dark dance."

The ritual's mystic surge steadied hearts, but throbs struck, shadows quaking like silk torn by unseen hands. Lira joined, her healing threads flaring, a vow to restore Cade's light, the shrine's core pulsing with fragile hope against the gathering storm.

Elders chanted, their lined faces resolute, hands weaving threads despite the surges as children hid behind stalls, clutching charms while shadows flickered, their small voices joining the chant, a defiant spark against the chaos.

Lira faced the clan, gestures rallying them, voice cutting through panic. "Cade's fading threatens our shadows—we go to heal him and save Sheng Xiao." A crescent portal swirled open under the cat statue, etched with Li Shou's sigils, surging with starlit whispers of the Prophecy's dance.

Lira clutched her crescent-moon healer's amulet, Kael's fingers lingering on hers, her pulse racing with unspoken longing, their eyes locking, her heart aching with warmth.

IV

"His light is my duty," she whispered, the amulet's runes flaring as she stepped toward her sacred charge.

They stepped into a shadowy void, silken shadows quaking at its edges, a chilling wail echoing—light and dark must dance—their mission to heal Cade a fragile spark against a darkness hiding ancient secrets, suspense heavy as Saanp's dunes loomed, threatening to swallow their hope.

V

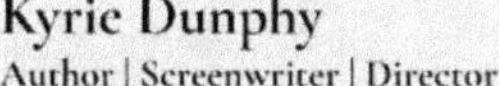

Kyrie Dunphy
Author | Screenwriter | Director

Kyrie Dunphy crafts immersive worlds of fantasy, science fiction, and horror for books, screen, and stage. A valedictorian with a BFA in Creative Writing from Full Sail University (2020), she published her debut anthology Fear the Lightning (2018) and the children's book The Wolf in Sheep's Avatar (2022). She also wrote the book and lyrics for the original musical Musical-ception.

Founder of UseMuse, a creative community platform for artists to connect and thrive, Kyrie lives in Orlando, Florida, channeling theme park magic and the eerie unknown into stories that ignite imaginations across generations.

kyriedunphy.com

www.ingramcontent.com/pod-product-compliance
Lightning Source LLC
Chambersburg PA
CBHW060813120726
47909CB00006B/1908